Falling into Place

Falling into Place

ALLISON ASHLEY

Montlake

Published by Montlake, Seattle

www.apub.com

EU product safety contact:
Amazon Media EU S. à r.l.
38, avenue John F. Kennedy, L-1855 Luxembourg
amazonpublishing-gpsr@amazon.com

ISBN-13: 9781662527999 (paperback)
ISBN-13: 9781662527982 (digital)

Cover design by Ploy Siripant
Cover images: © MVshop, © You1023, © Little_Monster_2070, © Madiwaso, © Lana Brow / Shutterstock

Printed in the United States of America

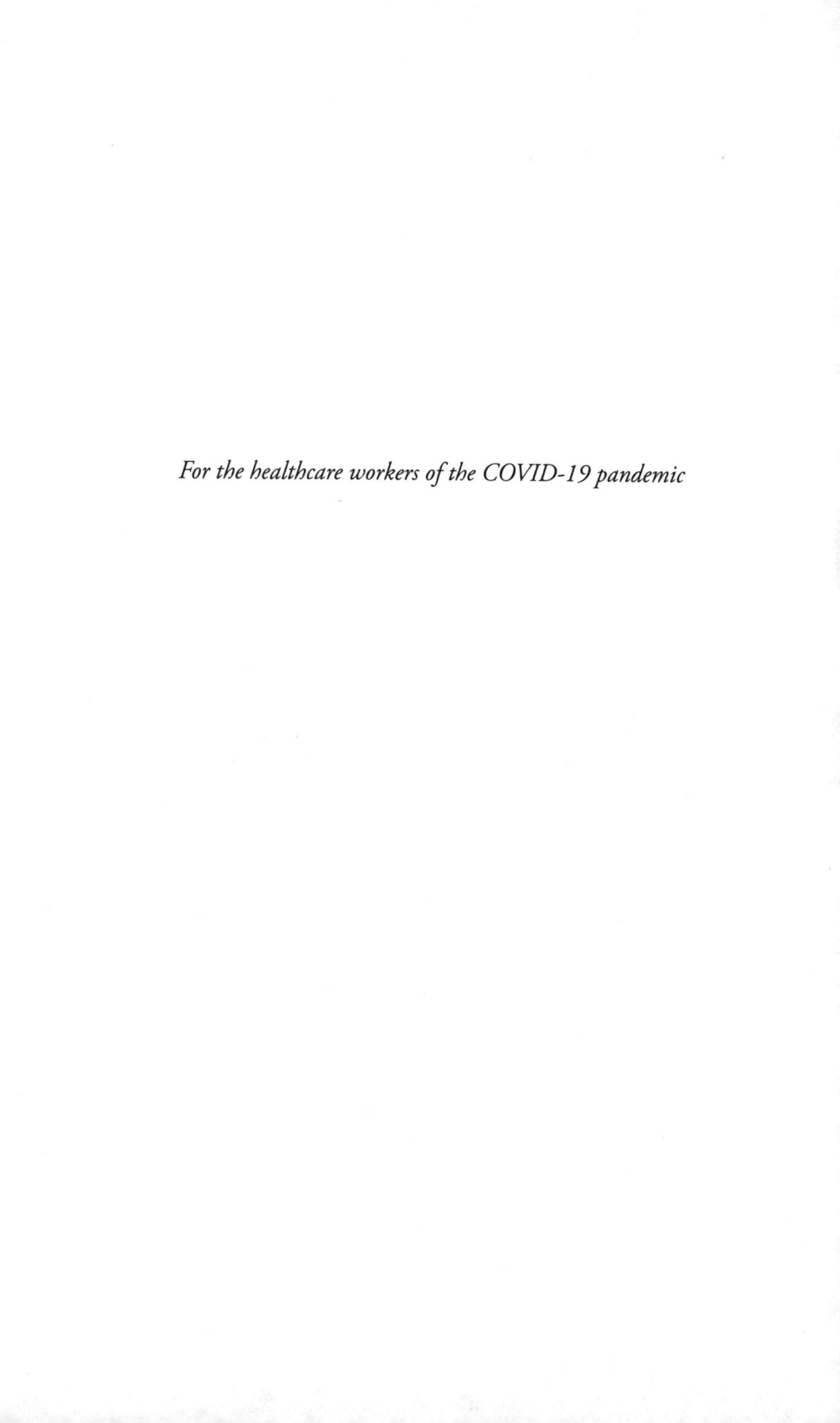

For the healthcare workers of the COVID-19 pandemic

CHAPTER ONE

Carly

> I went to a new Thai restaurant yesterday and it made me think of you. It was so good I thought about having it again tonight, but then I remembered it was Thursday and Thursday is Barrio's night. I can't seem to stop going there every week like we used to, but now I sit at the bar instead of at our regular table. Have you found a place over there you go every Thursday? Anyway. Miss you.
>
> —*Email from Carly Porter to Benjamin Wheeler*

"I would rather walk barefoot across broken glass than have sex with that man."

Extreme? Perhaps.

Overdramatic? Maybe.

Something one shouldn't say to their boss at 8:00 a.m. on a Monday morning before everyone had at least two cups of coffee? Probably.

But desperate times called for desperate measures.

Five minutes ago, Carly had walked into her longtime friend and part-time boss's office feeling fresh, hopeful, and a little nervous. But like, the *good* kind of nervous. The kind you get when you're about to cross the stage at graduation to receive that hard-earned degree or walk down the aisle toward the partner of your dreams. Maybe you didn't love that people would be staring at you, and you were slightly terrified you'd trip and fall and make a fool of yourself, but still, this was something you *wanted* to do. It was something good and exciting.

Today, Carly was the good kind of nervous because she'd been called into Mai's office for a one-on-one. The last two people who'd had a private meeting with either Mai or her business partner, Kyle, had been offered rare full-time, salaried positions at Mode Style, Oklahoma City's premier personal-styling business. Ever since moving back to her hometown two years ago, Carly had worked for Mode on a client-by-client basis as a contract employee. Which meant she'd had to keep her *other* job as an accountant that, while it paid the bills, bored her to tears.

She'd give anything to work in fashion full-time and had been killing herself to take on and go above and beyond for every client possible to prove herself. Her positive client-feedback rating was the highest in the company.

There was no way Mai hadn't noticed how hard she'd been working.

The excitement swirling through her veins meant she didn't notice Mai's solemn expression when Carly sat down on the other side of the desk. But when her boss-slash-friend spoke, her grim tone was unmistakable.

"Carly, we need to talk."

Carly's stomach dropped to her toes. "Oh." Her spine went straight and she gripped her hands together in her lap. "Um, okay?"

Was Mode going under? Was Mai leaving? Was Kyle?

Mai's cheeks puffed out as she slowly blew out a long breath. "Mrs. Princeton reached out to me over the weekend."

Carly frowned. "Kitty Princeton?"

"Yes. Your client's wife."

Though the term "client" was technically correct, it was also generous. Carly had felt more like a mix between a kindergarten teacher and an etiquette instructor during the hours she'd spent with the sixty-four-year-old oil tycoon. She'd spent more time than not politely (but firmly) declining his advances and attempting to redirect his focus from her breasts to appropriate subjects, such as current tie-width trends and popular street styles for more . . . seasoned men. She didn't have kids but wondered if maybe this was what it was like trying to dress a six-year-old who kept running off to play with his toys.

Unfortunately, the only toy Chet Princeton wanted to play with was . . . well, Carly.

"She called you on a weekend?"

Mai nodded. "Sent an email, too. And when I say what I'm about to say, I don't want you to panic, all right?"

Oh God.

"She contacted me to express concerns about your behavior toward her husband. She alleges that you've been . . . overly flirtatious with Mr. Princeton during your appointments."

"She *what*?"

The only reason Carly stopped there was Mai's flat expression that said, *I know this is complete bullshit, but let me finish*. "She said he's uncomfortable working with you, and she requested I assign a different stylist. She also suggested I consider . . . corrective action to address your unprofessional behavior. Now, don't look at me like that; I know it's not true."

"Thank God," Carly said. She felt sick. "Because I would rather walk barefoot across broken glass than have sex with that man."

Mai snorted, then put her hand up while she composed herself. "I'll accept that as your formal rebuttal to her allegations. I've known you a long time and know you wouldn't behave that way with a client, and on top of that I'm a member of the same country club as the Princetons. Everyone knows that guy has had more affairs than dollars in his bank account."

That was a lot of affairs.

Mai slid her red-framed cat-eye glasses from her nose and set them on the desk between them. "But . . ."

"But?"

"We can't afford to lose the Princetons—or their influential friends—as clients. And even though it's a baseless accusation, she did make a formal written complaint. So to cover Mode's ass, I have to document that I discussed the situation with you, and the entire team will be required to retake the sexual harassment and workplace professionalism training. No one will know what sparked the training update, so don't worry about bad press for you. I just have to make sure it doesn't turn into a PR nightmare for the company as a whole, okay?"

Carly nodded, thankful Mai trusted her but feeling sort of gross about the whole thing all the same. "I . . . feel like I should say I'm sorry, even though I didn't do anything wrong. Mr. Princeton is such a creep."

"Believe me, I know. And you're right, you have nothing to apologize for. It's more likely he does." Mai paused, leaned forward, and, with an elbow on the desk, pressed one palm to her forehead. "God, I should have asked you that first: Have there been any issues working with him? Has he done something to make you uncomfortable that I need to address? Important client or not, if he's crossed a line, he's gone."

Carly shook her head. She wasn't about to make this a bigger deal than it already was. "Nothing I can't handle. I appreciate it, though."

"Of course. I hope you always know you can come to me if something like that ever came up."

"I do," Carly said.

Mai smiled. "Well, thanks for coming in so early today. I know it's not the best way to start your week off."

Carly snorted. "You can say that again. And here I thought you were gonna offer me one of your coveted full-time positions." The second she said the words out loud, she regretted them. It sounded like she just expected Mai to hand it to her, rather than strategically outline everything she'd done to earn the role. She was Mai's best stylist, and they both knew it.

"You're a model employee," Mai said, echoing Carly's thoughts. "And you have the highest request rate from return clients of anyone on staff right now."

Why did she feel a *but* coming here, too?

"But hiring decisions aren't just up to me. I'm the style part of Mode, and Kyle's the business half. We're looking for someone with people skills and fashion intuition, yes—and you have those in spades. But we're also looking for people who bring fresh ideas. Innovation. Unique perspectives to keep us not only on the cutting edge of the fashion industry but also in the narrative of how our company fits into the broader picture of Midwest community and culture."

It wasn't the first time Carly had heard that. Mode's business model primarily revolved around stylists working via contract and by commission, and they only pulled people on full-time if they would have a more expansive role within the company.

"I believe in you, Carly," Mai said, likely reading Carly's silence as defeat. "Bring us something inspired that could take Mode to the next level, and you'd be very hard to say no to."

"That motherfucker."

Carly clinked her drink against the glass her best friend Sasha held up, then drank. "You can say that again."

"Do you think he's the one who put his wife up to it? To get you in trouble because he's pissed you said no? Or did she do it on her own?"

"I have no idea." Carly shrugged. "But it doesn't really matter. I know Mai believes me, but I don't know Kyle that well. Part of me wonders if this ruined my chances of ever getting a salaried position."

Most of the contract stylists had enough work that they didn't need to hold second jobs if they didn't want to. But Carly was unwilling to sacrifice having a consistent paycheck, and no matter how good she was, working on commission terrified her. Financial stability was nonnegotiable, and anyone who knew what her childhood was like wouldn't blame her for that.

"No way," Sasha argued. "They know how incredible you are. In a week they'll have forgotten all about it, and you can march back in there and demand a promotion. Be the badass I know that you are and go for what you want!"

Carly glared at her friend. "You mean to tell me that a week after being accused of sexual harassment at work, you'd walk straight up to your boss and demand a promotion?"

"Well. My sister's my boss, so. Probably."

"It's not that simple for me. Harassment allegations aside, Mode doesn't just want people who know fashion. They want people who bring 'fresh and innovative ideas' to the company." She air-quoted around Mai's key descriptors.

"You don't have those?"

"Not the kind they're looking for. The last person they hired is the one who pitched an athletics division and landed the Thunder contract. You think I can compete with the guy who gets to dress super-tall, super-sexy, super-famous NBA players?"

"Well, when you say it like that . . . no."

Carly took another long drink and spun around on her barstool. She gestured at their surroundings. "Take Variety. Never in a million years would I have come up with something as cool as this."

Ava, the owner who often doubled behind the bar, passed by at that moment and gave Carly a huge smile. "Bitch, you just made my whole day."

Carly laughed and gave a thumbs-up, then turned back to Sasha. "Remember when we first came here? You immediately wanted to cover it and did a whole piece in the magazine about it. I mean, a bar where people can gather and watch their favorite reality TV shows? Collectively gasp with housewives or literally cast their vote on who they think's about to get kicked off the island?" Tonight was *Bachelor* night, and she and Sasha rarely missed it. Witnessing the lavish dates, relationship drama, and rose ceremonies on a huge screen surrounded by other die-hard fans was a thousand times better than viewing from home. Plus, they awarded prizes to customers who correctly predicted the outcome of that evening's episode. "*This* is innovation."

"You're right. And that piece did do well," Sasha agreed. "Unlike anything else we've covered in the last nine months."

Carly had been scanning the room with appreciation when Sasha muttered that last part, so it took her a minute to pick up on it. She glanced over at her friend, assessing her more closely.

"What's going on?" Carly asked. "Is the magazine not doing well?"

Sasha was editor in chief of *LiveOKC*, an online and print magazine that focused on everything local in Oklahoma City and the surrounding suburbs. Part of a larger media company started by her parents more than thirty years ago and currently run by Sasha's sister, Macy, *LiveOKC* was a staple for keeping up with anything and everything happening in town, from boutiques to restaurants and all that fell in between.

From the age of nine, Sasha had planned on working at the magazine with her mom. But when her mom died unexpectedly in high school, *LiveOKC* became more than just a potential career that seemed interesting and fun. It became Sasha's entire life.

Sasha rubbed her temples. "No, it's not. We had our quarterly review this morning, and we've been behind on every metric for the last nine months. New subscriptions are consistently down, and local partners are starting to pull advertisements."

"Shit. Do you know why?"

Sasha shrugged. "Macy thinks there's too much competing for people's attention. You get, like, three seconds to hook someone, and if you fail, they're on to the next thing."

"You know how to do that, though," Carly said. "You're on top of all the social media stuff."

"It's not enough anymore. I try to keep up with the changing algorithms, but it feels impossible. Even if a random post does well, doing the same thing doesn't work a second time. It's exhausting, trying to keep up with the hot new thing, you know?" Sasha toyed with the straw in her glass. "*LiveOKC* won't survive if people just stop in and then forget about us; they need to keep coming back. I get what Mai's saying about valuing innovation for a business model, but whatever happened to good old loyalty and consistency? As a consumer, I don't always want to be surprised. Sometimes I want exactly what I want because I've had it before and know I liked it."

"Literally all I want in my life is consistency," Carly agreed. Growing up she'd had way too little of it. That was probably why she was chronically in long relationships—several years with a guy during college and one and a half with Benjamin, who she'd still be with if they hadn't agreed on taking a break while he was out of the country for an internship.

"Why does everything always have to be new and shiny?"

Carly gave her friend the side-eye. "Says the girl sitting at Oklahoma City's hottest new bar."

Sasha's glare would have turned a lesser woman into a statue, but they'd been friends long enough that Carly wasn't fazed. "Rude. I love the Hideout just as much as this place."

As much as Carly loved the Hideout, a hole-in-the-wall staple that had been around well before they could legally drink, the unique draw of this place couldn't be replicated anywhere else in town.

"You know what's weird, though?" Carly said, tipping her head. "Watching reality TV at a bar might be fresh, but reality TV itself isn't. I mean, God, what season is *The Bachelor* on now? Twenty? What about *Survivor*? *Big Brother*?"

"I don't know, like five million?" Sasha kept her eyes on the screen above the bar for a long moment. "How on earth is that possible when two of my favorite sitcoms over the last few years were canceled after one season? What is it about these shows people love so much?"

Carly definitely didn't have all the answers. "Maybe because humans are weird. We love watching other people live their lives, especially if we don't feel like we're living our own. Even if it's fake as hell. Can't find love? Watch someone else fall into it. Even if they're pretending, I eat it up every single time. Not enough adventure in your life? Watch castaways try to stay alive and win a competition from some remote island without electricity. Are they secretly sleeping in hotels and eating regular food when the cameras are off? Don't know, don't care. I'll pretend it's real all day long."

Sasha didn't reply right away, her attention locked on the lavish date between two strangers happening before their eyes. Carly tuned in, too, and neither said anything for a long moment.

Then Sasha said quietly, "You know, you're right."

Just as Carly noticed that look in her friend's eye—the same one she'd had when they were seventeen and stole and smoked several of her dad's cigars (bad idea) and then snuck into a rap concert at the Zoo Amphitheatre (100 percent worth it)—Sasha swiveled on her stool and grinned.

"I have an idea."

CHAPTER TWO

Brooks

"Who's that?"

"Oh, that's Dr. Martin. Don't worry about him; he doesn't yell and never gets mad if you page him in the middle of the night. But don't expect him to crack any jokes or go out with the crew after work. I don't know what skeletons are in his closet, but dude's private as fuck."

—Overheard at the 4W ICU Nursing Station

Ever thought something you were about to do was a terrible idea—possibly the worst idea of your entire life—then went ahead and did it anyway?

Yeah. Brooks knew the feeling.

He dropped his head into his hands, still a little shocked at what he'd just agreed to.

Stupidest man on the planet, probably. And the funny thing was, he'd known right away his sisters were up to something.

He first became mildly suspicious when he arrived at Macy's house for dinner last night and found his nephews and brother-in-law Mark gone. Sent to the arcade for the evening, or something. Usually, an invitation to come over was nothing but a ploy to get him to wrestle his nephews to the point of exhaustion before bed, and he was always happy to oblige.

Quiet in this house was never a good sign.

The nagging sensation intensified when he found Sasha at the kitchen table.

Despite the calm house and the fact Macy hadn't mentioned Sasha would be here, everything seemed normal at first glance. Neither sister appeared on the brink of tears, so hopefully no one was dying, had their heart broken, or needed help covering up a crime. Sasha was dressed for a night on the town, but she always was. Macy looked a little ragged around the edges, but that was pretty standard, too.

He was on service at the hospital, and they'd had six new admits today . . . Was it a full moon? He'd forgotten to check, so he probably looked closer to Macy's end of the scale.

Nothing in the kitchen seemed amiss. The family dog was passed out on his bed in the corner, and a few kids' toys sat discarded on the island.

His eye caught on Sasha again, because she'd always been the worst at keeping secrets, and that's when he noticed the massive spread of Pub W takeout on the table.

His favorite.

He froze in the kitchen doorway, alarm bells screaming in his head. "No."

Sasha tapped her bright-pink nails on the table. "What?"

"Whatever it is you want, the answer is no."

From her perch near the refrigerator, Macy glared at Sasha. "I told you Pub W was too much."

Sasha ignored her and frowned at him, tossing brown hair over her shoulder. "Your sisters can't invite you over for a meal? Just the three of us? We never hang out anymore."

"No."

"Would you sit down and hear us out?" Macy rotated and grabbed a bottle of his favorite craft beer from the artwork-covered fridge and a frosted glass from the freezer.

Wow. Whatever they wanted must be big.

He walked forward and took both. "Fine." He poured and sat down. Grabbing a plate, he loaded it with chicken nachos, because he sure as hell wasn't letting them go to waste.

A moment of silence passed while he ate. He kept his eyes down, adding jalapeño poppers and baked pretzels, enjoying the food and beer. While part of him would like to completely ignore his sisters' presence, he also wanted to get this thing moving.

To be clear, he loved his sisters more than life itself. But sometimes they could be a little . . . meddle-y.

"So what's up?" he prompted.

Macy glanced at Sasha, so Brooks followed suit. It wasn't a good sign that whatever they wanted to ask was his younger sister's idea.

"It's about the magazine," Sasha said, her voice lacking its usual enthusiasm. "It's not going so well."

Brooks set his napkin down. "What do you mean?"

LiveOKC was their mother's brainchild. After growing up in Oklahoma City, she'd moved to the West Coast to pursue a journalism degree, where she'd interned at a local lifestyle newspaper. When she graduated, she moved back home, determined to provide a stronger connection between the community and their city. What started as a weekly small business feature distributed with the Sunday paper became its own independent publication and, eventually, a multicity media company. Deborah Martin wanted to improve the reputation of the flyover state she called home, especially for the younger demographic. She wanted her hometown to be a place where people wanted to stay.

After she died, both Macy and Sasha eventually joined the company—Macy on the corporate media side and Sasha as the head of the magazine. Their mom had passed down her passion for their city, and after college they'd both been determined to honor her and the place they called home. Even though Brooks had deviated and gone into medicine, he had an emotional stake in the company—especially the magazine—and followed its content religiously.

For the Martin siblings, watching *LiveOKC* succeed wasn't only important, it was personal.

"I'm sorry I haven't brought it up before now, but it's not unusual for us to have low phases. I didn't want to panic unless it stayed down."

"I'm guessing it has?"

Sasha nodded. "We're down subscribers both in print and digital, seeing less traffic on the website, and our social media numbers have plateaued. People's inboxes are already too full, and new social platforms are popping up all the time. We're trying to keep up, but something's not working."

That didn't sound good. "Shit. I'm sorry." He was invested now that he knew it had to do with the family business, but still didn't know what it had to do with him. Did she need money?

Sure, he was a doctor now, but he'd just finished his fellowship and had a hell of a lot of student loans to repay.

"I've had two businesses pull their advertisements, and I'm afraid more will follow if we don't make it worthwhile for them to stay. Which won't happen if there's not interest in our content. I need to do something new to bring people back and attract new subscribers."

"Okay, that sounds like a good idea." His gaze involuntarily floated to the doorway of Macy's office, where three framed *LiveOKC* covers hung in a row behind her desk: one of the inaugural issue, one of the issue that had featured their mom and the creation story of the business, and a rotation of the current cover. Even though Macy had broader oversight than just the magazine, she said she wanted the reminder of what it was all for.

Carrying on their mom's legacy.

"So how can I help?"

Sasha hesitated. "Macy?"

Macy shook her head. "Nu-uh. You ask him. This is your thing."

"It was your idea!"

"No, it was *your* idea. I just suggested we use Brooks as our subject."

Whoa, *subject?* He'd marginally relaxed when he realized this might just be a group brainstorm to save a business they all cared about, but now? Apprehension crawled back up his spine.

Sasha crossed her arms. "This whole thing came up when you said you were worried about Brooks."

What?

He held up a hand and directed his attention to Macy. "Worried about me? Why?"

His older sister sighed heavily, sinking deeper into her chair. "Because all you do is work. When's the last time you went out with friends? Went on a date?"

"I see James all the time."

"James doesn't count."

"Why not? He's my best friend."

"You only see him at work!"

"We went out for beers a couple weeks ago."

"Okay, fine, so you have one friend you haven't completely cut out. What about women?"

Brooks scrubbed a hand down his face. "What about them?"

"Are you seeing anyone?"

"Depends on what you mean by that." Actually, regardless of how they aimed that question, his answer was the same. He'd had a perfect no-strings-attached arrangement with his old coresident, Ashley, but she'd taken a job in Minnesota several months back. Currently he wasn't seeing anyone in any sense of the word . . . But he didn't like where this was headed, and they didn't need to know that.

Sasha scrunched her nose. "Ew. We meant, like, dating. Going out. Getting to know someone."

"I spent the last three years in a grueling critical-care fellowship. Before that, I was in residency. And before that, I was busting my ass not to fail out of medical school. Not a lot of time for dating, as you might imagine. What do you want from me?"

"Your fellowship ended almost a year ago," Macy pointed out.

"Yeah, and I've been working in an overflowing ICU floor ever since. I'm the newest attending, and we're down two FTEs. That's how this stuff works."

"Brooks."

He mirrored her tone. "Macy."

"You got a *cat*."

"So?" He took a long gulp of beer. She better have stocked the fridge, because he'd need another in about thirty seconds.

"And you started gardening," Sasha put in.

His cheeks heated. "How did you know about that?"

"You posted a sad-looking picture of a tomato plant on Instagram."

One, he forgot he'd posted that.

Two, he was proud of that endeavor. Setting up that tiny raised bed in his backyard had been more work than he'd expected. "It won't seem so sad when I'm enjoying homemade salsa in a few months. Watch: It'll be better than Pub W's."

His sisters exchanged another look.

Macy leaned forward, clasping her hands together on the table as if she were a credentialed therapist. "We think you're depressed, Brooks."

"Do what, now?"

"To be fair, she's the one who said 'depressed,'" Sasha said. "I said you were lonely."

Brooks shifted his gaze between them, eyes wide. "Ease up, ladies. I'm not depressed or lonely. I'm just *busy*. I wanted a pet, so what? And my diet's been shit the last several years. My body composition is basically protein bars and caffeine. I liked the idea of having fresh vegetables around. What's the big deal?"

They stared back at him, Sasha with a sad, pseudopitying expression and Macy with a bland I-don't-believe-you-for-a-second look.

He crossed his arms. He loved his job and actually enjoyed being in the hospital. What was so wrong with that? "Should I revert back to my womanizing, asshole tendencies from high school? Is that what you want?"

"No," Sasha said immediately.

Macy remained calm. "Of course not. We want you to consider a standard and respectful adult romantic relationship."

In the split second before he launched into a speech about his happiness and self-worth not being tied to his relationship status, Sasha tossed out, "And we want you to save Mom's business while you do it."

His words caught in his throat and he frowned. "I don't see how those are connected."

"Did you know *The Bachelor* is one of the highest-ranked reality TV shows?"

He blinked, disoriented by the random question. "What?"

"Last season averaged five million viewers per episode, mostly young people. It's been on the air for over twenty years."

"Everyone hates that show," Brooks said, apprehension growing again.

"People *love* that show, despite the fact it's a fake, problematic mess. Everyone wants to watch people fall in love. They come back for it time and time again."

A thick black line connected the dots between his brain cells. "I don't like where you're going with this."

Sasha took a deep breath as if bracing herself. She darted an anxious look at Macy, who nodded at her like, *Go on*. "I want to feature you as a bachelor in *LiveOKC*. A single guy in Oklahoma City on the dating scene, showcasing some of the best places to take someone out, which would enhance our regular content, like restaurants and fun date locations. We could do a couple big pieces in the monthly print issue, and if people signed up for the newsletter, they'd get updates in between, like documenting your triumphs and failures."

"My *failures*?"

Macy shook her head and Sasha waved a nervous hand. "Not like bombing a date or anything. We won't do a post when that happens—"

"*When* it happens?" Good God, did they think he was a total amateur when it came to women?

Maybe he should bring up his high school exploits again. Didn't matter if it was sixteen years ago, he was. Smooth. As. Butter.

"*If*, Sasha," Macy put in helpfully. "If it happens."

Sasha fussed with the necklace around her neck. "This isn't coming out right. All I want is to feature you—an attractive, young doctor on the dating scene—on a search for love. It will get you back out there to meet people again. Have some fun. Plus, tons of local business owners want to be involved for the promotion, too. I pitched it to a few places just to feel things out and got a free four-month subscription to LoveInTheCity.com, gift cards to coffee shops, restaurants, and other places like that cool rock climbing gym in the grain silo for dates. You don't even have to spend money!"

Brooks stiffened despite this being the least-concerning part of her pitch. "I'd never use a gift card to pay on a first date."

Sasha kept going as if she'd lose him if she paused. "You only have to do it for the length of the dating app offer. Four months. And we're not going to, like, video your dates or anything. I just want to write a few articles and post updates every now and then, like when you go someplace really fun you want to tell people about. And only about things you approve. You could keep the names of the women private or use pseudonyms. You could write it yourself, almost like a dating journal, or I could do it for you."

She clenched her necklace in her fist. "Everyone I pitched it to got so excited, Brooks. It's like a dating tour of Oklahoma City. People would want to check it out for ideas even if they didn't care if you ever found love, but I guarantee people will follow along for that. This would give the magazine the push it needs. Bring back subscribers who got bored and bring in new ones. This will work. I know it."

He propped his elbow on the table and dropped his forehead in his hand. "This is . . . a lot, Sasha."

The room was silent for a beat, then came Macy's calm voice. "I thought so, too, at first. But I sat on it for a few days, and the more I thought about it, and the more I pictured you at the center of it all, the better I liked it."

"At first?" He glanced up. "How long have you two been cooking this up?"

"I've been thinking about it for weeks," Sasha admitted. "Trying to muster up the nerve to ask if you'd do it."

"What finally pushed you over the edge?"

She hesitated. "The tomato plant."

What did she have against lycopene? The nurses on the unit had been excited about free produce. "No salsa for you."

"Let us help you," Sasha pleaded. "And help *LiveOKC* at the same time. Please. For Mom."

Aw, hell. "Seriously?" he said. "That's a low blow, even for you."

"Forget about Mom," Macy said, even though she had to know that was impossible. "Worst-case scenario, you go on a few dates, approve a few articles Sasha writes, and get a new wardrobe out of the deal. Wish I could sign up, honestly."

Brooks paused. "Wait, a new wardrobe?"

"Oh, Mode is contributing a stylist and image consultant for the cause."

So many things about that sentence bothered him. Referring to his love life as a "cause," her apparent assumption he would eventually say yes, and the fact she thought he needed a stylist. Or image consultant, whatever the hell that was.

"What the hell is Mode?"

"It's a service sort of like Stitch Fix or Wantable, where you get a personal stylist to choose clothes tailored to your tastes and body type. But this one's local and you can meet with your stylist in person for shopping. Smaller scale. They try to find things from small stores and designers rather than chains or warehouses. You buy the clothes you want, give back the ones you don't."

"I thought you said I didn't have to spend money."

"The consultant fee will be waived, so you're basically getting a stylist for free. Mode's known for being the best. They've worked with some of the Thunder players! It's a steal, trust me."

"You need new clothes anyway," Macy said bluntly.

He regarded his faded jeans and T-shirt. "What's wrong with my clothes?"

"How much time do you have? I could spend fifteen minutes on those jeans alone."

Brooks glared at her. "Do you want me to do this or not?"

"Yes," Sasha cut in, directing her own scowl at Macy before focusing on him again. "Does it help that you know the stylist? My friend Carly works there, remember her? Working with her's better than a stranger."

Carly had been one of Sasha's closest friends in high school, and one of the few he hadn't messed around with. Only a year younger than him, Sasha's group of friends mixed with his often, and as the "hot older brother" and star of the basketball team, he'd received a lot of attention from the more outgoing ones.

At the time, he hadn't minded one bit.

He'd never hooked up with Carly, though. He hadn't known her all that well, but the words that came to mind when he thought about her were nice, smart, and shy. She'd gone to college out of state and stayed there several years but had moved home about two years ago. Sasha hadn't shut up about it when she found out Carly was coming back, and from what he could tell, the friends had picked up right where they'd left off.

It might be marginally better to have someone familiar, soft-spoken, and kind be the one to tell him his fashion sense sucked. Sort of like the way food poisoning was marginally better than the Ebola virus.

Sasha dropped her hands to her lap. She swallowed, her eyes turning glassy. "Please, Brooks?"

He closed his eyes. *Dammit.* He wanted to help her, but it sounded miserable. Just a step shy of torture. "I don't know. I need time to think about it."

She opened her mouth as if to argue, but seemed to think better of it. "Fine."

He went for more nachos and had only gotten his hands on one chip when she spoke again.

"How long do you think you'll need?"

"Don't rush him," Macy said quietly.

Sasha sighed. "Okay, you're right. Sorry. I've just been thinking about it nonstop, and I got excited. There's so much we could do with it, and I can't wait to see my brother finally fall in love."

He snorted. "Doubt that'll happen."

"Name one thing I put my mind to that I've failed at."

"Basketball," Brooks said at the same time Macy shouted, "Chess."

"Something I actually care about!"

Brooks swung his gaze to Macy. "She didn't specify."

"Agreed."

Sasha tried to glare at her older siblings and failed, never having been able to stay mad at them for long. She gave up and smiled, eyes bright. "Just wait. If you agree to this, I'll put every connection I have at your disposal, including all the available women in the greater metro area. Watch—you'll meet the love of your life, and who will you have to thank?"

"The stylist, probably, if things are as bad as you say." He angled his head. "Macy, too, because if anyone can talk me into this, it's her."

Turned out, it wasn't Macy who talked him into it. Brooks came to the conclusion on his own with a little indirect help from his friend James.

They'd hit the coffee shop near the hospital a few days after the meeting with his sisters, and while they waited for their drinks, James had surreptitiously tilted his head toward the barista. "What do you think of Aly?"

It had taken Brooks several seconds to realize who he was talking about. "What do you mean?"

His friend, usually confident bordering on arrogant, had appeared almost sheepish. "She's cute, right?"

Brooks blinked, disarmed. Now that he considered it, yeah, she was cute. Beautiful, even. "Definitely. Why?"

James shrugged, and Brooks could have sworn he blushed. It was hard to tell with his russet-brown skin and the fact Brooks could count on one hand the number of times he'd seen his friend embarrassed . . . but still. This was new. "I noticed her several weeks ago. I've come in a few times without you, and we've talked some. I was thinking about asking her out."

Something shifted in Brooks in that moment, a troubling internal realization even as he said, "Do it, man. You're a catch."

Brooks hadn't noticed Aly before.

He never noticed anyone. At least, not once he left the hospital.

Inside those sliding doors he felt at home. He felt prepared, confident, and useful. While he wasn't super social or one of the physicians that sat around cracking jokes in the break room, he knew everyone's name and they knew his. People respected him and took what he had to say seriously. He'd worked his ass off to become an intensivist, and watching over the people lying in those beds, their bodies at their most vulnerable, gave him the sense of purpose he'd been searching for.

But when he left, he just sort of checked out.

If he wasn't standing here right now, he wouldn't have been able to recall any of the employees working at this shop, which he frequented often. It wasn't that he didn't care—he loved this place. He tipped well and smiled and said thank you with every interaction. It was just . . . he'd been inside his own head for so long. Always studying, thinking about his patients, his next shift, that email blast with new clinical trial results he wanted to read, and when he'd be able to crash on his couch with his cat and a beer to watch the game without the code-blue alert screaming in his head. Honestly, he hadn't thought much of it, because it seemed normal to decompress after a shift, especially with the kind of work he did. Until he witnessed James, his colleague and friend who had just finished the same kind of grueling training program and kept the same schedule as Brooks, comment on a complete stranger he wanted to get to know.

Socializing with people other than his colleagues had become so foreign that he hadn't even realized he'd forgotten how to do it. Even though he'd never admit it to their faces, maybe his sisters were right. Maybe he was a little lonely. He just hoped Macy's worst-case scenario was on point and this whole dating thing wouldn't crash and burn.

He waited a couple of days just to make Sasha sweat, but he finally called her with his answer.

"Okay. I'll do it."

CHAPTER THREE

Carly

You won't believe the joint business pitch Sasha and I came up with. Not quite as bananas as that reptile café in Midtown, but close. I can't wait to tell you about it, let me know if you can talk sometime this week. Miss you.

—*Text message from Carly Porter to Benjamin Wheeler*

"He's in."

Sasha's announcement came the second Carly opened her apartment door. Half an hour ago, she'd sent a text:

Sasha: you home?
Carly: Yep.
Sasha: I'm coming over and I HAVE NEWS

There was only one *he* she could mean by that. Rather, there was only one *he* that mattered, if Sasha had been thinking about the plan they'd cooked up as incessantly as Carly.

She'd been a little hesitant when Sasha first blurted out, *We should do our own kind of reality show!* that night at Variety. It sounded pretty out there and more than a little complicated to coordinate. But Sasha had kept at it, texting Carly every few days with updates about things she was working on—assessing local business interest, meeting with the editorial team about content placement and the like—to make sure the plan could work. It was when Sasha suggested a formal partnership with Mode to dress the chosen bachelor that Carly decided to go all in. A collaboration like this could be just the type of innovative idea to prove to Mai and Kyle she was someone worth investing in.

If all went according to plan, this could give *LiveOKC* the bump it needed and land Carly a coveted permanent position at Mode. And over the last few weeks, all the logistics had fallen into place nicely . . . except one.

They had to find their bachelor.

"You found someone?"

Sasha danced her way into Carly's apartment, pausing when she twirled around and landed in the kitchen. She dropped her hands and shook her head. "God, I always feel like such a slob when I see your place. How do you keep it so perfect all the time? It's like a showroom."

"Focus, Sasha. Who's the bachelor?"

Her friend grinned as she leaned her hips back against the counter and crossed one ankle over the other. "None other than my very own brother, Brooks Martin."

Carly's mouth dropped open. "*Brooks?* How'd you get him to agree to that?"

"He was happy to help."

Carly cocked a disbelieving brow.

"Fine," Sasha said. "I bribed him with food, beer, and guilt. Macy helped."

"Ah." Carly smiled a little. The closeness between siblings had always been sweet and entertaining to watch for an only child like her. Based on her mother's less-than-stellar parenting style, it was probably best for society as a whole that Carly never had a brother or sister, but still. Part of her had always wanted one.

"Your brother might be the last person I ever expected to be part of this." And not necessarily because he was a bad choice. Brooks just wasn't someone who had crossed Carly's mind over the last several years. After he left for college when she and Sasha were about to start their senior year, it sort of felt like he'd dropped off the face of the earth. "Does he even need me? A stylist, I mean?"

Sasha barked out a laugh so loud, Carly's cat, Pepper, fell off his perch on the back of the couch. "Boy, does he."

Carly's eyes went wide. "That bad?"

"Oh, don't look at me like that. I know you love extensive makeovers more than the picky folks who already think they're as good as runway models."

It was true. Carly loved witnessing a complete transformation—not only on the outside but also what dressing well could do for a person's confidence. Fashion had been one of her only sources of it growing up, even when she'd had to get creative. Back then she couldn't risk spending much money, so she'd become a master at creating secondhand style. She loved teaching clients how to dress for different body types and thrived when presented with a challenge. That first look of awe tossed over their shoulder that said *Oh my gosh, I look . . . good?* was the best part, hands down.

If Brooks really needed that much help, it was proof good fashion sense didn't run in families. Sasha would never need help from a company like Mode. On the contrary, sometimes Carly's ideas stemmed from something her friend wore. For as long as they'd been friends, which bloomed somewhere in the middle of fourth grade, Sasha'd stood out.

While she'd never turned as many heads, Carly always worked to put her best foot forward when it came to her appearance, too. Like it or not, it was people's first impression of her. Even during her day job, where she walked into the office only to sit at the computer and work with numbers, she never had a hair out of place.

Her therapist would probably say Carly's tendency toward perfection was a way of concealing what really happened behind the aging, paint-chipped front door of her childhood home, but that didn't matter now. She was independent, successful, and happy, which was more than a lot of people could say.

"If you want to know the truth," Sasha said, likely interpreting Carly's musings as reluctance, which wasn't wrong, "I'm doing this to revitalize our business, yes. But I could have found another guy. Macy and I decided to ask Brooks because we think he needs this, too."

Brooks needed what? Help meeting women?

That was absurd.

Ridiculous.

Impossible.

"What do you mean?"

"He's spent the last decade and a half of his life in school and hospitals. Don't get me wrong—I'm proud of him. But he's not the same guy he was back in high school."

"Is that a bad thing?" Carly said without thinking. Yes, teenage Carly'd had a mild crush on him, along with the majority of their friends, but even then she'd had enough sense to recognize Brooks had some growing up to do.

Though at the time, it only seemed fair to give the Martin siblings a pass for temporary behavior changes after losing their mom so suddenly. Sasha had been sixteen and Brooks seventeen. Carly didn't know the oldest, Macy, very well but knew she'd been closer to twenty or twenty-one at the time.

Sasha had refused to come out of her room for a month after the accident, and when she'd returned, she'd made it clear she didn't want to talk about it.

At all.

Brooks, on the other hand, handled the loss of his mom in a stereotypical, dramatic Hollywood fashion. He went off the deep end and pivoted from popular-but-straitlaced basketball star to a partying risk-taker who rarely said no.

"For the most part, no," Sasha said, bringing Carly back to the question about comparing past Brooks with now. "He nearly destroyed himself his senior year, and I'm thankful he put that behavior behind him. But it's like he went too far in the other direction, you know? All he does is work. He hardly smiles anymore. He'll always answer our calls but never calls us himself. He has no social life to speak of. He's young and a doctor, for God's sake. He's finally out of training and has some free time, though you wouldn't know it talking to him. He should be on dates every weekend. Instead, he got a cat and started a garden. Macy thinks he's depressed."

"Hey, I have a cat. I'm not depressed."

"You go out. You have friends. It's not the same. I'm just worried about him, you know?"

It was hard to picture Brooks as his sister described him. After high school Carly had moved to Nebraska for almost ten years, so she'd missed a huge chunk of his life. But still, an image of him sitting alone in a dark living room was all wrong. He was too small there, the darkness larger than him, and that wasn't the guy she remembered. With all that dark hair, his long, lean body, and a killer smile, he'd filled every room to the brim with charisma and energy. He brought jokes and fun and excitement, no matter how ill-advised. When Brooks Martin sauntered through the doorway, everyone knew it, whether they laid eyes on him or not.

When he was nearby, people could feel it.

"Wow. I just . . . I had no idea."

"He doesn't really let Macy or me in anymore, but I'm hoping it will be different with you. I'll be honest: You have your work cut out for you. But I know you'll work that Carly Porter magic and transform more than just his wardrobe."

"The wardrobe's the easy part," Carly said, and Sasha laughed.

"Not this time."

Carly frowned. "Now you're making me nervous."

Sasha waved a hand. "Nah, you got this. I promise. Plus he's not married, so there's no chance you'll be accused of being a home-wrecker."

"Thank God," Carly said, thinking of all the training she'd just finished retaking, punctuated with her signature on Mode's new code of conduct. "I don't think I could afford another scandal. Even a completely made-up one."

"You and I both know you're the last person who would hook up with a client, and deep down, Mai knows it, too. In a few months, that awful Princeton woman will be the last thing on your mind as Mai's offering you a promotion and a raise, and you'll never have to use a calculator again. Now, let's go celebrate, yeah?"

"Yes. Let's."

"Where to?"

"Hideout?"

"Perfect."

That evening, after returning home and changing into sweatpants and a T-shirt, Carly settled onto the couch with her laptop.

She unlocked her phone and pulled up the contact Sasha had shared a few hours ago bearing Brooks's information, complete with his email address, phone number, and an adorable photo of him making a silly face to the camera.

This was the Brooks she remembered—energetic and fun, if a little overconfident, but just enough that it tipped more to the side of appealing than off-putting. He looked young in the photo, though she couldn't tell how young. It was hard to imagine this new version of the man Sasha had described earlier that evening.

Hardly smiles.

No social life.

Depressed.

Carly homed in on those hazel eyes, dark and bottomless but that had somehow always been so expressive and full of mischief, and wondered how such a transformation was possible.

On second thought, losing both parents in the span of a few years would probably do that to a lot of people . . . even if the response was a little delayed.

She opened a blank email and glanced at her cat. "Are we ready for this?"

Pepper stared at her with yellow eyes, flicking his tail in the air.

"Show a little excitement, will you? If this goes well, it could be our ticket to our dream job. And if I only have one job to worry about, that means I get to be home more often with you. Wouldn't you like that?"

Pepper blinked.

"I thought so," she said, and started typing.

Brooks Martin as her client. Well, this would certainly be interesting.

CHAPTER FOUR

Brooks

Brooks Martin, please report to the principal's office. NOW.

—Heard over the intercom at Freemont High School, senior year

The email came through late Monday evening while Brooks was sprawled out on his couch, reading about gardening in Oklahoma. As soon as he saw the sender, a stab of apprehension pierced his side.

Well, well, well. If it wasn't the consequences of his own actions.

To: Brooks.Martin@zzmail.com
From: Carly.Porter@modestyle.com

Brooks,

Well hi! It's been a while, huh? Hope things are going well and you're not dreading this email, because I'll be honest, I'm picturing you dreading this email. Sasha really cooked something up this time, didn't she? The good news is I'm confident with a few good outfits and avoiding any more of her meddling, we'll get through it together. And, you know, if this goes well, maybe you'll end up with the love of your life. Or get laid at the very least.

Brooks blinked at the screen, taken aback. Had Carly Porter just made a sex joke?

Anyway, Sasha mentioned your work schedule is pretty hectic so I'll just get straight to the point. At the bottom of the email there's a link to our website, feel free to check out the How It Works and FAQ pages to learn more. I'd like to schedule the initial consultation where I can answer any questions you have and learn about your style preferences. We can do it in person or via Zoom. In person is ideal but I'm flexible. Let me know what you think.

Carly

Brooks got up and grabbed a beer before following her advice to click on the link, this whole thing feeling more real the further he got.

Mode Style was a decent-size business, founded locally (likely why Sasha picked it) but had expanded beyond Oklahoma, employing several full-time consultants, social media experts, and marketing specialists in other large cities throughout the Midwest. They offered personal shopping, wardrobe styling, and image consulting services (which he understood only slightly better after reading the description).

His natural inclination was to request a virtual consult. He liked being at home, felt more comfortable behind a screen rather than face-to-face, and liked the idea of not being immediately judged for his clothes on their first meeting.

On the other hand, his sisters had implied he'd become some sort of recluse, which he'd grudgingly realized wasn't wrong. Maybe he needed a trial run with Carly before going on an actual date with a stranger, and this was as good an opportunity as any.

To: Carly.Porter@modestyle.com
From: Brooks.Martin@zzmail.com

Carly,
Dread is probably too strong a word. Am I looking forward to the next few months? No. But working with you is the least of my worries (please don't take that as a challenge).
I'd like to meet in person if we can. I'm on service this week, so my days are pretty long.
Maybe we could meet for coffee sometime tomorrow evening?

Brooks

Fifteen minutes later, his phone dinged.

To: Brooks.Martin@zzmail.com
From: Carly.Porter@modestyle.com

That's perfect—I have a different job during the day so I usually meet after hours, anyway. How about tomorrow at 6:30pm? Ever been to Coffee Slingers on Broadway?

Carly

To: Carly.Porter@modestyle.com

From: Brooks.Martin@zzmail.com

Love that place. See you then.

Brooks

To: Brooks.Martin@zzmail.com
From: Carly.Porter@modestyle.com

Perfect. If possible, could you follow the link at the bottom and fill out as much of this personal style questionnaire as you can before we meet?

Carly

He frowned at the screen. Homework already? Damn.

Brooks walked into Coffee Slingers at 6:24 the next evening. Ever since arriving three minutes late for rounds his first week as a resident at University Medical Center and receiving a public evisceration by the attending in front of the entire team, he'd never been late for anything again.

Like, literally never.

His gaze swept the shop. He didn't see anyone he recognized, so he headed toward an empty table to wait and keep an eye on the door.

"Brooks?"

He swiveled left, searching for the feminine voice. A (very) pretty brunette sat at the table he'd just passed, offering him a hesitant smile and a little wave.

He blinked. "Carly?"

Wow.

She looked . . . different. Fifteen years would do that to a person, he supposed. Why he expected the same girl with short blond hair and massive hoop earrings, he had no idea. He certainly didn't resemble the high school version of himself, thank God.

Her hair was brown, wavy, and long—so long he wasn't sure where it stopped—and he had the strangest urge to walk behind her or ask her to pull the mass over her shoulder so he could find out. Her features were similar to the girl he knew but matured and notably more confident than he remembered, even with her hesitant half smile.

He was nervous, too. Plus, he was staring at her like a total jackass.

"Hey. Sorry. I didn't recognize you."

She stood and offered her hand in a formal, professional gesture. "You look different, too."

Hard to say whether she meant that as a compliment. He shook her hand, firm but gentle, and after a beat of awkward silence he tipped his head to the counter. "Have you already ordered?"

"Not yet."

"Will you let me buy?" He'd need the bonus points when she saw how terrible he'd done on that questionnaire.

She hesitated for a beat, then shrugged. "Okay."

Another customer was at the counter, so they stepped up to wait. She stood quietly beside him, and he had no idea what to say, so he studied the menu as if he didn't know damn well he'd be ordering a quad Americano.

Thankfully, they didn't have to wait long. Carly ordered a latte, and once they were settled back at the table with their drinks, he eyed the thick leather binder on the table.

It seemed a little rude to jump right into the reason they were here, but he wanted to get this over with. He should probably ask how she was and what she'd been doing the last fifteen years, but the words wouldn't come.

Small talk wasn't something he did much of these days. His conversations usually either had purpose, like discussing patient status and treatment plans, or occurred with someone he'd known forever and felt comfortable enough with not to fill empty space with bullshit.

He took a drink of his Americano, keeping his eyes on the table.

"So you're a doctor now?"

He looked up and met her brown eyes. They were pretty. Warm and friendly and framed by long, dark lashes. "Yeah."

"And you work at a hospital?"

"Yeah. In the ICU."

"How much school did that take?"

"I finished last June." What were his sisters so worried about? Clearly he was a conversational wizard.

"Holy shit. You've been in school almost this whole time?"

"Pretty much." How did he not remember those eyes? Had he ever noticed them at all?

"And here I was proud of my four-year bachelor's degree."

"You should be," he said honestly. "That's a major accomplishment."

She muttered a few words that sounded both humorous and self-deprecating under her breath, bringing her cup to her lips.

Something about it relaxed him. "What's your degree in? Something with fashion?" Was that a thing?

She shook her head. "Nah, that sort of always came naturally to me. My degree's in accounting, actually."

"Oh." Seemed like a significant deviation from fashion, but when he thought about it, math for a career made sense for her, too. She'd always seemed ridiculously smart. "Is that your day job?"

"Yeah. I've been at Mode for two years now, though. It might not seem like long, but I've always had solid intuition when it comes to clothes. You'll be in good of hands with me, I promise."

Did she think he thought she wasn't good enough to work with him, or something? God, the idea of doing this with a stranger was ten times worse. "It's not like I'd know the difference. According to Sasha, I have no fashion sense." He glanced down, then back at her. "You probably already judged what I'm wearing, didn't you?"

"Of course not."

He didn't usually give a second thought to his clothes, so why he felt the need to defend himself was beyond him. "I only wear scrubs at work, and I don't have time to shop. Even if I did, now that my sisters made me all self-conscious about it, I probably shouldn't trust anything I might like—"

He stopped short when Carly laughed. It was one of those unexpected, full-bodied laughs, and he wasn't sure he'd ever heard it before.

It slid across his skin like a cool breeze on a stifling summer day.

"Relax, I didn't even notice what you were wearing," she said.

But she wouldn't meet his eyes.

The word slipped through his lips without thought. "Liar."

She met his gaze and blinked. Her lips twitched, confirming his suspicion, and even though he should probably be offended, he had the strangest urge to smile. This felt familiar, like the other night when he'd sat with his sisters.

Another tiny piece of pressure slipped from his shoulders, and he shook his head slowly, feigning astonishment. "Shouldn't this be a safe place? An honest environment between expert and client?"

She cupped her hands around the speckled ceramic mug. "Do you really want to do this now? I'd planned on easing you in."

He met her gaze straight on. When a new patient was admitted to his service, he had to figure out how bad things were before he could come up with a treatment plan. "Straightforward is best. I can take it."

Her left brow arched as she regarded him. Finally she sighed, seeming resigned. "It's the jeans."

The hell was wrong with these jeans? Macy had mentioned them, too. "What about them?"

"They're one, maybe two sizes too big. I see zero indication there's an ass anywhere in there."

He was so focused on them (his *favorite* pair) he nearly missed the second part of what she said. "Do . . . do I want people to see my ass?"

"One like that, yes." Other than the slight pink tint to her cheeks, she seemed perfectly professional and matter of fact as she said it. Businesslike.

Wait. "You looked at my ass?"

"Tried to," she said, unapologetic. "It's part of my job."

He was almost flattered, an emotion he hadn't experienced in years and that wasn't altogether unpleasant, until she added, "But as I said, I'm still not sure what I'm working with."

He watched her for a beat, unsure what to make of where this conversation had gone. And who it was with. "You're . . . not what I expected."

"What do you mean?"

"I thought you were shy."

"Quiet," she corrected. "I used to be quiet, but I've never been shy." She took a sip of her latte. "You'll see."

The way she tossed out those final two words felt like a grenade thrown into his lap, and she waved a hand as if ready to move on. "We'll talk more about pants later. Were you able to finish that questionnaire I sent?"

Still stuck a few seconds back on the *quiet, not shy* part, because same, he slid a hand across his mouth. "Yeah, I submitted it online, was that okay?"

She nodded and slid an iPad from the leather binder, then tapped the screen a few times. "Found you."

He nursed his coffee for a few moments while she scrolled through, trying to read her facial expressions. There were many, but he didn't know her well enough to interpret any of them.

Finally she nodded, which seemed universally a positive thing. "Height, weight, pant, shirt, and shoe sizes. Have you ever had formal measurements done? Like for a suit or a tailored dress shirt?"

"Not since Macy's wedding, which was almost ten years ago."

"That's fine." She made a note in the notebook to her left. "Color preferences include mostly neutrals, which is great. Classic, really." Her eyes flicked to his face, studying him. Just when he began to fidget under her perusal, she asked, "How do you feel about green?"

"Fine?"

She nodded and made another note.

"You said here purple, pink, orange, and yellow are nonpreferred colors. With your skin tone I agree with the orange and yellow. Are pink and purple hard no's, or are you open to trying them if I find something I think could work?"

He shrugged. "I guess I'd give them a try."

She made another note. "You left this one blank," she noted, pointing to the tablet and reading out loud, "What's your favorite part of your body?"

"I didn't think my answer would be helpful for this."

Her skin flushed and her mouth dropped open, and he realized how that sounded.

"My brain! Not my . . . Fuck. You know." He wanted to slide under the table. Maybe they should have gone for beers instead. "Sorry that I, um. Said that. Fuck, I mean."

Hell. He was in hell.

She put her hands to her face, and for a second he worried he'd totally blown this whole thing. He'd offended and embarrassed her, and now he'd have to tell Sasha this wasn't going to work . . . But then he heard a snort from between Carly's fingers.

When she dropped her hands and he saw her eyes, he couldn't help but smile back at her. He gripped the back of his neck, sure his face was as red as hers. He cleared his throat. "Anyway."

She leaned back and took a breath. "Well. You're right, your brain isn't what I was going for with this question. Dicks are equally unhelpful, in case you were wondering, though you wouldn't have been the first to answer with that."

He choked on his coffee.

She kept talking as if she hadn't just said "dicks" like it was any other word. As calm and collected as she'd been admitting she'd tried to assess his butt. "We can skip this question if you want, but if there's a certain area you'd like to bring attention to, this is the time to tell me."

He struggled to focus. *Body parts minus brain and dick.* "I honestly don't know."

He tried to exercise somewhat regularly at the twenty-four-hour gym near the hospital, but he wasn't obsessive about it and really only cared enough to ensure he remained fit and healthy. He was probably on the thinner side compared with other men he saw in the weight area, but he'd never felt self-conscious about it. His biceps weren't bulging out of any sleeves, and his pecs weren't defined enough to notice underneath a fitted shirt.

He clearly didn't know what kind of ass he was working with, but he wasn't about to stand up and ask for Carly's opinion.

"What do other men say to that question?" he asked.

"Forearms are a favorite. Arms, shoulders, butt. I'd say those are the most common."

"I don't think any of those are worth writing home about. For me, anyway."

She opened her mouth with a frown but closed it without saying anything.

"Can I say my eyes?" If not, he'd just say skip it. He was getting kind of desperate to move on.

Her gaze met his. "Why do you think I asked if you liked green?"

Oh.

Huh.

"Next, let's look at some styles, and you let me know if you'd ever wear something like that, okay?" She replaced the iPad in the leather binder and handed him a thick packet of flat-lay images of various men's fashion.

He spent the next ten billion years flipping through the stack, occasionally pausing when she had follow-up questions about what in particular he liked or disliked about something.

Relief coursed through him when he reached the final one.

"There. That wasn't so bad, was it?" she asked with a smile.

"Debatable."

"There's just one thing left before I start shopping. You can say no if you want to."

"Okay."

"I'm not sure how much you're wanting to buy. I assume Sasha wants me to dress you for the initial photos, any others that are taken for articles, and for your dates. Four months, right? How many do you think you'll go on?"

"Your guess is as good as mine. I haven't done this in a while, and I've never been on one of these apps. Maybe a couple?"

Carly made a strange noise. "I'd say you could meet as many women as you want."

"Is flattery part of the Mode package?" He wasn't complaining, just wondering.

"I'm just trying to prepare you. You could have several dates a week."

He shuddered internally. "I just want to help put *LiveOKC* back on track."

She tipped her head to the side. "Do you not want to fall in love? You're not in this for yourself even a little?"

"I don't know," he answered honestly.

She regarded him for a moment, and boy, did he want to know what she was thinking.

"I only ask because if you don't want to spring for a completely new wardrobe, I need to know what I'm starting with. You could send me pictures, or I could stop by sometime to take a look in your closet. If you'd rather skip that step, I can just work off what we've talked about today, but let me know as soon as you can. Sasha wants the first photo shoot to happen pretty quick."

He narrowed his eyes. "Is this a ploy to get in there and throw out everything you don't like? Because Sasha's been trying to do that for years, and I'm not giving in now."

She laughed. "I promise I won't get rid of anything without your express approval. You'd be surprised how much I can do with the things people already have. Sometimes it just takes a little creativity."

"I do science, remember? Repetitive, analytical, and concrete are my comfort zone. Pretty much the exact opposite of creative."

"Lucky for you, I can do both."

He thought for a few seconds. "Want to do it now?"

"Now?"

He shrugged. "Might as well, if you're not busy."

She tapped her phone and glanced at the illuminated screen, presumably to check the time.

A photo appeared, a candid shot of Carly's face slightly angled away from the camera as she looked at the ocean beyond. A colorful sunset lit up the sky behind her, breathtaking even in the picture, but it was the content, peaceful smile on her face that caught his eye.

When was the last time he'd looked that happy?

Hell, when was the last time he'd *been* that happy?

"That's a cool picture."

"Oh, thanks. My boyfriend took it." She paused as she regarded the screen, a small frown wrinkling her brow. Shaking her head slightly, her expression cleared. "I don't know why I just said that. Benjamin's not my boyfriend anymore—he's my ex, now. Habit, I guess."

"I'm sorry," he said, and it almost sounded like a question. Was that the appropriate response here? If she was still calling him her boyfriend by default, it must have been recent.

She shrugged. "It's . . . fine. It is what it is. He's in Seoul for an internship, and we agreed we didn't want to do the long-distance thing."

"Ah," he said, as if he were familiar with the mechanics of a major relationship decision like that.

"Anyway," she said. "I'm good to do it now if you are."

"Sure."

"Great." She gathered her things and stood. "Let's get out of here."

CHAPTER FIVE

Carly

> Got the pictures—very cool. I had no idea there were so many sharp angles in Korean architecture, and I loved the notes about the importance of harmony in design. Maybe one of these days we'll travel the world and sightsee together.
>
> *—Email from Carly Porter to Benjamin Wheeler*

Brooks lived in a nearby historic neighborhood only ten minutes from Coffee Slingers, which meant Carly didn't have much time to marinate on their meeting.

Not that she needed to have him figured out already, but listen, she liked being in the know. She worked behind the scenes on most things—like design and accounting—and paid attention to tiny details most people took for granted, whether it be clothing or a spreadsheet.

She liked being prepared, and she hated surprises.

The mystery of Brooks Martin would drive her crazy.

He'd seemed nervous and reserved when he first arrived, and had relaxed only marginally by the end.

When had he changed so much? Had something happened, or had he just grown out of his wild ways the same way she'd grown out of caring so much what other people thought about her? She still wanted to succeed, but now she just wanted it for herself. She'd always been her own biggest critic anyway.

Where was the confidence Brooks had worn like a well-loved sweatshirt? The fun-loving, enigmatic guy who'd shone so bright it had almost hurt to look at him? It was like he'd installed a dimmer switch and slid it all the way down, muffling the brightness she hoped was still buried in there, somewhere.

Rather than inviting and open, he was . . . not standoffish, exactly. She couldn't put her finger on it . . . Just not quite as warm. Less accessible.

He was still handsome, though, even if his good looks were more subtle. Current-day Brooks was a man who seemed like he wouldn't mind being overlooked, and if women weren't paying attention, they might do just that. But the longer she'd sat there assessing him, the more attractive he'd become.

And in those *awful* jeans! She'd lied through her teeth when she said she wouldn't throw anything away. They'd be gone the second she could get her hands on them.

She slowed to a stop when Brooks turned his Audi into a driveway. He parked and got out, walking to the porch of the single-story bungalow, where he waited for her with his hands in his pockets.

"This is so cute," she said as she made her way up the sidewalk, admiring the large oak towering over the yard, casting dappled shade over her steps. The front porch was long and narrow, and the railing looked freshly painted. The front door, too—a deep navy color that caught her eye right away. "I adore that color."

He seemed pleased. "Thanks. I wasn't sure about it, but I wanted a project. Thought about doing the table and chairs next. They came with the place."

A small wooden bistro set sat in the corner of the porch, and it had seen better days. "I'd totally do that in a lime green or yellow, but something tells me that's not in the cards for you." She glanced over at him and laughed. "Judging by the look of pure horror on your face, I'm right."

"It just sounds . . . bright."

Note: Slowly ease into bright colors when shopping for Brooks.

He unlocked the door, holding it open for her. A black-and-white blur darted across the room, and Carly let out a yelp before realizing it was only a cat. She took a few steps inside before she knelt and held out her hand.

"Meet Oreo," Brooks said, leaning against the doorjamb. "He's an okay roommate. Usually late paying rent and sort of has an attitude problem."

"That's cats for you," she said with a grin. The animal padded forward to sniff her, eventually allowing her to scratch underneath his jaw. "Nice to meet you, Oreo."

She rubbed him for another moment and stood. Oreo slithered in a figure eight around her ankles, purring and curling his tail around her calves.

Brooks regarded his pet with raised brows. "He's not usually into new people. The first time my friend James came over after I got him, he hid in the bathroom for three hours."

"James or Oreo?"

That earned her a tiny smile as they walked farther into the house. "Oreo."

"Maybe he smells my cat. I also have a freeloading roommate named Pepper."

"Yeah? Does Sasha give you a hard time about that?"

"No, why?"

He made a face. "She insinuated my getting a cat was pathetic or something. Like I was an old man destined to die alone because of him."

Carly rolled her eyes. "Where I'm from, we don't listen to Sasha."

His place was filled with homey-looking furnishings that were sort of haphazard and slightly mismatched, but somehow it worked. Probably because everything was based in neutrals without any aforementioned pops of color. Never a good idea for those to be unintentional.

The walls were decorated with a few unframed wrapped-canvas art pieces, which she slowed to study as she passed.

His voice came from behind her. "You make a good point, but I listened to her when I bought those."

"Local artist?" Carly guessed.

"Yeah. Her name is Bek, or something. Has a studio downtown."

They were beautiful. Abstract and eye catching but still muted in blues, greens, and whites, and quiet in a way that made you want to step closer to see what you might be missing. "Counterproposal: We listen to Sasha when it comes to art, but not when she's dissing our cats."

"Deal." He continued through the kitchen and into his bedroom. "Oreo's still following you, by the way."

She barely heard him because she'd just stepped into his bedroom and was struck by two things.

One: It smelled incredible in here, like pine and laundry detergent.

Two: While the rest of the house had been immaculate, this room was a disaster.

Okay, not a disaster, exactly. But his bed was unmade (she had a thing about that), loose papers covered the bedside table, several pairs of scrubs littered a chair in the corner, and two pairs of shoes lay right in the middle of the floor.

Was that a stethoscope on the doorknob?

"Sorry." He stood a few feet away, watching her, one hand passing across his jaw. "I wasn't expecting company."

"Don't be silly, it's fine." She glanced behind her, relieved to see the cat still there. She picked him up gently for something to do with her hands, or else she'd start tidying things up. "You should see my room."

Everything at her place was perfect, but he didn't know that. He didn't look convinced, so she changed the subject to the furball burrowing against her chest, purring like crazy. "I officially love this cat. I might have to steal him."

"He's one of those that's more like a dog than a cat."

"Those are the best kind."

He regarded Oreo for a moment. "Him, plus my garden, is what prompted this whole intervention, you know."

She peeked out his bedroom window, which overlooked the backyard. Sure enough, a tiny raised bed sat out in the back corner. "What's wrong with having a garden?"

He nodded a little, as if pleased someone was on his side. "Hell if I know." Then he stopped and twisted his lips to the side, looking strangely vulnerable. "I don't really know what I'm doing, though."

"With the garden?"

"Yeah. It was sort of a spontaneous decision, and in hindsight I probably should have done a little more research first." He leaned his upper back against the wall, and his gaze drifted from her, focusing through the window. "I'd just come off a rough week at work where we lost several patients, and . . . I don't know. I guess after seeing that, I sort of liked the idea of bringing something to life."

A soft breath whooshed through her lips as she regarded him and the distant look in his eyes. It was the most he'd said to her at once all day. "That's sad, Brooks. And sort of beautiful."

"It'll be beautiful if I can actually grow something. If not, I think I'll feel even worse."

The room filled with silence. What could she say to that? Her mind spun, desperate to think of something helpful. "My mom's a pretty serious gardener. She'll go on about it for hours if you let her. If you ever have any questions I'd be happy to ask her."

His eyes swung to hers. "Yeah? Thanks." He glanced back outside, then at her again, and after a few seconds he pushed off the wall as if he could displace the somber air between them. "Anyway. Sorry I took a turn down that road. Didn't mean to make it weird."

"I'm glad you did." She tipped her head toward the rumpled comforter on his bed. "Because ever since walking in here, I've been twitchy with the urge to make that. You crossed the weird line first, so I might as well—"

She let Oreo leap from her arms, but Brooks lurched forward and grabbed her wrist as she moved. "You're *not* making my bed."

She was well aware her quirkiness was showing. Didn't care, though. "I have to. I won't be able to sleep knowing it looks like that."

He let out an exhale that may have included a surprised laugh; it was hard to tell. "Seriously? Even if I let you—which I won't—by the time you go to bed, I'm just gonna mess it up again. There's no point."

She stared at the gray blanket and white sheets, and out of nowhere her brain conjured an image of Brooks tangled up in them. His long body spanning the length of the bed, shirtless. Maybe even naked.

And . . . sweaty?

"Carly? You okay?"

"Me? Sure." God, maybe she shouldn't have read that spicy romance novel last night. Her several-months-long dry spell since Benjamin left probably wasn't helping matters.

"Your face is all red. Is my unmade bed giving you hives?"

She cleared her throat and snapped back to reality. "What? No. I'm fine. Just the caffeine from the latte. Closet's that way?"

It was worse than she thought.

By all accounts, Brooks hadn't bought any new clothes in the last five years. Maybe longer, if you didn't count scrubs.

Carly often asked clients to describe their style in three words. They'd say things like *vintage. Classic. Edgy.* And her personal favorite: *timeless.*

Her, for example: *Flirty*, *eclectic*, and *fun*.

If she had to choose three words to describe the items she found in Brooks's closet?

Faded, outdated, mundane.

She'd kept these thoughts to herself, of course. He was already a flight risk, and her intuition told her he'd be resistant to too much change too fast. She was rarely wrong about those types of things. So she did her best to point out the (few) items she could work with and commend him on his tie selection.

"Sasha gives me one every year," he'd said, not sounding particularly pleased about it.

That explained why he had twelve ties with only two dress shirts and one suit, which, judging by the size, didn't fit properly.

She'd asked him to try on a few things for her, but by the third outfit change, he (1) was clearly losing patience and (2) caught her straightening out his comforter, so she announced she had enough to go with and got the hell out of there.

So yeah, it was bad, but she wasn't worried. She liked a challenge, and sometimes starting from a blank slate was the easiest way to go.

The next evening she went shopping. She'd been a little surprised at his insistence they keep a modest budget—he was a doctor, right?—but didn't pass judgment. One thing she'd become an expert at growing up was finding fashionable clothes anywhere, whether it was a department store, the mall, a secondhand store, or even a garage sale. Once, after her mom had spent her entire paycheck at the casino on the payday before freshman year, Carly did her back-to-school shopping at Goodwill and TJ Maxx and still managed to put together an updated closet she was happy with. Was it fun when clients wanted investment pieces and she got to shop at the high-end boutiques in town? Absolutely. Especially because she still couldn't stomach spending that kind of money on herself.

But she never let money stand in the way of reaching her goal to improve someone's wardrobe. Hadn't stopped her when she was a teenager, and it wouldn't stop her now.

Anyway, all that led her to start at reasonably priced Nordstrom Rack, which was hit or miss in the women's section but usually had a strong selection for men. She browsed for a while, grabbing a few things here and there with the photo shoot in mind.

She chose several shirts (smaller and more fitted than anything else he owned) and a few pairs of shorts (shorter and with fewer pockets than anything he owned . . . Could cargo shorts just die, already?). She'd grab a pair of chinos and jeans, too, in case he preferred pants.

It was six o'clock, so she took a chance he'd be off work and sent him some texts with pictures.

He replied immediately, vetoing all the shirts with patterns.

"Fine," she grumbled as she put them back, and the guy on the other side of the rack gave her a strange look.

Brooks: i like the gray one

Carly: Of course you do.

Brooks: it looks a little small though

Carly: Trust me.

Brooks: how much are you buying?

Carly: Don't worry about it.

Brooks: ok but I'm worried about it

Carly: I'm saying don't worry about it right now. You need to try some of this stuff on before you decide, okay? I can return anything.

Brooks: you sure?

Carly: Positive.

Carly: Please hold for shoe pictures.

Brooks: i don't need shoes

Carly: Hahahahahahahahaha

Brooks: wow

Brooks: are you this mean to all your clients?

Carly: You said you wanted honesty. "I can take it," you said.

Brooks: is it too late to back out

Carly: Yes. Here are the shoes. I'm buying at least two, so tell me which ones you like best and 'none' isn't an option.

Carly: [image]

Carly: [image]
Carly: [image]
Carly: [image]
Brooks: is that it? because none of those
Carly: Cool I'll pick then.

Smiling at the exchange, she gathered up the shoeboxes and clothes and made her way to the register, pleased with what she'd found. Her phone dinged with an incoming message, and she checked it when she got back to her car.

Brooks: hey will you ask your mom what's wrong with these?
Brooks: [image]
Brooks: they're my tomato plants and I think they're dying
Carly: Sure

She forwarded the image right away with a quick explanation that it was from the garden of a friend who was new at the endeavor. She sat in her car for a moment, looking at the photo and thinking about Brooks's words:

I guess after seeing that, I sort of liked the idea of bringing something to life.

He'd been talking about his job at the time, but she couldn't help but wonder how much the loss of his mom, and then his dad a few years later, may have bled into his desire to grow things and keep them alive. She hoped her mom had some grand idea to salvage the plants, because something told her Brooks Martin was in desperate need of a win.

CHAPTER SIX

Brooks

Brooks, what the hell was that? Get your head out of your ass, son.

—Coach McKee during the Freemont High state championship basketball game

"You won't believe what I've gotten myself into, Coach."

Coach McKee, or just Coach to Brooks, crossed one ankle over his opposite knee. He wore the same thing he always did—track pants, sneakers, and a T-shirt emblazoned with some rendition of Brooks's old high school basketball team. Coach retired three years ago, but Brooks knew for a fact he still attended every single game.

They'd just settled in at Coach's kitchen table, which was where they sat every time Brooks came over. His old coach (both in basketball and life, though Coach probably never meant to sign up for the latter) took his time stirring a spoonful of sugar into his coffee, then offered Brooks a bland expression that meant *Go on.*

"Sasha and Macy talked me into joining an online dating service and letting them tell the whole damn town about it."

"Online dating service?" Coach echoed, scratching his balding head. "What happened to meeting women the old-fashioned way?"

"Soda fountains aren't what they used to be."

"Watch yourself," Coach said. "I'm not *that* old."

"Where'd you meet Linda?"

"The picture show," Coach muttered.

Brooks laughed. "I might be able to meet someone at the movies, too, if I ever went."

"That right there's the problem with you kids these days," Coach said before taking a long sip of coffee. Brooks opted not to point out that as a thirty-three-year-old man, he was hardly a kid anymore. "Everyone's too busy looking at their phones to go places and talk to people's faces."

"Don't act like I didn't see that new reel you posted yesterday."

"I don't know what you're talking about."

"Anyway," Brooks said, his brief smile fading. "It's not the digital part I mind. In some ways it makes things easier for people like me."

"What do you mean, people like you?"

"I just mean I'm not really out on the town where I might strike up a random conversation with a woman. I haven't done that sort of thing since . . ." He trailed off. "Well, you know."

Coach's sharp gaze gentled. "You could, though. You're not the same person you were back then."

True, Brooks wasn't the same reckless kid he once was. But after years of buckling down to stay out of trouble and focus on school and his career, he didn't know how to get back out there. "I'm just not sure I'm any good at this anymore. Dating hasn't really been on my radar for a while, and I figured I still had plenty of time to wade back out there at some point. But Macy and Sasha make it sound like every second I'm at home, I'm wasting precious time and missing my chance to find someone."

"Nah. Everyone has their own timing for this stuff." Coach leaned back and rubbed the top of his head. "But if you're not ready, why did you agree to do it?"

Brooks slumped in his chair, the same one he always sat in. Coach liked to sit with his back against the wall—a habit he said held over from his years in the military—which put Brooks smack-dab in the middle of the kitchen. He had a nice view through the back window, though, where Linda had several bird feeders hanging from the eave. "It's not that I'm not ready, per se. I just hadn't even been thinking about it, I guess. Now that it's on my mind, I'm not completely opposed to it, even if the method for going about it wouldn't have been my first choice. But this whole thing is supposed to help boost *LiveOKC*, too. My mom's magazine, remember?"

"Sure. Sasha runs it now, right?"

"Yeah. I guess it's not doing so hot, and they cooked up this idea to showcase someone going through the dating scene in Oklahoma City." Brooks rubbed his eyes. "That's what I meant by telling everyone about it—there'll be pictures of me and articles about where I take people on dates and stuff."

"Well, hell," Coach said. "That does sound awful."

"Why anyone would care about someone else's dating life is beyond me, but apparently people love this stuff. Sasha and Macy seemed so convinced this could save the magazine from going under, so how could I say no?"

"'No.' Just like that."

"Helpful as always."

Coach just shrugged and rested his forearm on the table, the picture of ease. He might as well have said, *You got yourself into this mess, and I'm not swooping in to save you this time.*

Brooks didn't expect him to, but he wanted to complain about it to someone. Sasha and Macy were out for obvious reasons, and his buddy James still wouldn't have stopped laughing.

"Oh, and get this," Brooks added. "They're making me get a personal stylist to dress me. It's Carly Porter, remember her?"

Coach had been Brooks's basketball coach, but he'd also taught World History, so he'd know some students even if they weren't on his roster.

Coach glanced up, squinting. "Porter . . . Porter . . . She the one who's a congresswoman now?"

"That's Jane Porter. She was a year above me. Carly was Sasha's friend."

"Oh. Well, no, then. Don't remember her."

"Well, even if you did, I'd tell you to forget it. She's completely different than she was in high school. I thought she was sweet and shy, but now she has no problem telling me what I'm doing wrong. I mean, I'm not opposed to dressing a little better, I guess, but I want to be comfortable, too, you know?" He gestured at Coach. "You get to wear that around all the time, so you get it."

"Don't you wear scrubs all day?"

"Yeah, but I'm not supposed to wear them outside the hospital. I literally don't think I've ever seen you in anything else, no matter the location."

"Well, why would I? I wasn't trying to impress anyone. I'd already locked Linda down by the time I got the job at the school. Wouldn't have mattered, though," he said, a gleam in his eye. "It wasn't my fashion sense that caught her eye."

"What was it?"

"According to her, it was my charm, manners, and this dimple right here."

"Well, that's fucking adorable."

"Watch your mouth."

"Sorry, sir," Brooks said with a good-natured eye roll. Coach had dropped F-bombs all day during basketball practices. "Got any advice for me? As a man who's been married forty-five years?"

"Nope," Coach said. "Still don't know what I'm doing. But I can tell you one thing: I'm sure as hell going to enjoy watching you try to figure this out."

Three days later, Brooks sat at the nursing station, where he'd made a pit stop to call the radiologist who'd paged him with a stat CT result. A headache throbbed at his temple, probably because he'd been at the hospital since three in the morning. His overnight days were supposed to be over now that he was an attending, but sometimes he had trouble managing his patients from a distance. So when his fellow had called with a question about a new admit, he'd dragged his ass in. Yes, he probably could have talked things over with the trainee on the phone, but he wouldn't have been able to go back to sleep anyway. He liked to lay eyes on new patients himself to make sure nothing felt off.

He'd just ended the call when his phone buzzed with a text message. He leaned his hip against the counter and unlocked it again.

Carly: I should have bought the gingham shirt. Why did I let you say no?

Brooks: should I know what that is

Carly: The blue checkered one?

Brooks: the plaid one?

Carly: Not plaid. Gingham.

Brooks: it's 7am and this is what you're thinking about?

Carly: Sasha's gonna kill me for dressing you in something so boring for your photos. If you don't find a wife she'll bring it back to this very moment and blame me.

Brooks: relax

Brooks: tell her it's my fault

Carly: Obviously it IS your fault. What do you have against patterns?

Brooks: i like simplicity

Carly: Your complex medical degree says otherwise.

Brooks: maybe that's why. everything is so complicated here. i say words like atelectasis and dexmedetomidine and refractory hypoxemia and i know what they all mean. when i get home my brain shuts off

Carly: Show off

Brooks: you started it with your fancy word for plaid

Carly: What time is the photographer getting there?

Brooks: 5

Carly: Ugh. I have so much work to do today but all I can think about is the shirt that got away

He slid his phone back into his pocket, and one of the nurses he often worked with paused on her way past him.

"Dr. Martin?"

"Yeah?"

"You okay?"

He glanced up at her, confused. "Yeah?"

She didn't look convinced. "You were smiling."

He was? Huh. But also, "You thought that meant something was wrong?"

"No. Maybe?" She winced. "Sorry, I'm just not sure I've ever seen you smile. Sort of weirded me out, I guess." She continued on her way, leaving him stunned.

Well.

Note to self: Smile more at work.

Brooks got held up trying to leave after the department meeting that afternoon, which meant he didn't have time to hit the gym before he went home.

Then he spilled his coffee getting out of the car. His early wake-up meant at this point he was running on fumes, so this was particularly distressing.

And when he walked into his house, he discovered Oreo had scratched the upholstery of the entire right side of one of his armchairs.

All things considered, he was in a terrible mood when Carly knocked on his door at four thirty.

She didn't seem to notice, bustling in without so much as looking at him with her arms full of boxes and shopping bags dangling from her fingers. She started talking without slowing down, so he quickly closed the front door and followed her.

"I should have come earlier; I'm worried we won't have enough time. Should I set up in your room?" She took off without waiting for a response. "I'll lay out my suggestions in order of preference, and we can see which one you like best . . . Oh, hi, Oreo."

Seeing her drop all her crap to cuddle his cat might have improved his mood if (1) he wasn't pissed at Oreo and (2) it weren't for the next words out of her mouth.

"For God's sake, Brooks."

"What?"

"Do you ever make your bed?"

"No." There were two sides to the age-old argument, and he was firmly in the there's-no-point camp.

"I can't work like this."

"Guess we'll have to cancel, then." He tried to mask his annoyance with humor but wasn't sure if it panned out. He was tired, undercaffeinated, and had very few fucks left, which he was saving for the unsuspecting photographer Sasha would be bringing. Carly deserved respect, and kindness, too, but if she could handle Sasha on a regular basis, one bad mood of his wouldn't faze her.

Carly pursed her lips and deposited Oreo on the floor. She didn't spare Brooks a single glance and went for his bed, tossing his pillows into a pile and pulling his top sheet toward the head of the bed.

"Carly, *stop*."

"I need somewhere to lay this stuff out," she clipped.

He nudged her aside. "I'll do it. You're not making my bed for me. Move."

She gave him the side-eye but backed away. After a few long seconds of silence, he sighed. "I'm sorry. I'm tired." He looked over and her face softened.

"Me too. I barely slept last night because of that damn shirt."

"You're not serious."

"I am. Got any coffee?"

"I did but it's all over my driveway."

A tiny grin cracked her lips. "No wonder you're in a bad mood. Have some in the kitchen? I can make a pot while you finish that."

He nodded. "Make it extra strong."

She didn't bat an eye. Was she also a freak who could drink coffee and go straight to bed, like him? Sasha insisted he was some sort of robot every time they were out for dinner and he ordered full-caffeine coffee with dessert.

Five minutes later, his bed was made, and she returned with two steaming cups of coffee in University Hospital mugs. He'd resisted the temptation to peek in the bags she'd brought and watched apprehensively as she pulled each item out and laid it carefully on the bed. Yes, she'd sent him pictures, but it wasn't all that easy to see the clothes on his phone and he wouldn't put it past her to throw in something unapproved.

This is for Sasha. This is for Macy. This is for Mom.

When she finished arranging and smoothing everything out, she stepped back and held the coffee mug in front of her face, peeking over the top. "Well? What do you think?"

He sucked down the dark liquid and approached with caution. Three outfits stared back at him.

A pair of khaki pants that looked way too narrow for his legs with a brown leather belt and white polo shirt.

Navy shorts (shit, would they even go to his knees?) and a gray shirt that looked like a polo but had no collar—he remembered approving that one.

And light-blue-striped (at least, he thought they were; they looked weird) shorts with a plain white T-shirt and a green sweater.

"A sweater?" was the first thing he said. "It's supposed to be eighty-five degrees today."

"It's just for the picture. The green will go great with your eyes, and women can't resist a man in a cozy-looking sweater."

"What the hell are those shorts?"

"Which ones? The seersucker?"

He'd never heard that word before in his life.

She didn't provide additional information and instead suggested, "Why don't you try the chinos and polo first?"

It did seem the least offensive of the three.

"Okay." Maybe the pants wouldn't be as tight as they looked.

With his coffee in one hand and the clothes in the other, he disappeared into the bathroom. He checked his watch as he shucked off his blue scrubs—they had fifteen minutes before the others would arrive.

"Wait, shouldn't I have an undershirt?" he called through the door.

He heard what sounded suspiciously like laughter covered by a cough. "No."

He frowned at himself in the mirror. No undershirt with a polo? With a sigh he did as directed and put it on, and damn, that was soft against his skin. He pulled on the pants, which fit perfect in the waist, at least, and walked back out with the belt in hand.

"I know skinny's the style, or whatever, but I just don't feel comfortable—"

Carly hushed him with a finger to her lips and immediately circled him, eyes traveling up and down his person critically. "They're slim fit, not skinny." She stepped back with a fist pressed to her chin. "Tuck it in and put the belt on."

"Are these a little short?"

"No."

He set the belt on the dresser and went to work stuffing the polo into his waistband, cocking an eyebrow at her tone. "You're bossy when you're styling." As he slid the leather through the belt loops, he caught her eye, and she looked away. He avoided her gaze while he finished, too, because there was something strangely intimate about doing anything with a belt, even if he was putting it on rather than taking it off.

When he finished, he held out his arms. "Well?"

She looked him over again and stepped right up to his front, smoothing her hands along his shoulders and chest, surprising him with how easily she put her hands on him. "This looks pretty good," she murmured, twisting around to look behind him. "I knew there was a butt in there."

"Carly Porter."

"What?"

He just blinked at her.

"Sorry, did I embarrass you?"

"No. Maybe. I don't know."

She shrugged. "It's my job to make your assets stand out here, Brooks. Pun intended. How do you feel in this? Good? Want to try something else?"

"I don't know." The fabric hugged his thighs when he moved, which felt weird. Things just felt . . . tight and on display. A terrifying thought suddenly occurred to him: What was going on in the groin area? The polo had been untucked and covering him when he walked out . . . Shit. He quickly turned back around to stand in the doorway of the bathroom as if he was looking at the whole thing together in the mirror while surreptitiously making sure his junk wasn't, like, on exhibit without the extra breathing room.

Carly's head popped over his shoulder as if she stood on tiptoes. "I like this," she said. "You look hot. But I want to see the gray Henley before we decide for sure."

A pleasant warmth settled beneath his rib cage. *Hot?* He hadn't been called that in years.

She gave him a smile and an eyebrow wag before turning on her heel.

He watched her through the mirror, a small smile on his face, considering this new Carly. One that poked fun at his clothes, wagged her eyebrows at him, and looked at his butt and called it part of her job.

She seemed to love it. The job, that is, not his ass.

Which is how I want it, I think.

"I'm surprised you don't do this full time," he said. "You're in the zone right now, I can tell. I can't imagine putting numbers into a spreadsheet gives you the same feeling."

"It doesn't," she agreed. "And I'm working on it. I'm actually hoping this whole project with Sasha will impress my boss enough to make that happen."

"Really?" Damn, Carly's job was riding on this, too? That might be too much pressure.

"Yep." She handed him the shorts and shirt with a meaningful glance toward the bathroom. "Which is why I'm determined to make you look as good as possible every chance I get."

Definitely too much pressure.

"These are too short," he said once he was dressed.

"Unlikely."

"They are."

"I got a nine-inch inseam. I could have gone with seven."

The hell did that mean?

"Just let me see," she demanded.

He swung open the door and halted in the doorway, arms crossed over his chest. The feminine appreciation in her gaze nearly stopped him from complaining further, but then he felt the draft of the air conditioning all the way up his legs. "They're, like, midthigh!"

Her eyes tracked back and forth between his for a moment, as if trying to assess how distressed he really was. "Hey. I know this isn't what you're used to, and I don't want you to be uncomfortable. But I dress a lot of men, and I promise they're not too short. This is very much the style right now. I'm picturing close-up photos for the post anyway, so you don't have to show any leg if you don't want to." She beckoned him forward so she could circle him once more. "This is good. You have great arms. Those forearms could bring in a lot of attention."

They could?

"We need to unbutton these two, though." She reached up to slip the top two buttons out. "There."

A whiff of vanilla and the coffee she'd made flooded his senses as she moved. He stood like a statue, feeling like a Ken doll with the way she poked and smoothed and tugged at his shirt.

"Let's try a French tuck."

"A what?"

She pinched the bridge of her nose. "Tuck in just the front."

"Shouldn't I put the belt back on?"

"No."

Man, his instincts were pure shit.

The front door opened and Sasha's voice floated in from the entryway.

"You know what," Carly said quickly, "Never mind, I like it like that." She whipped around and grabbed a pair of white sneakers. "Put these on."

He opened his mouth, but she quickly added, "No socks," and he snapped it shut.

In less than thirty minutes he believed everything his sisters had said. He knew nothing about fashion. No undershirt, no socks, more fitted, shorter. Sweaters in summer and whatever the fuck a seersucker was.

"Brooks?"

"Back here," Carly called at the same time Sasha entered his bedroom with a small woman carrying a massive camera.

Oreo, who he'd forgotten about once they started with the clothes, shot across the room and leaped into Carly's arms.

"Whoa," she said, barely getting ahold of him.

He eyed his cat curiously. "Nice catch."

Sasha approached him with a smile. "Wow, brother. You look great." She glanced over her shoulder to where Carly was talking softly to his cat. "Nice job."

"Why are you so sure I didn't pick this out?" he asked.

His sister just laughed. "The clothes are great, but what's going on with your hair?"

He blinked and reached up to slide his fingers through it. He hadn't even looked at it since he got out of the shower before heading to work early this morning.

"I say we leave it as is," Carly said. "It's kind of messy but in that casual, tousled way. Some men spend a lot of time trying to make their hair behave like that."

Sasha squinted and looked again, then nodded. "Yes. Good. Brooks, this is Cam, the photographer. Cam, this is your handsome subject."

Cam, a woman with long dark hair and blue glasses, stepped forward, and Brooks held out his hand. "Nice to meet you."

She met his gaze with a huge smile and shook his hand. "Likewise."

Sasha had suggested they do the photos at his home, either in the sparsely furnished living room or in the backyard, which boasted several large oaks like the one in the front.

"So where do you want me?" he asked.

The way Carly looked at him in that moment had him second-guessing his choice of words, but no one else seemed to notice.

"Lighting outside is perfect right now." Cam peered through his bedroom window. "Can we go out back?"

They filed through the house to the back door, where Carly caught his arm. "Can Oreo go outside? He doesn't seem to want me to put him down."

Brooks ran a soft hand down Oreo's back, accidentally brushing Carly's fingers. "He doesn't go outside much. I think he'll be fine once the other two are out of the house. He just doesn't like a lot of people around, but apparently he already considers you a friend."

She did a cute little thing where she pursed her lips and lifted her brows. "Oreo, you flatter me."

"Brooks!" Sasha yelled. Startled, he looked up to find Cam holding the door open, watching them, and Sasha glaring at him through the window.

He grunted and took Oreo from Carly, depositing him on the couch before ushering her outside.

Sasha pointed. "Go stand over there."

"Careful to keep those shoes clean," Carly added. "It rained last night."

"Two more steps back," Cam said. "A little more. Stop."

Brooks swung his gaze between the three of them, a little taken aback at being simultaneously ordered around by three women.

No wonder his mom had been so ruffled before her own cover photo shoot—a morning he remembered like it was yesterday. She'd been so nervous about her makeup and what to wear that Macy and Sasha had stepped up to help her get ready while he and his dad had offered to make breakfast. They made a huge mess in the kitchen, attempting to make Belgian waffles from scratch, and hadn't produced anything edible. His mom had said she was too nervous to eat anyway, so they all packed up for the photo shoot and went out for brunch after. The cover had turned out perfect, of course, and was one of the three displays at Macy's house.

Cam approached him and turned his body this way and that, taking a few test shots, instructing him to relax a little more, lean on his back foot, and smile as if he wasn't in hell right now.

She took several photos and immediately lowered the camera to review the images. As Sasha crowded next to her to look and give her input, Brooks leaned back against the tree and noticed Carly bending over his garden a few yards away. She had her phone out and it looked as if she was taking pictures.

Just as he was about to ask what she was doing, Cam was there, walking him to a different location and taking more pictures.

"Brooks!" Sasha wasted no time redirecting his attention. "Smile!"

He took a deep breath and resisted the urge to throw in the towel and cancel this whole thing here and now.

"Not like that, you're forcing it. You're supposed to look happy to be Oklahoma City's most eligible bachelor!"

It's just four months. A few meals and a few articles. You know how to place an intraosseous IV line, surely you can do this.

"Seriously," Sasha said after he tried again. "You're killing me."

"God, Sasha," Carly called from her spot by the garden. "*I'm* about to slap you and I'm not even the one you're yelling at."

The expression on Sasha's face was so comical, he looked straight at Carly.

And he smiled.

CHAPTER SEVEN

Brooks

"Those poor kids."

"Which ones?"

"The Martin siblings. Over there, by the meat counter? Lost their mom last year. Accident on I-35 during that storm. Haven't seen the dad out in public since. I heard at the nail salon he's so depressed he barely speaks. I think the older sister's taking care of the other two. Such a shame."

—Whispered in the baking aisle of Homeland grocery store, sixteen years ago

"It's go time."

Brooks cocked an eyebrow, holding the door open as Sasha entered his house like a woman on a mission. His other brow joined the first when Macy appeared in the doorway.

"What are you doing here?"

"You think I was gonna miss this?" she asked as she passed.

Brooks sighed and moved to close the door, but a hand shot out.

"Whoa." Macy's husband, Mark, had nearly been hit in the face. "Easy, bud."

Brooks allowed Mark entrance (and gave him a pass for the *bud*) but extended his other arm. "What the hell?"

"Come on," Mark said with a laugh. "Macy said if my parents agreed to take the kids I could come watch."

After he closed the door, Brooks leaned the back of his head against it. "I thought this part was supposed to be about me. Does this require an audience?"

Sasha spoke from where she knelt on the floor, messing with the laptop she'd opened on his coffee table. "We're all engaged in the process."

Macy sat on the couch. "What she means is we don't think you'll do it right."

"How could I mess up my own dating profile?"

Sasha and Macy laughed simultaneously for far too long, and Mark just looked at him with something like pity.

"I hate you all." He pushed off the door and headed for the kitchen. This was going to be a long night, and he'd need a beer or three to get through it.

"I'm here in solidarity against the Martin women," Mark whispered as Brooks brushed past him. "Give me a signal, like a wink or head scratch, and I'll fake a migraine so they have to take me home."

Brooks bumped his fist. That was more like it. "I'll get you a beer."

When he returned, his sisters were huddled together on the couch, Sasha furiously typing as if she had a term paper due in the morning. But he'd never actually seen her work this hard for anything school related.

He sat in the armchair and waited for a few seconds, expecting them to pause and ask for input.

"What are you doing?" he asked when they didn't.

"Filling out the 'About Me' section. It's free text," Macy said without looking up. Sasha didn't seem to have heard him.

"Need anything from me?" he deadpanned.

"Nope." Apparently Sasha *had* heard him.

Mark just shook his head and took a pull from his beer.

Not that Brooks was surprised—this was about how it had gone with the write-up for the debut article, which would go live on the website first, followed by the print issue. Sasha wrote the whole thing, which he only let slide because it was mostly describing how the entire endeavor would go down.

He'd put up a dating profile.

Go on real dates (no setups like on *The Bachelor*).

Report back about the venues and, if he wanted to, how the dates went (good or bad). Sasha promised readers they'd be along for the ride if he met someone special, despite his skepticism it would happen.

The one thing he'd been allowed to choose was the photo in the spread, and only because he'd put his foot down. Sasha had wanted one of the more brooding images, but he fought for the one where he was smiling, remembering it was Carly's snarky comment that had lightened his mood that day.

The incessant tap of Sasha's fingers against the keyboard did the exact opposite, grating on his nerves more with each second that passed.

"That's perfect," Macy murmured. "Oh, wait." She grabbed the laptop and typed something of her own, then handed it back to Sasha, who read the addition and smiled.

"Nice," she said appreciatively.

"Seriously," Brooks said loudly.

"Shh, calm down. I'm just doing a few basics, like you're a man, no kids, you're a doctor, you're from Oklahoma, blah blah blah."

"Can we skip my profession?"

Sasha looked up and frowned. "What? Why?"

He shrugged. "I don't know, I just feel like women only want to go out with me because I'm a doctor."

"Why do you think that?" Macy asked at the same time Sasha said, "What women want to go out with you?"

He eyed Sasha. "If the notion is so shocking, why did you ask me to do this?"

"I didn't mean it that way, obviously. You haven't been going on dates, so how would I know women had been suggesting them?"

"It doesn't happen a lot, but I only get approached by women at the hospital where they know what I do. Maybe they think I'm rich, or something?" If they saw his student loan statements they'd probably run in the other direction. Plus, the general public tended to put doctors on a pretty high pedestal, and if that's what he was starting with, there was a good chance he'd let them down.

Sasha pursed her lips. "You don't go anywhere except work, so that's the only place women *can* notice you."

Okay, fair.

But as a rule, he preferred not to admit when Sasha was right. "Regardless, I'd rather start with something more important, like common interests or values."

Macy looked on the verge of arguing, but Sasha spoke first. "Fine. I'll just put you work in health care."

"Thanks."

"Okay, now we're getting to the questions." Sasha settled back into the cushions. "What are you passionate about?"

Brooks eyed her fingers hovering over the keyboard. "Can't I just do this myself?" When she'd said she'd come over tonight, he'd envisioned sitting at the kitchen table on his own, giving serious consideration to these questions, with Sasha available to help if he wasn't sure how to answer something.

"You type too slow."

"I do not."

"Just answer the question, Brooks," Macy said.

Brooks signaled at Mark with a wink, but his brother-in-law was looking at his phone and didn't notice. Brooks sighed. Evidence-based medicine and broad-scale education about the importance of advanced directives probably weren't good choices for this.

"Um, helping people, I guess? Health and wellness?"

Sasha nodded. "What else?"

"I don't know."

After a pause, Macy suggested they come back to that one. "What's next?"

"What are two things you like doing with leisure time?"

"I don't know."

"Brooks!"

"What? For fourteen years I didn't have leisure time. Since then, I've sort of wandered around, unsure what to do with myself when I'm not working, worried I should be studying for an exam or preparing a Grand Rounds presentation." Nearly a year later, and he still didn't know how to relax. "I started that garden a few weeks ago. Can we put that?"

Sasha's expression said *no*. "Do you read?"

"Sometimes." Usually medical journals.

"Watch TV?"

"Yeah, sports, usually."

She typed something, and Brooks made a mental note to double-check her answers before they submitted anything.

"What are three things you're thankful for?"

That one was easy. "My sisters, my nephews, and basketball."

Sasha sniffled and Macy put her hand to her heart.

Mark coughed.

"Oh, um." Brooks tapped his knee with his fist. "Right, and my brother-in-law."

"How about I just put family, friends, and basketball?" Sasha's voice sounded a little wobbly.

"Great."

They continued on like that for an hour, moving through several different sections of the profile. Just when they were finishing up, his phone dinged.

Carly: My mom thinks the tomatoes don't get enough sun. She wants to know if that part of the garden gets a lot of shade.

Shit, he didn't know. He thought he'd picked a good part of the yard, but there were several trees nearby. The thought that he'd already killed everything he'd planted was depressing, but he tried not to go there yet. He set an alert on his phone to remind him to check and made a joke to make himself feel better.

Brooks: definitely not as much as my sisters have thrown my way tonight

Carly: What's going on?

Brooks: they came over to set up my dating profile

Carly: Both of them?

Brooks: yes

Carly: Are you okay?

Brooks: no

Brooks: save me

Carly: Why didn't you just do it yourself?

Brooks: Sasha offered to help but now i know it was a trick

Carly: She's sneaky. She once convinced me to go see a horror movie with her even though she knew I hated them. The title was really obscure and she convinced me it was a romance. I slept with the light on and a bat under my pillow for two weeks.

"Who are you talking to?" Macy asked.

He looked up. "What?"

"You're smiling at your phone."

Both his sisters were looking at him now. He attempted another SOS signal to Mark, but the bastard was still focused on his phone.

It wouldn't be a big deal to tell them it was Carly. They knew she was his stylist and that they'd be talking and spending time together. But the way they were looking at him told him they'd read something into it that was all wrong, and he didn't have it in him to deal with it.

"Just a friend. No one important."

Highlights from the dating profile of Brooks Martin:

What are three things you couldn't do without?
-Coffee
-Sneakers
-Thunder basketball

What life experiences have shaped you the most?
-Achieving my degree
-The death of someone close to me
-Growing up with two sisters

What person shaped you the most?
-My high school basketball coach

I spend a lot of time thinking about:
-Coffee
-The meaning of life
-Health care in America
-My cat
-Tomatoes
-Kindness
-The metric system
-What really happened to Amelia Earhart
-Coffee

I like:
-Going to the same coffee shop so often that the barista knows my regular drink
-Airports
-The huge oak tree in my front yard
-The way my nephews scream when I jump out at them while playing hide-and-seek
-When my phone autocorrects normal words to ridiculous ones
-Recycling
-Eggs over easy
-The roar of the crowd when the Thunder make an unexpected comeback
Four things I'm good at:
-Driving
-Opening jars
-Finding the best local coffee shop in any given city
-Killing spiders

Something new I recently learned is:
-Seersucker is a kind of fabric (I think)

My self-summary: I'm gonna be honest here. I've been focused on my career for a long time. Like, over a decade. After going through the process of filling out this profile, I've realized maybe my sisters are right (they're the ones who put me up to this): I've sort of forgotten how to have fun. I've become an introvert, which I think is okay sometimes, because after a hard day I think I'll always be the kind of person who wants to come home to the comfort of my home (and my dog-cat) rather than blow off steam at a bar, and because I work in health care sometimes my brain just needs peace and quiet to recharge. And I think that's important for anyone I might date to know that about me.

But I want to get back out into the world and figure out what, besides my job, I enjoy. I want to learn how to play and have fun again. Because I was fun, once, I swear. I know it's in there somewhere because it comes out every once in a while and surprises the hell out of me, in a good way. I want something to look forward to.

If anyone out there is going through the same thing, or if you aren't but you're okay with a guy who's kind of quiet but who might surprise you and who cares about doing good in this world, while at the same time hoping he's bettering himself, we might be a good fit.

Or not, but we won't know if we don't try, right? I guess that's another thing you can expect from me: honesty. And if my sisters' experience with dating has told me anything it's that not all men put that quality high on their list, and that's a shame. Case in point: I made my sisters let me fill out this section on my own, and after they read it, they both laughed and asked if I was messing with them. When they realized I was serious they tried to delete it and rewrite it for me. I won this round, but be warned I have two sisters who like to meddle in my life and think they're always right (they're about 50/50).

Anyway, looking forward to meeting you.

CHAPTER EIGHT

Carly

Dear Carly,

Congratulations! After thoughtful review and consideration of your application materials, you've been selected as a recipient of the G. Stanley Pearce Foundation Undergraduate Scholarship. We look forward to welcoming you to campus in the fall.

—*Letter from Creighton University, senior year*

"I think I'll dress you like an Englishman."

Brooks met her gaze from across the dress-shirt-covered table. "Sorry?"

Carly ran her hand across a silk tie paired with a lavender oxford. "After the photo shoot I was thinking about your overall style and where I wanted to go from there. I think you could pull off more than you think in terms of colors and fabrics, but you won't be comfortable. The defining feature of English fashion for men is restraint. Clothes make a statement, but they never shout and they help people notice *you*, not what you're wearing. Your wardrobe will be intentional but not loud. You know?"

He stood a little straighter and crossed his arms. "I want to argue but that actually sounds pretty good."

"Hi-hi, sorry I'm late!" a feminine voice called out through the clothing racks. Carly turned to find Cam making her way around a display of argyle socks, holding her camera protectively to her chest.

In exchange for a 15 percent discount on their purchase, Sasha had promised the owner of Empire, a men's clothing boutique, she'd print a candid of Carly and Brooks shopping for date attire. Mode would get a mention out of it, too, so despite Brooks's snarky *Are they gonna photograph me taking a shit, too?* text when they got the email, Carly was on board with it.

"No problem," Carly said with a smile. "We were just getting started."

Brooks said nothing, his expression sullen.

Carly glared at him and mouthed, *Fifteen percent off.*

He nodded, sighed, and dutifully said, "Hi, Cam," as if he were an eight-year-old kid whose mother was making him greet the great-aunt-twice-removed at a family reunion.

Cam didn't seem bothered and looked around, glancing through her lens and adjusting a few knobs on her camera. "This won't take long; I just need a few good shots for us to pick from. I'd like to get something organic rather than posed, so just proceed as if I'm not here. I'll stay out of the way."

"Got it." Carly resumed her perusal of dress shirts, and Brooks came around the table to stand next to her, his posture stiff and more awkward than it had been two minutes ago. His gaze kept darting to Cam and back.

Carly elbowed him. "Just focus on me."

"I'm trying," he muttered. "So how much do I have to buy today?"

Brooks's dating profile had gone live and Sasha had put up an entire page on the *LiveOKC* website dedicated to the endeavor. It included date ideas where people could vote for their favorite, with links to everything, of course, and an "About Brooks" section.

When Carly checked this morning, the comments had been out of control with women clamoring for a chance to date him. The print issue would be out next week, which would probably only heighten the frenzy. "That depends. How many dates have you set up?"

"Just one so far. Next Friday."

A buttery-yellow linen button-up caught her eye for Vaughn, a twenty-three-year-old client she'd started working with last week. She grabbed one in his size and laughed at Brooks's expression. "This isn't for you." Relief filled his features. "Where are you taking her?"

"I have no idea. I haven't been on a date like this in years. What's the norm?"

"You could always let her pick, but first dates are less stressful than they used to be. You don't have to do a full-on dinner when you're not even sure if you want to spend that much time together yet." A chambray shirt called to her from the top of the table, and as she reached for it, she shivered when the cool air conditioning brushed her lower back when her shirt rode up. "Grabbing a drink or a cup of coffee is pretty standard. Takes some of the pressure off."

When she straightened, Brooks snapped his eyes up from her waist with a blink. "I could just take her to Coffee Slingers?"

"Sure. That way if it's clear early on there's not a connection, you finish your drink and get the hell out of there."

Brooks angled his head. "Sounds like you've done that before."

"Many times," she admitted.

"Really? That bad?"

"The awkward silences, inappropriate questions, suggesting we just head to his place after five minutes of talking."

Concern etched across his forehead. "Maybe I don't want to do this."

"They're not all like that," she said quickly. "They can be pretty great, too. The first time I went out with Benjamin, we hit it off right away and ended up talking for three hours straight. After a date like that, it's like you float home on a cloud, wondering if you just had your last first date."

He'd been listening, eyes on hers, but his gaze shifted to a rack of slacks to his left. "It sounds like you miss him."

She shifted on her feet. "I mean, we're still friends, and I'd miss any friend that moved away. Seoul's fourteen hours ahead so it's not easy, but we keep in touch. Texting and sometimes email since we're on completely different schedules."

"How long were you together?"

"A year and a half."

"That's a long time."

"Yeah."

"Have you dated anyone since he left?"

"Not yet." But she would, soon. Probably. Maybe.

She grabbed a short-sleeved shirt from a rack. "Anyway, we can just find something for a casual first date today, if you want. We can meet up again when you have more plans."

Brooks eyed the piece she'd just grabbed. "Are you sure? I don't want you to feel like you have to shop with me before every date. Is that what you usually do for clients?"

"Sometimes. But even if it wasn't, you're not a regular client, you're a friend. Plus, Sasha has some ideas for you. Depending on which offers you end up taking—like the white-water-rafting place downtown or the new escape room on Twenty-Third, we might need to go in completely different directions."

"I'm definitely gonna let Sasha get me suite tickets to a Thunder summer league game," he added. "But I won't need you for that. I've got Thunder gear covered."

Carly laughed. Loud. "You do *not* have that covered. I saw your closet, and you will not wear a T-shirt or a jersey"—she shuddered—"on my watch."

Her volume attracted a saleswoman, who approached and didn't hide a blatant assessment of Brooks. Most of the employees at Empire knew Carly and would have let her be, but this one must be new. "Can I help you two find anything?"

Brooks looked like a deer in headlights, and Carly offered a wan smile. "We're good, thank you."

The woman nodded. "Okay, my name is April, just let me know if I can help," she said to Brooks.

Carly sifted through a stack of dark-wash jeans and held up his size. "What do you think of these?"

He shrugged, then his face cleared as if he'd remembered something. "Hey, that reminds me. You didn't happen to accidentally grab a pair of my jeans that day you were at my house, did you? When you packed up the clothes to return?"

She busied herself with a collection of cotton polos. "Hmm?"

"They were a pair of Levi's. I can't find them."

"Huh. No, I didn't see them."

The warmth of his body alerted her he'd moved closer. "Carly."

She found a size medium and yanked the hanger off the bar. "We should try this; white is a good color for you."

One of his hands gently grabbed her shoulder, shifting her in his direction. She looked up to find him looking at her intently, a spark of accusation in his eyes. With a touch of mischief.

Wow, she'd forgotten about this side of him. The one that had all the girls at their high school walking around with hearts for eyes.

"They were the ones I was wearing that day at the coffee shop and you said you couldn't see my ass," he said matter-of-factly. "Are you sure you haven't seen them?"

The distant click of a shutter reminded her Cam was nearby. She tried to step away from him. "Why would I have?"

"Because you hated them and you won't look at me."

"I don't think I like what you're suggesting."

His lips twitched as if fighting a smile, but he let her go.

She shoved the items she'd gathered so far at his chest. "Go try these on."

"All at once?"

It was a good thing Cam was just taking stills, because a video recording might have picked up her muttered "Wiseass" before she instructed him to start with jeans and the green crew neck.

She followed him to the fitting-room area, and a few minutes later, he walked out in navy chinos and the white polo.

"That's not what I asked for."

"I know. How does it look?"

She waved him closer and stood from the chair she'd sunk into. "Good." Really good. *Click, click.* "I was right about the white."

"Everything still just feels . . . tight."

She pinched the soft fabric between her fingers and tugged. "Look how much room is in here. It's not tight, you're just used to wearing shapeless clothes that fit like a garbage bag."

"Wow. I wasn't sure before, but now I'm positive you stole my jeans."

She ignored him. Well, his words, anyway. It was hard to ignore his body in the confined space, the nearby triple-paned mirror accentuating his lean, muscled form. "You should buy this. The navy goes with anything. What's next?"

He shrugged and went back in. Cam announced she'd gotten enough, and as she left, Brooks shouted a goodbye from the fitting room. Carly slipped out while he changed to grab a few more items and tossed them over the door.

Eventually, he came out in a pair of distressed jeans and the green shirt, and Carly's breath caught in her throat. She covered her reaction with a whistle, hoping a sassy response would distract him.

Eyes going wide, Brooks placed his hand, palm open, dramatically on his chest. "Is this what it feels like to be objectified?"

"Yes. Welcome to life as a woman."

She'd never whistled at a client before, but this was Brooks. A (sort of) friend she'd known most of her life, and a man who needed a confidence boost.

"I'm just teasing," she said. "But seriously. Can't you see how much better that looks? The lines are so much cleaner. You're casual but sophisticated. Sexy and easy-going. It's the perfect combination for a first date."

His lips parted. "I look . . . sexy?"

He glanced at himself in the mirror, white teeth pressed into his full bottom lip as he frowned. He ran one hand across his stomach and turned back to her. She tilted her face up to his, searching his eyes. She'd never ask a real client this question, but he was different. And they no longer had an audience. "Do you really not know how attractive you are?"

Gripping the back of his flushed neck, he cast his gaze once again to his reflection and back to her. "I don't know. I feel like I'm too much of a science geek to be sexy."

"Nerds are hot right now." Now and always, if you asked her. Peter Parker over Spiderman anytime, anywhere.

"Really?"

"Yep."

"I guess it's just been so long since I considered my appearance to be something that mattered."

"It's not all that matters," she agreed, still a little unbalanced at the sight of him. The man should wear green every day. "But even if it's been a while, don't you remember how much attention you got in high school? Every girl at our school wanted you back then, and you've only gotten better with age."

His hazel eyes were steady on hers, expression unreadable. "Every girl?"

Was he asking if she'd been one of them, or was this a way to boost his ego? She'd give it to him. "Pretty much."

He didn't say anything for a moment, watching her, and she had the urge to fidget under his perusal. Bite her lip or step away or move closer . . . something. It was her job to help her clients find their confidence, but something about this felt different. Heavier.

"I'm not proud of the person I was then," he finally said.

There was a lot she wanted to ask to follow up on that, but when another guy brushed past them to an open fitting room, she decided now wasn't the time.

Brooks had turned back to the mirror, brow furrowed and posture tight. What was on his mind?

Much of his life was unknown to her, so for the most part there was nothing she could say that might make him feel better. She had no idea what demons lurked, no inkling of the kind of encouragement he needed to realize he was a man worth getting to know. But there was one thing she did know, and it was the thing she'd been hired to help with. So she'd give him one last thought and move on for now, certain she'd come back to this moment and analyze it when she got home.

She leaned forward to speak softly, privately. She was close enough to smell his clean, spicy scent and resisted a sudden, somewhat alarming urge to bury her face in his chest.

"I know I've given you a hard time about your style. First impressions matter, so it's my job to bring out the best in the way you present yourself. But believe me when I say this: I'm adding a few details to the package you're already working with, yes, but it doesn't really matter. You don't need it. You're a very handsome man, and the fact you don't seem to know it only makes you more attractive. That saleswoman was even checking you out earlier."

"She . . . she was?"

"Yes. Believe me, when it comes to how you look, you have nothing to worry about. Nothing at all."

He blinked a few times and slid his hands into his pockets in a move that didn't speak of discomfort, but more like humility. Then his lips spread into a self-deprecating smile. "Time will tell if you're right. But even if you are, looks will only get me so far."

"What do you mean?"

"I'm not good at the other stuff, either. Like . . . small talk, for example. I don't remember the last time I went out with someone I didn't already know inside and out, like my sister, or my brother-in-law, or my best friend James."

"Don't you talk to strangers all the time at work? Your patients?"

He shook his head. "Most of my patients are sedated and on ventilators. I talk to their families, sure. But that's different. I'm in my comfort zone talking about medicine and technology and my treatment plan. I'm not asking them about the weather, or whatever."

"The weather? Wow, is that what you consider small talk?"

He tossed his hands up in the air. "See?"

"You seem to do fine talking to me."

"I know you, sort of. And we're not talking about personal stuff, either."

She considered him for a moment and the muscles flexing in his jaw as if he was clenching his teeth from stress.

"So let's change that."

His expression was a giant question mark.

"Let's buy your stuff—those jeans for sure, and whatever else you like—and grab dinner. You can practice small talk with me. That way it won't be so scary on your first date."

His lips flattened. "I don't think I said it *scared* me."

"Your face said otherwise."

"Okay, let's do it." He turned to head back to the fitting room, then paused and twisted around again. "At least tell me this: Did you just hide my old jeans, or did you throw them out?"

"I have no idea what you're talking about."

CHAPTER NINE

Carly

Single in OKC? In a new relationship and looking for somewhere fresh to take your partner? Or just need to put some excitement back into date night with your spouse? Follow local thirtysomething Brooks as he embarks on a dating tour of the OKC metro, showcasing all the best spots to check out from the new and unexpected to some hidden gems to revisit. Make sure to sign up here for updates and follow us on socials for bonus content!

—Excerpt from pop-up on LiveOKC website

Half an hour later, Carly was on a date with Brooks Martin.

It wasn't a real one, but still. Her inner teenager did a backflip when he slid into the booth across from her and asked for two drink menus to get them started. If only her middle school nemesis Becky Bennett, who once called Carly "a frumpy girl no guy wanted to kiss," could see her now.

"Wait," he said, forehead already furrowed. "I can drink on a date, right? Is that a faux pas?"

"Totally acceptable. Not everyone drinks, though, so you might want to feel your date out first. And hopefully it goes without saying that getting sloppy probably isn't in your best interest, but otherwise I say it can be a nice way to take the edge off an already nerve-racking situation."

"The last time I got wasted was before I was even legal to drink, so I think we're good."

"College really changed you, huh?" she observed.

"Yeah, I finally got my head on straight." He picked up a roll of napkin-wrapped silverware and twisted it between his fingers. "Anyway, I'm ready to learn. Teach me your ways, Wise One."

Carly laughed. "I'm not claiming to be an expert, but I've been on my share of dates and go out quite a bit with Sasha, where I'm bound to meet new people. I usually start off with things like where they're from, what they do for a living, or if they've done anything new and exciting around town lately."

He nodded. "Okay, yeah. That doesn't sound so bad."

"It's not, but it still takes practice," she said. "Wanna try?"

"Now?"

"That's what we're here for, right? Pretend you don't know me and we're on a first date."

"I thought I didn't have to do an entire dinner on a first date."

She wouldn't be deterred by stalling tactics. "You let me pick and this is what I wanted. Because you're a gentleman you didn't argue."

A smile tipped the corner of his mouth.

"We don't know each other, but I just sat down and you're struck by my impossible beauty and impeccable fashion sense, and you want nothing more than to impress the hell out of me." She made a show of getting comfortable and held out her hand. "Hi, Brooks? I'm Carly."

He stared at her hand for a beat before he sighed heavily. He shook it. "Hi, um. Carly. It's nice to meet you."

She placed her hand in her lap and just smiled at him.

Several seconds passed. He blinked.

A few more, and she lifted her brows.

He gave a little cough and tapped the table lightly with his fist, glancing around the room.

She counted to five. Slowly. "Brooks!"

"What?"

"I gave you lots of ideas of things to say. Let's *go*."

He smoothed out his shirt and nodded. "So, where are you from?"

"Oklahoma City. I grew up just a few miles from here."

"Really? Me too."

She feigned surprise. "No way. I wonder if we've ever crossed paths before?"

"Nah, I don't think so."

"How can you be sure?"

His gaze was direct. "I'd remember you."

Warmth flushed across her skin, and she leaned in as if to impart a secret. "Excellent flirting. That would totally work on a real date."

He didn't respond right away, but eventually offered her a smile. "So, what do you do for a living?"

"I'm a personal stylist," she said. "I mostly work with young professionals on limited budgets and prioritize clothing recycling to reduce waste by shopping at resale shops around town."

"Wow, I could have used something like that during residency interviews." He regarded her closely, dropping the facade. "Do you really do that? Work with regular people like me when it's not, you know, Sasha-mandated? Because I gotta be honest, I would have thought stylists were only for the rich and famous."

"I take whatever Mode gives me," she said honestly. "But my boss knows I have a knack for creative shopping and staying within a budget, and honestly, those are my favorite clients. It can take a lot of time and effort to piece something together from discount- and used-clothing stores, but it's not impossible and completely worth it. It just takes some creativity, and I want everyone I work with to feel good about themselves, no matter how much money they have."

Brooks looked like he wanted to say more, but the server chose that moment to sidle up for their drink orders. Carly didn't miss the way the young woman's eyes lingered on Brooks.

When she departed, Carly lifted one brow. "I think our waitress would be happy to fill date slot Number Two. Or Three, if you want to double back for April from Empire's number."

Looking bewildered, Brooks glanced in the direction the woman had gone. How was this man so clueless? "I'd never ask another woman out when I was already on a date."

"Are you saying that to avoid another date? Because you're just delaying the inevitable, you know. Sasha will make sure of it."

He groaned and tipped his head back. "Can you let me get through this practice and my first real date first? I can't look that far ahead."

"Okay, yes. Sorry." She smiled brightly, straightened her spine, and fluffed her hair to make a show of resuming their playacting. "What about you, Brooks? What do you do for a living?"

"I'm a physician."

"Really?" She batted her eyelashes. "Wow. You must be really smart."

He nodded sagely. "Very."

She laughed. "Did you always want to be a doctor?"

"No. I was always good at science, though, so I majored in biology in undergrad and it just sort of went from there. When I thought about careers in science that could help people, it seemed like one where I could have the biggest impact."

Carly shuddered. "I was terrible at science." Her first (and, please note, *only*) C on an exam was on a physics test, and after almost passing out during the first frog-dissection day, she faked the flu for the rest of the week to get out of it.

"I've always wondered if I would have gone into medicine if I hadn't been good at it from the start. I love what I do and I'm glad I did, but if I'm honest I started down this path just because it was easy for me. I didn't have anything I was passionate about back then. But what if I'd loved art? Or the idea of being a lawyer? I have zero creativity and hate arguing, so could I ever have made those work? I guess I just got lucky the thing I'm good at ended up being something I enjoy, too."

"It's an incredible thing to do with your life. I can't imagine it's easy, though."

"It's not. Especially in the ICU, where I have a front-row seat to people watching their loved ones slip away. There's a lot of people I can't save, and some days it's hard as hell." A shadow briefly passed over his features.

Something about that moment made her wish they were closer so she could lean into him or give him a gentle touch. It wasn't the first time she'd wondered if the one thing Brooks Martin needed was a good old-fashioned hug.

Not your job.

She might be able to pick him up with a different question, though. "What's your favorite part about it?"

His eyes dropped to the table while he thought, and he reached across to rub one shoulder with the opposite hand. "I love the challenge. I know I just made it sound horrible, but it can be rewarding, too. It's a pretty cool feeling to know I have the training to take care of just about anyone and anything. I mean, when other doctors don't know what to do and they're overwhelmed, they send their patients to *me*. Sometimes on the hard days I reach for an inner strength I didn't even know I had, and it reminds me what I'm capable of. And when I'm able to pull someone back from the brink of death, I feel like fucking Superman."

"God, Brooks. That's incredible." The exhilaration on his face in that moment was palpable, and contagious.

His cheeks went pink. "Also, there's a major shortage of intensivists. So, you know. Job security."

"Now, *that* I understand."

A line formed between his brows. "I'd have thought accounting was a pretty solid gig."

"Oh, it is," she clarified. "That's why I do it. Even though I could pick up enough clients at Mode to make similar money, it would be commission based and dependent on client volume, so it could change in an instant. That's the kind of insecurity I'm uncomfortable with and why I'm eyeing one of their salaried positions. Hence, this collaboration with Sasha."

"Ah." He smiled softly. "Don't worry. We'll get you that job you want."

"I hope you're right," she said. "But stop breaking character and getting us off track. Now ask me if I've seen any good movies lately."

He chuckled. "So, Carly, have you seen any good movies lately?"

"At the theater? No. But my Netflix queue has gotten a lot of action lately."

"Yeah? What kind of movies do you like?"

"Don't laugh," she warned, because she couldn't think of anything but her real-life answer for this fake persona. "I'm a sucker for anything with romance."

"Why would I laugh?"

"Because a lot of men would, I guess? A bunch of people at my accounting office went to see some rom-com together after work a couple of weeks ago, and this one guy who sits next to me said he'd rather sit through a week of finance meetings than two hours of some pathetic love story."

"Dude sounds like a dick."

"He is. Oh, and he also said that Hollywood love is totally fake, doesn't exist in real life, and only gives women unrealistic expectations."

"Wow. Imagine being a dick and so fucking wrong at the same time."

"You may be shocked to hear this, but he's currently single." Carly absentmindedly toyed with the napkin in her lap as she studied him. "I gotta say, of all the things I thought you might have strong feelings about, romance films wasn't one of them."

"It's not the movie thing that bothers me," he started. "It's this guy saying love like that doesn't exist in real life."

"You think it does?"

"I know it does." Something in him changed in that moment, and for some reason it made Carly brace herself for his next words.

"It's exactly what my parents had."

CHAPTER TEN

Brooks

Deborah Truman attended college in California, which is where she met Paul Martin. They fell madly in love, got married three months later, and Paul followed her back to Oklahoma so she could pursue her dream of starting a local news source dedicated to the people and community of her hometown. Anyone who met Deborah and Paul knew right away they were head-over-heels for each other, and theirs was truly a romance for the ages.

—Reverend Thornhill at Deborah Martin's funeral

He shouldn't have brought them up. Dead parents were probably off-limits for a first date, even a pretend first date with a girl he sort of knew in high school and was enjoying getting to know again as an adult.

He preferred not to talk about them at all, truth be told. While he was a master at discussing difficult topics with his patients (occasionally) and their families (often), he wasn't so great at handling his own baggage. Lucky for him he'd gotten good at avoiding it.

But it just pissed him off, hearing that some dude was out there suggesting love was some unattainable fantasy or something that only existed in movies. There were couples who experienced passionate, all-consuming love that transcended body and soul and drove a person to dedicate their entire life to making someone else happy.

He knew because he'd seen it.

Carly didn't know what to say, that much was clear. Even though he hadn't meant to make her uncomfortable, she had this sort of awkward, agonized look of remorse on her face. Thankfully the server came with alcohol in tow, and they placed their food order. But the interruption was short lived.

"I'm sorry," she said softly when they were alone again.

He shook his head. "Don't be. Those memories are the ones I love most. Instead of thinking about how I felt the moment I found out my mom was gone, or the way my dad nearly disappeared as a person after that, I prefer to think about the fact they still held hands wherever they went. The way my dad had to touch her any time she was close by, even if he was just passing her in the kitchen. He'd kiss her cheek or slide his fingers across her waist. Or if he wanted to get a rise out of us about how gross they were, he'd smack her right on the ass."

Carly laughed a little at that, and he was glad. They were good memories.

"They weren't so in love that they neglected us, but their relationship was a priority. They had regular date nights and took weekends away, just the two of them. They genuinely loved being in each other's company, even after twenty-three years of marriage and three kids. The way my dad looked at her sometimes . . . It was like he felt so much for her he didn't know what to do with it." So much he didn't know how to live after she was gone.

He couldn't meet her eyes, afraid he'd find discomfort or, worse, pity in her gaze. But the words she spoke were soft and genuine, and he glanced up.

"That's so beautiful. You're lucky to have had such a good example set for you."

This was veering far, far away from small-talk territory, but . . . "Did you not?"

Her gaze dropped to the table and she didn't reply for a long moment.

Shit. Should have gone with his gut and kept quiet. "You don't have to answer that."

She shook her head. "No, it's okay. I was just trying to think of a nice way to say my dad ran off when I was a baby and my mom loved gambling too much to ever make the effort again with another man, but there's just not a nice way to say that. She hardly made the effort with me, so no, I didn't have that kind of example."

"Did Sasha know?" he said without thinking. *Really? That's what you're going with? Next time try a simple* I'm sorry *or* That sounds difficult.

But . . . wow. This was completely new information. He'd never picked up even an inkling of that from her back in high school, which was especially shocking, given his sister was a major gossip and the worst at keeping secrets. How was it he'd known all about Trisha Hampton's pregnancy scare and the dating history of every member of the student council, but not this?

"Yeah. Probably the only one that did, actually. I'm sure you don't remember this, but I stayed with your family for an entire week during sophomore year because my mom blew all her money at the casino and we couldn't afford groceries. Sasha saved me from seven days straight of packaged ramen noodles and frozen peas."

No, he didn't remember that. He'd been pretty focused on everything having to do with himself back then. What would he have done—if anything—had he known? "I'm so sorry, Carly."

She smiled, but something about it didn't feel genuine. "It wasn't all bad. Sometimes she won big and took me out to celebrate. We'd dine at the finest restaurants and go shopping for an entire new wardrobe. I learned quickly to buy a few things in different sizes, so that if my body changed, I'd still have nice things to wear if she lost it all again."

He was speechless. His stomach hurt for her and what that must have been like. No wonder she was so cautious about money.

Then her foot tapped his under the table. "She's been clean for ten years now. She's doing really well."

He blew out a breath. "That's good."

She scratched the side of her nose. "So, I didn't mean to unload all that on you. What were we even talking about?"

"You were trying to help me with small talk."

"Right. That went well."

He laughed. To get back on track, he tried to think of another good first-date topic of discussion. "So what do you like to do for fun?"

"Shop and watch movies. I love trying new restaurants, and if I so much as hear a whisper about bar trivia, I'll be there." She toyed with the straw in her cocktail glass. "This will make me sound like an old woman, but I also like to crochet."

Brooks couldn't help it, he laughed. "Really?"

"I made Pepper a sweater last month."

"It's May."

She shrugged. "He's an indoor cat."

"Would you make one for Oreo?"

"Sure, what size is he?"

How the hell was he supposed to know? Were cat sizes even a thing?

She laughed, one of those full-bodied ones he still hadn't forgotten from the first time they got together a few weeks ago. "God, you should see your face. I'm kidding. Cat size is universal."

He dropped his head back against the booth. Who was this woman?

"Oh, here's a trick you can use on a date," she said, hardly missing a beat. "If things are getting a little awkward and I'm looking for something to say, I just look around the room and find inspiration."

"Like . . . how, exactly?"

Her eyes wandered around the large room until she stilled and pointed to a frame on the wall. "There. I'd point out that painting and say I liked the colors or something, and ask if they were into art. Or . . . when we're looking at the menu, I think of some food I've never tried but have always wanted to and ask them if they have anything like that.

Or something else food related, like if they had to eat one single food every day for the rest of their lives, what would it be?"

Brooks just blinked at her. Those were all great ideas, but he didn't trust himself to come up with anything like that on the fly.

"If I'm already feeling pretty comfortable and we're hitting it off, I might lean in and ask if he thinks anyone else in the room is on a first date. It takes the attention off us, and it can lead to a fun conversation guessing the backstories of the people around you."

He glanced around the room, pausing when he landed on a couple at the bar. He tipped his head in their direction. "They're on a first date, for sure."

Carly followed his gaze. "Totally."

"He's wearing hair gel and trying real hard to make her laugh," he started.

"And she's laughing way too loud and keeps touching his arm," she finished. "Ten bucks says they leave together within the hour."

"What? No way."

"Why not?"

"She's way out of that guy's league. That would be like . . . like you and me leaving together after dinner."

"Well, we probably will, seeing how I drove you here," Carly said, grinning. "And that's ridiculous. I'm not even a little out of your league."

He snorted. "Please."

"Why on earth would you say that?"

Maybe he should shut this down, but it was an objective fact that she was gorgeous. He waved an arm in her general direction. "Look at you."

"I can't," she said. "Not when I'm looking at you."

His heart stopped in his chest.

She leaned forward, mischief in her eyes. "Fix your face, my guy. That's what it will feel like when a woman flirts with you, and you can't stare at them like they just said the earth is flat."

Brooks barked out a laugh and turned back to meet her brown eyes. "You're an enigma, Carly Porter."

She raised her brows and took a long sip of her cocktail. "I'm sure you're right, but what do you mean?"

He tried to put it into words. "You're just surprising, I guess. Just when I think I've got you figured out you change it up on me."

"I still don't follow."

She regarded him across the table, one brow raised. Everything about her was just so damn inviting, and he couldn't believe how easy it was to talk to her. Something told him even if they "practiced" like this every day for a year, it still wouldn't be this easy with someone else.

"When I first met you at Coffee Slingers, I'd been expecting the quiet book nerd I remembered from high school. And you're still sort of that person, because you work with numbers and you crochet sweaters for your cat. But you're also completely different. You go to bars all the time with Sasha. You're funny and sarcastic and you say things about my ass and waitresses checking me out, and it's all very confusing."

She seemed amused by his summary. "Maybe I always was that person. I don't recall you trying to get to know me back then."

His initial reaction was to think what a shame that was, but then he remembered what happened to anything he touched during that time of his life. "Thank God for that," he said, shaking his head. "I'd have ruined you."

"You weren't *that* bad," she said, but they both knew he had been. "But either way, I think you get a pass after losing your mom, and virtually your dad, at the same time."

Her words startled him at first. On the rare occasion someone had a reason to mention his dad, they offered their condolences for his death, which had happened after a major heart attack during Brooks's third year of medical school. But with the way Carly said it, she knew it felt like they'd lost him long before that. That after his mom had died, his dad had become a shell of his former self, barely able to hold on to his job and having zero energy to devote to his children. He'd been so absent that Macy'd had to step up occasionally as a parental figure, but she'd been in college and had her own life to worry about.

Most people didn't know that part, but with as close as Carly and Sasha had been back then, it made sense Carly understood both.

The sound of shattering glass pierced the air, and both of them startled in the direction of a server who'd dropped an entire tray of drinks. The restaurant went silent for a beat before the low hum of conversation picked up again.

Brooks blew out a long breath and directed a wan smile across the table. "Well. I've come to the conclusion you and I can't make small talk. It's serious business with us or nothing at all."

"Right? Damn."

"I hope I can keep it lighter with my dates."

"Quick, tell me a joke."

He froze, and she burst out laughing. "Your face! You look like I just asked you to recite the periodic table from memory."

Now she was talking. "Hydrogen, helium, lithium, beryllium—"

"Oh my God, stop." She snorted. "Do not do that on a date."

"Why? You're laughing, aren't you?"

She was really beautiful when she laughed.

"And here I was feeling like the geek at this table with my crocheted cat sweaters. Seriously, berylli-whatever? Who even knows that?"

He shrugged. "I had to memorize it in med school. It's one of those things that never left me. And I bet some women would find it extremely sexy."

She scrunched her nose. "Impressive, maybe. Sexy might be pushing it."

"You're right, showing them my mediocre garden is what will get them into bed."

"If that's your end goal you should be thankful you can't find those horrid jeans."

He jabbed a finger at her. "I *knew* it. What did you do with them?"

There went those eyelashes again, batting. “Nothing. I’m just saying it’s probably best you can’t find them, because they were basically a woman repellant.”

“I’m worth more than the clothes I wear, you know.”

“Believe me, I know that more than anyone. When my mom first started gambling and before I learned to plan ahead, there were times all I had to wear were things we’d picked up at the nearest garage sale. I refused to let it define me, but it sure as hell stung when kids hurled insults at my back.” He had the urge to reach across the table and grab her hand, but she said it so matter-of-factly he could almost believe it didn’t bother her now. “Your clothes should be the least interesting thing about you, but first impressions matter. I just want to help you put your best self out there the first time you meet someone, okay? That means jeans that show her at least a glimpse of your ass.”

He laughed and crossed one ankle across his knee under the table. “Okay, okay. Fine. If I can return the favor, might I suggest that on your next date, maybe don’t bring up the cat sweaters?”

“If you promise not to cite the elements, I won’t bring up my crochet. Deal?”

He grinned, unable to think of the last time he’d smiled this much. The nurses at work should see him now.

“Deal.”

CHAPTER ELEVEN

Carly

> Yes, the food here's incredible but no, I haven't found a margarita as good as the one at Barrios. I can't stand the thought of you sitting at the bar alone every week—promise me you'll take Sasha next time?
>
> —*Email from Benjamin Wheeler to Carly Porter*

"Why didn't you tell me your brother was smoking hot?"

Carly couldn't help but laugh at the look of distress on Sasha's face. "Ew, because he's my *brother*," Sasha said. "Which means he's not."

Their friend Kendall was having none of it. She flipped her phone around on the table so that it faced Sasha and Carly, displaying the *LiveOKC* website, and jammed her finger into Brooks's smiling face. "He most certainly is. He's got that sexy, smart, STEM vibe going on. Back me up here, Carly."

"I'll agree and take some credit," Carly said, regarding the photo she'd looked at way more than was appropriate, probably. "Properly fitting clothes really took Brooks to the next level."

"I've known you for four years and not once have you offered to set us up," Kendall whined. "Where have you been hiding him?"

"He's been hiding himself," Sasha defended. "And if you want to date him, you gotta do it through the app and for everyone in town to see. Arranging something behind the scenes with someone I know would defeat the whole purpose."

"Also, he should probably be the one in charge of who he dates," Carly put in with a laugh. Sasha's tendency to manhandle things to her liking came in handy sometimes, but it could also be too much. "This isn't Regency England among the peerage."

"Fine, I'll do it." Kendall pulled out her phone. "God knows I'm on enough dating apps already. What's one more?"

Carly checked her watch. "He's actually having coffee with someone as we speak."

He'd texted her in a panic two hours ago, certain the outfit they'd picked out was all wrong and that he'd crash and burn in the conversation department within minutes. She'd talked him down by suggesting he recite the periodic table to himself. Slowly. "I wonder how it's going."

For his sake, she hoped he'd settled in just like he had with her. What had people thought when they saw her and Brooks together that night, looking like they were on a real date? Had they seemed stilted and awkward, like many first dates were, or had they looked as relaxed as she'd felt? At times, their conversation had bordered on intimate, and while she got the feeling he didn't have those often, it hadn't felt weird. Not even a little.

Would he tell the woman he was with tonight about his parents? Would he open up about his job or tell her she looked beautiful?

"She's a vet tech, right?" Sasha asked, startling Carly out of her thoughts. "He wouldn't give me the login to his account, and I couldn't get much out of him about her."

Carly wouldn't let Sasha within ten miles of her dating app account, either. "Yeah, I think so. He thought maybe they'd have some things in common, both being in the medical field."

"Should I call him to check in?"

Kendall laughed, and Carly said, "God, no," despite having the urge to do the exact same thing herself.

"Leave the poor man alone," Kendall said, not looking up from where she was setting up the new account on her phone. "What about you, Carly? Still on your dating hiatus until Benjamin gets back?"

"Excuse me. I'm not on a dating hiatus."

Kendall looked up to give her the side-eye. "Have you been on a date since he left?"

"I . . . well. No."

"She's been hanging out with Chet Princeton, didn't you hear?" Sasha deadpanned.

Kendall's jaw dropped. Anyone who knew anything about this town knew about that man and his exploits.

"Ew, I am not," Carly said, glaring at Sasha. "I hate you."

Sasha just cackled, and Kendall said, "Not funny."

"Agreed," Carly said, but went right back to Kendall's question. "I'm just busy right now, okay? This whole thing with Brooks is taking a lot of my attention on top of my other Mode clients and, you know, my *real* job. So I hardly have any free time right now anyway."

Sasha made a show of assessing the bar they sat in and the drinks on their table. "You made time to meet up with us for Friday happy hour . . ."

"Would you prefer I ditch you two to pick up some rando at the bar?"

Her friend shrugged. "That might be better than holding out in hopes Benjamin wants to pick things back up when he gets back."

Her friends didn't dislike Benjamin, per se . . . They just found him a little dull. Sasha's exact words the night she met him had been, "He's like the guy on that *New Girl* episode that spends the entire half hour talking about model trains and his favorite types of cheese."

"That's not what I'm doing," Carly defended. She and Benjamin hadn't even talked about what might happen when he got back. Though, except for that minor horny moment the first time she went to Brooks's house, she'd been fine on her own during the five months he'd been gone. Seven more didn't seem impossible or, in her opinion, unreasonable to consider for the right guy, but that wasn't something her friends would agree with. "And I'd prove it with Plaid Oxford Guy by the dartboard, because I'd give him a 10/10 on that crisp sleeve roll, but I'm meeting my mom for dinner in an hour."

"You could have a quickie in the bathroom," Kendall said, eyes still on her screen.

"Hmm," Sasha said thoughtfully, and turned around to assess their options. "Maybe I'll consider that with Blue Hat over there."

"You'd probably mess up your hair," Carly pointed out. "And wrinkle that Veronica Beard skirt."

Eyes wide, Sasha put a hand to her blond curls. "You're right. Not worth it."

"It might be," Kendall said, then tossed her phone down triumphantly. "Done! Brooks Martin, here I come."

Sasha pursed her lips.

"What? You don't want me to go out with him?" Kendall asked.

"No, it's not that. I think you're great, obviously, or I wouldn't be friends with you. I just realized how much attention he's getting all of a sudden. It probably feels like a lot."

"I think it might be good for him," Carly said. He had seemed a little overwhelmed when he let her look through all the matches he had, but a lot flattered, too. "Remind him what a catch he is."

Sasha cocked a brow, and Carly held up her hands. "I'm not saying *I* want to catch him. You should know after that whole Princeton issue and my dream position riding on this whole thing, I'm the last person who would go after a client. But I have spent a lot of time with him lately, and I'm invested in his success and hope he finds someone that makes him happy."

"I, on the other hand, have no such professional hang-ups," Kendall said. "So go ahead and wrap your brain around it, Sasha, dear. Because soon I plan on being the one sharing a latte with him. Oh my God, what if I marry him and we're sisters-in-law?"

Sasha laughed. Carly smiled, too, but a strange sensation bloomed in her gut at the thought. Kendall and Brooks? Married? Something about it didn't sit that well with her, but why? Kendall was smart, driven, and loyal. She had a successful career as a real estate agent and could always be counted in for a night of fun on the town. She'd be a great catch and deserved to find happiness as much as anyone.

For Brooks, though? Carly just couldn't see it working out long term.

"I could get on board with adding you to the family," Sasha said. "But let's not get ahead of ourselves. It took some convincing to get him to even consider dating, so I think marriage is probably pretty far from his mind."

"We'll see about that," Kendall said with a grin, and Carly secretly wished for some of that confidence.

They moved on to topics other than Brooks for the next half hour, then Carly bid her friends goodbye. But as soon as she was in the car driving across town to her mom's, the man of the hour crept right back into her thoughts. She couldn't help thinking about his date and wondering if he would ever compare his dates with the evening he'd spent with her.

A little while later, she pulled into the driveway of her childhood home, which had once been her grandparents' and was the same house where her mom grew up. If it hadn't already been paid off when Carly and her mom moved in after her grandparents died, there was no telling when it would have been taken away from them.

Maybe that time in eighth grade when her mom lost her job and gambled away her severance package in the span of two weeks. Or anytime Carly's sophomore year . . . That had been rough.

But because they'd had this house, only water and electricity bills occasionally went unpaid. When things started getting shut off, her mom typically realized she'd gone too far and stayed clean for several paychecks to get everything back and restore basic needs like clothes, food, and books for school. There was just no telling how long she'd go before she got sucked back in again.

A foreclosure wouldn't have been so easy to come back from.

Carly let herself in through the front door and walked slowly through the familiar furnishings. It all looked the same as it had when she was a kid, but tidier. Smelled better, too, like lemon and detergent. Her mom hadn't given much thought to cleanliness in the years she'd struggled with addiction, and Carly had always been terrified of what friends might see when they stopped by her house. It was probably the reason she'd never invited people over, and why she was so obsessed with keeping her own space clean now.

She'd spent most of her time in her room, alternating between escaping into a book or movie and studying like her life depended on it. In a way, it had. She hadn't been nearly as focused on guys and parties like her peers—she'd just wanted to get out and finally be in control of her life. Her own future.

Mom was doing so much better now, though, spending her free time working in her garden, cooking, or going on walks rather than hitting the nearest casino. Carly's gaze passed over the five- and ten-year pins her mom had earned for abstinence, shining and proud in their usual place on the bookcase, and she smiled. Yes, the decisions her mom once made had hurt her, crossed the line into neglectful at times, and had a lasting impact on her to this day. But shortly after Carly had left for college her mom had entered rehab, progressed through a twelve-step program similar to that for AA, and turned her life around. It wasn't immediate, but as her mom had made improvements on her own, the same could be said for hers and Carly's relationship.

She was the only family Carly had, and while she couldn't forget her mom's past mistakes, she had accepted her apology and agreed to move on.

"Mom?" Carly called out as she stepped onto the small patio. On the bistro table to her left lay a spread of bread and cheese, plates, utensils, and two bowls.

"Out here." Her mom's voice came from somewhere in the garden. "Just grabbing some herbs for the gazpacho. Could you get it from the fridge?"

"Sure."

When Carly returned, her mom was sitting at the table picking cilantro leaves from the stems. Once she added a handful and mixed it together, her mom used a ladle to scoop a serving of soup while Carly filled her plate with way too much cheese.

"How's work?" Carly asked. Her mom had recently been promoted to senior administrative assistant at the ad agency where she worked, and while she'd been thrilled with the move, she'd been nervous about the added responsibilities. "Has it been better this week?"

"So much better. I only needed time to settle in, I think."

"Really?" Carly feigned surprise. "Weird."

Her mom rolled her eyes. "Yes, I know. It's exactly what you said would happen."

Carly just grinned and took a bite of sharp cheddar.

"I never understood when people talked about loving their job. I figured going to work was just a means to an end, you know?" her mom said. "But I get it now. I look forward to it every single day and never dread going to work like I did when I was in retail. I love knowing that I'm the most organized person in the entire office and everything will run smoothly because of me." She looked down at the table. "I've never felt so useful, fulfilled, and . . . well, proud of myself, I guess."

"I love that for you, Mom," Carly said. She was proud of her, too.

"I partly have you to thank, you know."

"Me? Why?"

"Seeing how passionate you are about your job made me want the same thing. At Mode, I mean," she clarified. "I know you don't mind accounting, but I've never seen you get as excited over math as you do for the Nordstrom Anniversary Sale."

"Who in their right mind would be excited about anything more than the Nordstrom Anniversary Sale?"

"Not you, clearly, which just proves how perfect personal styling is for you. I'll never forget that story about the science teacher you helped last year. Chris, or something?"

"Christian," Carly said, and couldn't help but smile. She'd adored working with that client—a middle-aged English teacher who'd contacted Mode for help finding something to wear to a school fundraiser he'd worked all year for. He and Carly bonded over their favorite books as they wandered through TJ Maxx. As a teacher, he'd had a limited budget for clothes, and she'd taught him all her tips and tricks for sifting through the overfilled racks at discount department stores. "He met his husband, Nick, at that event. It all started with a compliment about the shoes we'd picked out, and the rest was history."

"I still remember how you lit up talking about it, and thinking how badly I wanted a job that made me that happy. Honestly, I'm a little surprised you haven't tried making a career out of it."

Carly shifted in her chair. She usually kept her thoughts about balancing both jobs to herself when it came to her mom. As far as her mom knew, she was perfectly content sticking with accounting and dabbling in fashion on the side . . . as more of a hobby. She'd never hinted at the fact she wanted to put everything she had into personal styling and definitely hadn't mentioned the reasons she was hesitant to do so. Her fears of financial insecurity stemmed directly from her mom's decisions during Carly's childhood, and she didn't want to say anything that might make her mom feel guilty.

"Maybe someday," Carly said noncommittally.

That seemed to be enough for Carly's mom, because she sat back with a smile. "So have you heard from Benjamin lately?" Her mom had adored Benjamin from the moment she'd met him and might have taken the breakup harder than Carly had.

"We FaceTimed a couple of days ago, which was nice. I hadn't seen his face for weeks. He was at a lunch thing and I was about to go to bed, so we didn't talk long. But he's still really enjoying it and said he met someone based out of Texas who'll be a great job contact when he finishes up."

Her mom waggled her eyebrows. "That sounds promising! Texas is a lot closer than South Korea."

"That's what I said."

After taking a sip of water, her mom gripped her hands in her lap and cleared her throat, then picked up her glass and put it down again.

Carly frowned. "What's up, Mom?"

Her mom smoothed a few flyaways from her face. "I, um, have something else I wanted to talk to you about. I've sort of been . . . seeing someone."

"Dr. Gantz?" Her mom (and Carly, occasionally) had seen a therapist off and on since rehab. Was she struggling with temptation again?

"No. Not that. I meant I've been seeing a man. Romantically."

Carly's brain briefly tripped over *romantically* before settling on surprise. "Wow, really? For how long?"

"Two months."

"Two months!"

Her mom winced. "I know, I just wanted to make sure it was really . . . *real* before I said anything. And I think it is. Real, I mean."

"Oh my God. Are you blushing?"

"No?"

"You so are! Tell me about him. How'd you meet? What does he do?"

"We met online. They have a site for 'mature adults,'" her mom said, as if offended by the term. "And he's a financial planner. We messaged for a few weeks before we met in person, and we've gone out four times now. He knows about my gambling history and that I've been clean for a while now. He's divorced, no kids. He's really nice, Carly. I like him a lot."

Carly smiled. "That's amazing, Mom. I'm happy for you. When can I meet him?"

Her mom nodded, as if that had been where she was going with this. "I told him about you, of course, and said it was important to me that you two meet. I wanted to talk to you about it and make sure you were comfortable before I arranged anything."

It was strange, because her mom had dated very little. None at all before Carly went to college (that she knew of), and only a couple of times since. Her mom seemed content to be alone, but just like Carly keeping her thoughts about career changes to herself, maybe her mom had done the same.

Had she been worried Carly might be jealous, since she was nowhere near settling down?

"Of course I am," she said with a genuine smile. "I can't wait."

Encouraged, her mom's eyes lit up. "Great! Maybe we can get lunch or dinner in the next few weeks?"

"Sure, Mom. That sounds perfect."

Carly spent several hours with her mom, then stopped at the grocery store on her way home. It was almost midnight when she settled down with the remote to queue up *The Proposal*, and her phone dinged with a text message.

Brooks: look

Brooks: [image]

Brooks: i took this earlier and your mom was right. fucking tree

Brooks: i don't mean that, i love that tree. but the majestic bastard is casting shade on my tomato plants all afternoon.

He'd sent all four messages before she could get a single response out, and her smile grew with each one.

Carly: Bummer. I don't think they'd survive you trying to move them, either. Maybe next year?

Brooks: oh next year it's on. i'm gonna pot them and find the perfect spot. do you think your mom would come check out my yard and tell me where?

Carly: I'm sure she'd love to.

Brooks: BUT

Brooks: LOOK

Brooks: [image]

Brooks: the cucumbers have flowers

Brooks: that's good right

Carly: Heck if I know

Carly: Stand by

Carly: Ok my mom said that's where the cucumbers will grow.

Carly: You did it!

Brooks: let's not get ahead of ourselves. i won't celebrate till i hold a big cucumber in my hand

Carly nearly fell off the couch.

Brooks: ah, shit

Brooks: never mind

It took her a full minute to stop laughing and type out her next message.

Carly: Please tell me you didn't discuss this with your date tonight . . .

Carly: (Was that a smooth segway? Because you know I'm dying to hear how it went)

Brooks: haha, i did not mention my garden

Brooks: but it went pretty good

Brooks: she left about twenty minutes ago

She left? As in, his house? He'd brought the woman back to his house on the first date?

Carly dropped her phone to her lap and rubbed her eyes, now recognizing the ugly feeling in her chest—the same one she'd had while chatting about Kendall dating him, earlier—as jealousy. Which the rational part of her brain acknowledged was ridiculous and uncalled for.

Where was this coming from all of a sudden? She wasn't interested in Brooks. Not as more than a client and a friend. Hell, because of his relation to Sasha, he was almost like family. Was she feeling possessive because of the work she'd put in, preparing him for this moment? Helping him shop and practice small talk didn't mean she deserved credit for how well things were going, or any claim on the funny, sweet guy he'd been hiding beneath that serious, analytical veneer.

Whatever the reason, she had to get a grip. Even before the PR near miss with the Princetons, Carly had considered all clients firmly off the table, and now that decision was more than a personal rule, it was a company one, too. She had no intention of considering Brooks in a romantic sense, but apparently some primitive part of her brain needed the reminder. Pushing the unwelcome feelings down, she focused on keeping up her encouragement of his success. It was good news that this first date seemed to go well, but Brooks could use some extra confidence in the bank for the one that would crash and burn. A bad date somewhere in the mix was inevitable.

She picked her phone back up.

Carly: !!!

Carly: She came to your place??

Carly: You baller

Brooks: she said she wanted to meet oreo! she works with animals!

Brooks: it wasn't like that

Brooks: well, it wasn't like that at first

Okay, off the table or not, she didn't want any more details in that direction.

Carly: I take it this means the conversation part went well?

Brooks: yes, thanks to you

Brooks: i used your trick to guess backstories of the other customers and she loved it

Brooks: turns out I can be kind of funny?

Carly: You're totally funny

Carly: Well done

Carly: I'm happy for you.

Brooks: me too, actually. it was more fun than i expected

Carly: What's next? A second date with tonight's winner? A first date with someone new?

Carly: I.e., how much help will you need from me next week?

Brooks: for clothes or for general dating tips?

Carly: Clothes, because clearly my job preparing you for date conversation is done.

Brooks: i wouldn't say that

Brooks: it could have been a fluke

Carly: I doubt it, but just know I'm here for whatever you need.

That night when Carly fell asleep, she had a dream that she was on a date with a man who made her laugh and her skin tingle. The next morning she woke up with a silly smile on her face, still a little groggy but slowly remembering the details of the scene that had played out overnight. But then her smile faded as everything came back to her, and she groaned loud enough for Pepper to meow in response.

Even though it was just a dream and it meant absolutely nothing, it didn't bode well for her that the man sitting across from her was none other than Brooks Martin.

CHAPTER TWELVE

Brooks

Local bachelor Brooks Martin was spotted at Hall's Pizza Kitchen with a date last night. Things looked pretty cozy in the corner booth . . . has he found a keeper already?

—Threads post by Hannah Reinholdt, Oklahoma native and social media influencer

It turned out, dating was fun.

Who knew?

Not Brooks, who'd pretty much steered clear for the last fifteen years or so. While the rationale he'd given to his sisters for his lack of relationships—namely that he'd been way too busy focusing on his career—was true, he also just hadn't been interested in building something that might completely decimate him if he ever lost it. He'd primarily relied on understandings with a few women who were looking for the same thing he was: no dates, no strings, no emotions. Hell, sometimes there wasn't even talking. Just a way to find release in the midst of their stressful lives, which oftentimes only consisted of fifteen minutes here or there.

After seeing what the loss of his mom had done to his dad, Brooks sort of lost faith in the whole idea of finding "his other half," because he didn't want to become so dependent on someone that he'd be unable to function if something happened to them. Witnessing heartbroken spouses fall apart when patients passed in his ICU didn't particularly help matters.

But through his epiphany about James and these first several weeks meeting new women, he'd realized he didn't have to take it all so seriously. Dating didn't have to be about immediately locking someone down as a life partner or forging some unbreakable emotional connection with someone. It could also mean interacting with new people, exploring common interests, and engaging with the community around him—none of which he'd done in ages.

Six weeks had passed since Sasha had launched Brooks onto the dating scene, and he'd been on five first dates and two second dates. All in all, he didn't hate it. He *had* hated going on a local radio show and *Sip & See OKC*, a morning television show in Norman, to talk about himself and his favorite date-location discoveries around town. Sasha'd said publicity events like that were key to bringing attention to him and the magazine and reminded him why they were doing all this in the first place. So he'd agreed to those two bookings, but only those two.

The best part was, most of the women he'd met were great. After Abbey, the vet tech, there was Leslie, the seventh-grade science teacher. He'd taken advantage of Sasha's offer to book one of those wine-and-painting classes, and they'd laughed their asses off when Brooks's dog turned out looking more like a Sasquatch.

"I do science, not art," he'd defended, and Linh had called that a sorry excuse after the seven-year-old sitting across the table showcased her (very obviously a canine) finished product.

Then there was Amanda, a consultant who also wrote historical fiction novels on the side, and who'd pulled most of the weight to get them out of the time-travel-themed escape room they'd signed up for. Afterward, they'd stopped for a burger, where she'd talked about traveling the world with her art historian father. Even though he'd retired, her job still took her all over, and she hoped her next novel would sell well enough that she could quit consulting. She hoped to move to France within the next year or two to be better situated for book research. Because Brooks was committed to staying near his family and wasn't open to relocation, this discovery meant they ultimately thanked each other for a fun evening and agreed a second date wasn't in the cards.

He'd had the most fun with Desiree, an attorney he'd met for a game of pickleball. They spent hours trash-talking each other on the court and getting to know each other during periodic beer breaks, and had so much fun that they'd arranged Date Number Two before parting ways that first night. Unfortunately, when she'd come back to his place after another enjoyable evening at dinner and a movie, he'd learned the hard way she was severely allergic to cats. Apparently she'd missed his brief mention of Oreo in his *LiveOKC* write-up and dating profile, and he'd had to raid his bathroom for Benadryl before waiting outside with her for an Uber.

He wasn't quite ready to give up Oreo for a woman. Not yet, anyway.

Sure, there were awkward moments, and no, everything hadn't gone perfectly (see: Izzy, the personal trainer who'd stepped away for a phone call five minutes into their coffee date, never to return). But he was learning a lot about himself, like the fact that he liked sashimi and was deeply fascinated by the competitive senior pickleball circuit.

He met with Carly regularly, too, because even though they hadn't purchased many items to pad his closet, he still wasn't great at choosing something to wear. How Carly was able to mix and match to come up with a million different outfits from six pieces of clothing, he'd never know. They texted often, too, because she gave great advice and he didn't have anyone else he felt comfortable asking, like was it a good sign Linh had texted him two days after their date to say she had a good time (yes) and was it a bad idea to risk ordering the Fifth Amendment taco at the Midtown taco joint on a date (absolutely yes). He'd also kept her up to date on his garden progress and whined about something Sasha'd changed in one of the articles he wrote up.

Sometimes he texted her for no reason at all. Just because he wanted to.

She'd become sort of a safe place for him throughout this ordeal, and he was glad she didn't seem to mind because he wasn't even halfway done yet. Maybe she was just humoring him because she stood to gain something she really wanted out of his success, too, but he couldn't help but hope she enjoyed talking to him as much as he did her. Enough that they'd remain friends even after this whole thing was over, because now that Carly Porter was back in his life, he honestly couldn't imagine it without her.

"Linda said she saw you on one of her morning shows."

Brooks set down his coffee mug and scratched his jaw. "What did she think?"

It was early on a Saturday morning, and Brooks had stopped by Coach's place on his way home from the gym. He'd missed the last two weeks—the first because he'd been on service at the hospital, and then again last week because of Carly. She'd driven to Tulsa to check out a few stores that didn't have OKC locations and was so excited to give him first dibs on some items she'd bought that would work well for both him and another one of her clients that she invited herself over on her way back into town. She hadn't arrived until after nine, and as they often did, they'd started talking. She hadn't left until after midnight.

Instead of their usual spot in the kitchen, Coach had set up the chessboard on the back patio. Brooks never stopped trying to best the old man, even if he rarely succeeded.

Coach moved a pawn, then rested one hand on his belly, which had grown significantly rounder since his retirement. "She said you did great. I think the word she used was 'charming.'"

"Really?" Linda McKee was a no-bullshit kind of woman, so that was high praise, indeed. "I thought I came off awkward as hell."

"Well, she said you were that, too."

Brooks barked out a laugh. "I'll take what I can get." They both fell silent for a moment while Brooks regarded the board, and Coach only spoke again after Brooks made his move.

"So how's that whole thing going?"

"Honestly? It's not that bad," Brooks admitted. "I'm kind of enjoying it."

"You did have a little pep in your step this morning. I think I see a little spark coming back to your eyes. Have you met a special lady? Is that why you bailed last week?"

Brooks didn't miss the *coming back* part of Coach's comment, further broadening the number of people who'd noticed his antisocial tendencies over the last several years. "Nah, nothing like that. I'm just having fun right now."

Coach frowned, pausing with his hand on his rook. "You can have fun *and* meet someone special, you know."

"Easy. I'm just getting back out there, alright? I don't need that kind of pressure."

After making his decision—playing his bishop, not his rook—Coach sat back, palms out like, *Fine*. "I just don't want to see you open yourself up only to close yourself off again."

Brooks made a face. "You sound like Carly."

"Carly?"

"Porter, remember? The stylist Sasha's making me meet with?"

Coach's expression cleared and he nodded.

"She said something similar the other day. Last Friday night, actually, which is why I didn't come last week. We stayed up talking way too late, and since you only want to be social at the ass crack of dawn, I couldn't drag myself out of bed."

Coach cocked a brow. "Fashion people make house calls?"

"If they need to, I guess. I think I might be getting special treatment with this one, though, since she's Sasha's friend." Brooks cracked a small grin. "She's sort of become my dating guide, too. She let me practice small talk since I hadn't done that in forever. Honestly, I was more nervous about that part than anything else, but at one point, I was telling her about the work I do and how it's one of the only places I feel confident and in my element, and I realized I sort of felt like that sitting there with her, too. It made me think maybe I can do this, you know?"

"Well, it's good you have her around. You definitely needed all the help you can get."

"Just for that . . ." Brooks started, and made his move.

Coach blinked. "Shit." He sat for a long moment, staring at the board.

He had several options to get out of the trap Brooks set, but it was anyone's guess which one he'd take. Things could get pretty quiet when they played chess, depending on how intense the game got. The two times Brooks had beat Coach, he'd been uncharacteristically talkative. Hoping to keep his opponent distracted, Brooks kept going. "She's helping me with my garden, too."

"Who is?" Coach said to the board.

"Carly."

"She's a gardener, too?"

"Her mom is. She sends her mom all my questions and pictures of my plants."

Grunting, Coach continued staring at the game. "You could have just asked me. You know Linda's got a green thumb."

"True," Brooks said. "I hadn't even thought about that. I'll keep that in mind."

His phone buzzed in his pocket, and because Coach was taking his sweet time, Brooks figured he had a pass to check it. Carly had sent him an image of a tiny, bright-purple sweater with the caption Think Oreo will like it?

"What are you smiling at?"

Brooks looked up to find Coach's eyes on him. "Oh, just a picture Carly sent me." He chuckled. "She, uh . . . she makes sweaters for cats."

Coach frowned again, but kept his attention on Brooks for a long moment. "This Carly woman. Have you thought about asking her out?"

"Like, on a date?"

Coach nodded.

"No. Definitely not." Brooks locked his phone and put it face down on the table. "She's just a friend. It's not like that with her."

"Really? Because you haven't told me a single detail about any of these women you're supposedly having fun with, but in the last three minutes I've learned Carly has a cat, gives good advice, was at your house late last Friday, and has a gardener for a mother."

"I—" Brooks started, then stopped. Cleared his throat. "I don't see Carly like that. We've spent a lot of time together lately, but mostly because we have to. It's nothing more than that."

"She's not pretty?"

"What?"

"Since you're not interested in her, I'm assuming she must be ugly."

"Good God, Coach. You can't just call someone ugly. Haven't you heard that old saying if you can't say something nice, don't say anything at all?"

"I'm an old man. I can do whatever I want."

"Hard disagree. Human decency never expires."

"I don't see you correcting me."

"Carly's the opposite of ugly. She's a knockout, okay?" As soon as the words left his mouth, Brooks scrambled to clarify before Coach could take that and run ten miles with it. "Objectively speaking, I mean. Anyone would think so. But her looks are neither here nor there."

Coach nodded, like he was on the same page now. "She's boring, then? Doesn't make you laugh."

"What? No, she's one of the funniest women I know." He suddenly remembered the fashion pun she'd casually dropped during a conversation last week. "But in this sort of sneaky, unsuspecting way which makes it even better. I probably laugh more when I'm with her than anyone else."

"Hmm." Coach scratched at his cheek, which he used to keep clean shaven but had let grow out after he retired. "Wait, I've got it: She's too critical. Always wants to make sure you know when you're doing something wrong, right?"

"No! She . . . Wait a minute. I see what you're doing." Sneaky son of a bitch.

"Oh, so there is a brain in that head of yours? I was beginning to wonder."

"Damn, Coach. Coming at me like that before nine in the morning?"

"I call it like I see it. Something's changing in you, and if you're spending as much time with her as you say, it sounds like she might be the reason. You smile like a complete jackass when you talk about her, too. I figure either you think I'm stupid, or you're lying to yourself. And I'm pretty sure we both know which one it is."

Brooks just stared at Coach, processing. He liked to think he was an intelligent guy. He was a physician for God's sake, and chose one of the most complex specialties available in medicine. Unfortunately, despite all the training he'd been required to take during fellowship, emotional intelligence had never been his strong suit.

Did . . . did he have feelings for Carly Porter?

"I. . . I don't know," he finally managed. "But even if you're right, it can't happen while I'm committed to this magazine thing. I've gotta see it through for Sasha and Macy. And for my mom."

"Why can't this Carly be the one you go out with and take pictures with and write this crap about? Then everyone wins."

Brooks scrubbed a hand down his face, any and all thoughts of chess strategy disappearing altogether. "She's part of the team making the whole thing happen, and she mentioned its success somehow being important for her job, too. I don't think it's an option."

"So you wait, then," Coach said, as if it were just that simple. "How much longer do you have to be auctioned off?"

"What? God, I'm not . . . That's not . . ." Brooks pinched the bridge of his nose. "You know what, never mind. I have two and a half months to go."

"That's not too bad. If she's the one for you, she'll be worth the wait."

Brooks kept his expression carefully neutral. Even if he was a little rough around the edges, Coach adored his wife and was absolutely a commitment man. It wouldn't do any good to tell him Brooks wasn't looking for "the one." On the contrary, he wanted to steer clear of anything resembling it.

But when it came to spending time with someone he enjoyed being around and had fun with, Coach was right: Carly stood out, well above the rest. Obviously he found her attractive, and if by some coincidence she felt the same about him—and understood he wasn't interested in anything deeper—he could probably get on board with taking things one step past friendship.

He just had to figure out if that was what he wanted. If it was, and even if he managed to wait until the *LiveOKC* project was over, starting something with his sister's best friend would be complicated in more ways than one, for both of them.

He wasn't sure an added level of complexity was a good idea, and honestly, he wasn't convinced she'd find him worth the trouble.

CHAPTER THIRTEEN

Brooks

Just be yourself. Trust me—it's better to learn up front you're not compatible than fake it early on and realize your mistake when it's too late and you've wasted both of your time.

—Carly Porter to Brooks Martin

Coach was in the doghouse.

After the man who was like a second father to Brooks had opened his big mouth, Brooks had spent the rest of the weekend thinking about their conversation.

And about Carly.

He got in his head about it, and it started wreaking havoc on his dates. He went out with three women over the next two weeks, and he couldn't seem to stop himself from comparing each of them to Carly. Wondering how she might have answered a certain question differently, or if she'd have been willing to order four appetizers from the brewery downtown and divvy them up as their meal (Danielle had not been so inclined).

Though, to be fair, the third date was a failure all on its own, without any inadvertent help from Coach or Carly.

Sasha partnered with several small businesses in the Paseo Arts District and suggested he take a date on a First Friday Gallery Walk, a monthly event where every store in the area stayed open late for the public to walk through their shops and stop at the various restaurants along the way. He thought it sounded cool, so that's where he invited Taryn, the graphic designer he'd been messaging, to meet him.

She showed up in some sort of sequin skirt and shiny red platform shoes, which seemed like a strange choice for a casual perusal of art galleries in a district that could only be described as full-on hipster.

Then again, he only looked presentable tonight because of Carly, and who knew what he'd have worn if left to his own devices. So he gave Taryn the benefit of the doubt.

The first stop was a gallery of sculptures, and Taryn giggled each time they passed any with partial nudity, earning side-eyes from the other observers.

She's probably nervous. You're a doctor and not everyone's as comfortable with the human body as you.

He asked a few questions (he was basically a small-talk master by this point) as they made their way to the next gallery, some of which she answered and others he had to repeat because she was distracted, looking at her phone.

Wasn't that, like, Rule Number One of a first date? No phones except for emergency? If it wasn't, he'd motion for a formal addition.

At one point, she asked if they could go downtown to hit some clubs after this. Apparently she had a DJ friend working the music at Shotz, and she liked getting there early to be close to the booth. The dance floor got wild when the strobes started, a detail she'd imparted with the gravity of a business owner laying off her entire staff. He'd never heard of Shotz—and yes, when she held up their Instagram page for him to see, he made note of the spelling. It didn't sound like his scene at all.

Flashing lights and music so loud you couldn't hear yourself think wasn't his definition of a good time, not to mention he was a shit dancer.

Confusion seeped in, too, because hadn't she said in her messages she liked folk and indie rock, like him?

He suggested they stay on Paseo a little longer, wondering how he'd get out of going downtown. Their conversation was awkward and stilted, and he wondered how the hell they'd had such good conversations when messaging on the app over the past week. Judging by tonight, they had absolutely nothing in common. He even brought up Thunder basketball because she'd said in a message she loved going to games, but tonight she gave him a sort of nervous look and admitted to not going to any baseball games last year.

He stopped in the middle of the sidewalk, now more suspicious than confused. "The Thunder's a *basketball* team. You said you were a huge fan, like me."

She balled up her fists and pressed them together near her abdomen, shifting on her feet. "Okay, um . . . There's something you should know."

Oh boy. "Okay."

Her eyes darted to the sidewalk. "I wasn't the one messaging you, exactly."

They were blocking the crowd flow, so he moved closer to the building, gently tapping her elbow to encourage her to follow. "Sorry?"

"My, um, sister? She was the one talking to you. I saw you on that *Sip & See OKC* morning show, and I wanted to meet you so bad. You're, like, so cute and seemed like such a nice guy. You wouldn't believe the assholes out there."

His cheeks heated both at the compliment and the fact she'd just admitted to duping him. He wouldn't turn it around and tell her she was kind of an asshole for lying to him, even if it sort of felt true.

"But I don't know, I guess I wasn't sure you'd like me, so I asked my sister to help me."

"So you didn't think we'd be compatible, but instead of moving on you asked your sister to lie and pretend to be you so I'd want to ask you out?"

"I thought maybe we just needed to meet. I know I'm supposed to, like, be good at texting and messages and stuff. But I'm so much better in person. I love to dance and know all the best clubs in town. I figured since you were the brother of the girl who runs such a fun magazine you were probably a lot like her, but maybe you just didn't put that on your dating profile."

He kept his voice neutral, more resigned than angry. "Nope. I'm just as boring as I seemed."

"Oh."

"I see you're not going to refute the boring part," he muttered. "Listen, I'm sorry you've had some bad experiences. Men can be jerks. But I thought I was meeting a woman who likes the same kind of music and loves my favorite sports team. I want to spend time with someone I can talk to and who shares the same interests as me, like a low-key Friday night where we walk around to look at art and drink coffee and craft beer. Doing shots and dancing at a club isn't really my style, so I'm just not sure how much fun we'd have together, you know?"

She nodded, scrunching her nose. "I'm sorry." She fiddled with her purse strap for a few seconds. "So, I think I'm gonna go."

"I'll walk you back to your car."

They remained silent as they went, and he was thankful she'd parked nearby.

He thought about telling her it was nice to meet her, but instead he scratched at his jaw. He really had wanted to meet the woman he'd messaged with. "So, this sister . . . ?"

"She's gay."

Well, damn. He couldn't catch a break.

It was only eight o'clock when he got in his car. Despite usually being such a homebody, he didn't feel like going home just yet. It was as if his mind had committed itself to being social most of the night and he didn't know how to turn it off.

He could go to Macy's to see his nephews, but he wasn't really dressed for wrestling, and Carly would kill him if he ripped these pants. Then he remembered she'd texted him earlier that afternoon about finding a perfect royal-blue shirt for him (*Carly-approved for Thunder games!!* she'd said) while out shopping with another client. He turned on the car to get the air going and grabbed his phone from where he'd tossed it on the passenger seat.

Brooks: perfect? i'll be the judge of that. but thanks.

Carly: You'll love it. Feel free to come by and grab it whenever.

Brooks: you seem awfully confident I won't want you to return it, but okay

Brooks: i'm out and about now, are you busy?

As soon as he pressed send, he cringed. It was Friday night; surely she had plans.

Carly: Nope, you can come now.

Carly: Wait, didn't you have a date tonight?

Brooks: yeah, it was Not Good™

Carly: Oh no, what happened?

Brooks: don't ask

He'd never been to Carly's place and asked for her address. She lived in an apartment just ten minutes away, and soon he stood outside her door. He crossed his arms, then dropped them to his sides. And reached up to smooth his hair. What was that tug behind his belly button, and why hadn't he felt it two hours ago before meeting his date?

When she opened it to let him in, he took in her red cheeks and puffy eyes and went on high alert, everything in him going tense. "What's wrong?"

It was that motherfucker Benjamin, wasn't it? He'd never liked that guy. He'd never met him, but it didn't matter.

She waved a hand with a sniff and a grin. "Nothing, I was just watching *The Notebook*. I was too invested to turn it off after you texted, but maybe I should have." He stepped inside and she shut the door. "I cry every single time."

He'd never understood that. "I've never cried at a movie," he admitted.

She froze midstride. "Never?"

"Nope."

Everyone has a weakness, Coach had said to him once. He'd had a minor breakdown in the locker room after a visiting player taunted him with his mom's death, and Coach had been his usual hard-assed self, trying to get him back out there. *The trick is to figure out what your opponent's is but never let them see yours.*

He hadn't cried in public since. Not even at his dad's funeral—he'd managed to keep the tears contained until he was in his car. Alone.

Carly just blinked at him. "Have you seen *Titanic*?"

"Yeah."

"*Marley and Me*?"

"Yep."

"*Toy Story 3*?"

"Close, but no dice."

"*The Fault in Our Stars*?"

"How long is this gonna go on?"

"I've just never heard of such a thing." She crossed her arms, and he registered the white tank top and black leggings she wore. He'd never seen her in loungewear before. Her brown hair was pulled back in a ponytail, and she wore a pair of clear-framed glasses. Something about her natural, relaxed state and the crumpled tissues in her hand made him want to step closer and do something completely irrational, like pull her into his arms.

Or maybe that was residual protectiveness from seconds before when he thought she was missing her asshole ex-boyfriend.

He didn't let himself consider the third option: Coach was right and he did, in fact, have a thing for Carly Porter. Seeing this whole pseudo-*Bachelor* thing to the end was important to him and his family, and sneaking off to mess around with his stylist wouldn't do anyone any good.

"You look great, by the way," she said. Her gaze tracked to his shoes and back up. "You must have an excellent stylist."

"She's okay."

She arched a single brow.

"A little bossy, to be honest."

She laughed. "You like when I tell you what to do."

He did, actually. Which was strange, because he'd been ordered around so much in residency and fellowship that his absolute favorite part of being an attending was making the decisions on his own, independent of anyone else. Sure, he always sought out advice when presented with a particularly difficult case, but asking for input was his choice.

With Carly, she pretended he had a say, but they both knew he didn't.

"You look good, too," he said without thinking.

"Oh." Her cheeks flushed and she smiled at him. "So you're really not gonna tell me about the date?"

"Not worth it. Trust me."

"I'm sorry, Brooks. I've been there. Dating's hard."

He ran a hand through his hair. "It's been what? Two months since Sasha put up that first post? Just two more to go." He gave her a wide-eyed look and she laughed.

"Aren't you supposed to be writing things up for her? About your dates or something? I don't remember seeing anything last week."

"Yeah, I texted her in a panic a few days ago because I've run out of things to say, so she said we could do it as a Q&A format and sent me questions to answer. I haven't looked at them yet."

"Judging by how you did on your style questionnaire, I'm not sure that was Sasha's best idea."

"Hey, I tried my best on that!"

"We don't give participation points at Mode. You skipped half the questions, including the one asking you to name your favorite body part."

"You said my answer wasn't useful."

"I can't dress your brain, can I?" She gave him a pointed look. "At least when that guy said his dick, I was able to shift the conversation to pants."

There she went again. "How can you say that so casually?" He could talk about penises in the medical sense without embarrassment all day, but the D-word coming out of Carly's mouth didn't feel the same.

At all.

"Say what? Dick?"

He took a deep breath. In through his nose, out through his mouth.

"Because I'm an adult," she said, as if that explained everything.

Which it kind of did.

Yes, he'd brought it up, but he couldn't talk to Carly about dicks any longer. He was about to bring up the shirt—the entire reason he'd stopped by—when a gray-striped cat sauntered into the room.

"Is this the infamous Pepper?"

She walked to the small table next to the couch and picked up a half-full glass of wine. "Infamous? Do I talk about him that much?"

"No. But he's a cat, so I figure an accolade like that will start me out on his good side."

"He's a dog-cat, remember? You don't have to pander to his whims."

Brooks smiled and crouched as the cat approached. "Hey, bud." Pepper allowed him to slide a hand down his back, arching and flicking his tail. "Maybe we should get him and Oreo together for playtime. Do cats do that?"

Her brows came together in thought. "Ours might."

He almost suggested they make a date out of it, but that would probably be a bad idea.

Pepper leaned into his hand and Brooks smiled and looked up at her. Big mistake—she was smiling back at them with a sort of dreamy expression that was making him less inclined to care about the fact she was his stylist and wasn't one of the women he was supposed to be dating. In public, anyway . . .

He quickly looked away before he entertained that thought any further, and his gaze landed on the paused scene on the television.

"Is that Ryan Gosling?"

"The one and only."

"So that's why you're watching this movie."

"What? No, it's not. It's objectively one of the best movies of all time."

"Dude's a good-looking guy; I'm not judging. I'll take your word for it being the best. I never saw it."

"You've never seen *The Notebook*?" Her reaction was worse than when he'd said he thought he wasn't supposed to wear black and brown together (all neutrals match, apparently).

"Nope."

"Sit." She pointed to the couch. "I'm starting it over."

CHAPTER FOURTEEN

Carly

"Did you see the ballot box for Homecoming King at lunch? Who did you vote for?"

"Brooks Martin, who else?"

"Same. Last week he smiled at me in the hallway, and I swear I almost passed out. What about you, Carly? Who did you vote for?"

"Who did I what? Oh, I didn't. I went to the library during lunch."

—Gym class at Freemont High, sophomore year

This wasn't her best idea.

Carly was already struggling with Brooks inserting himself into situations where he shouldn't be—there'd been that dream the other night, and then yesterday, she imagined sharing a table at Coffee Slingers with him for no reason at all when she'd stopped in for coffee—and somehow she'd thought it would be a good idea to invite him to watch a romantic movie with her?

Big regrets for that third glass of wine.

There were sexy parts, for crying out loud. She lived alone and only had a couch, which felt small enough to fit inside a Barbie Dreamhouse with the way Brooks's body took up space. He'd sat about as far away from her as humanly possible, but warmth seemed to radiate off him during the heated scenes and Carly kept her eyes glued to the screen, cheeks burning.

Adult enough to casually say "dick," my ass.

His pine-tinged scent was detectable at this range, and it saturated her senses and crossed a few wires in her brain. What would it be like to be the woman Brooks watched movies with on the regular? Was he a cuddler who could be easily distracted for a hot make-out session, or did he like to focus and catch every detail to discuss as soon as the credits rolled?

What was his favorite movie?

What was the last one he'd seen? She had so many questions. So many things she wanted to learn about him but didn't really have the right to know. He was her client and she was part of the team preparing him to meet other women, and if she did anything to encourage these feelings, her job could be at risk.

Last but certainly not least, he wasn't interested in her like that.

The movie ended and she shut off her wayward thoughts, putting on a confident, teasing demeanor. "Well?"

"Sorry, no tears."

"What are you, made of stone?"

One corner of his mouth tipped up, but it wasn't the full smile she'd come to covet. "Something like that."

"Okay, so no crying. But did you at least like it?"

"Sure, it wasn't bad. I love James Garner. He reminds me a little of Coach McKee. Remember him?"

It sounded familiar . . . She squinted her eyes as she thought. "Wasn't he the football coach at our high school?"

A gentle fondness passed over Brooks's expression. "Basketball." He paused. "He was my coach for four years and helped get me back on track after my mom died. Not before I made some big mistakes, but at the end of senior year, I finally listened."

She'd had no idea. She hadn't really paid attention to the school sports teams back then. Was Coach McKee the one responsible for the change in him? "It sounds like he was really special to you."

"He was. Still is, actually. We've kept in touch."

"Really? I love that. Last year, I helped Mrs. Knipplemeier find something to wear to her daughter's wedding. Remember her?"

Brooks snorted. "Name a single teenage boy with a teacher named Knipplemeier who didn't spend all year cracking jokes behind her back, and I'll show you a liar. She's probably the only teacher I'll literally never forget."

Carly laughed. "I was so prudish back then I couldn't say her name without blushing."

"I had no such qualms," Brooks said, grinning. He stretched his arms high above his head. "Mind if I use your bathroom?"

"Sure, it's that hallway right there, the door on the left."

He got up and paused as soon as he hit the middle of the hallway, the bathroom to his left and her bedroom to the right. He glanced over his shoulder at her, one brow raised. "Now *that* is an immaculately made bed."

She laughed. "I told you, I have a thing." Her room had been the one place in her control as a kid, and she'd taken meticulous care of everything inside those four walls. She kept her bargain clothes clean and perfectly folded, her bookcase full of used books dust-free and organized, and found some measure of stress relief in the process of making her bed every morning.

He turned in place. "Actually, your entire place is spotless. Organized, clutter-free, nothing out of place, and not a single dust bunny. I seem to remember the first time you saw the disarray of my room you said I should see your place, as if yours was just as messy. You're a dirty little liar, aren't you?"

The way her stomach dropped at the way he casually called her "dirty" wasn't normal at all. "I believe it's called being polite."

"Lying is polite?"

"I was trying to make you feel better!"

"Is that what you told yourself when you stole my jeans?"

She couldn't help it, she laughed. With a snort and everything.

He just nodded and continued into the bathroom, calling out one last thing before he shut the door. "I knew it."

She leaned back on the couch and picked up the remote and was still flipping through movies when he plopped back down beside her.

"What's next?" he asked.

"Next?"

"You're not gonna give up that easy, are you? Surely there's another movie you think might make me cry."

"I do, but I'm not sure I want to put myself through another tearjerker. Unlike you, I did cry tonight. Both times. I need something uplifting now."

"Probably for the best. I have a process, and I don't think you could break me anyway."

"You have a process?"

He nodded. "If I'm in a situation where I don't want to cry, especially if I'm in public somewhere, I start singing 'Baby Got Back' in my head."

"I'm not sure that counts as singing."

"Whatever it is, it works every time."

"What's so wrong with crying in public?"

"Nothing. I actually admire people who are comfortable showing emotion like that, but after I cried in the locker room junior year the week after my mom died, I sort of got turned off on the whole idea. For myself, anyway. High school guys can be a bunch of assholes."

"That's horrible, and they were assholes." Sometimes the girls hadn't been any better.

"Why weren't we friends back then?" he asked. "I knew several of Sasha's friends, but you were always sort of a mystery."

"Eh, I liked it that way. I didn't want many people close enough to see what my life was really like, so I tried to fly under the radar. Keep my distance."

Brooks smiled ruefully. "Sounds familiar."

"It's like we've sort of switched places, isn't it?"

"A little, yeah. I have no intention of going back to the Extreme Brooks that I was in high school, but I see now I went a little too far in the other direction. I'm on my way to something in the middle, thanks to you."

She bent forward in a dramatic little bow. "I can't take all the credit, though. Maybe just like, ninety percent."

He laughed. "I'm just glad you agreed. To help me, I mean." His hazel eyes assessed her face, and he hesitated a beat, as if debating what to say next. "It's been more fun than I thought it would be."

She hummed in victory. "Fashion *is* fun."

"I don't think it's the clothes I enjoy," he said quietly.

Her heart hiccuped, and she just stared at him. As she considered how unwise it might be to ask what he meant by that, he spoke again. "What do you think would have happened if we'd noticed each other back then?"

"Excuse me, don't try to both-sides this. You were Brooks Martin. Not noticing you wasn't an option."

She couldn't tell if he was pleased by that or not. "What did you notice?" he asked, a raw vulnerability in his gaze.

A strange sensation jump-started in her chest. She sifted through memories, pulling some off the dusty shelves and leaving others where they were. "You were . . . charming. Bold. Spontaneous. Everything I wasn't."

He said nothing, but the hand he'd rested on the back of the couch shifted, brushing her hair back from her shoulder. His fingers touched her bare skin there, and her breath caught as a sizzle of fire rushed down her spine.

Was he . . . interested in her? His steady, heated gaze said so. His breath seemed to come a little quicker, chest rising and falling in time with hers. His eyes dropped to her lips, then shifted back to meet her eyes. His brow furrowed and he worried his lower lip with his teeth, as if he were considering something, or holding himself back from it.

"What would you have done if I'd flirted with you like I did with Sasha's other friends? If I'd asked you out?"

She opted for humor because the moment felt heavier than she was prepared for. "I'd have passed straight out, that's what." Though, she wasn't altogether confident it wasn't true.

"Come on."

"The sexy, popular upperclassman and star of the basketball team noticing me, the shy, studious girl who cut her own hair to save money? That's, like, the plot of every teenage rom-com."

His brows pinched together, but her brain had trouble focusing on anything except his thumb moving back and forth across her skin. "I thought you said you didn't want people to notice you. That you tried to stay under the radar."

God, since when were there so many nerve endings at the edge of her shoulder? She swallowed. "There would have been . . . exceptions."

His gaze turned electric. "Would you have made an exception?" he asked, voice a little rough. "For me?"

"I . . ." she started, but the words wouldn't come. *Yes. Absolutely.*

Had he leaned closer? Had she? His eyes, nose, lips . . . They didn't seem as far away.

All the signs were there that he wanted to lean in, and while her body was here for it, her brain panicked, asking rapid-fire questions: What was happening? What did it mean? Was this a terrible idea? What the hell was she doing?

A shrill ringtone sliced through the air. She sucked in a startled breath, and Brooks jerked back like a fifteen-year-old with his hand on the school fire alarm. She blindly reached for her phone.

The display showed an incoming FaceTime call from Benjamin Wheeler, complete with his contact photo that was a candid of the two of them at Christmas last year.

Brooks's eyes shifted from the screen to her face, and his expression shuttered. He stood. "I'd better go. Sorry I stayed so late."

He was halfway to the door before she caught up to the movement and stood. Phone still vibrating in her hand, she silenced the call and tossed it back to the couch. She'd completely forgotten that Benjamin said he'd try to call her tonight.

The timing could not have been worse. Or maybe better . . . because what was she thinking, almost kissing Brooks?

Still, she didn't want it to be weird, and didn't want to leave things on an awkward note. "No, you don't have to . . . I'll call him later."

He dug his keys out of his pocket, probably just so he didn't have to look at her, because there's no way that fancy Audi wasn't push-start. "I have to be at the hospital early tomorrow."

"On a Saturday?"

"It's orientation for our new class of critical-care fellows. I'm leading it."

"Oh, okay." Fine, that was a decent excuse. "Hang on, at least let me get that shirt for you."

She retrieved the bag from her room and handed it to him. "Do you want to try it on first? Make sure you like it before you take it?"

He shook his head. "I trust you." Damn, he really wanted to get out of there.

"Okay. Just, um, let me know what you think. If you want."

"Sure. I'll talk to you later." Then he was gone.

The door closed behind him, and she dropped her forehead against it. It took all of thirty seconds for the weight of what they'd just barely sidestepped to settle across her shoulders. Yeah, in the moment she hadn't intended to stop him, but she had way too much on the line with this project to throw it all away in a moment of weakness. She'd worked too hard and wanted that Mode position too bad. Especially after the phone call she'd gotten from Mai earlier today.

She'd been in the car, headed home from a bone-dry day of inputting numbers into spreadsheets, when Mai's number lit up her console. Her boss wanted to congratulate her on how well the *LiveOKC* partnership was going. She had nice things to say about Brooks's attire in the various media sources he'd appeared in—print, television, and digital alike. But most importantly she'd shared a sharp increase in client contracts, one in particular from one of the *Sip & See OKC* morning show hosts, which could lead to great publicity for the company as the stylists for someone so regularly in the public eye.

"Strategic partnerships like what you've done with this magazine are exactly the type of thing we're looking for," Mai had said. "I hadn't realized the connections you had, not only with *LiveOKC* but also with the entire Martin Media Group. They have several outlets we could pursue in the future. I have a meeting with Kyle next week, and I plan to discuss your success with this. I'll be in touch."

Carly couldn't take her eye off the prize. Not right now.

Handsome, charming, and smart or not, Brooks Martin was just as off-limits now as he'd been from day one, and Carly had to be more careful.

A hopeful part of her brain popped off with a reminder that when this was all over, if he hadn't found someone he wanted to be with, maybe they could test the waters. The prospect filled her with the same kind of excited energy she felt when she was waiting for a client to emerge from the dressing room in an outfit she just knew would turn out perfect, which, to be honest, was a little alarming.

Brooks may be rediscovering his skills in conversation and flirtation, but was he actually ready for an emotional connection?

What would Sasha think?

What about Benjamin? What would happen when he came back?

And speaking of Benjamin, how the hell had she gotten so distracted by Brooks that she forgot they were supposed to talk tonight? They'd agreed on a time and everything, and she'd been looking forward to it all week.

She pushed off the door and went back to the couch, Pepper circling her ankles after she sat. Her cat had traded off between her and Brooks's laps all evening, and it didn't escape her notice that he seemed to love Brooks. He'd never cared for Benjamin, but he also didn't seem to like Sasha, so Carly'd never held it against him.

She gently nudged him to the side, and he promptly leaped up to the spot Brooks had vacated and curled up, while she picked up her phone and settled in to call Benjamin back.

CHAPTER FIFTEEN

Brooks

Are you keeping up with OKC's local Bachelor, Brooks Martin? Tell us in the comments!

—LiveOKC Instagram post

What has been your favorite date location so far? OKC City Tours (link here) hooked me up with a rooftop spot for the downtown Fourth of July fireworks show. We just hung out with drinks and appetizers and watched the sky from the best vantage point in town. I gotta say, it was pretty magical.

Have you met anyone special? I've met some lovely women, but nothing serious yet. (Don't worry, dear readers, I'll keep you updated. —Sasha)

What advice do you have for OKC singles creating a dating profile on LoveInTheCity? Be yourself. Being someone you're not will waste both of your time. I think there's someone out there for everyone, so why waste your time meeting people you have nothing in common with? Be honest (but not too honest—I probably should have skipped the cat hairball story, apologies to Date #3) and maybe even a little vulnerable. That's the kind of thing I put out there and what I hope to find in return.

Any embarrassing moments you want to share? I'll just say this: if you take a woman to listen to a band play at a local bar, maybe check to make sure the lead singer isn't her ex. Who sings mostly love songs he wrote about her.

Yeah.

Any what-not-to-do advice? Don't bring a cucumber from your garden as a gift for your date. I thought it would be nice and sort of funny. It was neither. #creeper

Name three things about this process that have surprised you.

1. In a lot of ways it's not as bad as I thought it would be. Overall we're all just looking to make a connection and find someone to spend time with.

2. Pie Junkie has the best dessert in town. Holy crap, where has that place been all my life?

3. Having a personal stylist has really helped my confidence through this whole process. It's been a long time since I cared much about how I dressed, but she told me first impressions matter, and while I'm loath to admit it, she's right. Even the shopping

isn't so bad. I know, I'm just as surprised as you. If you're interested, check out Mode Style.

Carly: You got cucumbers?? I can't believe you didn't tell me!

Brooks: oh hey, i got cucumbers

Brooks: how did you know?

Carly: *LiveOKC* newsletter just hit my inbox. That's so exciting! I'm proud of you, you little gardener, you.

Brooks: i prefer Garden Master

Brooks: Green Giant

Brooks: SuperGardener

Carly: Garden Gnome

Brooks: no

Carly: How was the date last night? Did you wear the shoes?

Brooks: yes but no one noticed because they're shoes

Carly: If she didn't compliment that delightful pair of footwear I don't even know what life is anymore.

Brooks: do you have a fetish I need to know about?

Carly: Obsession, not fetish. I love shoes in a completely nonsexual way.

Brooks: wow, yeah. important distinction

Carly: Seriously how was the date?

Brooks: it was fine

Carly: Just fine?

Brooks: yeah. probably won't go for a second date.

Carly: Have you considered maybe you're looking for reasons not to have second dates? There's no way this many women don't want to go out with you again.

He couldn't, wouldn't, tell her the truth, which was there were so many times he'd found himself wishing it was Carly across from him—instead of the perfectly pleasant woman named Jillian—that he'd cut the date short. Jillian didn't know that, of course. He'd planned a walk around the Myriad Gardens and then going for ice cream after, but had nixed the dessert part. Not because he hadn't liked her. On the contrary, it was the best date he'd been on so far (minus him bringing a cucumber—that was awkward). She was funny and outgoing, and they had a fair amount in common. She was beautiful and held a successful career as a physical therapist, which gave them the topic of health care as something to fall back on if conversation ever stalled.

Which surprisingly, it never did.

Still, she wasn't Carly.

He couldn't stop thinking about her. Her quiet but snarky personality and how fucking beautiful she was when dressed up or while lounging at her house (seeing her relaxed like that had been . . . a mistake). She cried while watching movies and was obsessed with perfect lines and throw pillows on her impeccably made bed (which just made him want to mess it up, preferably *with* her).

He'd made an emergency visit to Coach's house last night and spent an hour talking about her, and yeah, he *had* thought about telling her about his cucumber success. He'd felt a ridiculous and probably slightly pathetic amount of pride when he had pulled those first two vegetables from the vine, and she'd been the first person he'd wanted to tell. She'd get excited with him and wouldn't make him feel like a total loser for celebrating his accomplishment. But that night at her apartment where he'd almost kissed her had freaked him out. He wasn't the kind of guy who made moves on a woman who was his sister's best friend that he'd hired (well, sort of) to perform a service, and who was obviously still hung up on her ex.

Hell, he was barely the kind of guy who made moves.

He should probably put some distance there.

Which would be difficult tonight since he would see her out for Sasha's birthday. That reminded him . . .

Brooks: what should i wear tonight?

Carly: For Sasha's thing? Whatever you want. Fassler Hall is super casual.

Brooks: okay

Brooks: but i need you to tell me exactly what to wear that's what you do

Carly: Have you not paid attention when I've explained the reasons for pairing things? The goal is to learn how to do it yourself.

Brooks: okay

Brooks: can you just tell me though

Carly: Give it a try on your own. You have better instincts than you think.

Brooks: where did you hide my favorite jeans?

Carly: I have no idea what you're talking about but regardless those are always the wrong choice

Carly: I believe in you, Brooks. You can do this.

He pursed his lips, annoyed, but also amused. He crossed his arms and walked into his closet, standing before his options. He'd stay in here as long as it took, because if the way he'd felt when she'd gushed about his cucumbers just now was any indication, little made him feel as good as when he made Carly Porter proud.

He hadn't felt this nervous in a long time.

He walked into the massive beer hall, posture stiff and hands stuffed into his pockets as he surveyed the room for anyone he recognized in the group celebrating Sasha's birthday. Which would be one of his sisters or Carly.

Sasha had told him to bring James, but the bastard bailed to go to dinner with his new girlfriend. For years, James had long been his go-to on the rare night he wanted social interaction. He understood Brooks's call schedule, and they always had plenty to talk about. When it came to women, he and James had kept similar lifestyles during training. Meaning they hadn't done relationships. And for the first several months after starting real jobs, just like Brooks, James hadn't broken tradition.

Until Aly, the barista. Brooks hadn't thought it would last long, because nothing with James ever lasted long. But it had been a couple of months now, and when Brooks had caught James at the hospital to catch up last week, his friend had seemed pretty damn happy.

"Why do you look distraught?" a familiar feminine voice said from behind him, bringing him back to the present.

Brooks immediately relaxed. "Because you wouldn't tell me what to wear."

"Looks great from the back. Turn around and let's see the whole picture."

Was she referring to his ass again?

Maybe he should have told Sasha he was sick. Or on call tonight.

He turned around to face Carly, and the second she filled his gaze his throat seized up. His hands screamed at him to let them touch her. Slide his fingers through that long, brown hair or move his palm down the green, silky tank top that fluttered around her skin with the breeze flowing through the open windows. He tried to swallow but it was no use, because that black skirt was so short her legs seemed miles longer than seemed possible. He didn't give a flying flip about shoes, but he liked that he could see her pink-tipped toes in whatever heeled sandals she wore, tall enough that the top of her head was near his chin, sending her vanilla scent his direction.

"Nice shoes," he said, unable to clear the rasp from his tone.

He definitely shouldn't have come.

Her eyebrows danced with humor as those warm brown irises drank him in, and did he imagine that flash of heat in her eyes?

"You did good, Brooks," she said with a smile. She tucked hair behind one ear, sending a gold earring twirling. "Real good."

Mesmerized by the light flashing on the jewelry, it took him a second to respond. "I threw everything you've ever picked out for me on my bed, closed my eyes, and grabbed something."

She laughed and his heart swelled. "No, you didn't."

"I'm serious." He'd come up with the short-sleeved gray Henley in one hand and navy chinos in the other. He still thought the pants were too tight and too short, but he'd wear them every fucking day if she'd keep looking at him like that.

"At least tell me you hung everything back up after."

"Right before I made my bed."

She groaned and it went straight to his groin. "Come on," she said, shaking her head. "Everyone's over here."

He followed her to a rambunctious group near the back of the room, crowded around a table with a giant two-foot-tall game of Jenga on the wooden, picnic-style table.

Sasha yelped and nearly spilled her beer when she saw him, jumping up to give him a hug. "You came!"

"Happy birthday, sis." Macy sidled up on his other side, and he put an arm around her. "And hello to our ringleader."

Sasha addressed the twelve or so people gathered around. "This is my long-lost brother, whom most of you have heard about but never seen in the flesh."

He waved awkwardly.

A chorus of *hey*s and *welcome*s went around before they were once again focused on the ongoing game, and the tension left him when their eyes moved on.

"Ready for trivia?" Macy asked Carly.

"Always." She checked her watch and said, "Game starts in ten. Either of you want anything from the bar before we start?"

"Sure," Brooks said. "I'll come with you."

"Grab me one of their hefeweizens, will you?" Macy asked him, and turned to find a seat.

Brooks and Carly wove through a few tables to the long bar top, found a place between other patrons to squeeze in and place their orders.

"Ever been here before?" she asked.

He shook his head. "No, seems cool, though. I bet it's packed on weekends."

"It'll get pretty busy tonight, too. Trivia nights are always a hit."

Some guy standing next to Carly leered at her from behind, and Brooks glared at him over her shoulder.

"Hey, you two!" A blonde with a bright smile approached. She held out her hand. "I'm Kendall. Nice to finally meet you, I've heard a lot about you from Sasha and Carly."

"Don't believe anything Sasha said." He was curious what she'd heard from Carly, though.

Kendall laughed. "She said you're a hot doctor. And unless you're not really a doctor, I see no lies."

"Kendall's the shy one of the group," Carly said, her tone teasing but with an undercurrent of something else. Brooks shot her a side-eye and almost whispered something in response, but Kendall had sidled up next to him and bumped his shoulder with hers.

"Buy me a beer?"

"Sure." He hadn't been flirted with so openly in a while. It felt nice, but he was keenly aware of Carly standing on his opposite side. "Order whatever you like."

The bartender returned with his and Carly's drinks, and Carly quickly walked away, leaving him and Kendall at the bar while she waited for hers.

She hopped up on a vacated barstool and rotated to face him. "Ever played bar trivia before?"

He shook his head. "I know Sasha loves it, though. I'm not surprised she picked this for her birthday. What kind of questions do they ask?"

"Sometimes there's a theme, like Harry Potter or nineties music. Tonight's just general trivia so there'll be a mix of everything. Pop culture, history, music. Anything, really."

"Good to know. Are there prizes?"

"Gift cards. But it's more of a pride thing in our group. It's all about bragging rights."

They continued talking while they waited for her drink, and he learned she was an Ohio native, moved to Oklahoma in middle school, and a real estate agent. She loved country music (did he know Chris Stapleton was playing downtown next week?) and was super into hot yoga (he was welcome to come with her next Wednesday to give it a try). The conversation required virtually no help on his part to keep afloat, which was kind of nice.

When the bartender brought her beer, they stayed at the bar for a few minutes longer, but then Sasha called out across the tables that it was almost game time.

Once back with the group, he handed Macy her beer and took an open seat. Kendall sat beside him, and he forced himself not to look around to find where Carly had settled.

"Okay, everyone," a voice boomed from overhead. "You know the drill."

Heads nodded and everyone around him grabbed little pieces of paper and pencils that a restaurant employee had dropped in the center of every table.

"I actually don't know the drill," he whispered to Kendall. "Help a guy out?"

"Three people to a team. You're with me, and let's grab"—she half stood and tapped the shoulder of a guy to her left—"Jeff. Get over here." Jeff shot her a dreamy-eyed look and happily obeyed.

"He wins a lot," Kendall whispered as Jeff moved seats. "Okay, so there are twenty questions. We pick a team name and they ask all the questions and we write the answers down before we turn in our papers. No googling or anything, and I'd keep your phone in your pocket if I were you. People get pretty crazy if they think you're cheating. Usually takes them about twenty minutes to review everything and announce the winners. Top three teams get prizes. In our group, top team gets a free round from the losers."

"Who cares about drinks," Jeff put in. "It's all pride."

Brooks held out his hand. "Hey, man. Sorry if I ruin this for you. First timer."

Jeff eyed him as they shook hands, but Kendall waved the game card in the air. "You're a doctor. You've gotta be super smart."

Chances were the questions weren't about sedatives or metabolic acidosis, but . . . "I'll do my best."

The emcee boomed out a welcome and a cheer went up, followed by everyone taking a drink of their chosen beverage. He went through a quick review of rules, rehashing the No Google portion with particular intensity.

"Told you," Kendall whispered, and Brooks chuckled.

She smelled nice. Not quite as appealing as the vanilla scent he'd noticed whenever Carly was around, but still nice.

Carly was about two yards away, within his line of vision, but she wasn't looking at him. She laughed at something the guy next to her said, and he almost smiled just watching her face light up.

"Here we go!"

The room went silent as everyone crouched together with their groups, tiny pencils in hand.

"Question one: Singer Stefani Germanotta is more commonly known by what name?"

Brooks hadn't even processed the question before Kendall had furiously scribbled a response on their paper. He didn't see a point in checking to see what she'd written, because he had no idea and wouldn't know if it was correct or not.

"Question two: How much does the Chewbacca costume weigh?"

What the actual hell were these questions?

"Eight pounds," Jeff whisper-yelled, straight faced. "It's eight pounds. Write it down."

"Got it." Kendall rubbed her hands together. "Off to a good start."

"Question three: How many times has Kim Kardashian been married?"

Seriously, how did anyone know any of these?

He glanced up and caught Carly looking straight at him. She was laughing.

He pointed at himself, feigning affront, as if to say, *You laughing at me?*

She didn't even try to stop and nodded, then gave him a thumbs-up. *You're doing great.*

He wanted to send her a snarky text but didn't want Jeff to kick his ass. By the time he refocused on the question at hand he noticed Kendall had already written down *three*.

Brooks wasn't even sure which one Kim was.

"Question four: What is the body's largest organ?"

"Skin," he said automatically, though based on the raucous laughter that filled the room, several people had suggested something very different.

"He's a doctor. Listen to him," Jeff said.

Apparently Brooks was too much of a doctor and Jeff was taking this too seriously for either of them to consider a dick joke along with the rest of the room.

That made him think of the guys who put that sort of thing on Carly's style questionnaire, and he sought her out again. She must have felt his gaze because she glanced up. He pointed to his head and mouthed, *brain?*

Dick, she mouthed back, and shit, he knew exactly how that word sounded coming out of her mouth. He wished he didn't find it so sexy, but lately there really wasn't a thing about her he didn't.

He only knew answers to two more questions—which country produced the most coffee in the world (Brazil) and which NBA team temporarily relocated to Oklahoma City after a natural disaster in their home state (New Orleans Hornets), but even so, he enjoyed himself. Kendall knew everything related to pop culture and Jeff had a lot of history and geographic knowledge, and he thought they had a pretty decent chance of ending up in the top three.

Kendall turned in their game card with their team name—Doc Martin, which he had to admit was pretty clever and made him wonder why no one called him that at work—proudly written at the top. The entire birthday group reconvened to hang out together as the trivia hosts tabulated the answers, asking what other teams had put for various questions.

"You knew the basketball one, didn't you?" Carly asked, slipping onto the bench beside him.

"Yup. And you knew the most expensive fabric in the world, didn't you? What is it?"

"Vicuña wool. It's something like two grand per yard."

"Holy shit. Never buy that for me."

She snorted. "I wouldn't even buy that for myself."

"We'd probably make a pretty good trivia team, you and me."

"Yeah, I'd carry us most of the way, but you'd swoop in with the weird anatomy and sports questions."

He wanted to argue he knew some pop culture stuff, but she was right. He stopped by the bar for another beer, and by the time he made it back to the tables, the emcee was once again tapping the mic.

"Here we go, everyone. In third place with seventeen questions correct is . . ." He paused dramatically for several beats. "Let's Get Trivial!"

A group of people several tables away jumped up and yelled in celebration as everyone else clapped.

"With eighteen questions correct, second place goes to . . . I Am Smartacus!" After allowing that team to celebrate, audio of a drumroll played over the speakers. "And we actually have two teams with near perfect scores tonight, giving us a tie for first place. Congratulations to the Red Hot Trivia Peppers and Doc Martin, each with nineteen points!"

Jeff leaped across the table with a whoop to throw an arm around Brooks's neck, knocking over several thankfully empty beer glasses in the process.

"Whoa. Yeah, great job, man." Brooks clapped him on the back. The second Jeff released him, a very different body pressed up against his other side.

"We won!" Kendall said excitedly, giving him a squeeze. "You won your first-ever trivia game!"

Brooks grinned and hugged her back, weirdly proud of the accomplishment. Sasha gave him a thumbs-up from across the table, and over Kendall's shoulder he happened to catch Carly looking their way, a strange expression on her face. Before his brain could really process it, though, she met his gaze and immediately smiled and gave him exaggerated jazz hands.

Kendall pulled away and her face took over his field of vision, blocking Carly, who stood in a small group several feet away. "That was fun."

"Yeah, it was."

"So, I have to be honest. I've followed along with your dating posts on Sasha's blog."

"Oh, yeah? What do you think?" He hoped it was real and sort of funny and was giving some local businesses recognition, but part of him wondered if all it did was make him look like a pathetic dating novice. Or a huge geek. Or both.

"I love it. I recently joined LoveInTheCity, too, and have had a few less-than-stellar dates." She looked up at him from under long lashes, twisting her lips to the side. "Actually, I'd been thinking about asking Sasha to introduce us. After tonight, I really think we'd have fun together."

He sensed what was coming and wondered where Carly was or if she could overhear their conversation. Which was stupid, because why did it matter?

"What do you think? Will you take me out, Dr. Martin?"

He regarded her smiling, confident, upturned face, certain she was very different from what he considered to be his type. If they'd had a lot in common from the dating site questions, they'd have been matched through the software, but he hadn't seen her name anywhere. She was outgoing, loud, and fun. She was a lot like Sasha, come to think of it, which explained why they were friends.

Either way, he'd enjoyed hanging out with her tonight, so what did he have to lose?

"Sure, I'd love to."

CHAPTER SIXTEEN

Carly

> Hey. I just wanted to check in and make sure you're really fine with what we talked about yesterday. Give me a call later if you want.
>
> —*Text message from Benjamin Wheeler to Carly Porter*

Carly's week started off incredible and then went straight to hell.

At least her one win was a big one: *She got the job.*

As in, Mai and Kyle agreed that on top of her stellar style instincts and customer relationships, her work with *LiveOKC* and connections for future media collaborations were proof she was a strong, well-rounded investment for the company. They'd called her into Kyle's office on Monday and made the formal offer, and she'd been so happy she hugged them both and cried.

She'd even successfully negotiated the salary, something her younger self never would have been able to do. She didn't even wait an hour after arriving at Bailey Accounting later that morning before submitting her two weeks' notice.

She rode that high for a good twenty-four hours before things started going downhill, and as the hits kept coming, Pepper seemed more and more concerned.

"Would you stop looking at me like that? I'm fine."

Her cat blinked slowly, flicking his tail once, his black-and-yellow gaze giving Carly a bland *Yeah, right* look.

Carly sighed. "Okay. I'm not fine. I mean, I am, but I could be better. Are you happy?"

Cat-blink.

"This week hasn't been the best, I'll give you that. But you know what? I've got my dream job, I have a roof over my head, and I have great friends. So my love life isn't in great shape, but that's not the end of the world."

And really, the job thing was huge. Amazing. Everything she'd been working toward at Mode. She sort of hated that she let completely different issues dim the light of that accomplishment, but she couldn't seem to help it.

Pepper jumped off the side table, pushing a copy of Kennedy Ryan's latest romance onto the floor as she went.

"You did that on purpose," Carly muttered, picking up the book and centering it back onto the stack where it belonged. She slipped on her shoes and tucked her phone into her purse with a sigh.

It had been seven days since Sasha's birthday party. Three weeks since the night Brooks had come over after his failed date and watched *The Notebook* with her. Both nights had led her to two very important realizations.

One: She liked Brooks. Like, a lot. Which was unfortunate, since there wasn't a single thing she could do about it, both because it could risk her job and because he was maybe falling in love with one of her closest friends.

Which led her to number two: She did *not* like seeing him with Kendall. And not because it was Kendall—her friend was lovely and great and deserved an incredible man like Brooks. No, it was just that

(1) Kendall wasn't Brooks's type at all, and (2) Carly wouldn't like seeing his arms wrapped around another woman no matter who it was (except Sasha, of course).

She'd given more thought to how she might approach Brooks after the *LiveOKC* thing was finished, because even if she wasn't one to take big risks, she also didn't particularly enjoy living in regret. The more time that passed without him connecting with someone, the more likely she was to have an actual shot. If she could wait until he wasn't her client and they were both single, there'd be nothing holding her back.

But then Kendall came into the picture and excitedly informed Carly a few days after the birthday party that she and Brooks had made plans.

Date plans.

Which, of course, was the whole point for Brooks and being part of this whole Bachelor series.

So, yeah. That sucked.

He'd tried his hand at dressing himself last night and had sent her a picture to make sure she approved. She had, and how. The man pulled off flat-front shorts and leather sneakers like a damn Ralph Lauren model. An assessment Kendall was sure to agree with.

That also sucked.

The final event topping off the shitty parts of her week was yesterday's phone call with Benjamin. They hadn't been in touch for a few weeks, and with the whole Brooks/Kendall thing sending her into a rare state of loneliness, she'd taken a chance Benjamin wasn't busy and called him. He'd answered, and during their conversation she blurted out a question she'd had for months but never could bring herself to ask.

"Have you dated anyone since you've been gone?"

"What?" Benjamin had asked, clearly not expecting that.

"I'm just wondering if you've . . . you know. Gone out with anyone over there."

He'd paused for a long moment, then said, "Are you sure you want to talk about this?"

If that in itself didn't answer her question, him stating straight up he'd been casually seeing one of his co-interns for a few months sure did. It had not only surprised her but also made her feel sort of pathetic that she hadn't done the same, a truth she'd tried and failed to keep out of her voice.

She'd made an excuse to get off the phone pretty quickly after that.

Thank God Carly had a client to meet this morning, or else she would have spent the entire day wallowing in a pool of self-pity. Glancing at the clock, she cast one last glare at Pepper and swiped her keys from the table. "Be good while I'm gone."

The meeting was scheduled at a tea shop in Nichols Hills, near some of the best independent shopping venues in Oklahoma City. Carly walked in one minute before ten and spotted a dark-haired woman near the window with an expectant look on her face.

"Jacque?" The woman nodded and Carly held out her hand with a smile. "I'm Carly. Nice to meet you."

"You too."

"I see you've got a drink. Mind if I grab a tea before we start?"

"Not at all."

Once she'd procured an Earl Grey with several drizzles of honey, Carly parked herself across from Jacque. "So have you ever done anything like this before? I've gotta give props to your husband—that's a pretty thoughtful gift, if you ask me."

"No, I haven't," Jacque admitted. "I can't believe my husband even thought of it."

"I have to agree." Carly laughed. "I don't know many men who would gift their wives an afternoon of shopping. Nothing against flowers or chocolates, but I'd pick this over those any day."

A sad sort of smile settled on Jacque's lips. "I was trying to get ready for our first date night since our twins were born and broke down in the middle of the closet because nothing fits the same as it used to. He's so wonderful and said all the right things, like how beautiful I am no matter what. But all I see is this six-month postpartum body, and I just . . ."

She looked down at her hands for a few seconds, then took a breath and lifted her eyes. "Anyway, bless that man, a few days later I had this gift certificate in my inbox."

"He's right, you are beautiful," Carly said. "And my job is to help you see it, too."

Jacque toyed with the string of her discarded tea bag, expression polite but skeptical. "You've got your work cut out for you."

"It's a good thing I'm amazing at my job," Carly said with a smile, undeterred. "Okay if I tell you a little about how this usually works?"

"Sure."

"For this package, I'm basically at your beck and call for three hours. We could spend that time any number of ways, and the timer won't start until we make a plan."

She nodded. "Okay, what are my options?"

"Some clients like to take me to their house, where I can help make recommendations based on what's already in their closet, because sometimes it just takes a little creativity to style things in a new way. Others want to hit some stores and use me as a personal shopper to help them pick things out and pair them together. We could always do both—see what you've got and strategize what new pieces we want to add. And a few times I've had people just want to sit and chat while we look through websites, talking about style ideas and concepts. When your husband contacted Mode, he mentioned shopping and that you two would set a budget together, but that may have changed?"

"No, that's true. We talked about it, and he said he wanted me to buy whatever I wanted." She chewed her lip. "But I'm, um, not very comfortable spending a lot of money." Her cheeks flushed pink. "I'm sorry. I looked at your website, and I'm sure you're used to working with people with a lot of cash to spend, but I just don't think I can. The size of our family basically doubled, and one of the twins has had some medical issues we're still paying for. I . . . I hope that's okay."

Carly's heart squeezed, remembering all the times growing up she'd tried to find confidence for herself on a budget. "That's definitely okay."

It was more than okay, if the sudden fizz of excitement in her stomach was any indication. Jacque was right: The majority of Mode's clientele was high-income individuals, and while it was fun being able to shop for them without restriction, Jacque felt more like Carly's people.

"Okay, thank you." Jacque looked down at her lap. "I thought about trying to shop on my own first . . . but I didn't even know where to start."

"I have a ton of ideas for us. Believe it or not, I know all the best reasonably priced places around town, and some are real hidden gems. Let's chat a little more about your style and the things you like to wear, then we can head out. Sound good?"

Something like relief flashed in Jacque's eyes. "That sounds great."

Her husband had technically only paid for three hours of Carly's time, but she spent close to five with Jacque. She couldn't remember the last time she'd felt this inspired and energized by a client. Each smile and look of pleasant surprise on Jacque's face when she came out of the dressing room in a new outfit was like winning the lottery.

She may not be saving lives like what Brooks did for a living, but for Carly, this was its own type of healing.

After making a simple dinner and changing into loungewear, Carly settled onto her couch. Seconds later, her phone lit up with a text from Brooks.

Staring at the screen, she hesitated to unlock it. She'd been waiting for him to message her about his date with Kendall, because he usually told her about his dates. If he didn't, she usually asked.

Did she want to know how things had gone?

No. Especially not if it had gone well, which made her some kind of asshole, probably.

Kendall had texted her twice today, and she hadn't looked, afraid of what she might find. *We're already in love!* or *I think this is finally it, he's the one!*

Carly could think of nothing worse than those two hitting it off and witnessing their perfect, beautiful love story as a bystander. Because if anyone would have the romance-film-style love that rarely existed in real life, the universe would pick them just to spite her.

A second text from Brooks came through. She couldn't avoid him forever, so she bit the bullet and looked.

Brooks: [image]

Brooks: come get some of this

Two things happened simultaneously: An overloud laugh burst from her lips, and she nearly sank to the floor in relief. Which was a weird combination.

Carly: Is . . . is this a sext?

Brooks: what? no they're my cucumbers

Brooks: i bet your mom wants some too

Bless his heart.

Carly: That's a lot of cucumbers

Brooks: the vines have taken over the entire garden and i need help unloading some of these. i can't possibly eat them all

Carly: Why don't you pickle them?

Brooks: what?

Carly: You know. Make pickles out of them.

Brooks: ???

Carly: Tell me you know pickles are made from cucumbers

Brooks: oh

Brooks: yeah I knew that

Carly: OH MY GOD

Carly: You didn't

Carly: HAHAHAHAHA

Brooks: this feels like a good time to remind you I know the entire periodic table by heart

Carly: I'm literally wheezing I'm laughing so hard

Brooks: are you taking some of these or not?

Brooks: nevermind I'll just take them all to work

Carly: No no, I want some. I love cucumbers. And, incidentally, pickles.

Brooks: i hate pickles. but i love cucumbers, how is this possible

Carly: Did you know sauerkraut is cabbage?

Brooks: yes

Carly: Raisins are grapes

Brooks: 🖕

Carly: Just checking

Brooks: i just need to know how many cucumbers you want

Carly: I'll take 3

Brooks: ok. i'll pick out the best ones for you

Carly: And one for my mom

Brooks: K

Had he texted Kendall to see if she wanted any? Or had he brought some to her on their date last night?

She pressed her phone to her chest and closed her eyes. What if he'd invited Kendall back to his place last night and Kendall had been the first one to see his spread? Had she, in fact, been the one to pick the best cucumbers?

Oh, hell. She was about to cry over a vegetable.

She jumped at a sudden knock at her door. She wasn't expecting anyone, but made her way to the peephole, ensuring she didn't make noise in the event it was someone she didn't want to talk to, like her chatty neighbor. She wasn't in the mood for a discussion about natural methods of wasp repellant just now.

When she saw who stood on the other side, she frowned and backed up to swing the door open.

"Kendall?"

Her friend arched one eyebrow like it was her job and marched inside. Carly closed the door and turned around to find Kendall next to the couch with one hand on her hip.

"Why are you avoiding my texts?"

"What? I'm not. Sorry, I've just been . . . busy."

Kendall's second eyebrow joined the first. "Well, I hope you're not busy anymore, because I need to talk to you. As you know, I went on a date with Brooks last night."

Oh no. This was it. She was about to ask Carly if she'd be her maid of honor at their wedding and why hadn't she looked at the texts because at least then she'd have been able to scream in frustration as she answered the affirmative (because of course she would)?

"Oh, right." There, she sounded cool. Casual. "How'd it go?"

Kendall snorted. "Not good, Carly. Not good at all."

"Oh, no, why not?" That had actually been genuine.

Mostly.

"Because he's completely and one hundred percent hung up on you."

CHAPTER SEVENTEEN

Brooks

"Should we take some dinner up to Dad?"

"I left a sandwich outside his room an hour ago."

"Should I go check to see if he ate it?"

"I don't know. I think he just wants to be left alone."

—Conversation between Sasha and Brooks Martin, senior year

Brooks tended to get lost in his work when he was in the unit. It was one of his favorite things about the job. When he swiped his badge and walked through the self-propelled double doors, he could leave everything else behind for a little while.

Memories.

Regrets.

Thoughts of doing things to Carly Porter he had no business entertaining.

All things that kept him up at night, and that he welcomed a reprieve from.

But doing so also meant he got a little intense about certain tasks, which was why that Monday morning he was trying to look up lab results on his phone while power walking down the hall and ran smack into someone. Automatically, he put a hand out, his fingers grasping a feminine shoulder. "Whoa, sorry."

"That's okay—oh, Dr. Martin! Hi."

Nikki, one of the new critical-care fellows he'd met when he led their orientation a few weeks ago, smiled up at him.

He dropped his arm and slid his phone into the pocket of his white coat. "Hey, Nikki. How's everything going so far?"

"Good, just finishing up with all the onboarding stuff. I start my first month in cardio with Stetman next week."

He winced. Stetman was a real asshole to the first-years. Brooks swore the man got off on making sure each of them cried at least twice before he was finished with them. "Good luck."

"Thanks. I'm actually on my way to Schwartz Rounds. Are you heading that way? I could save you a seat."

He frowned a little, trying to place the name. He'd heard of it but couldn't quite remember what it was. "Schwartz Rounds?"

"Oh, have you never gone before? It's where providers get together to discuss recent patient experiences that meant a lot to them, or that were especially hard for them. Share how they felt about it, that kind of thing. We had them at my residency program, and I never missed one."

He remembered now. The second he'd seen the description as a place where health care workers could "discuss emotional issues they face," he'd deleted the email. "Nah, I don't go to those."

"Why not?"

"I guess I'm not really into all that touchy-feely stuff."

"Oh, that's right."

He gave her a strange look. The way she'd said that sounded like it was something she expected of him, but that was impossible. They barely knew each other.

She winced. "Sorry, that didn't sound right. It's just . . . well, you know. The fellows talk. Us first-years ask the seconds and thirds about the attendings. Ask what we need to know, right? Like who's gonna grill us about the patient in front of the entire crew, or who's obsessed with local antibiotic resistance patterns. I like to make a good first impression, so I wanted all the dirt."

He blinked, considering the connection in her words. "So the dirt on me is that I never show up to Schwartz Rounds?"

"No. They just said you're pretty straightforward as a physician. Everyone says you're a great doctor and take good care of patients. You're just not one of the emotional ones who likes to connect with your patients or their families." She squinted her eyes a little, as if trying to ascertain if she'd upset him. "They didn't mean it as a bad thing."

"That I don't like to connect with my patients doesn't sound like a bad thing?"

"Not necessarily. There are tons of doctors like you. Some are the best ones in the field. And to be honest, I get it. Especially in critical care, when we know we won't see all our patients walk out of here, there has to be some level of detachment to stay professional and avoid burnout." She shrugged. "Maybe one day I'll get there, too, but for now, tapping into the human, emotional part is what I love most. It's nice to know I'm not the only one feeling a certain way, you know? I like to lean on my colleagues on the hard days."

When he had a hard day, he just forced it down and went about his business. He'd learned the hard way that when things got tough, he just had to keep going and get through it. "Everyone finds what works for them, I guess."

"That's true." She checked her watch. "I'd better get going, I don't want to be late. See you later, Dr. Martin."

"Yeah. See ya." He watched her walk away with a frown, then shook out of it and retrieved his phone.

He had work to do.

When Brooks walked into Macy's house later that evening and found Mark and the boys gone again, he panicked. The last time that had happened, he basically signed away all his free time for four months.

"Why do you look like that?" Macy asked from where she lounged in the armchair.

"Like what?"

"Like you're about to turn around and leave a Brooks-shaped hole in my front door."

"You invited me for dinner, but the boys are gone," he admitted. "That doesn't usually work out well for me."

"I'd argue it's worked out pretty well for you," Sasha said from the kitchen doorway. "But they're here. They're just upstairs."

He narrowed his eyes. It was too quiet for that to be true.

"Transformers-movie marathon," Macy added, reading his skepticism.

"Can I go up there instead?"

"No," Macy and Sasha said in unison.

He crossed his arms, but his little show of resistance didn't faze either of them. Macy stood and gestured for him to follow. "Come on. Food's in my office."

"In your office?" Why would they have dinner in there?

"We can spread out around my desk. I thought it was fitting that we meet in there for this. Anyway, it's just frozen pizza, so it's nothing fancy."

Frozen pizza meant they probably weren't going to ask him for any favors tonight, so he followed her.

Macy's office was the one room in the house that was off-limits to the kids, so it was by far the tidiest. She sat in the padded leather chair behind the desk while Brooks pulled up an accent chair for Sasha and an ottoman for himself. He was trying to be chivalrous, but it was so low that he ended up at nipple-level to the edge of the desk.

Behind Macy's head, the three large frames hung where they always did, but when he saw what was displayed behind the glass in the third one, he groaned. "Oh God, why did you do that?"

Macy twisted around to regard the enlarged image as she spoke. "My brother was basically the centerfold in our magazine. Of course I was going to show it off."

"No one else comes in here! And for God's sake, do *not* call me a centerfold."

"Fine. Main story, then."

"You usually only put up the covers."

"I made an exception for a full-page photo."

"I still don't understand why it had to be so big," he grumbled. Though deep down, it was kind of cool to see himself beside his mother, forever captured in the frame beside his, pride for everything she'd accomplished clear as day on her face.

Macy just smiled and divvied up pizza onto three paper plates.

"I'll get straight to the point so you stop stressing out," Macy said to Brooks, and Sasha nodded her support of this plan. "Sasha's been afraid to jinx it so she hasn't said anything, but I wanted to let you know the Bachelor series is working. Everyone's talking about it. And therefore, everyone's talking about *LiveOKC*."

"Really?" Brooks said, pleasantly surprised. He'd steered clear of the articles and posts, trying to focus just on the dating app. Maybe the comment sections would give him a boost, but he knew they could be nasty, too. He figured he didn't need that kind of feedback.

"Really."

"Wood, please," Sasha ordered, and the three of them dutifully knocked their knuckles against the desk, even though neither he nor Macy were particularly superstitious.

"I just wanted to let you know so you'd . . . I don't know, be assured what you're doing is worth it, I guess. I know it was unconventional and a lot to ask."

"Especially of you," Sasha added.

"But from the business perspective," Macy continued, "it's doing exactly what we need it to."

"Good," Brooks said, his mother's smile looming large behind his sister. "That's really good. That's what this was all for, right?"

"Partly," Macy agreed. "But it was also about you. So I also wanted to formally check in and see how you're doing. Sasha seems to think you're enjoying yourself, too, but we both know she can embellish."

"Hey!"

Brooks snorted and Macy asked, "Where's the lie?"

Sasha scowled and said nothing.

"So?" Macy prompted. "How are you doing with this whole thing?"

While they all wanted to keep their mom's dream alive, he believed his sisters honestly thought the whole endeavor would be good for him, too. Family business or not, they wouldn't have asked him to do it otherwise. So he gave them a mostly honest answer, omitting the part about his growing infatuation with his personal stylist.

"I am having a good time," he said. "You two were right. I'd turned into kind of a loner and forgotten what it was like to get out and meet new people. It's been fun. More than I thought it would be."

Some degree of tightness left Macy's shoulders, reminding Brooks how she'd often felt responsible for her younger siblings. He'd doubtless caused her a few gray hairs over the years. "Have you met anyone you really like?"

Yes, but not through the app. And he liked her more than he'd ever liked anyone else, like ever, which was a little unnerving.

"I . . . don't know," he hedged, unsure what else to say.

Macy squinted at him, and from his left Sasha leaned toward him. He squirmed and took a massive bite of pizza.

"Oh my God, you have," Sasha exclaimed. "When? Who is it? I can't believe I didn't pick up on it in the articles! Is it serious?"

"Whoa," Brooks mumbled through his full mouth, palms up.

"Sorry, sorry," Sasha said, duly chagrined. "You're right. Too much."

"What she meant to say was, you're giving off some kind of vibe that I'm sure is unintentional, but we're your sisters so naturally we picked up on it," Macy said, ever the calm, rational one. "So we'd like more information if you're willing to share."

Calm, rational, and damned effective—because he was *this* close to putting everything on the table and asking them for advice. He just as quickly decided against it, though, because while Macy would be reasonable, Sasha might flip out. She'd hated it when he messed around with her friends in high school, and none of those girls had been anywhere near as close to Sasha as Carly.

"I'll pass," he said. Sasha squeaked in dismay, so he added, "For now. Let me see how it goes first, okay? When I'm ready to talk about it, you'll be the first ones I come to."

"Of course," said Macy.

Sasha nodded and kept quiet, her face red with the effort.

It was silent for a moment, then he said, "What do you think Mom would have thought about all this, anyway?"

"With us running the business, or using her only son as the center of our revival campaign?" Macy asked.

He laughed. "Both."

"I think she'd have loved anything that brought us together," she said, "and that connected us more with our community."

"That's what her whole life was about," Sasha agreed. "Family and community."

Brooks smiled as an unexpected gratitude settled along his rib cage. "That and Ralph's pineapple pizza."

His sisters burst out laughing.

"She had the worst taste in food," Sasha said, then shuddered. "Fruit doesn't belong on pizza."

"I didn't mind it," Macy said. "But only when we got it from Ralph's."

"So every Friday night, then," Brooks said. It had been a family tradition to order pizza from the local joint every week for movie night. They'd stopped ordering it after she died, and as far as he knew, no one in the Martin family had gone back since.

They spent the next half hour eating and reminiscing, then Sasha stepped out to take a phone call, leaving Macy and Brooks alone in the office.

His eye caught on her wedding ring and, still on the two-foot-tall ottoman, he leaned forward to rest his forearms across his knees. "Can I ask you a question?"

Macy looked up from where she'd been tapping at her own phone and set it down to give him her full attention. "Sure."

"Do you ever worry about what happened with Dad?"

"What do you mean?"

"You married Mark, so you obviously love him. You loved him enough to choose him to share your life and start a family with. But after watching how Dad all but disappeared when Mom died, do you ever worry about the same thing happening if anything ever happens to Mark? What if you couldn't function for yourself or your kids?"

Rationally, he knew his dad's situation wasn't typical. Grief was expected, and it took time to restore a sense of normalcy after such a significant and shocking loss. The difference was most people found a new way to operate and move on, somehow.

His dad never had.

Brooks understood the medical side now, after learning about brain chemistry and various types of clinical depression in med school, and he knew his dad hadn't received the proper help he probably should have. But during those teenage years when Brooks was just trying to make it through, he'd harbored some pretty serious resentment. Yeah, his dad was sad and grieving, but they all were. Had Mom really been the only thing his dad cared about in life? The only thing that made him happy? What about Brooks? What about Sasha and Macy? What about the friend group they met up with at least once a month for card games?

Did they cease to matter without his mom?

He'd needed his dad in those days more than ever. So even to this day it was still hard for Brooks to separate what he experienced back then—feeling the visceral loss of not only his mom but also basically his dad, too—and not associate that with what could happen when you fell in love.

"No, not really," Macy said slowly. "I mean, sometimes I get in my head, like when Mark's traveling or something, and I convince myself something terrible will happen and I'll never see him again. I'll call him in a panic and won't settle down until he answers. Even though it doesn't happen often, I worry more about something happening to *him* rather than how *I'd* react if it ever actually did." She propped one elbow on the desk and put her chin in her hand. "I mean, no one really knows how they'll respond to something like that, but I can't fathom abandoning the boys. That's when they'd need me the most."

His first thought was, *Exactly*, so apparently he wasn't completely resentment-free.

"Why do you ask? Do you worry about that?"

He had worried about it. After seeing the impact his mom's death had on his dad, he'd basically decided he'd never be so dependent on another person that he'd risk being put in that situation. He'd successfully avoided thinking about it much after his dad passed away . . . until Carly popped back into his life. There'd been a few times recently when he'd wondered if she had the potential to be that kind of person for him. Someone that, if he let himself become too attached to her, he wouldn't be able to live without.

He definitely wasn't ready to get into specifics, though. "Not a lot. Obviously it doesn't really relate to me right now. But it crosses my mind sometimes."

"Keep in mind I was sort of removed from the worst of it because I'd already moved out. So it makes sense his behavior affected you differently than it did me."

"Yeah, I guess."

"Do yo—" Macy started, but a thunder of footsteps tracked through the kitchen seconds before his nephews burst into the room.

"Uncle Brooks!"

Before he knew it, Brooks was on his back on the floor, laughing and wrestling and trying to protect his junk from sharp elbows and knobby knees.

"Boys!" Macy barked. "Haven't we talked about staying out of Mommy's office? Uncle Brooks and I were having a conversation."

"It's fi—*oomph*, easy buddy," Brooks grunted. "Fine."

More than fine, actually, because he probably shouldn't have initiated that conversation in the first place. He'd started it but now he was done talking about it, and thankfully Sasha and Mark joining them in the office to watch the WWE match ensured Macy wouldn't try to circle back to it. Tonight, anyway. She'd definitely pin him on it again someday, but he'd avoid it for as long as he possibly could.

After all, he'd gotten pretty good at that.

CHAPTER EIGHTEEN

Carly

> We expect employees to always act ethically, responsibly, and respectfully when dealing with company partners, clients, and our company image.
>
> Employees will avoid personal, financial, or other potential conflicts of interest that may hinder their ability to perform expected job duties.
>
> —*Code of Conduct, Mode Style*

Carly was freaking out.

Cucumbers. You're just here for cucumbers.

And yet, she remained frozen in her car outside Brooks's house, staring at his front door, Kendall's words from the night before scrolling through her mind like a Broadway marquee.

He talked about you all night. I could tell it wasn't on purpose, but he just sort of kept coming back to you.

You should see the look on his face when he talks about you. Literally all I want in life is for a man to look like that when he talks about me.

Please put that man out of his misery.

She'd come because she told him she'd be by today, but after hearing all that? What was she supposed to do, just stroll in there and act normal? Like she felt nothing and knew nothing and that nothing would change?

Half of her wanted to talk to him, but the other half maintained it was pointless.

Was it best to get it out in the open, maybe talk it out, because trying to hide mutual feelings that grew stronger every day could cause problems on its own? Normally it wouldn't have had her tied up in knots, because once she'd become an adult and gained some experience in the relationship department, she rarely had trouble telling a man she was into him. But in this moment, instead of butterflies it felt like a swarm of hornets dive-bombing inside her stomach. Something about admitting it to Brooks Martin . . . and more, admitting it to him when maybe he felt the same . . . It was important. Bigger and more significant than anything she'd done before, and that gave her pause.

Also, the fact they absolutely, positively could *not* act on it right now really fucking sucked. But she'd literally *just* landed that job, and she wasn't about to let a man get in her way, that man being Brooks Martin or not. Two points to the Carly who wanted to keep her mouth shut.

When an older woman walking her dog gave Carly the side-eye as she sat in her car staring at his house, she finally got out, no closer to deciding what she'd do. Talk to him? Don't talk to him? Make a run for the cucumbers and get the hell out of there?

She rubbed at her eyes as she walked unsteadily to his door and knocked.

A few moments later he opened it, looking rumpled and sexy in gray sweatpants and a white T-shirt, his dark hair in adorable disarray.

In her purely professional opinion, he had the hot loungewear look down pat. Vivid imagery of the dream she'd had last night—of her and Brooks making good use of a vacant hospital room—cycled through her brain, and she reached out to steady herself on the doorjamb.

"Hey," he said with a smile, lifting one arm to run a hand through his hair. *Gah*. "Come in. Sorry I didn't get dressed for you. I usually just go from sweatpants to scrubs and back again when I don't have plans."

"You never have to get dressed for me." She stopped short, halfway through the door, and turned wide eyes on him. "Um, I meant get dressed *up*. For me."

He laughed and put a gentle hand on the small of her back to urge her forward enough for him to close the door. The touch burned straight through her shirt, burrowed beneath her skin, and radiated to every single nerve ending.

Oreo pranced into the room and made a beeline toward her. She picked him up and nuzzled his head, happy to take the distraction.

"He missed you," Brooks said. He stood near the armchair, relaxed with his hands in his pockets, looking at her like he was happy she was in this room with him.

Cat. Cat. Focus on the cat. "I started making him another sweater."

Brooks tucked his lips between his teeth.

"Don't look at me like that." She cocked a brow at him and some of her anxiety settled, replaced by something more pleasant. "Just wait until you see it on him. You're gonna love it."

"I don't doubt it," he said, clearly trying to hold in a laugh.

With each look and word spoken, just being in his presence and the reminder of how comfortable it was . . . made it all seem easier.

Being with him felt natural. Maybe they could figure this out.

She glanced through to the kitchen, then brought her eyes back to his dancing hazel ones. "I know you think the fact that I crochet cat sweaters makes me a huge nerd, but you're the one with a dozen cucumbers laid out on your counter."

"Fourteen," he corrected, his ears turning pink. "Got two more this morning."

That was all it took. That sweet look of pride that he'd successfully grown a vegetable all on his own.

"I like you," she blurted.

His body stilled and his brows came together. "What?"

Oh God. That happened.

Might as well keep going . . . but, just . . . what was she supposed to do with her hands? "I like you, Brooks. As in, I have feelings for you. Lots of them. Technically they're not all good, I guess, because sometimes you're frustrating." His stunned expression shifted a little at that, forming a crooked grin. "Like when you can't see how good you look in a straight-leg jean or when you're moody because you haven't had enough caffeine. But mostly they're wonderful, warm, sparkly feelings that make me happy and make me want to be closer to you. You're so smart and kind of nerdy, and sweet and thoughtful. And funny, even when you're not trying to be. So . . . I, um. Yeah. I like you and that's all."

His smile was sweet and languid and adorable. She couldn't help but smile back at him, even though her stomach had tied itself back into knots.

"I like you, too," he said, grin widening. He gripped his chin with his thumb on one side and fingers on the other, and slid them down as he nodded slowly. "I also have feelings. *Lots* of them."

Then he started toward her.

"No!" she cried.

He froze and his hands shot up like she'd yelled this was a stickup.

"Sorry. I just, I mean, we can't act on it right now, and I'm not sure what I'll do if you come close."

"Carly," he said roughly, hands falling to his sides.

"I know," she groaned, and again apologized. "I wasn't sure if I'd tell you or not, and maybe I shouldn't have because you're my client and I can't date you as long as you're that, and now this will just be miserable for both of us. But I couldn't help it. You just . . . You made me."

"What? I didn't do anything."

"Yes, you did. You knew I was coming over and you wore those."

He glanced down and frowned. "Sweatpants?"

"Exactly. Then you smiled at me and teased me, and you have all your produce so carefully lined up—did you arrange it by size? Honestly, what was I supposed to do?"

"I don't know, maybe not show up here in those shoes and with those dangly earrings and gorgeous eyes and tell me you like me, then make me stand over here like I'm in time-out?"

She sniffed. "You can sit over there. If you want."

"I don't want," he said thickly.

"Oh."

They stared at each other.

"I also don't want to date you."

"Oh," she said again, then, "Wait, what?"

"You said you can't date a client, and that's fine. I shouldn't date you right now, either."

"Yes. Good. I agree."

"No dating."

"Right."

He studied her for a long moment, and she felt his perusal like a gentle caress. Then, he said, "How do we feel about kissing?"

"Abou—what?"

"Kissing. How do you feel about that?"

"I—"

"Because here's the thing: Kissing isn't the same thing as dating. Wouldn't you agree?"

"I agree with that specific sentence, yes. But—"

"Because, and hear me out, I think we should go ahead and get that part taken care of. Get it out of the way, or else we're going to be thinking about it for the next month until this whole magazine thing is over. We both have reasons to see it through to the end, but that doesn't mean I'm not going to want you the entire time."

She let out a long, slow exhale. "Same."

"So that's a yes, then?" he asked. "I can kiss you? Just the once, for the time being. I promise."

Her pulse throbbed from her collarbone to her fingertips. She wanted that more than she wanted early access to next year's Nordstrom Anniversary Sale. "Okay. Yes. Please."

Then he was moving, coming up against her in three long strides, both hands drifting across her cheeks in a move that was somehow firm and gentle at the same time, and the next thing she knew his open mouth was hot against hers, tipping her head back as a deep groan rumbled from his chest into hers. It felt like he wanted to climb inside her, and she twisted his shirt in her fist to make it easier for him, to pull him closer. She buried her other hand in his hair, and he walked her backward until her shoulders hit the wall. Arching into him, she kissed him deeply, so instantaneously addicted to him that she whimpered when he flattened one palm against the wall and pulled back.

His mouth left hers but didn't go far, instead moving to rasp into her ear, "Twice? Two times. That's all I'm asking."

"Yes to two." Her hands snaked down his back to grip the ass she'd been dying to investigate. "Maybe three, four tops—"

He kissed her again and dipped down to grip her upper thighs, lifting her, and it was the single hottest thing that had ever happened to her. She wrapped her legs around his waist as he used his hips to pin her to the wall, his full lips determined and insistent. She gave herself over to the moment, clinging to his shoulders and moaning when he did something filthy with his tongue. When she needed a second to breathe and it seemed like he did, too, she tipped her head back.

"So," she panted. "Is that . . . a cucumber in your pants, or . . . ?"

Brooks did a sort of sharp exhale-laugh thing, and his breath brushed the sensitive skin along her neck, making her shiver as she smiled.

"How do you do that?" he asked, gently sliding her down the front of his body until her feet were back on the ground. His pupils were dilated and his breath came fast. "Turn me on and make me laugh at the same time?"

"It's a gift."

He pressed his forehead against hers. "God, I can't believe I got to do that. Part of me has wanted it since the first time you said 'dicks' in that coffee shop."

She slid her hands down to palm his butt again. "And I'm happy to report this ass was worth the hype."

"Holy shit," he said gruffly. "You can't do that."

"What? This?" She pulled his hips harder against her.

He made a choking noise. "Fuck. Yes."

"Why not?"

"Because. Even though we decided on thirty-seven kisses before we wait, I don't want to get carried away. We have to be careful."

"Careful. Right." She nodded. "But before we do that, can we keep doing this? Just for a little bit."

"Good idea."

He kissed her hard, dipping his tongue into her mouth and turning her into a vessel of pure sensation. He could suggest just about anything right now and she'd be all in, so it was a good thing he'd come to his senses and drawn a line somewhere.

They remained that way for long moments, wrapped up in each other and barely coming up for air. For a man who'd claimed just a few short months ago to be unfamiliar with the dating scene, he sure knew how to use his mouth. First kisses could be fumbling and awkward, but there was none of that with Brooks.

Kissing him felt like coming home.

A strange beeping came from somewhere to her right, stopped, then started up again.

She whimpered when he pulled back, the disappointment shining in his eyes indicating he didn't really want to stop, either. "That's the hospital."

"Oh."

He slowly peeled himself back and walked to the end table, coming back with his phone. He bent down to kiss her forehead and said, "Let me see what they need. Don't move."

He took the call in the kitchen, and his serious doctor voice saying all sorts of fancy medical jargon did nothing to cool the embers still smoldering in her bloodstream. She smoothed her thumb across her lower lip, processing everything that had just happened. Brooks Martin. Brooks-fucking-Martin just had his hands on her body and his mouth on her mouth and said he couldn't believe he was touching her. *Her*, Carly Porter.

Smiling, she flopped onto the couch and pressed her face into a throw pillow, inhaling his spicy scent before kicking her legs and squealing with glee.

A throat cleared behind her and she scrambled to sit up. Brooks stood there, one hand gripping his neck, eyebrows raised.

"That was for high school me," she explained.

"Ah."

They just looked at each other for a moment, then he threw a celebratory fist in the air with a deep and rowdy, "Yeeeeah!"

She clapped a hand over her mouth.

He dropped his arm, nonchalant. "That was for present-day me."

Laughing, she got up and walked toward him. He put his phone down and opened his arms. It was a perfect hug with her cheek against his chest and his against her hair, despite the chuckles of disbelief and exhilaration passing between them.

"Do you have to go in?" she asked, referring to the call.

"No. Not yet, anyway."

"Good."

"Can you hang out for a bit?"

"Yeah. I can."

"I'm glad you came over," he said, lips in her hair.

"Me too."

CHAPTER NINETEEN

Brooks

"Hey, man. Nice job on rounds today. You handled your own when Richter tried to pimp you in front of the whole team."

"Thanks, I think I just got lucky. I'm Brooks, by the way. You a first-year, too?"

"Yeah. I'm James. Wanna grab a beer after this? I could use one after today."

—Resident call room, University Hospital, PGY-1

"Who is she?"

Brooks glanced up from his watch. "Who is who?"

From his spot beside Brooks in the back row of the conference room, James huffed out a quiet laugh. "The woman you're thinking about. I've never seen you so antsy. Got somewhere to be?"

"I don't know what you're talking about," Brooks murmured.

"Don't play that with me." James propped one ankle on the opposite knee and leaned back with his fingers behind his head, feigning interest in Dr. Lim. "You're seeing someone when you get off, aren't you?"

"Nope." Not that he didn't want to, though—he'd have loved to head straight to Carly's place right after work if it was an option, and every day after. But he'd already made plans to meet a woman named Madison for a drink tonight, something he'd questioned last night.

"Should I cancel the dates I have left?" he'd asked Carly as he'd run his fingers up and down her arm. "There are only two, but still. It feels kind of shitty going to meet another woman after this."

She'd promised keeping the dates after making out with her didn't make him an asshole, because no one expected exclusivity with a first date. "That even goes for this," she'd said, waving a finger between them. "You never know, you might fall in love on the spot and forget all about me."

He'd played it cool because they'd literally just kissed for the first time, but that was about as likely as him going on a solo shopping spree just because. A little part of her had seemed relieved, though, when he said he didn't intend to set up any others and that Sasha would just have to deal with it. Pathetic as it may be, the idea of Carly being jealous over him was strangely satisfying.

James still didn't look convinced, but he let it go. In truth, Brooks wouldn't mind telling his best friend about Carly. In fact, he'd love to talk to someone else other than Coach about her. He could go on for days about her incredible personality and that she was so easy to talk to they could cover topics from his ass to their favorite musicians and even his mom's accident without awkwardness. That she took his fashion missteps in stride, and rather than making him feel embarrassed about his ignorance, she made him feel attractive and confident every time he tried something new, even though she looked like a runway model in anything that touched her skin, from one of those short dresses with high shoes to leggings with a tank top and bare feet. He'd smile when he talked about her tidiness and obsession with crisp sheets on a perfectly made bed and her penchant to cry at movies.

But lately James had been strutting about like the all-knowing guru of women and relationships, despite his current state of bliss being based on the first time he'd seen a woman for more than a week in a decade. Brooks didn't want to give him the satisfaction, and besides, it hadn't even been twenty-four hours since he'd found out Carly was into him. Plus they'd agreed to avoid being anywhere in public together for the next few weeks.

They needed to be careful, sure, but as far as he was concerned, seeing each other in private was another story. Yes, they'd said last night that it was just until the magazine ran the farewell article, but he wasn't confident either of them would stick by it.

Hell, after starting with one kiss on the table, they'd ended up awake until two in the morning, watching movies and making out like horny teenagers, and she'd only gone home when a page sent him to the hospital.

As if she knew he was talking about her, his phone buzzed and her name popped up.

Carly: I'm this close to falling asleep at my desk.

Brooks: why? didn't get much sleep last night?

Carly: No, some guy kept me up super late

Brooks: man, what a dick

Brooks: he probably left a giant hickey on your neck, too

Carly: About that.

Carly: I had to wear a TURTLENECK to work. It's August! I look ridiculous!

Brooks: not sorry

A few long moments passed before her reply finally came through: Me neither. He couldn't help the asinine smile that spread across his face in that moment.

Brooks: want to grab coffee over lunch? we both need some

Carly: That's the opposite of avoiding public interaction.

Brooks: yes it is

Brooks: want to?

Brooks: i won't touch you, i promise

Carly: I do, but there's no way in hell I'm going anywhere else in this shirt. My accounting coworkers will be the only witnesses.

Brooks: how about i bring it to your office?

Brooks: we can just meet in the parking lot like a drug deal

Brooks: you get coffee, i get to see you. win/win

Carly: You don't have to do that.

Brooks: i can't have you falling asleep on the job, i feel responsible

Carly: Obviously you are.

Carly: OK, but you can't touch me in the parking lot, either

Brooks: fine

After that, Brooks was even more antsy to get out of this damned department meeting. When it finally adjourned, Brooks and James stood to follow the flood of white coats filing out of the room.

"You gonna bring this woman tomorrow night?" James asked.

Brooks frowned. "Tomorrow?"

James gave him a look like, *Come on.* "The Humane Society gala? Dr. Lim's—you know, our chief—big annual fundraiser? I know you bought a ticket, because I talked you into it and made you swear you'd come with me. Then walked you to his assistant's office to watch you buy it."

"Shit, I forgot all about that," Brooks said. The whole Bachelor thing and recent hyperfixation on Carly had really thrown his schedule off. "That was back when we'd both have been going stag and would have each other to get drunk with. You're probably bringing Aly now, aren't you?"

James grinned. "I am. And you can bring your mystery lady."

"Nope. Too soon." And too public.

James' phone buzzed. "Gotta take this." He started walking backward with the phone in his hand. "Whether you bring a date or not, I'd better see you there tomorrow. The chief will notice if you're gone, and no one wants that kind of attention from their boss."

Carly was, in fact, wearing a turtleneck, and he couldn't help but laugh at the glower she aimed at him as she exited the building and walked toward his car.

"You still look hot," he said when she was close enough.

"I should," she said. "I'm sweating like a glass of iced tea in July."

"I thought that might be the case," he said, and held out his hand. "So I got you cold brew."

The wrinkle between her brows smoothed out as she took the cup. She tipped it to her lips for a long sip and sighed. "Mmm. Thank you."

"Anytime." He leaned his hips against his Audi. Her hair was pulled up in a high ponytail, and together with the black fabric wrapped around her neck, her dangly gold earrings stood out even more. What was it about those that drove him so wild? "How's your day?"

"Dragging," she said, and set the cup on the hood. "Now that the end is near and I only have a few days left, typing numbers into a spreadsheet is even more boring than before."

"Wait," he said. "What do you mean? Did you quit?"

Her eyes went wide. "Oh, I haven't told you yet! I guess I got a little distracted last night," she started, and the way her cheeks turned pink was adorable. "I got the promotion at Mode. They were so happy with how the *LiveOKC* collaboration turned out, they offered me a full-time position. So now I literally get to do fashion all day, every day."

Her eyes were so bright, her smile so big, and his heart so full for her, he acted on impulse. He lurched forward and wrapped her in his arms, lifting her feet off the ground. "Oh my God, Carly, that's amazing. You deserve it. Congratulations."

Even though her arms wrapped around his shoulders, she didn't relax against him, and he remembered he'd promised not to touch her. He went to put her down. "Sorry."

But when her feet touched down and he thought she'd step back, she stayed up on her toes and tightened her hold. "Just one more second," she whispered. She lingered there in his arms for another long moment, her face buried along his collarbone. He pecked her quickly on her hair—he couldn't help it—and gently moved away. Not another soul was around, so they were fine. Still, he wasn't supposed to do that.

She kept her eyes down, but he saw the corners of her mouth lifted in a smile. She took two more steps back, and lifted her gaze in admonishment. "Stay there or I'm going back inside."

"Yes, ma'am."

"How's yours? Day, I mean?"

"Not too bad. No issues with patients and my buddy James was working, too. We got to catch up a little."

"Did you meet him at the hospital?"

"Sort of, we did residency together. He went into cardiology so we weren't in the exact same program after that, but we still crossed paths quite a bit. It's hard to make friends, working as much as we did, but since James was in the same boat, it was just easy with him."

"Ah yes, the trauma bond is real." She tipped her head, squinting at him. "Didn't you keep in touch with any of your high school friends? You were always surrounded by people. Whenever I saw a crowd, I'd think, 'Brooks Martin must be in there somewhere.'"

She grinned at him when she said it, beautiful and happy, and he wondered for the hundredth time how he'd ever overlooked this girl back then. His seventeen-year-old ego definitely wouldn't have needed words like that, though. And he'd meant what he said that night on their practice date, that he wouldn't have been good for her as a teenager.

Hell, he still probably wasn't, but he didn't want to think about that right now.

"I might have been popular," he said, not out of arrogance but as objective fact, "but I didn't have a lot of friends. Good ones, I mean. I wish I'd had someone like James back then, like Sasha had you."

"Not even the guys on the basketball team?"

"I mean, we hung out and stuff, sure. But we were also all jockeying to be the best and outshine each other, on the court or off. I'm not sure guys have the same friendships that girls do at that age."

Or maybe it had just been him.

"That kind of sucks. It seems like that's when we all need it the most."

He regarded the building behind her, thinking. "Coach filled that role for me sometimes. When he caught me getting really low, he'd give me one of his tough-love pep talks and knock me out of it." He'd been more of a friend than most of the guys at school, that was for sure.

Carly was quiet for a beat, and he looked over to find her frowning.

"What are you thinking?" he asked.

"I was thinking I'm not sure tough is the kind of love people need when they're hurting."

He considered that for a moment. From the little Brooks knew about his early life, Coach hadn't had it easy and was a big believer in both mental and physical strength and self-reliance. "You might be right, but it worked for me back then. He knew how hard things could be, and I think he just wanted to prepare us to be successful in this world."

"Well," Carly said. "You turned out pretty amazing, so I guess whatever he did worked."

"Amazing? Really?" He definitely didn't agree, but he wouldn't mind hearing her say it again.

"Really," she confirmed.

God, he wanted to kiss her.

That's when a man came through the glass doors, and his office wear reminded Brooks of the favor he had to ask.

"So I need your help with something. It's kind of an emergency."

She frowned. "What is it?"

"I need a suit."

She'd been reaching for her drink, still on the hood, and her hand froze midair. "Sorry?"

He grinned. "Carly Porter," he started, as if he were about to ask her a life-changing question. "I need you to help me find a suit."

"I've been trying to get you to let me buy you a suit for months."

"I know. I didn't think I needed one, but now I do."

She was silent for a beat, then squealed and clapped a hand across her mouth, eyes wide. "I really get to do it? For real?"

"If I'd known it would make you this happy, I'd have let you do it a long time ago."

She snorted. "I believe the last time I brought it up your exact words were, 'Give it up, Carly, I don't need a fucking suit.'"

He shrugged. "That was before you kissed me. I'm a new man."

"Before you kissed me, you mean."

"Well, yeah. That. Plus I have a fancy gala thing for work I forgot about."

"Ah," she said. "Got it. When is it?"

"Tomorrow."

"Tomorrow?"

"Yeah."

"There's no way I can get a suit for you by tomorrow. It has to be measured and tailored."

"Can't you find something close enough?"

"Off the rack?" she sputtered.

He blinked, glancing around the empty parking lot. "Yeah?"

"Absolutely not."

"Well, that's our only option, I'm afraid. What if, by some miracle, you find one that's around my size because you're just that good, and I promise I'll get it tailored after? For all future use?"

"That's a lot to ask, Brooks."

She sounded so serious. "I know," he said, grinning as he tried to match the severity of her tone. "I'm sorry."

She finally let out a long exhale and said, "Okay. I accept this mission."

"Thank you."

"As long as I can come over early and watch you get dressed."

"To do what now?"

"You have no idea how sexy it is to watch a man get dressed. Especially a suit. Putting on the tie and shrugging on the jacket?" Her voice was thick and breathy, which would become a problem for him if it went on much longer. "Don't you ever put on cuff links without me."

Heat flushed up his neck. "I won't."

"Good." She picked up the cup again and took another drink. "Good thing I don't have plans tonight. Sounds like I'll be shopping."

"If anyone can make this happen, it's you."

"That's true," she said confidently. "So what's the woman you're meeting tonight's story? I mean, if it's not too weird for me to ask that now, after . . ." She trailed off, and now all he could think about was the way the inside of her mouth tasted.

Focus, man.

"I don't mind if you don't," he said. "Her name's Madison . . ." He paused, trying to remember her last name, but it wouldn't come to him. "Madison. She's a sales rep for a drug company. Seems nice. Doesn't like cats but has club-level season tickets to the Thunder, so I figured I'd give her a chance."

Carly snorted. "I bet you did."

"I *meant* we obviously have that in common," he defended. "Not that I asked her out for tickets."

"Mm-hmm."

She was clearly unconvinced, but he moved on to a more important question. "How would you feel about going to a Thunder game?" He was a little shocked they hadn't talked about this before. She might be the one exception of a woman he'd still want to hang with even if she hated basketball.

"I mean, if I'm with you and you buy me beer and snacks, I'm in."

"I've never wanted to kiss you more."

Carly pursed her lips, but her eyes flashed. "I'd better get back inside, then."

He grinned. "Probably a good idea."

"Also, I'm burning the hell up out here."

That got a full laugh out of him. "See you tomorrow?"

"Yep. Thanks for the coffee." She gave him a little wave and walked away.

He got in his car and made his way back to work, and when he came cross "Purple Rain" as he skimmed radio stations, he smacked the steering wheel.

"Princeton," he muttered to himself, remembering tonight's date's last name.

Madison Princeton.

CHAPTER TWENTY

Carly

You can have anything you want in life, if you dress for it.

—Quote by costume designer Edith Head, on a Post-it in Carly Porter's closet

The evening was doomed from the start.

The good thing was Carly had been able to find a decent suit on sale, and in Brooks's size. Yes, she'd still hold him to the promise to get it tailored for a more personalized fit after tonight, but what she'd come up with would do quite nicely.

She showed up at Brooks's house at six o'clock on the dot with his suit over her arm. When he opened the door, he immediately zeroed in on her lips, and she knew right away she'd made a serious miscalculation.

She put a hand over her bright red mouth. "I thought this might make sure we were good," she whispered. "Because I might go grab a drink after this and thought I wouldn't want to mess up my lipstick."

He'd fisted his hands near his sides and swallowed thickly, his Adam's apple bobbing in his throat. "Our brains work very differently."

Oh.

With superhuman strength, she made it past his incredible smelling, freshly showered body without touching him. She paused to greet Oreo, careful not to drop the garment bag, aware of Brooks hovering nearby.

"How was the date?" she asked, standing.

"She wasn't you."

Her heart squeezed, but she tried to keep her expression neutral. He wasn't the type of guy to say pretty things just to score points, which made the simple statement a thousand times better.

He gave her a half smile. "She was pretty cool, actually. Refreshingly honest. She admitted she's casually dating another guy she's really into, and she just agreed to the date because her mom doesn't like the guy and she'd promised she'd keep her options open. I guess her mom and her friends have been following the series pretty religiously, so they flipped out when she said she was meeting me. I told her I was into someone, too, and that I was happy to stand in anytime to keep her mom off her back."

"Dang, I'm surprised she put all that out in the open."

"She didn't really mean to, but we just sort of ended up there. I guess her parents are all rich and fancy, and she stands to inherit a shit ton of money. So she wants to stay in their good graces."

"Wow." Carly leaned one shoulder against the wall. "Would you marry someone you weren't that into for money?"

A strange expression flashed across his features, there and gone so quick she might have imagined it.

"I'm not sure," he said. "Would you?"

"I don't know, either." As unromantic as it was, guaranteed financial stability sounded pretty nice. "Anyway, let's get moving, I don't want you to be late for your party."

But then she entered his bedroom and laid eyes on his bed.

His neat, perfectly made bed.

He ran into her from behind because she'd stopped so suddenly, then turned sideways to slide past her, a worried smile on his face. "Did I do it right?"

"It's perfect." Her poor heart couldn't handle it.

And *then.*

The man got dressed.

She looked up from her phone just as he came out of his closet in gray slacks and a crisp white dress shirt, open at the collar (which was crooked: even hotter), revealing a sliver of skin lightly dusted with hair. He held one arm extended, fiddling with the sleeve button with the other hand.

She scooted to the edge of the bed. "Come here. I'll help you."

He arched a brow at her tone, which yes, was more than a touch bossy, but came willingly.

Instead of buttoning the cuff she rolled the sleeve up, just below his elbow, and asked him to move back.

He took one step away from her, looking slightly confused but mostly amused. "Here?"

She nodded. "Do the other one."

"Roll up my sleeve?"

She bit her lip and nodded again. She may never have this opportunity again, and this wasn't one she'd pass up.

He rolled the fabric up in phases, moving slow for her benefit probably, the muscles in his forearms flexing.

His eyes never left hers, enjoying this as much as she was.

Her voice came out breathy. "Now cross your arms."

"Like this?"

She released a slow exhale. "Yeah." That image would be burned into her brain for all time, perfect for calling upon when she was old and bedridden and looking for memories from when she was young and full of life.

He seemed to revel in her studying him for a few moments, the corners of his mouth tipping up. Then his gaze darted to the side and back to her. "Okay, now I feel weird."

"Tie, next."

"I really do think you have a fetish."

"With a sexy doctor getting dressed up while I watch? Yes, I absolutely do."

He grinned, neck flushing pink, and grabbed the tie. He flipped up the collar and turned to face the mirror above the dresser, sliding the tie around his throat. It was tempting to get up and help—stand in front of him or maybe sit on the dresser and pull him between her legs while she folded a perfect half Windsor. But she couldn't move just now with this view.

The slacks fit remarkably well and looked great on his ass as he leaned forward just a little, tucking his full bottom lip between his teeth with focus. The fabric made a slight brushing sound every so often when it slid across his shirt or as he pulled the silk through the knot. She was momentarily distracted by his hair, too, which he hadn't done yet. Would he let her watch him fix it, too? Or maybe . . . maybe she could rub the product through the thick strands herself?

"I haven't worn a tie since my last job interview." He turned to face her and held his hands out. "Well?"

"I'm impressed," she managed to get out. Her whole body was on fire. She stood on wobbly legs and approached him. "It's just a touch uneven . . . There." She let her hands rest on his hard chest after she straightened it. The fresh, spicy scent of his soap surrounding her was just delicious, and his body so warm. She leaned in, just a little.

His breath hitched, and he didn't move for a few seconds. She should move back, now. Walk away. Abort mission.

Heart in her throat, she couldn't seem to make herself go.

"Look at me," he rasped as he covered her hands with his, pressing them harder into his body. His chest rose and fell as his fingers slowly moved down her arms and curved around her shoulders, one hand cupping her neck as his thumb brushed her earlobe.

She shivered and tilted her face up to find his heated gaze on her eyes, then drop to her mouth. His heart raced beneath her palm, and the silent tension in the moment was thick with barely restrained energy. Her stomach clenched when his thumb took another sweep, this time along the sensitive skin behind her ear, and she went up on her toes, the need to touch her lips to his a million times stronger than her desire to preserve her makeup.

It was one of those kisses that wasn't demanding on the surface but carried expectation in its promise of what it could become. The way his fingers curled into her hair and her stranglehold on his tie that turned her knuckles white communicated what they both wanted.

The pull between them was intoxicating.

Without warning, he was gone.

"Give me a second," he said brusquely, and walked out of the room.

She blinked, her heart still racing, and pressed her palms flat against her stomach as she stared at the empty doorway. God, it took mere seconds for her to get lost in this man. Probably wasn't the best idea to get him all hot and bothered before going to a work function . . . She couldn't blame him for needing a second to cool off.

She needed several.

Less than a minute later, he came back into the room, strides long and purposeful. He tossed his phone on the dresser while the other hand yanked at his tie, his gaze locked on her face.

His hand gripped the back of her head. "Gala's off," he rasped, and kissed her.

She kissed him back for a beat before her brain caught up, and she pulled her face back. "Wait, what?"

He stared at her mouth with unfocused eyes. His hand was at her thigh, sliding underneath the hem of her sundress to grip her skin. "I called James." He dipped his head and kissed her jaw, then inhaled deeply as if he could pull her straight into his lungs. "Told him to tell the chief I'm sorry but I couldn't make it."

"Oh," she said, and it sounded like a question. She leaned her head back with a sigh. Of their own volition, her hands went to work undoing the tie he'd just spent several minutes tying. "Are you sure?"

"Never been more," he murmured against her skin. Once his tie was undone, he snapped it free and tossed it behind him. He stopped for a second. "Wait, are you supposed to be somewhere?"

"Nope." She untucked his shirt and slid her hands underneath in search of his warm, bare skin. Kendall would understand.

He ducked his head even lower, and his lips met her shoulder as he slowly slid the strap of her dress down. It usually took her longer to get in the right headspace for sex, but he'd basically just done a reverse striptease for her, which, as a fashion expert, had the same effect that taking clothes off probably had on most people.

Also, it had been way too long.

She was hot and bothered and impatient, and needed his body on hers now. She'd never needed someone as bad as she needed Brooks, something she should probably evaluate later.

She stepped back and pulled the dress over her head, letting it fall to the floor in one fluid motion. She'd taken off her shoes when she'd come in, so she stood before him barefoot and wearing only her black bra and matching underwear.

His hand covered his mouth and he tipped his head back for a second, closing his eyes as he inhaled deeply. A sliver of self-consciousness fluttered through her, but then he was moving, working the buttons on his shirt with impressive speed, and the oxford joined her dress on the floor. His strong arms closed around her waist, lifting her and tossing her onto the bed with a delighted squeak.

She opened her mouth to say something, and he gave her a stern look (wow).

"If you're about to say something about messing up the bed, I don't want to hear it."

A delighted laugh bubbled up, surprising her. When was the last time she'd laughed—or even smiled—during sex? Yes, sometimes it was serious and intense, but gosh, it could also be fun.

"Actually it was a cucumber joke."

He put a knee on the bed and pinched her side lightly, and she yelped and scrambled to make room as he joined her. One hand wrapped around her thigh and his lips slid along her hip, stilling her movement. His tongue traced from her hip bone to her belly button, and her smile slowly faded as sensation took over and her mouth fell open on a sigh.

She ran her hands along his shoulders and down the ridges of his arms as he worked his way up her body, slowly, kissing trails and paths and discovering where she liked to be touched and the many, many places she was ticklish. The rest of their clothes came off, and feeling his naked body against hers was better than the slide of a silk chemise on her skin.

By the time he made it back up she was ready to fuse her lips to his and feel his skilled tongue in her mouth, but he paused, hovering above her with palms pressing into the mattress. Their gazes locked and his expression was so sweet and affectionate, all she could do was lie there and let it wash over her like a cool breeze on a summer day.

"Are you done laughing?" He smiled crookedly, his eyes moving back and forth between hers.

"I hope not," she said honestly. "I don't remember the last time I've been this happy."

His chin fell to his chest for the briefest moment, as if that was more than he could take. Was it too much? Should she not have said that?

But he just lowered his body closer to hers, pulling a gasp from her lungs, and touched his forehead to hers. "Me either."

CHAPTER TWENTY-ONE

Brooks

THE MARTIN SPECIAL

1 large Hawaiian, extra pineapple

1 large Meat Mania, easy sauce

1 order cinnamon knots

1 liter Coca-Cola

—Ralph's Pizzeria Custom Register Entry

Brooks felt drugged. Or drunk.

Or something.

His muscles were loose and relaxed, his vision was blurry, and he was uncommonly affectionate to the point he wanted to tell the warm body beside him how much he adored her.

All of it was probably just the orgasm(s) talking, but either way, he needed to take it down a notch.

"First one didn't count," he managed.

It had been a while. He'd tried to make it up to her.

"Second one sure as hell did," she returned, her chest still rising and falling rapidly.

He rolled onto his side and pulled her back to his chest, breathing her in. She covered his hand with hers and wove their fingers together against her stomach.

"Brooks Martin, are you a cuddler?"

"Not usually, no."

She tilted her head back to look over her shoulder, meeting his eyes. Her cheeks were still flushed and her lips swollen from his kiss.

He lifted his head to kiss her temple, then let it fall back to the pillow. He slipped his knee between her thighs. "I'm sorry I didn't wear your suit."

"Right now, I literally couldn't care less."

Neither could he. "I'll make it up to you."

"You already did."

Okay, but he wanted to do it again.

And again.

He slid his fingers through her silky hair, all the way down her back to the edges, and put his thumb on the small bump of her spine. He moved it up and down a few notches, counting, enjoying the soft, smooth feel of her skin. "Wow. L3."

"What?"

"When we first met up at Coffee Slingers, I was surprised how long your hair was. And how dark."

She laughed. "Yeah, I was in a short blond phase in high school. Did you like that better?"

"No. I liked this and wondered exactly how long it was, which was a completely inappropriate thing to be thinking about at the time. But now I know it goes to your L3 vertebrae."

"Whoa. Nerd alert."

"I think you like that about me."

"Let's find out. What's the twelfth element?"

"Magnesium."

"Kiss me."

He did, and a few seconds later her stomach growled and he laughed. "Looks like we need to feed you something, though. What sounds good?"

She thought for a moment. "Something we can order in, because I don't want to go anywhere, and we *can't* go anywhere. Together, anyway."

"Fine by me."

"I sort of want pizza. How about Ralph's?"

He froze. She must have felt it because she scooted forward to twist around and look back at him again. "What's wrong?"

His parents had loved Ralph's. If memory served, they'd only missed having it one Friday night when a stomach bug had ravaged the house and no one could get out of bed without getting sick. He'd looked forward to Friday nights, even as a hormonal preteen and teenager when it wasn't cool to hang out with your family.

He hadn't had it since his parents died. None of them had.

Out of nowhere, Nikki's voice popped into his head, reminding him that everyone at work saw him as unemotional and someone who didn't like to connect with people. She'd said she liked to get through hard things by leaning on others. This moment, right here, right now, could be a chance for him to try that. He could tell Carly about Ralph's and what it meant to him and that thinking about the fact he'd never share it again with his entire family, all five of them, felt like a shard of glass slowly puncturing his heart, draining warmth and happiness from his very soul.

He could tell her, and maybe lean on her. If there was anyone in the world he'd share that with, it was her.

But as he regarded her lying beside him, her brown eyes wide and concerned, the words died in his throat. He pasted a smile on his face and shook his head. "Nothing. I'm great. Ralph's sounds perfect."

After placing their order on Uber Eats for contactless delivery, Carly slipped on one of Brooks's old college T-shirts—which was sexy as hell—and settled onto the couch in the living room. He searched through his Hulu queue while she cuddled into his side and ran a hand down Oreo's back.

"I showed my mom the picture of your garden haul," she said. "She was impressed. She's getting ready for her second planting of the season, so I stole a bag of her carrot seeds for you."

"You *stole* them? Way to set me up for a good first impression with your mother."

"I can give them back."

"No, I want them. Are you sure I can plant them? It's so hot right now." August in Oklahoma usually boasted triple-digit heat and constant humidity and was the one time every year Brooks serious considered relocating.

She shrugged. "If my mom's doing it, I promise it's fine."

He wasn't totally convinced, but he definitely didn't know better. "Okay, but if they don't grow I'm blaming you."

She laughed, then gave him a gorgeous smile before resting her head on his shoulder. "They'll grow."

An absurd warmth bloomed in his chest at her confidence in him. It had been a long time since he'd felt like he had to prove something to anyone but himself, but over these last few weeks he'd found himself wanting to make Carly proud.

He found a sitcom she'd mentioned liking once and ran his fingers through her hair. Two weeks ago he'd never have thought he'd be here, with this smart, beautiful woman pressed up against him, sharing his usually solitary space.

"I'm not sure I'll be any good at this," he blurted out.

"Won't be good at what?"

"Being a partner. Even a casual one," he added. "I'm used to being alone. I work weird hours sometimes. Until recently, I haven't had a social life in more than a decade."

She sat up, crossing her legs on the couch and turning to face him. "I don't care about that. When I start at Mode full time, I'll keep weird hours, too. A lot of clients can only meet in the evenings or on weekends. And I don't need a man to be social—I can do that on my own if I want to. That's not what I want you for."

His mouth twitched, relief filling him. "Oh? What do you want me for?"

She pursed her lips. "I just mean I like you, Brooks Martin, as you are. I know the reason we reconnected and why Sasha wanted you to do this whole Bachelor thing. I know your job can be hard and some days you probably just need to coast. I know you have a cat and like to watch TV at home and probably only like to go out in the fall for Thunder games. I also know you're more fun than you give yourself credit for. I'm not looking for someone to keep a social calendar like Sasha does, or even like I used to. I want someone I enjoy spending time with and who I want to get naked with."

Something ached below his sternum, and he tried to ignore the accompanying warning that Carly was someone he could get attached to if he wasn't careful. Sex and talking, that's all this was. Friendship and companionship and a lot of touching.

"Is that so?"

"It is."

He leaned close, loving the way her breath hitched when their lips were barely an inch apart. He probably should have focused on all the other nice things she'd said, but . . . "You want to keep getting naked with me?"

"Very much, yes."

He kissed her softly. "I'm all for that, in case it wasn't clear. But you keep beating me to the punch, just like when you said you liked me. I should have said it a long time ago, but there just seemed to be so many reasons why I shouldn't."

"I probably shouldn't have, either. We still have to be careful."

"I know. We will." He wouldn't risk all of Sasha's hard work. In fact, he was fully content to just hide away with Carly in the privacy of his house until the coast was clear, and then maybe even longer just to make sure. "But I'm so fucking happy you did."

She plucked at his sweatpants. "I was so nervous I sat in my car for fifteen minutes before I finally came to the door. And I still didn't know if I'd tell you how I felt. Because my job matters and so does Sasha's, and I know you care about keeping the magazine alive, too. But then you were just so cute about your cucumbers I couldn't hold it in any longer."

"That's what finally did it for you? My produce?"

"Obviously."

"Weird, I kind of thought it was the jeans I wore when we first met."

She didn't miss a beat. "I do love a charity project."

"Damn," he said, clapping his free hand across his heart.

They both laughed, smiling at each other, but then her expression transformed into something serious, contemplative.

"It's been a slow build for me," she said. "Even from the start, I couldn't help but notice you. The ways you've changed, the parts of you that remind me of the old Brooks. I wanted to keep things professional, so I worked really hard to keep any thoughts of you as more than a client at bay. But the more time we spent together, the more I liked you, and the harder that was to ignore. It wasn't until you had the date with Kendall that I realized how into you I was. You've never been just a client to me, so it always felt different. The idea of you and one of my closest friends together made me miserable."

"I'd never have agreed to go out with her if I'd thought I had a chance with you." His steady gaze never left her face, and he reached out to wrap a piece of her ponytail around his finger. "She's a great person, and in another life I might have had a lot of fun with her. But all I wanted that night at trivia was to be next to you. I felt so obvious."

"Same." She slid her hand up his forearm. "This doesn't have to be something scary and serious, okay? Honestly, I don't do well with change, and I just made a huge one with my job that I'm glad I did but is still a little terrifying. I'm going to want to take this—us—slow, anyway, you know? See where it goes. Can we do that?"

"Yes." Relief flooded him, cool and soothing. "Slow is good." He slanted his mouth across hers again, because he couldn't get enough of the taste of her.

"And speaking of change and your job, we need to celebrate. Sometime later when, you know, I can take you out and do it right."

"I'd love that," she said.

"Does the promotion mean you get to do more with the ideas you told me about a while back? Finding used clothes and helping people who have a tighter budget for shopping and stuff? Because I still think about that and how many people you could help."

"I hope so," Carly said. "I suggested it once to Mai, that we do some targeted marketing toward that part of our community. She wasn't super excited about it, so I let it go. But maybe now I'll revisit it with her." She rubbed her thumb across his skin, lost in thought. "Thrift shopping is actually the whole reason I fell in love with fashion, did you know that?"

"No, I didn't."

"The first time I remember getting excited about clothes was in sixth grade. We obviously didn't have a lot of money, and I mainly wore hand-me-downs from neighbors or things my mom picked up at garage sales. They didn't fit me well because we took what we could get, and when I hit middle school it became painfully obvious other kids were going to judge and tease me about it. One day I asked my mom if we could go to Goodwill together, because I wanted to see for myself what my options were. I found this flowy pink skirt and I fell in love."

The only item of clothing he'd ever loved were those damned jeans. God, he missed them.

"The skirt was all worn," she continued. "And in hindsight was more suited for a costume closet than something a preteen girl would wear to school, but it didn't matter. I'd never owned anything like it, and I wore it around all weekend, feeling like a princess.

"For the first time in . . . well, ever, I had confidence when I went to school on Monday. It was far from high fashion and didn't have a brand name others would notice, but there was just something different about me that day. *In* me, even. I had the courage to talk to a girl at school and made one of my first real friends. I wore that skirt as often as I could, and started going with my mom every time she went searching for clothing bargains. I developed a knack for finding things I loved in the most unusual places and found my own style. I discovered creativity and how to be bold. I learned how to express myself using what I had to work with." She smiled, tugging at the fabric near his thigh again, almost like she needed something to do with her hands. "Anyway, I guess that's why I love that kind of styling. It's where I fell in love with it."

"I can't believe I've never heard that story," he said. "You're amazing, you know that?"

"You think so?"

"I know so. You turned something tough into something beautiful, and you're helping other people with it. What's better than that?"

Her soft smile was everything.

"Hearing that story reminds me a little of the day I knew I wanted to go into critical care," he said. "There was this patient who was near death when I'd started the rotation, and on my last day one month later, I watched her walk out of there on her own two feet. Even the attending was surprised at her recovery, but none of it would have been possible without that medical team. I'd lost both my parents by then, and I was having a hard time believing anything ever ended well. I'd already changed quite a bit, but instead of just being focused and introverted, I was on a path toward flat-out pessimism about life. Seeing that patient turn around sparked a passion in me I didn't know I had, and it's the outcome I'll never stop chasing. That's how you look when you talk about helping people find their confidence—you light up. There's nothing better than finding your passion and turning that into what you do with your life, you know?"

"You're so right," she said, and the way she looked at him in that moment made him feel on top of the world.

A rustling sound came from the front door, and they both stilled, listening. Then Brooks's phone dinged with an Uber Eats alert.

"Pizza's here."

"Oooh, yes," Carly said, rising.

She went to the door and opened it, but when he noticed from the corner of his eye that she didn't bend down to get the boxes, Brooks looked over.

And found himself looking at Sasha, standing on his porch, staring straight at them.

CHAPTER TWENTY-TWO

Carly

Could you just leave my friends alone? Aren't there enough seniors for you to hit on?

—Sasha to Brooks Martin, junior year

It took Carly several seconds to process what she was looking at.

Her best friend, whose brother she'd just slept with, stood there, holding her dinner.

Carly steeled herself for some comment about her obvious state of undress, but instead, Sasha pinned her brother with a hard, singular stare as she marched inside.

"You ordered *Ralph's*?"

Carly swung her focus to Brooks, who sat like a deer in headlights, eyes wide and mouth ajar. Weirdly, though, she was pretty sure his discomfort wasn't because she was here or the fact they'd just been caught in a compromising situation.

No, his focus was on . . . the pizza?

"Uh." He popped his knuckles, shoulders high and tense. "Yeah, we—"

"How long have you been doing this?" Sasha demanded.

What was Carly missing? Why was Sasha reacting so strongly, and why was Brooks acting like he'd done something wrong?

He swallowed, and Carly's breath caught at the pain in his eyes. "I haven't. I mean, this is the first time. I swear."

A long, deep exhale audibly left Sasha's body. "Thank God. I had it once last year and I felt like shit for days. This makes me feel so much better."

"You had Ralph's?" Brooks asked. "Without Macy and me?"

From where she still hid by the now-closed front door, Carly couldn't see Sasha's expression but imagined it wasn't pretty as her friend dropped the boxes on his coffee table with considerable force.

Brooks nodded, looking duly chagrined. "Right."

"What are you even doing here?" Sasha asked him.

"What are *you* doing here?" he countered.

"I came for the cucumbers you promised me. I expected to let myself into an empty house, because you're supposed to be at your work thing." It was then that Sasha seemed to remember Carly, and she whipped back around to look at her. "What is this? Is something going on between you two?"

Carly tugged at the hem of his T-shirt, as if bringing it lower on her thighs would make this look less suspicious. "It's . . . not what it looks like?"

Brooks dropped his head into his hands.

"You're not wearing pants. And that's Brooks's shirt."

Oh God. Carly wrapped her arms around herself, balancing one bare foot on top of the other. "I, um . . ." She looked to Brooks for direction. Sasha was her friend, sure, but she was his sister. They really should have figured out how to handle this before they . . . you know.

"Seriously," Sasha said, voice rising. "What the fuck?"

Brooks stood. "Hey, easy. Sit down, okay?"

"I don't want to sit down. I want you to tell me what's going on, and somehow that it won't be what I think it is." She aimed an accusing glare at Carly, something Carly had rarely had cause to be on the receiving end of. It didn't feel good. "Because what I think is that my best friend is messing around with my brother, not only behind my back—which is bad enough—but also when he's supposed to be her client that she's helping in a professional capacity." She spun around on Brooks. "And what I also think is that my brother, who's the very public face of a current multi-issue article series, made a move on my best friend instead of one of the many, many women he's dated as part of said series." She paused, and when no one spoke, she said, "Someone *please* tell me I'm wrong."

"You're . . . not," Brooks started.

Sasha balled her hands into fists and pressed them to her forehead.

"Listen," he continued. "This hasn't been like, going on for a while. It just happened."

"Literally two days ago," Carly put in.

"I don't care!" Sasha cried. "Do you know how this could make me look? Make the magazine look? There are already plenty of skeptics trying to call this whole thing fake, but I never let it bother me because I knew it wasn't, and anyone who met Brooks or the women he'd gone out with would know it was real. The *authenticity* of what it's like to be single in your thirties and how to make the most of navigating the good and the bad that come with that was the whole fucking point! If anyone knew you"—she pointed at Carly—"a member of the team that's supposed to be setting him up for success, was secretly seeing him behind the scenes, God, they'd think I did this just as a publicity stunt!"

"Well," Brooks said carefully, "that is sort of what it was, right? To boost interest?"

Carly winced, wishing he'd pushed back on the authenticity part because he had been honest in every interaction so far. Nothing was staged or fake, and he'd put a lot of himself into this whole thing.

Sasha bristled, clearly not appreciating his response, either. "I did this because I love what the magazine stands for and what it does for our city. I believe in the importance of small businesses and community events and elevating opportunities to bring people together. It was Mom's vision first, and now it's mine. I thought you understood that. I thought you had that vision, too."

Brooks gripped the back of his neck. "I did. I do. I'm sorry." He approached her and went to put a hand on her shoulder, but she stepped back. He dropped his arm to his side. "I didn't mean that how it sounded. I'm just . . . I wasn't prepared to talk about this now. Hell, Carly and I have barely talked about it."

"Oh my *God*," Sasha exclaimed.

"What he means," Carly interrupted, "is that neither of us meant for this to happen. We didn't plan it, and we realize the timing's not ideal. But no one else knows, and we'll keep it that way. We won't be seen in public together or do anything that would seem unprofessional. Neither of us want to risk what you've worked so hard for."

Sasha snorted. "Is that supposed to make me feel better? Thank you," she said, voice thick with sarcasm, "for keeping your liaison secret for the last few weeks of this project. God, couldn't you have just kept it in your pants until we were through?"

Carly didn't know what to say to that.

"I'm sorry," Brooks said again.

"Honestly, I'm not sure who I'm more surprised about," Sasha said. "Brooks, I didn't know you had it in you anymore. I guess that guy you were in high school's still in there somewhere, going after all my friends, isn't he? Maybe I should have seen that coming and picked a different stylist."

"Whoa, hey," Brooks said, tone firmer. "It's not like that."

Sasha just shrugged, like his intentions didn't matter, and turned on Carly. "Honestly, though, I never would have expected this from you, especially after what just happened with that sleazy client. If anyone knows how dangerous bad press can be for a company, it's you. You just saw how Mai reacted when she was in that situation, so how could you do something like this and risk not only my business but yours, too?"

Brooks shot her a frown, and Carly just looked at the floor. Sasha was right. She'd been selfish, and stupid.

"I—" Carly started, but Sasha held out a hand.

"Don't. I'm leaving."

"Wait," Carly said at the same time Brooks said, "Let's talk about this."

But Sasha was already at the door. "I need to think, okay? Figure out what I'm going to do, if anything. Don't call me. Either of you."

Then she was gone.

The room was eerily silent, Carly standing on one side and Brooks on the other. Her heart was in her throat, and she worried she might burst into tears any minute.

She chanced a look at him, and his eyes were on her, wary and concerned. "Are you going to leave too?"

"What?"

"That was . . . rough. I mean, she wasn't wrong about any of it and we probably deserved it, but it still kind of sucked."

Carly just nodded, trying to regain a sense of equilibrium. It was like she'd had the wind knocked out of her.

He dragged a hand down his face. "I just thought, maybe . . . now you'd be regretting everything and would want to leave." His voice was low and troubled, like the thought made him miserable.

"She was right about some things, and we hurt her. I hate that, and I hate that she found out this way. We should have handled this differently." She reached across her body and rubbed one hand up and down the opposite arm. "But I don't regret anything that's happened with you, and I don't want to leave."

His shoulders relaxed. "Good. I don't want you to, either." He crossed the room and pulled her into his arms. "I'm sorry I put you in this position."

"Technically I think I started it. Both times."

"Give me some time and I'll even the score."

She smiled against his chest. "Okay."

"Just let her cool off, okay? It'll be alright."

Her smile faded, but she kept her forehead against his warm body, letting it and his words comfort her, even though she wasn't sure they were true.

"So what's the deal with Ralph's?"

They'd somberly settled back around the coffee table and divvied up slices of pizza in relative silence. It had cooled considerably during delivery and the conversation with Sasha, so Brooks popped their pieces in the microwave and had just handed Carly a plate when she asked the question.

He rolled his lips together for a moment, as if considering how to answer. He put his plate on the table and rubbed his hands together between his knees. "It was my parents' favorite restaurant. We used to order it in every Friday night, and we'd all make a big deal about my mom getting pineapple while the rest of us wanted meat on meat. It was sort of our family thing, and even as teenagers, none of us left the house on Friday nights until after we'd had dinner together. We didn't have a ton of family traditions, but that was one. It stopped the second my mom died."

A pressure point emerged beneath her ribs. "You haven't had it since?"

"Not until now."

"I'm so sorry, I had no idea," she said. "We could have had something else. I wish you'd told me."

"I should have. I thought about it, but . . ." He looked down at his hands, clasped together. "I'm not good at talking about things. And I thought maybe having it with someone who made me happy would be kind of nice. Like maybe it would feel like it used to."

"Oh." A piece of her frustration slipped away.

"I'll work on it," he said, and she knew he meant it. "Talking to you about that stuff, I mean. But you have some explaining to do yourself, you know."

She paused with her piece of pizza halfway to her mouth. "What do you mean?"

"Who's this sleazy client Sasha mentioned? Did something happen?"

Carly put her food back on the plate and balanced it on her lap. "Yes and no. I had a married client who was . . . flirty." Based on the hard look in Brooks's eyes just from that, she figured it was best not to elaborate further. "I ignored it at first, but it got to the point I had to shut him down. A few days later, his wife called my boss and accused me of hitting on her husband."

"What the hell?"

"Obviously, it wasn't true. Thank goodness Mai believed me—I guess this guy has a reputation for running around on his wife, and he's not discreet. So I didn't get in trouble, but just to cover her ass Mai made us take all this training about professionalism and appropriate client relations. Wrote up a new policy we all had to sign. All that happened right before Sasha pitched this *Bachelor* idea."

"Oh my God, Carly." Brooks sank back into the cushions, palms over his eyes. "Why didn't you tell me? This is a big fucking deal. It's not just, like, something taboo or frowned upon—you could lose your entire job over this, couldn't you?"

"Well . . . yeah. But no one's gonna find out, right?"

"Sasha just did," he pointed out.

"She might be mad at me, but she wouldn't rat me out." She wasn't the vindictive sort, and saying it out loud made Carly feel even shittier for doing this to her. "Besides, that wouldn't help her situation, either."

"True." He sighed and pushed back up to a sitting position. "Okay. Well, we're officially in ultrastealth mode. I've already done enough damage, I won't add your job to it."

"Should . . . should we just stay away from each other until the final article goes up?" Carly asked. "About four more weeks, right?"

Brooks cleared his throat. "Yeah. We could try that."

Carly frowned. "Really?"

"Sure. I can wait if you can."

She regarded his sweet, hazel eyes and thick, dark hair that was honestly still a little messy from sex. She swallowed. "I can wait."

"Okay. Good. We'll stop and revisit things when it's over."

"Right."

They stared at each other for a beat, then both faced forward. Carly took a bite of pizza and Brooks a pull from his beer.

The bottle hit the table with a clatter. "Or we could not stop and just be really, really careful."

Carly was nodding before he finished speaking. "Yes. Let's do that."

He groaned with relief, and she almost laughed. "Good."

They finished their dinner, and after she helped take the box and dishes to the kitchen, he stopped in front of her and brushed a strand of hair behind her ear. Carly leaned into him, wrapping her arms around his waist as he pulled her in. She took a deep breath and exhaled slowly, then did it again, relaxing with each one.

Today had been a lot—some of it in wonderful ways and some not.

His chin came to rest on the top of her head, and his arms held steady across her back as if he were perfectly content to stay like this for a good, long while.

Few things felt as good as standing in a man's arms. The best hugs made her feel safe and wanted without expectation.

"Hugs are underrated."

"I was just thinking the same thing." Her cheek found the perfect spot against the curve of his shoulder. "Especially hugs with men. I love my girlfriends, but boobs get in the way."

He choked on a laugh, and her head moved against his chest. "I'd have to disagree. Boobs are my favorite part."

"That's because you don't have any. Trying to hug another woman means arranging four of them between us."

"I can honestly say I've never thought about that."

"You're going to now, though, aren't you?"

"Frequently."

Feeling more like herself, she gave him a quick smack on the ass and pulled back. "I'd better go."

"What? Why?"

The fact that he didn't want her to leave sent a rush of warmth through her. "I don't know, because it's late and I still have work to do?"

He just looked at her, blinked, and gripped the back of his neck with one hand. "But we just talked about boobs and stuff."

She couldn't help but laugh. "Wanna come to my place? I thought I'd be home hours ago, and I really did have some prep work to do for a client I'm meeting tomorrow. But I can put on another movie that makes most people cry and see if you have a heart in there somewhere, and when I'm done, we can do stuff."

"Would this be, like, a sleepover?"

"I don't hate the idea of you in my bed."

A huge grin split across his face. "Can I bring Oreo? Introduce him and Pepper?"

Damn, this man was adorable. "Sure."

He grabbed her wrist and pulled her in for a kiss. "Let me grab a few things."

It was remarkably difficult to focus with Brooks sitting a few feet away, but she managed it for the entire length of *The English Patient*.

He didn't shed a tear.

"Something's wrong with you," she said as the credits began.

"Probably," he agreed. "But I'm not the one with color-coded bookshelves and appliances on my counter lined up by size."

"You should see my closet," she quipped, and immediately regretted it when he rose from the couch.

"Oooh, yes. I do want to see that."

She pushed her chair away from the desk and lunged for him. "No!"

In the quiet apartment she realized how loud and desperate that had sounded.

He stilled and slowly turned to face her. He tilted his head and blinked. "Why? Whatcha got in there?"

She giggled nervously. Smoothed her shirt and picked at her thumbnail. "What? Nothing. I just . . . I'm a stylist. It's my Zen space. I'm very, um, particular about it, is all."

He lifted his chin a notch, eyeing her. "I won't touch anything, promise. I'll take off my shoes and wash my hands and cross myself before I go in."

She narrowed her gaze. "You're making fun of me."

"You're hiding something."

"No, I'm not."

"Then let me check out your closet. You've been in mine and examined every single thing I own—" His eyes went wide and he sucked in a breath, his mouth dropping open. "That's it."

She said nothing.

He pointed toward her room. "My jeans are in there, aren't they?"

She hesitated a second too long. "No."

"Carly Porter. Don't lie to me."

She tucked her lips between her teeth.

He shook his head slowly, a grave expression on his face as he made his dramatic announcement. "I'm going in."

At this point, there was no use trying to stop him. Pinching the bridge of her nose, she followed him into her room, where Oreo and Pepper had claimed opposite corners, curled up, and were completely ignoring each other.

She sat on her bed, grabbed a navy throw pillow and hugged it to her chest, waiting.

Several minutes later he emerged from her walk-in closet . . .

. . . wearing those atrocious pants.

He stopped in the doorway, sliding his palms this way and that along the denim at his waist and down his thighs. "So. Damn. Comfortable."

She wouldn't normally say this about a client's clothes, but they were past that and the flash of challenge in his eye couldn't go unheeded. "So. Fucking. Hideous."

He was fighting a smile. "Wow. That bad?"

She quirked a brow. She'd die on this hill. "Yes. That bad."

"Huh." He put his thumb and forefinger to his chin. "I seem to remember you once telling me it's not the piece of clothing, but how the person wears it."

"Those jeans were excluded from that comment."

"Really?" A muscle flexed in his jaw and he regarded her carefully as he reached behind his head with one hand and in one fluid motion tugged his shirt off. "How about now?"

Okay. So, the thing was, the man had a nice body. She'd never been very attracted to those huge guys who spent hours at the gym to be all muscly and veiny. She gravitated more toward lean and fit, and the modest chest, defined abs, and masculine-without-being-overly-large arms filling her vision were very much her preferred eye candy.

She also had a mild obsession with romance films, so when he raked his long, clean (and talented, she'd learned a few hours ago) fingers through his hair and reached up to grip the doorframe, several parts of her body took notice.

In conclusion, she was very, very attracted to him. Even, apparently, in the jeans.

In. The. Jeans.

She was also very, very stubborn. With considerable effort, she schooled her features to what she hoped was bored and unaffected. She didn't trust her voice not to come out breathy and wanting, though, so she kept quiet.

He licked his bottom lip and smiled as he let his arms fall and took a few steps toward her, eyes locked on hers. He reached down and flicked open the button, and they slid an inch down his hips, revealing his left hip bone and a mouthwatering view of that beautiful V. "Now?"

Her grip on the pillow tightened. "I hate those jeans so much," she said in a near whisper, swallowing thickly, "that I want you to take them off right this minute."

"You do?"

She nodded. Vigorously, her intention to appear unaffected be damned. She was on fire.

"I will if you tell me I look good in them."

She squeezed her eyelids shut. "Brooks, it's not you. You're so hot my mouth is watering. But no one, and I mean no one, would look good in those."

"I'm sorry to hear that." He rebuttoned them and walked away, tossing a victorious grin over his shoulder. From the hallway, he called out, "Which movie should we watch next?"

Carly threw the pillow to the floor and fell backward on the bed, covering her face with her hands. She groaned. "*Fine*. You win, I love the jeans and you look good *in* the jeans and get your fine ass back in here right this second!"

One second later she heard the thump of denim hit the floor and two seconds later he was on the bed, laughing and kissing her all over.

She frowned while she ran her hands down his back and arched her neck to give him better access. "I'm not sorry I stole them, though."

He kissed her hard and deep, sliding his hand into the waistband of her leggings.

"Neither am I."

CHAPTER TWENTY-THREE

Brooks

Good evening. Is this the residence of Deborah Martin? May I come in for a moment?

—Officer Gary Sanchez to Paul, Brooks, and Sasha Martin

It had been a while since Brooks had been to Macy's without Sasha. But she'd called and asked him to come by, and he wasn't altogether surprised to find their third sibling absent.

She still wouldn't talk to him.

He spent an hour in the backyard with the boys before Macy sent them upstairs to wind down, then told Brooks he could stay on the deck. She returned a few minutes later with two beers and settled in beside him on the wooden steps.

"So," she said.

"So."

"I talked to Sasha."

"I figured." He took a pull and lowered the bottle to dangle between his knees. "For what it's worth, I'm sorry. Even though I didn't really think it mattered at this point when we're so close to the end, and when I planned to follow through with the dates I had left, I understand Sasha's side, too. I'd never want to make her look bad. Or you, for that matter. I know how hard you've both worked to keep Mom's dream alive."

"It's more than that, now," Macy said. "It's our dream, too. We may have picked up the baton, but we've added our own flair. I like to think we've turned her baby into something even bigger and better than she could have ever imagined."

God, he felt about two inches tall. "You have. I'm so proud of you both, and I'm sorry I almost fucked it up."

Macy let out a long sigh. "It's not as bad as all that. Is it ideal? No, but I also think Sasha's overreacting a little. Whether it was real or not, people were entertained and learned more about Oklahoma City. Thousands of people discovered *LiveOKC* because of you. You helped boost our visibility beyond anything we've ever seen, and I doubt anything could undo that. I think Sasha just views the authenticity piece as putting her personal reputation on the line, which is fair, especially because she's the one on the ground working directly with local partners. But this wouldn't make or break the business, okay?"

He swallowed hard, letting her words sink in. "Okay. Yeah, that helps. I still wish I'd maybe handled it better, but let's be honest—I don't have a clue what the hell I'm doing."

"Obviously."

Macy being Macy, blunt as always.

"I didn't expect to feel this way about Carly. And I definitely didn't expect her to reciprocate."

"That's mostly why I called," Macy said. "I wanted to check in. See if there's anything you want to talk about."

She was giving him space to resume their conversation from before—about his dad. Which he appreciated, but he didn't want to. Not anymore and not right now. Bringing that up again would confuse him, and after the last few days with Carly he just wanted to live in that bubble for a little while. Ignore all his baggage and be happy and carefree for once. Maybe it was stupid and maybe it was shortsighted, but it's where he was at the moment.

"No."

He felt her side-eye burning into his skull, but he held strong.

"Okay, I have a question, then. It would be pretty great if things could work out between you two, but with Carly and Sasha being so close, it could also get very messy if it doesn't. So I have to ask, do you think you're ready for something serious?"

"We agreed to take things slow."

"What does that mean?"

He wasn't sure, exactly. "It means slow. We're not putting a label on it right now."

"Slow doesn't mean you're not building something. That's the whole point of starting in the first place, right? I just want to make sure you're prepared for what could come next. And that you're ready for that."

The last thing he wanted to do was hurt Carly, so he replied with an honest question. "How would I know if I'm ready?"

"For starters, recognize that attraction only gets you so far. You also have to be understanding and support each other. Communication is key, and you have to know you can be completely open, honest, and vulnerable with that person." Macy looked at him with reluctance. "Communication has never been a strong suit for you."

She wasn't wrong, but defensiveness flared anyway. "I talk to people all day. Half my job is communicating things to nurses, other doctors, and families of patients." It wasn't easy to translate an intense medical condition into words family members could understand.

"In a relationship you have to be able to talk about *you*," Macy said gently. "About things that make you happy and things that don't. What hurt you in the past and what hurts you still. You have to be able to communicate how you feel, whether it's good, bad, or ugly."

He propped his elbow on his knee and rubbed his forehead. Took a swig of beer for good measure.

"Do you think you can do that?"

Could he tell her everything? "I've been more open with Carly than anyone else."

"That's not the same thing."

"Well, it's all I've got right now."

While Macy was one of those people who could wait in silence all day if it meant getting her point across or gathering the information she wanted, she also knew when not to push.

She reached over and squeezed his arm. "If what Sasha said is true, it's still early. You don't have to have all the answers now, but those are some things to start thinking about if this continues. You'll figure it out, okay? You have time."

Would he, though?

How could he when he didn't even know what he wanted or what he was ready for? He was completely enamored with Carly and wanted to be with her, but there were qualifiers. He wanted to have dinner and go on walks and grab coffee with her, but he couldn't tell her how dark his thoughts had become in that year after his mom died. He wanted her beside him when he woke up in the morning and he wanted to talk to her about his ideas for a garden next season and maybe taking a ski trip come winter, but he still preferred to go home alone to decompress after a hard time at work. He didn't want her to see the rough, damaged parts because she made him feel lighter than he had in years, and she made him happy.

He wanted to stay there.

And he wanted to make her feel the same. Show her how much he cared about her, admired her, and wanted her. Why would he want to bring her down with things like death and regret that plagued him on a regular basis?

He left Macy's that evening feeling more confused than when he'd arrived, wondering how on earth he could get his shit together before

Carly gave up on him. They said time healed all wounds, but it had been seventeen damned years and he was still here, so.

Carly had been at an employee-only Mode get-together that evening and had come over after it ended, and he'd considered bringing up his conversation with his sister. Maybe asking what she thought about it all or telling her about Nikki and Schwartz Rounds and how he wondered if there was something wrong with him because despite it being one of the highest-attended conferences in the health system, he had no desire to go. That would be a step in the right direction, right?

But when she arrived and immediately put her hands on him, he'd realized she was interested in spending the night pursuing other endeavors. He considered when he might bring it up again as they stumbled into his bedroom, but his attention was quickly diverted and everything but Carly faded into darkness.

"Dude. You look high."

Brooks couldn't even think of a witty reply, so he just grinned. "Maybe I am. Think they'll fire me?"

James laughed. "Hell, no. You're the only one willing to take call all the time. And we both know you're clean as a whistle. That's love I see in your eye, you son of a bitch."

"I wouldn't go that far," Brooks laughed. "But I have had a pretty great few days."

The understatement of the decade. The last five days had been phenomenal. He'd probably smiled, laughed, and talked more than in the last few years combined. The sex was pretty great, too.

He'd never had both with the same woman before.

"Does that mean you're done with the whole public-dating thing?"

"Don't tell me you actually followed that."

James looked appalled. "Of course I followed it. Entertaining as hell, tell Sasha I said well done. You, on the other hand, are lucky you actually found someone. You were a disaster."

Brooks had the urge to throw his coffee at his friend, but they were in the public cafeteria and two doctors going at it probably wouldn't be great PR. Although, it was five thirty in the morning and there was hardly anyone around . . .

"Seriously, tell me about her. I've been waiting for this moment."

"Stop acting like you weren't in the same boat a few months ago," Brooks said.

"I'm not. But when it feels right, you just know, and that's how it is with Aly. Even if we've only been together a few months, it feels like I've known her all my life. I can't imagine my life without her. I want that for you, man."

"Easy," Brooks said. "It's way too early for all that."

"I knew on my second date with Aly."

Brooks glanced down at his coffee and wrapped both hands around the warm cup. He opened his mouth to admit to his best friend just how ridiculously into Carly Porter he was, but the shrill beep of his pager cut him off. He bent over his waist to check the number. A single, meaningful look passed between them as Brooks stood.

James waved him off. "We'll talk later."

Brooks dialed the back line to the ER attending physician as he walked quickly down the hall. Sanjay answered on the second ring. "Hey, sorry to bother you but your fellow's tied up and they said you were around to take call."

"No problem. What's up?"

"Nasty MVA. Single-vehicle accident with all this rain. Two adults in the car, one pronounced dead at the scene. The other's intubated and stable for now. CT showed . . ."

Brooks saw all sorts of traumatic injuries, most of which he could handle with professional objectivity. Occasionally, though, a car accident would sound so similar to what happened all those years ago, being involved in the case caused a visceral reaction.

Single-vehicle accident in the rain.

Pronounced dead at the scene.

Sanjay listed known injuries and described all measures taken so far in the ER. Brooks lost his breath for a split second but regained it when he passed the familiar signage directing him to 3W ICU. He couldn't think about the similarities or the way he'd vomited all over the police officer who'd showed up that night to give his family the news. He couldn't think about the funeral or the fact that he couldn't remember the last thing he'd said to his mom because he'd had no idea that's what it'd be.

This wasn't him, it wasn't his mom, and he was at work. Taking care of broken bodies was his job. There was a survivor and maybe he could save this one.

"Has family been informed?" Brooks asked, pushing through the double doors of the unit.

"Yeah." Brooks frowned at Sanjay's tone. "The couple's seventeen-year-old son. He knows his mom's gone, and I swear, Brooks, that might have been one of the hardest fucking things I've ever done. He'll be in the waiting room. I told him you'd come talk to him once you've assessed his dad's situation. I hope your news is better than mine was."

A wave of dizziness washed over Brooks. He mumbled something to Sanjay and ended the call, pressing one hand into the wall. He searched the hallway and lurched for the nearest staff bathroom.

His knees hit the tile as the coffee burned its way up his throat.

CHAPTER TWENTY-FOUR

Carly

I'm a sucker for friends to lovers. Especially when it's one of those slow burns that sneaks up on them. Like, he's known her for years and they have that closeness and trust of a deep friendship, and bam! One day, he wakes up and realizes he's madly in love.

—Carly Porter at the office book club, last spring

Carly hadn't talked to Sasha for a week, which was the longest they'd ever gone, even when Carly lived two states away. She didn't blame Sasha for her silence, but still, it ate at her all week and only abated when she showed up at Social Capital for Kendall's birthday Saturday evening. Sasha was there, too, and Carly kept her distance at first, wanting to give Sasha whatever space she needed. But when Sasha complimented Carly's purse—a vintage find she'd stumbled across at an estate sale last week—Carly knew they'd be okay. It may take a few weeks and some groveling on Carly's part, but they'd get there.

When the party was over, her first thought as she walked to her car was to call Brooks, but she hesitated after pulling up his contact.

They hadn't talked in two days. Not really. He'd called yesterday after work but hadn't sounded good. He'd told her his shift had been rough and he'd stayed several hours over. She'd asked if he wanted to come over and she'd make him dinner, hoping he'd agree and talk to her about what had been so difficult. She couldn't imagine having a job like his and would probably need regular therapy to keep some semblance of a healthy mental state if she did.

He'd declined in a way that tugged at her heart, and she'd let him go. She hadn't stopped thinking about him, though.

With a frown, she put her phone down and turned on the ignition. She grabbed takeout on the way home and ate in front of the television. When the clock neared eight, she glanced at her phone again, wondering if Brooks was okay. She wasn't the kind of person who processed difficult things alone, but she could appreciate their differences there. She didn't want to push if he wasn't ready to talk.

As if her thoughts had summoned him, her phone rang.

"Hey," she said with a smile. "I was just thinking about you."

"Quick, who makes shoes with the red soles?"

"Christian Louboutin, why?"

"I'm at Fassler Hall with Jeff for trivia."

That was so much better than her mental image of him at home, alone and upset. "Brooks Martin, are you cheating?"

"We already turned our answers in, I just wanted to know if I was right."

"Were you?"

He laughed. "Not even close."

"Should have asked me to come," she said, only half joking.

"I would have," he said, followed by a shuffling noise as if he were getting up and walking. His voice lowered. "But Jeff said this was a guy's team only. No girls allowed. And yes, he said it like that, like we're in fifth grade and just put up a 'Keep Out' sign on our tree house to keep the cooties away."

Jeff did take trivia very seriously. She avoided being on his team at all costs.

Suddenly the background noise was gone, like he'd stepped outside. "What are you up to?"

"Nothing, just hanging out at home." *Wishing you were here.*

"Game's almost over, mind if I come over after?"

"I'd love that."

"Brooks!" Jeff shrieked in the background. "Get in here!"

Carly laughed. "You'd better go."

Brooks's voice was muffled as he yelled back, "I'm coming, man." Then, in a clear whisper into the phone, "This was a mistake."

"Yes, it was."

"See you soon."

Brooks arrived an hour later.

"Did you win?" she asked as they settled on the couch.

He extended his arm across the back. "Nope."

"I'm sorry."

He smiled. "I don't care. I doubt Jeff will ever ask me to come again, though. I think my performance that first time set up unrealistic expectations and he thought I'd be more helpful."

"Rookie mistake," she teased.

"Right?" His attention was diverted when Pepper entered the room, and he leaned over to scratch him.

"You don't do that often," she stated. "Go out with people you don't know very well."

"You mean when I'm not being dragged by my sister? True. But I actually had fun. Maybe the whole magazine thing was good for me."

She cleared her throat, and he grinned at her.

"In more ways than one." He leaned forward and propped his forearms on his knees, his hands extended. He looked down. "I'm sorry I've been a little MIA."

"Don't apologize." She put her hand on his back. "I'm sorry work was tough. Do you want to talk about it?"

"Not really." She felt his heavy sigh through her fingers. "But maybe I should."

She wanted to scoot over and wrap her arms around him. Instead, she remained where she was, listening and waiting, with her hand on his back. Giving him space but letting him know she was here.

"There's this seventeen-year-old kid. His parents were in a car accident. His mom didn't make it and his dad is on a vent in the ICU." His head dropped lower and he pressed his thumbs against the bridge of his nose, closing his eyes. "It's still touch-and-go for his dad right now. I had to tell him that, and to try to explain the injuries and what we were doing to try to help him. And the whole time I was talking it was just . . ." He trailed off and took a few long inhales. Carly's heart hurt for the kid and for Brooks, her throat tightening with each breath.

His voice shook a little when he spoke again. "It felt like I was looking at myself. And part of me knew I was in a unique position to be there for this kid. I mean, I've literally been in his shoes and I know the gut-wrenching agony he's feeling, and yet all I could do was stand there, several feet away, talking in some robotic voice like I didn't feel every word like barbed wire straight to my gut." He turned his face away. "When he started crying, I left. I fucking left, Carly. I called pastoral care to send someone to talk to him."

Tears burned beneath her eyelids. She wished with everything in her she knew what to say, but she didn't. She moved closer and wrapped her arms around him, resting her chin on his shoulder. She slid her palm across his cheek and turned his face to look at her, their noses touching. His eyes were sad but dry, reflecting a pain deeper than words could heal. "I'm so, so sorry."

"What's wrong with me?" he whispered.

She kissed the corner of his mouth. "Nothing. You're a human who was put in an impossible situation. I can't even imagine how hard that was for you. And you didn't leave him alone, you made sure someone better qualified for things like that took care of him. It's not your job to carry a burden that heavy on your own. You're a great doctor and an even better man."

He covered her hand with his and they sat like that for a long moment, breathing steadily. She pulled him closer and ran her fingers through his hair, then did it again. After a few minutes he hummed in pleasure. "That feels nice."

"Sometimes when I was a kid my mom used to stroke my hair when I was sick or upset about something. I don't know why, but it always made me feel better."

He considered that for a moment, leaning heavily into her. "It reminds me I'm not alone."

"You're not. I'm glad you told me what happened."

He was silent for so long she didn't think he'd reply, but then he said, "I don't deserve you."

"Are you kidding? You're the one out there saving lives."

"I don't save everyone."

She paused her ministrations. "And when you don't, it's not your fault. You know that, right?"

He shrugged.

"Some things are outside our control."

"Says the biggest control freak I know." She heard the tiniest smile in his voice, and it released a fraction of tension from the moment. But the curve of his shoulders and unfocused look in his eyes said he was exhausted. He needed rest.

"Want to watch a movie?" she suggested. "I won't even pick one that should but won't make you cry. We can go with something light."

"Sure," he said. "That sounds great."

Carly woke up the next morning her favorite way: with a warm body beside her. His large fingers traced a line from her shoulder to her hip and back up, featherlight and tender.

She opened her eyes and found his gaze on her. Normally she'd be self-conscious because she wasn't one of those peaceful sleepers who woke up looking the same as when she went to bed. She slept with a mouth guard, drooled when she slept hard (which she usually did after sex), and her hair was always a hot mess.

But the look in his eyes as he gazed at her stopped her heart. Some unnamed emotion rose up inside her chest and gathered in her throat. "Why are you looking at me like that?" she whispered. She hoped he would never stop.

His expression remained serious and contemplative as he moved his finger to her shoulder to start another trail down her skin. "I was just noticing some things."

"Noticing things?"

He nodded. "I'm a scientist. I observe."

She had the urge to smile, but the intensity in his eyes stopped her.

He swallowed as he brushed his finger just beneath her jaw. "Your pulse is visible here. Steady and strong, and I felt your heart beating." His palm flattened just below her collarbone. "I saw the rise and fall of your chest; the way your lungs expanded with air all on their own without the help of a machine." His thumb gently traced her eyebrow. "I watched your eyelids flutter as you woke up, and your eyes became lucid as they focused on me, and your lips curved into a smile when you recognized me." His chin trembled, so slight she might have imagined it. "So many tiny details that people hovering around hospital beds day and night are desperate to see from their loved ones, and I realized what a gift they are. What a gift you are."

There was not one single word she could utter. Nothing to do justice for the way he'd effectively just stolen her breath and taken her heart into his hands.

The only possible response was to kiss him with everything she had, which is exactly what she did. And when her lips touched his, she came to a significant but unsurprising realization.

She was falling in love with Brooks Martin.

CHAPTER TWENTY-FIVE

Brooks

I'm proud of you.

—Coach McKee to Brooks Martin, University Medical School graduation

One week later when Brooks was on his way to Coach's house for Saturday morning coffee, something didn't feel right. He couldn't put his finger on it, exactly, but he checked his calendar to make sure there wasn't somewhere else he was supposed to be, and confirmed his text thread with Coach that they'd agreed to get together today.

Maybe it was a full moon. He always felt edgy on full moons, as was typical for health care professionals everywhere.

He was thinking about what he'd tell Coach about Carly this week—like how fucking happy he was and that yes, Coach was right about her all along—when he turned onto Coach's street.

Red and blue lights flashed bright, momentarily disarming Brooks before he processed the ambulance parked outside the house. The feeling didn't fade even when, after he'd thrown the car into park and run inside, he'd found Coach alive and well, yelling at the EMTs that it was "just a little chest pain" and everyone was "overreacting."

Brooks convinced him to let them run some tests, and that a brief stay in the hospital wasn't the end of the world. When it turned out their "overreaction" was, in fact, a mild heart attack, Coach became marginally more amenable to listening to what the doctors had to say.

Coach was admitted for observation, and Brooks felt better when he knew Coach's every bodily function was monitored and the best cardiac medical care in the state was mere feet away.

Yet . . . something still felt off.

Brooks didn't leave the hospital that day, and either rotated with Linda or sat in Coach's room with her, playing cards and shooting the shit to keep them occupied. James wasn't on service, but after hearing a close friend of Brooks's was in the cardiac unit, he popped in to introduce himself.

By the time night fell, Linda looked dead on her feet. Hospital accommodations weren't ideal for getting a good night's sleep, so Brooks convinced her to head home and promised he'd stay with Coach all night. He expected a discharge tomorrow or the day after, and he'd have had a hard time leaving whether Linda stayed or not.

He lingered around Coach's room for a few hours, chatting with employees he knew, then settled into the leather recliner with the remote in his hand. Coach was out cold, snoring louder than a freight train, so Brooks figured sleep wouldn't be something he'd get much of himself.

After several episodes of *Friends* on Nick at Nite, his stomach growled. He checked his watch—right at three in the morning—and stood. But just when he put his hand on the sliding door to grab something from the vending machine, a loud alarm filled the air.

Brooks jerked around, searching for the source.

The cardiac monitor.

Flatlined.

Several machines immediately detected abnormalities and began alarming in quick succession.

"Sarah!" Brooks yelled for the nurse taking care of Coach tonight. "Crash cart, now!"

He dropped everything in his hands—his phone, his coffee cup, his wallet, and lurched for the bed. The backrest had been propped up and he lowered it manually with a crash, pressing his fingers against Coach's neck.

"Please, please, please," he chanted, despite the equipment having already told him what he needed to know. "Fuck."

He clasped his hands together, centered the heel of his lower hand over Coach's sternum, and went up on the balls of his feet.

He pushed. "One, two, three . . ." Over and over. "Four, five, six, seven . . ."

He hadn't even made it through one round before Sarah came running, a second nurse behind her with the crash cart and three more on their heels.

"Two of epi," he yelled as a rib cracked under his weight. "One, two, three . . ."

Training and adrenaline took over while his subconscious drifted off into memory.

Red and blue lights flashed in the rearview mirror. Brooks's forehead fell against the steering wheel.

Macy was going to kill him.

His dad wouldn't, because he didn't care, and his mom wouldn't, because she was dead.

Something tapped on the window, startling him. He rolled it down, wincing and shielding his eyes from the bright flashlight shining on his face.

"Son, do you know how fast you were going?"

"Yes. I mean. Um, no, ma—I mean, sir." Shit.

The police officer leaned down and took one sniff, then stepped back. "Step out of the car."

He failed the field sobriety test with flying colors, and minutes later found himself sitting on the curb with his hands cuffed behind his back while the officer ran his information.

Fucking idiot. *He was too drunk to think much else, but that seemed appropriate and he said it over and over. It kept being true.*

He was eighteen now. This would go on his permanent record. Not that he had any plans to do anything worthwhile anytime soon, but maybe he would have someday. A DUI was a felony, right? They'd definitely find the weed in his car if they searched it, too. Would colleges even want him after this? Employers? Would his sisters?

Would anyone?

He sat there in the dark with his head against his knees for what felt like forever. Long enough to sober up a bit, and the shame of what he'd done settled on his shoulders like a ton of bricks.

What the hell was taking this cop so long? If he was going to jail he just wanted to get it over with already.

Headlights flashed across him, and he ducked his head lower, not wanting someone he knew to drive by and see him like this. He'd get up and move behind something but didn't want it to look like he was trying to run. Some modicum of sense reminded him he was in enough trouble as it was.

A car door slammed and a figure walked toward him. It took Brooks a few seconds to realize who it was.

Coach McKee stopped at the hood of Brooks's car and leaned against it, everything about him radiating disappointment.

"What are you doing here?" Brooks asked.

"Greg called me. We're friends, go way back."

Greg must be the cop.

"Said he'd pulled over someone I might know, and if I wanted to come pick him up it would save him a hell of a lot of paperwork." Coach crossed his arms and leveled a hard stare. "You reek of alcohol, kid."

Brooks said nothing.

"What the fuck were you thinking, driving like this?"

He'd been yelled at by Coach enough during practice to know it was best to stay silent.

"You realize you could have killed yourself? Is that what you want?"

Brooks shrugged. "It doesn't matter."

"Stop mumbling and talk to me like a man. You're eighteen and acting like you think you're some big shot now, huh? Prove it."

"Go to hell." Yeah, he was still plenty drunk. No matter how pissed he was, he'd never have said that to Coach sober.

"What did you say?"

Brooks clenched his jaw and looked up, rage and pain burning a hole through his veins. "I said it doesn't matter. It doesn't matter what happens to me."

Coach pushed off the car and strode forward, leaning down to get in Brooks's face. "The hell it doesn't. You could have killed someone else, did you think about that, you selfish kid? You want someone else to end up like your mom because you thought you'd get wasted and get behind the wheel?"

Brooks shot to his feet. Out of the corner of his eye he saw the police cruiser door swing open, but Coach glanced that way and held his palm out, shaking his head.

"Don't you dare talk about my mom," he seethed.

Coach didn't back down. "Look at yourself. You think she'd be proud of you? Proud of this? If your mother saw you now, she'd be ashamed of you. Don't taint her memory this way. Don't shame her with the man you're turning into."

Of course she'd be ashamed of him. She'd look at him like Coach was now, with disbelief and disappointment and despair. And it would hurt like a motherfucker.

But she'd still love him. No matter what he said, no matter what he did, no matter where he went. Mothers were the only people in the world who were supposed to love their kids with total abandon. Without condition. He used to think his dad felt that way, too, but he wasn't so sure anymore.

If his mom saw him right now, he'd want to crawl into a hole and hide.

But she would have loved him.

That realization is what broke him.

Coach saw it coming and his arms were open when Brooks fell into them, sobs racking his body.

He wailed and screamed while Coach kept him upright, his hands still locked behind his back. A year's worth of suppressed grief poured out all at once, and his tears for a beloved parent lost was enough to fill the ocean seven times over.

He cried for the pain she might have felt, though the doctors had said it had been instant. He cried for his sisters. He cried for the memories they'd never made and the advice he desperately needed from his dad but would never hear. He cried because he wanted to hug his mom just one more time, breathe her perfume into his lungs again.

He cried for the kid he was before she died and before his dad may as well have, because he'd been happy and kind and good, but he was gone. And he cried because he'd become a person he wouldn't have wanted his mom to see, but he didn't know how to be anything else. Everything hurt and the things he'd done over the past year had been the only things he could to numb the pain.

"It's okay." Coach's voice broke, and Brooks cried harder. "You're okay. I've got you, son."

"I hate this," he hiccupped. "I hate it."

"I know."

"I can't do this."

"Yes, you can." Coach grabbed him by the shoulders and looked him in the eye, his own eyes red-rimmed. "I know it doesn't feel like it now. But you can do this. You will."

It sure as hell didn't feel like it.

It had taken him a while to get ahold of himself, and eventually the cop had come over to remove the handcuffs and let Coach drive Brooks home. They hadn't gone to his house right away, though. They drove around for a while and talked. Coach had given him his signature tough love and told him he had to change the path he was on. That the next time Brooks made a mistake like that, he wouldn't be there to bail him out.

Brooks hadn't known it at the time, but when he woke up safe in his bed the following morning and thought about what happened the night before, it had been the start of a new life for him.

A life where he would focus on being good again.

One where he would make something of himself and make his mom, and Coach, proud.

And one where he'd never let his emotions take over his life like that ever again.

"Dr. Martin."

Sarah's face came slowly into focus.

"It's been thirty-seven minutes," she said gently.

Brooks surveyed the scene around him. One of the respiratory therapists had taken over compressions. The nurse keeping record was watching and timing, ready to let him know when they could give another dose. But after this long with wide-open fluids, four doses of epinephrine, and persistent asystole, he knew it was futile.

Coach was gone.

"Stop."

All eyes were on him. As the senior physician in the room, it was his responsibility to make the call.

He listlessly looked at his watch. "Time of death: three forty-one," he said, and walked out of the room.

CHAPTER TWENTY-SIX

Carly

Which careers have the best job security?

—Carly Porter's Google search history, senior year

Carly shot up in bed, unsure what had woken her.

A knock sounded at her door.

She glanced at the clock. It was six in the morning, which was way too early for anyone to be at her door. Just as she'd decided to ignore whoever it was and crawl back under the covers, she happened to glance at her phone screen.

Three texts and a missed call from Brooks.

The knock came again and she swung her legs out of bed and rushed to the door.

He stood on the other side with slumped shoulders and his shirt all wrinkled. She was still processing his unkempt appearance when he swayed to the side as if he might fall over.

She reached out to grab his arm. "Brooks?"

His gaze collided with hers and she gasped. His usually bright hazel eyes were dull and haunted.

She tugged lightly and he followed her inside. "What's wrong?"

He rubbed a hand down his face. "Coach died."

Her stomach dropped and she pressed a hand to her chest. "Oh no." He'd texted her about Coach's heart attack, and they'd talked pretty late last night after he'd decided to stay with him so Coach's wife could get some sleep. She put her arms around him. "Was it . . . were you there when he . . . ?"

He nodded.

"I'm so sorry." She brushed a lock of his hair back. "What can I do? What do you need?"

"Nothing, don't do anything. I'm sorry I stopped by like this and woke you up. I just, I don't know. I just sort of ended up here."

Her heart ached. "I'm glad you came. I'm sorry I didn't hear your call, my phone was on silent. Can I get you something to drink? Are you hungry?"

"No."

"Do you want to talk about it?"

"No."

He looked dead on his feet.

"Why don't you come lie down? See if you can go to sleep here, with me?"

He nodded, shoulders relaxing. "Can I take a shower first?"

Fifteen minutes later he came out of her bathroom in just his boxer briefs, hair damp and shoulders red from the steady stream of hot water. Carly was in bed, waiting, her heart drifting in search of him. She'd peeked in to give him a fresh towel from the laundry room and the image of him standing there under the steam, head bowed and eyes closed, hands flat against the tile, would forever be burned in her memory.

He'd already lost his parents, and now, too, the man who seemed to have filled a role as a second father figure. How much more would he have to endure?

He stretched out beside her and they met in the middle, lying on their sides and weaving their arms and legs together. He buried his face in her hair and she pressed her lips to his chest. They remained that way in the silence for several long moments, breathing steadily in the somber silence.

Carly didn't know how it felt to lose someone close to her. Her grandparents had passed when she was a baby, and she'd been lucky to not have dealt with the death of a loved one since. Everyone experienced it at one point or another, but some losses would hit harder than others. Some probably felt like a blow to the gut. How long did the pain linger? When did it fade to something manageable, only resurfacing on special dates like birthdays and holidays? Were some losses so deep the ache never truly went away?

He'd be hurting longer than the time they'd lie here together, but if being here with him could give him any measure of peace even for a moment, she'd stay here as long as it took.

He was still so long she wondered if he'd fallen asleep, but then his fingers fanned out across her back and his upper body shifted. His lips met her forehead and trailed down her cheek, coming to rest in a sweet kiss on her mouth. She kissed him back tentatively, unsure what his intention was, communicating as best she could that she was perfectly content in this moment just as it was.

Then he sucked her lower lip into his wet mouth and her stomach clenched. She opened her eyes and he pulled back a little, his gaze fierce and pleading. She tilted her face up, close enough for their lips to touch again, because if their roles were reversed, she might want him to help her forget, too.

Carly slowly emerged from sleep several hours later, stretching her limbs as her brain gradually came online. Her chest constricted at the memory from just a few hours prior.

Brooks, moving above her, inside her, holding her close with his face buried against her neck as he breathed words against her skin.

Please.

I love you.

Make it stop.

Three words uttered for the first time that should have made her heart burst with joy, but she wasn't altogether sure he'd even realized what he was saying. He'd seemed outside himself, and in that moment she would have done anything for him, done anything to take away his hurt and make it stop.

"I love you," she'd murmured into his hair, the words true and much easier to say than she'd imagined, but he'd seemed too far gone to hear.

She shivered, colder than usual when Brooks stayed over, and rolled over to find his side of the bed empty. Frowning, she ran a hand over the cool sheets and lifted onto her elbows to glance toward the bathroom. The light was off.

She slipped on a tank top and sweatpants and padded into the hallway, expecting to hear him in the kitchen or catch the hum of the television. But the TV was off and the kitchen was dark.

Maybe he went out for coffee? She had no idea how long ago he'd left, but that seemed like something he would do.

It was 10:00 a.m., just four hours after he'd shown up at her door. She'd sort of passed out after they slept together, her body and emotions spent. She'd thought he was in the same boat.

They'd fallen asleep together, right?

Just in case, she circled the counter and checked the coffee table for a note, then went back to her room to see if he'd sent her a text.

Nothing.

She sent off a text that simply said, *You okay?* and made herself a pot of coffee. When he didn't reply right away, she assumed he must have gone home for some reason and probably fallen asleep.

It hadn't been long ago that he'd gone silent after having that difficult case at work, and despite saying he wanted to get better at talking through things and not retreating into himself, she understood it wasn't a habit that he could break overnight. Still, this felt . . . different.

When it had happened before, he hadn't slept with her, said he loved her, and snuck out of her bed without a word.

Was he embarrassed he'd allowed himself to be vulnerable in front of her? Maybe it was naive, but she'd hoped they were close enough by now that he wouldn't feel that way. Before she could get too far down that road, her phone lit up with a text.

Mom: Is this outfit OK for Café 501? Never been there.

Shit. Carly glanced at the clock. She was meeting her mom and the new boyfriend, Lance, for Sunday brunch and was gonna be late if she didn't get ready. The guy had made reservations at one of Carly's favorite restaurants, which meant either her mom had tipped him off in the hope of earning brownie points or he'd just gotten lucky. Either way, she needed to put aside her brooding about Brooks and focus.

Carly: That's perfect. See you soon.

She took the quickest shower of her life and made it to the restaurant just in time. Her mom was glowing, her occasional high-pitched laughter the only thing that tipped off how nervous she was.

"I just want you to like him," her mom whispered when Lance was in the restroom.

"Relax, Mom. He's great."

It wasn't a lie, exactly. Lance was perfectly nice, polite, and intelligent. He was easy to talk to and seemed to really like her mom, which was what mattered most. He reminded Carly a lot of Benjamin, actually. Still, Carly wasn't completely taken with him for her mom. There were no red flags, which was good, and she couldn't quite pinpoint what it was . . . but everything about them together was just sort of flat. She'd say none of this, though, because her mom seemed happy, and Carly wasn't in the best place to be judging anything romantic right now. She struggled to keep from thinking about Brooks, which was probably to blame for her pessimistic attitude. By the end of the meal her mom had a content smile on her face, and Carly counted it a success.

She checked her phone as she walked out, thinking surely Brooks had called or texted her back by now.

Still nothing.

She stayed out of the house and kept herself as busy as possible for the entire day. She shopped for clients, browsed the bookstore, and went grocery shopping. It was after eight when she got home. By this point, anger had set in, and after she unlocked her apartment door and stepped inside, she tossed her purse on the table with more force than necessary.

Where the hell was he?

Carly woke with a start. Her leg was asleep and her neck ached, and the faint sound of music floated through the air.

She sat up from where she'd apparently fallen asleep on the couch, orienting herself to place and time. Monday morning, sometime after sunrise because light streamed through the sheer curtains behind her. The music kept going, and she suddenly realized it was her ringtone.

Brooks? Did he finally call?

It took her several seconds to locate her phone stuck between two couch cushions. She looked at the screen and disappointment filled her yet again.

"Hey, Mai," she greeted, trying to sound chipper and not like she just woke up.

"Carly, how are you?" Something in her boss's tone felt off, and Carly sat up straighter.

"I'm okay," she answered honestly, urgently scrolling through her brain to make sure she hadn't missed some sort of meeting or appointment. She still wasn't used to the fact this job didn't require her to show up and clock in at a certain time, and being at home on Monday morning felt a little like cheating. "How are you?"

"I've been better. I have something to discuss with you, and I'd like to do it in person. Could you come by the office this morning?"

Oh God. "Sure. Is everything okay?" Was she in trouble?

"Let's talk about it when you get here."

Her stomach flipped with unease. "I can be there in an hour, is that okay?" Her hair was a complete mess, so she had to do something about that before going in.

"I'll make myself available. See you soon."

Hands shaking, Carly ended the call and put her phone down, her mind racing through the possibilities. A client issue? A company layoff? She'd recently met Jacque at the outlet mall to help her find something for her anniversary dinner and hadn't charged her a fee for it. She'd just wanted to help, but her business-minded boss might not see it that way.

Was it possible Mai heard something about Carly and Brooks's relationship?

Pepper regarded her from the back of the couch. She gave him a quick scratch and got up, trying to convince herself it probably wasn't as bad as all that.

Maybe it wasn't anything bad, at all.

An hour later, Carly walked through the glass doors of the downtown high-rise that housed Mode's offices. As promised, Mai was waiting for Carly as soon as she arrived.

Mai closed her office door and gestured to a chair. "Have a seat."

Carly did as asked and resisted the urge to fold her arms across her stomach like a child in the principal's office. Mai sat on the opposite side of her desk.

"I appreciate you coming in, and I want to get right to the point. But first, I want to ask if there's anything you want to tell me. Anything you think I should know that might negatively impact the company."

The underhanded question caught Carly off guard, and she was quite frankly exhausted after yesterday. So even though it was unlike her, Carly replied with a question of her own, her tone more irritated than it probably should have been when speaking to her boss. "Is there something specific you want to ask me about?"

Mai pivoted easily. "You completed the updated professionalism training over the summer, correct?"

Oh God. This had to be about Brooks. But what had she heard, and why was she concerned about it?

For now, Carly stuck to the specific question at hand. "Yes."

"And signed that you'd comply with the code of conduct outlined in that training?"

"I did."

"Someone brought to my attention that you may have violated that policy with a client. Brooks Martin. Is that true?"

Who could have brought that to her attention? Sasha was the only one who knew about them, and there's no way she'd have ratted them out, right? Carly didn't know what to do. She wasn't the type to lie, especially not at work and not to someone she'd considered a friend for so long. But in this moment she understood why someone would, out of desperation to keep their job.

"I . . . I don't—" She stumbled, trying to think past the panic fogging her brain. "I don't know what this could be about. We've worked closely throughout the whole series, though we're pretty much done, now. Did someone mistake one of our shopping appointments as something . . . more?"

Mai stood and came to Carly's side of the desk, leaning back against it. She pulled out her phone and tapped the screen. "Listen, Carly. I'll be straight with you. Mrs. Princeton said she saw you and Brooks together and that things looked . . . more than professional. She has photos."

Mai handed Carly the phone.

The photos were grainy and far away, as if taken from inside a building, but it was Brooks and Carly, alright. In the parking lot of her accounting firm the day he brought her coffee. She swiped to see a series of three photos.

One of them just standing there, talking. One with their arms around each other, when he'd hugged her after learning about her job.

And the last one just before they broke apart, with his lips in her hair.

They didn't look good, she'd give Mai that. Then something Mai had said seemed to click in her brain.

"Wait, Mrs. Princeton? Chet, my ex-client's wife?"

"Yes."

"Why the hell is she taking pictures of me?" That was creepy as hell.

"I only know what she told me—that she was meeting with her financial planner and was waiting in the lobby. She saw you come off the elevator and recognized you for . . . obvious reasons. From the window she saw who you were meeting."

Carly was about to ask why on earth this woman would care, and note that her personal vendetta against Carly (that was completely unfounded) was going a little too far. But with Mai's next words, it all made sense.

"She recognized Brooks, too, from the Bachelor series. She said she'd followed it religiously from the start and even encouraged her daughter, Madison, to sign up for the dating app in hopes she'd be a match. Evidently, she was."

Her stomach rolled, her fingers turning to ice. She had the sudden urge to crawl underneath the desk and hide.

Shit.

Madison Princeton. Brooks had mentioned a Madison but couldn't remember her last name. She was the woman he'd gone out with the day after these photos were taken.

"She believes you and Brooks were together when he went out with her daughter and that he got her hopes up for no reason. Understandably, she's extremely upset about it."

This was bad. Even though Brooks had said Madison wanted to be with someone else and was using Brooks as a pawn to get her mom off her back, it wouldn't help for Carly to bring that up. The truth of the matter was, she had gone against company policy and there was photo evidence. She could try to explain the images away—say they looked worse than they were—but they had done much worse in private. Either way, the damage was done.

First with Chet, now this. Mai deserved her honesty.

"I didn't expect to feel this way about him," Carly admitted quietly, staring at the image on the phone still in her hand. "I never meant for this to happen. It's real, what I feel for him. If that even matters."

Mai sighed. She took the phone, laid it on the desk, and massaged her temples. "You've put me in a terrible position, Carly."

"I'm sorry." And she was.

A few moments of silence passed before Mai spoke again. "I believe that none of this was deliberate, and that you weren't acting with sinister intent. But you broke company policy. Someone else saw, and you confirmed it. Even if you and Brooks are in a genuine relationship now, I can't ignore those facts. Even if I wanted to, HR wouldn't let me. I hope you understand . . . my hands are tied."

Carly knew what was coming, but she still flinched at Mai's next words.

"I'm going to have to let you go."

CHAPTER TWENTY-SEVEN

Brooks

When I'm at a loss for how to manage a patient, I phone a friend. Medicine isn't independent work, it's a group project. You've got access to a whole host of experts and specialists in this building, so for the sake of every patient you take care of, use them every chance you get.

—Dr. Brooks Martin to the critical-care fellows, last winter

Brooks peeled his eyes open in tiny increments, allowing his pupils to adjust to the light and the room to slowly come into focus. His temples throbbed and his mouth felt like it was stuffed with cotton balls. His stomach was on edge, and it was a toss-up whether he was hungry or needed to vomit. Puffy eyes and a dry throat rounded out the disgraced picture he must make.

Oh, and he really had to pee.

He grunted as he rolled to the side and put his feet on the floor.

Easy. Definitely not hungry.

Oreo jumped onto the bed with ease and sat on his haunches, staring with his flat copper gaze.

"Don't judge me."

He used the restroom and after washing his hands, planted his palms beside the sink and locked his elbows, studying his reflection in the mirror.

He hated himself.

It had been a day and a half since Coach had died and he'd shown up at Carly's door.

He didn't even remember driving to her apartment yesterday morning. He'd called Linda to deliver the news himself, and her anguished howl would be burned into his brain forever. He'd just sort of left the hospital in a haze and found himself there, like going anywhere else hadn't even occurred to him.

She was the only person he'd wanted to see. He'd just wanted to be in her general vicinity and nothing more. To hug her and hear her voice and lie down beside her and sleep for days with her body breathing and living next to his.

But as he'd lain there with her in his arms, his lips on her hair and her sweet breath warm against his chest, the excruciating hole in his chest hadn't abated.

Not even a little.

Maybe grief turned him a little mad, or maybe the frenzy had been there all along and he'd just suppressed it. Either way, he'd ended up using her body to drive away the demons, chasing the relief only sex could bring, even if just for a moment. It hadn't worked out for him the way it used to, though. With Carly, it wasn't just about the physical. It never had been.

He was in love with her. When he closed his eyes, he saw her, and when he went to sleep, he dreamed of her. No part of him wanted to be apart from her, even the dark ones. And that was the whole problem. Even as he was sinking lower and lower, he just pulled her along with him. Instead of talking about what had happened or how he was feeling, he'd fucked her to forget.

When that didn't work, and the combined memories of Linda and his dad's reactions to learning the loves of their lives were gone forever pushed front and center in his brain, he'd panicked. As much as he'd told himself she wasn't, Carly had become that person for him. Someone he couldn't imagine living without, and he'd resonated more with his dad in that moment than ever before.

All the events of the day had crashed down on him, and that last realization had been too much. He couldn't get out of there fast enough.

He'd come home, gotten drunk, and stayed that way. One look at his phone showed she'd called and texted a few times, probably checking on him.

He hadn't even noticed, and obviously hadn't responded.

Sinking to his haunches, he ran his hands through his hair. He'd snuck out of her apartment like a coward and basically ghosted her.

She had to be furious. He would be.

As he considered how he might be able to fix this, a tiny voice asked if he should even try.

Carly deserved more than a man who could hang around when things were good but randomly disappeared when his emotions got too big to handle.

He obviously had issues. He'd known it from the start and should have known better than to let himself fall into a false sense of security with Carly. He'd just ignored all the reasons he'd avoided relationships in the past, and at the first sign of discomfort, slipped back into his comfort zone.

Clearly, a few weeks of bliss didn't translate to long-term-relationship capability.

At the sound of his doorbell, his heart stopped. Was it her?

He shot back up to a standing position way faster than advisable in his current condition. He had to pause so he wouldn't vomit, and the doorbell rang again before he slowly shuffled his way through the house and answered the door.

Sasha reared back and put a hand over her nose. "My God."

"You act like you've never smelled whiskey before," he said flatly. It was probably coming out of his pores at this point.

"I hope you're not supposed to be at work right now."

He wasn't, thank God.

Macy glared at her sister and stepped forward to envelop Brooks in a hug.

"Don't jostle me," he warned.

She ignored him. "We heard about Coach."

"News travels fast."

Macy pulled back but left her hands on his shoulders. "Are you okay?"

"No."

She nodded as if she'd figured as much.

He moved to the side to let them in. He eyed Sasha carefully, because other than his email to her with his final piece for the magazine, they hadn't spoken since the day she discovered Carly at his house. But when he sat down on the couch, she sat beside him and leaned into him.

"What can we do?" she asked.

"Nothing. There's nothing anyone can do."

"When did it happen?" Macy asked.

"Yesterday morning. Early. Linda's a mess."

"I bet," Macy said. "It was a shock."

He nodded.

"Why didn't you call us?" Sasha asked. "Did you just come straight home and start drinking?"

"I went to Carly's first."

Sasha stiffened, and he laughed humorlessly.

"You don't need to worry about that anymore, Sash. I'm pretty sure I fucked that up."

"What?" she asked at the same time Macy said, "What do you mean?"

He propped his elbows on his knees and dropped his head into his hands. "I'm in love with her."

Sasha gasped. "You're what?"

"Yeah. I couldn't believe it, either."

They sat with that for a minute.

"Why is that a bad thing?" Macy asked gently.

"Because I don't know how to do this. Because it terrifies me. I don't know how to talk about things that are hard for me, and one of those things is the fact that I watched Dad waste away because of love and that's why I never wanted any part of it. I've actively avoided it my entire adult life. I didn't mean to fall for Carly, but now that I have, I can't imagine letting her go. But it's like there's two halves of me, and it's anyone's guess which one will win on any given day. The guy that's optimistic and thinks he can figure this out versus the one who knows better and who reminds me I'm nowhere near partner material. The second one's the guy who showed up to Carly's yesterday. The man that pulled me out of my self-destruction had died right in front of me, and I took that as an invitation to slide right back into it."

He swallowed hard, staring blankly at the dark TV across from him.

Sasha squeezed his shoulder, and Macy moved from the chair to his other side, her palm on his back.

The attempts at comfort were futile at this point, but he appreciated their presence all the same. He was so damned lucky to have them.

"You're not back in it," Macy said. "High School Brooks wouldn't even be having this conversation with us."

He rolled that around in his mind for a moment.

That was true.

"You're different now," Sasha said from his other side. "You had a bad day because something terrible happened. You're human. But look, you recognize it wasn't the healthiest way to react and you'll do better next time. What did you do to mess things up with Carly, anyway? Did you pick a fight with her?" Sasha asked.

"No."

He felt Macy's concentration on his face. "Did you upset her, somehow?"

"I don't know. Probably."

"What do you mean, you don't know?"

"I haven't talked to her."

Sasha frowned. "Wait, so when you went to her place . . . ?"

He twisted the heel of his hand into his forehead. "Listen. I was in a bad place when I showed up there. I wouldn't talk to her about what happened even though I know she wanted me to. She was wonderful and took care of me, and after she fell asleep I panicked and snuck out. She was obviously worried after she woke up and called me several times, but by that point I was drunk or passed out."

Sasha gave him a disappointed look that was eerily similar to their late mother's. "Well, yeah. You acted like an ass. But you're not giving her enough credit. She's not into drama and wants to get to the bottom of things. You made a mistake and need to grovel, but saying you fucked up the whole relationship—which is still super weird to think about, by the way—seems a little overdramatic. She's a reasonable person and you just need to talk to her."

He'd never groveled before, but not because he'd never messed up. Usually his mistakes negatively affected him more than anyone else. He'd never hurt someone he cared so much about to the point that he needed to make amends.

"I don't know how."

"Dammit, Brooks," Sasha snapped.

He startled, and glanced over at Macy. Her eyes were wide, too.

"I'm so tired of hearing you say *I can't* or *I don't know how* when it comes to your own happiness. I know how you are at work, and I know you'd never give up like that on your patients. No matter how bad the situation is, you'll keep working and keep digging and press on to find answers or anything that might help, even when the chance of success is next to nothing. Why is it you never afford yourself that kind of determination?"

I don't know was on the tip of his tongue, but he thought that might piss her off even more. It might have been a rhetorical question anyway, because she kept right on going.

"Figure it the hell out, okay? Ask for help. Go to therapy. Read a self-help book. Don't you have resources at work for this sort of thing?"

He did. He'd just never used them.

"If you really want to be that optimistic guy and tell the other one to get lost, you *can*, but it's gonna take some work. If you want to be the kind of man Carly deserves and that will give you both a happy life together, you have to face your issues head-on. If you think you weren't a good partner yesterday, start being one today, and an even better one tomorrow. Do the work to make yourself worthy of this woman. Because deep down, I know you are. You're not broken beyond repair, you're just a little rusty in a few places."

He just stared at her, mouth ajar.

"Damn, Sasha," Macy said, pride shining in her tone. "That was . . ."

"Awesome and kind of harsh," Brooks filled in, then double-checked with Macy to make sure. "It was, right? I might still be a little drunk, so I can't be sure I read it right."

"It was," Macy confirmed. "The perfect mix of encouragement and tough love. I couldn't have done it better, myself."

Sasha lifted one shoulder. "I call it like I see it."

"You know who else used to talk to me like that?"

"Coach?" Sasha guessed.

"Well, yeah," he admitted. "But I was talking about Mom."

Both of his sisters' faces softened.

"She was good at that," Macy said. "Sometimes too good."

"There were times I couldn't tell if she was proud of me or mad at me," Sasha said with a laugh.

"Exactly," Brooks said. "That's what that just felt like." He mimicked her higher pitched voice. "You're a disaster, Brooks. Like, an absolute catastrophe. But I think you can fix it, probably. Good luck with it."

Macy laughed, and Sasha just regarded him without a trace of repentance.

"You'd have gotten there eventually, I think, but present circumstances have given you an opportunity to step it up right here and now," she said. "And if you think Carly's worth the effort, you don't have another choice."

CHAPTER TWENTY-EIGHT

Carly

Hey, where's the best place to find kitchen cabinet organizers? And don't say you don't know. I've seen your apartment.

—Text message from Kendall to Carly Porter, one year ago

Her entire adult life, Carly had worked so hard to avoid ever realizing her greatest fear that she'd never considered how she might react if it actually happened.

If you'd asked her a week ago how she might handle the prospect of unemployment, she'd have guessed it would be something along the lines of hysteria or a full-blown panic attack. Maybe even to the point she'd be on her knees, tearfully begging Mai to reconsider. She'd furiously search internet job boards and apply for twenty jobs by noon, because even though she was a saver and had a perfectly respectable safety net in her bank account, she never wanted to actually *use* it.

But when she'd left Mode's office that day, she had just felt numb. She'd gone home in a sort of trance, her body going through the motions to get to her car, drive home, and unlock her apartment. She fed Pepper, poured herself a glass of wine (adopting airport rules because no one was there to stop her), and settled in on her couch with the remote.

She sat there for hours, only getting up to pee, and wouldn't have thought her day could get any worse.

Then Brooks called.

"Hi," she said, too weary to say, *Where the hell have you been?* like she'd been prepared to yesterday.

"Hey," he said.

She closed her eyes, tears building beneath them. It was so good to hear his voice. Especially after this morning.

"I'm sorry." His voice cracked.

She was so raw that the anger from yesterday dissipated like smoke. She wished he was here. Why had he called instead of coming over?

"God, Carly, I'm sorry for how I treated you this weekend." He sighed, and she could picture him at home, on his couch, or maybe at the kitchen table with a cup of coffee, raking a hand through his hair. "I was sort of in shock, I think, and went to a dark place inside my head. I used you to get out of it, and when that still didn't work, I ran away. You deserve better than that, and I'm embarrassed and ashamed of myself. I hope you can forgive me."

All she wanted in this moment was to fold herself into his body and feel his warm strength around her. "I accept your apology about the disappearing part only. I was fully engaged and on board for everything else." She'd give anything for him to take her mind off the conversation with Mai this morning, which didn't feel much different from what he'd done early Sunday morning and seemed to think he needed to apologize for. "Sometimes when you're hurting, it helps to just get lost in someone you trust. I could easily do the same with you."

She almost told him about getting fired right then and there, but she couldn't make the words come. It almost didn't feel real, yet. The news would make him feel even worse, too, because it was sort of because of him, and he didn't need another weight stacked on his shoulders right now.

"But," he started, "if our roles were reversed, you'd also talk to me about what had upset you when you were ready. Whether it was later that day, the next day, or a few days later. You'd trust me with the talking part, too."

She frowned. "You won't?" He was new at this, sure, but weren't they getting there?

"I don't know. I've never trusted anyone with those parts of me, really." A door opened and closed in the background, as if he'd walked outside. "I gave bits and pieces to Coach once, and sometimes I've talked a little to my sisters. I've even opened up some to you. But there's a hell of a lot more in here, buried deep and that I've never dealt with. Things I haven't even let myself dwell on. I learned how to distract myself with things like school and work, which I thought was better than sex and alcohol. But I just traded one diversion for another, and I'm realizing maybe that hasn't been the healthiest thing. Both for me and any relationship I might want to have."

His voice was careful and hesitant, like he was leading up to something. Dread slowly settled in her stomach and spread, sending ice trickling through her veins.

"I . . . God, I care about you so much, Carly. But I think I need some time to figure a few things out. I need to work on communication and how I handle stress. I need to work through what happened with my parents and the horrible things I see in the hospital, and to learn how deal with all of that in a different way. I don't know what will happen when I dig into those dark moments, and I—I don't know. I just don't want to bring you down with me. I want to be able to be there for you and to shoulder your burdens when you need me, but I don't know if I can do that when I'm already on my knees from the weight of mine."

She blinked twice, then rubbed her eyes with one hand, her head starting to pound. Was this really happening right now? Literally hours after she'd lost her job for being with this man?

"Are you saying this is over?" she asked bluntly.

She thought she heard a sniffle, but couldn't be sure. "I'm saying I have to make sure I'm worthy of you," Brooks said slowly. "And I . . . I think I need to get there on my own before we can be together."

Well. There it was.

She almost laughed at the absurdity of it all. The irony of him saying he couldn't be there for her on the exact day she needed him to. But he didn't know she'd just lost her job, and even in her current state she recognized he was taking a big step admitting he needed help. It wasn't his fault every part of her life was falling apart.

No job. No Brooks. Sasha still wasn't speaking to her. Kendall was visiting her parents in Ohio, so Carly didn't even have her to fall back on.

This was officially rock bottom.

Her eyes were glassy, but no tears spilled over. She dug her fingernails into her palm just shy of pain, released, then did it again.

"I don't know what to say," she finally said. "I wasn't expecting this." Any of it.

"I'm sorry." He sounded as miserable as she felt. "I'm so fucking sorry."

"You said that already."

"I know," he said. "That's why I have to do this. I can't keep doing things I have to apologize for."

A few tears escaped and tracked down her cheek. "Are you sure this is what you want?"

"No." She took a small measure of comfort in that. "But I'm sure I want to give us the best chance, and in order to do that I have to step back and fix some things. I just . . . Something tells me things will get worse in here before they get better."

She just sat there, lashes wet and eyes unfocused. There really wasn't anything she could do, was there? If there was, she didn't have the energy to recognize it.

"I don't know how yet, but Carly, I will fix this," he promised.

She shook her head, eyes closed, throat tight. "What happens if, by the time you think you're ready, I've moved on?" She didn't know if such a thing was possible, but if he could walk away, surely she could find someone else, too. Someday.

He said nothing for a long moment. "If you were happy, I'd find a way to live with that," he said, voice rough like he had razor blades in his throat.

If you were happy. She'd thought she was happy before Brooks, but the word took on a whole new meaning after him. He made her laugh and made her think, and when she was around him, she felt beautiful and adored. She'd never known uninhibited joy or what it felt like to truly *crave* someone. She'd been living at a six, perfectly content and satisfied, until Brooks showed her what life was like at a ten. Which was all well and good until he removed himself from the equation.

On the other hand, it was also very possible the choices she'd made because of her feelings for him had ruined her life. In more ways than one. So all things considered, maybe this was for the best.

Tears flowed down her cheeks in earnest now. Now that they'd started, she couldn't stop them. She had to get off the phone.

"I have to go." She didn't wait for his reply and ended the call, sank back into the cushions, and let the flood take over.

Carly barely moved for three days. She had nowhere to go professionally and had zero interest in social functions. The beauty of food-delivery apps meant she didn't even have to leave to eat and had meals delivered to her doorstep twice a day. For hours on end, she zoned blessedly out as she binged series after series, and for the most part, that kept her calm. But occasionally something tripped her memory—about being unemployed or worse, about Brooks—and she'd break down again.

After ignoring her calls and texts for several days, her mom stopped by unannounced, banging on the door until Carly finally let her in. With wide eyes her mom had taken in the disaster that was Carly's apartment—food containers on the counter, dishes in the sink, random clothes and books strewn around the living room, and demanded to know what had happened. After Carly told her everything—from falling for Brooks to alienating her best friend and getting fired, and finally him deciding to call things off—her mom made her take a shower then tucked her back in on the couch, cleaned the place up, and made Carly her first home-cooked meal in five days. She'd also offered Carly money, which she politely declined. She'd go crawling back to her old accounting firm soon enough.

An hour after her mom left with a promise she'd check back in tomorrow, another knock sounded on the front door. Carly looked around as she got up, wondering if her mom forgot something. Maybe she'd gone against Carly's orders and told Sasha what happened, and her oldest friend decided to come check on her, too.

But the person standing on her *Got Wine?* welcome mat was the last person she expected to see.

"Benjamin?"

He looked exactly the same as the day he left nine months ago, from his cropped blond hair and wire-rimmed glasses to the University of Oklahoma T-shirt he wore at least twice a month.

Benjamin gave her a shy sort of smile. "Hey."

"What are you doing here?"

"I, uh, came back early. Can I come in?"

"Sure," she said, stepping back. "Yeah, of course. Come in."

He crossed the threshold but didn't go far, and turned to her with arms open and an expectant expression. She walked into his embrace, inhaling the familiar scent of his laundry detergent and trying not to compare it to the way it felt when Brooks hugged her.

"It's good to see you," he said into her hair.

"You too."

He lingered there for a beat, then released her and walked farther into the living room. Pepper lifted his head from where he'd sprawled out in the middle of the couch, but made no move to vacate. Benjamin stopped in the middle of the rug and looked around for a moment.

"Not much has changed in here," he said, smiling at her.

Thank God he hadn't shown up a few hours sooner. "You know me," she said. "Creature of habit."

He remained standing there and rubbed the back of his neck, as if he wasn't sure what to do next. They hadn't spoken since their conversation about dating other people, and to be honest, once things had started up with Brooks she hadn't thought about Benjamin all that much.

"Can I get you something to drink?" she asked, remembering her manners.

"Sure, I'll take a water. It's so hard to stay hydrated when I'm traveling."

"When did you get back?" she asked, grabbing a glass from the cabinet.

"Today."

"Today? As in, you flew back from South Korea *today?*"

"Well, technically the trip started yesterday, but yeah. I hope it's okay I came over. I . . . I didn't want to wait to see you."

She filled up the glass and brought it to him, then nudged Pepper off the couch so they could sit down. She wasn't sure what to make of him being back in the States or of coming directly to her place, and asking about the former seemed like the safest place to start. "Did something happen to bring you back early?"

"The director of our program quit unexpectedly. It kind of shook things up at the company, especially with their internship program, so they cut us loose early."

"Oh no, I'm so sorry."

Benjamin opened the drawer in the end table to grab a coaster and set the glass on top. "It's okay. I'll figure out my next steps in the next couple of days. They still offered to give us letters of recommendation, so I'm not worried about finding a job somewhere." He ran his palms up and down his thighs, which he usually only did when he was nervous. "But I, uh, I didn't come over to talk about my job. Not right now, at least."

"Okay," she said, waiting.

He locked eyes with her. "I missed you while I was gone."

"I missed you, too," she returned, though with notably less enthusiasm. She could chalk up her lukewarm sentiment to the week she'd had, but it was more than that. Even if it was over, her time with Brooks changed her, and at this point she wasn't sure what that meant. For her, or for her *and* Benjamin—because it seemed like that's where he was going with this.

"Would you go to dinner with me tonight?" he asked. "So we can talk?"

With the history they had, she could at least hear him out. There were plenty of things she needed to update him on, too. "Sure."

"What is today?" he asked, looking up and squinting. "Jet lag has me off on my schedule."

In her state, Carly hardly knew, either. "Thursday?" She was pretty sure that was right.

"Thursday, huh?" He grinned.

She smiled back. She knew exactly what he was thinking.

He wagged his eyebrows. "You wanna?"

She nodded. "Barrios, here we come."

CHAPTER TWENTY-NINE

Carly

> I'm sorry for everything I put you through, and I hope you can find it in your heart to forgive me.
>
> *—Excerpt from letter from June Porter to Carly Porter, during Step 9 of her recovery program*

The first thing Carly thought when she stepped into her mom's backyard was how much Brooks would love her mom's garden.

She rubbed her sternum and focused her attention on the patio and her mother, who waited for her at the wrought-iron table.

Her mom stood and wrapped her in a tight hug. "You look better today."

"I feel better. Thanks for taking care of me this week."

"I'm happy you let me."

Carly regarded the table where they usually chatted. "Could we take a walk?" she asked, too antsy to sit.

"Sure. Just let me change my shoes."

Five minutes later, they strolled down the neighborhood sidewalk in silence.

"You're awfully quiet," Carly noted.

"You texted to say you were coming over for advice, and you haven't asked for that since you were twelve. I'm a little outside my element, here."

"Fair," Carly said with a small smile, then blew out a breath. "Benjamin came back early."

Even from her side view, Carly saw her mom's face light up. She'd always loved Benjamin. "He did? That's wonderful!"

"Yep. Showed up at my door two days ago," Carly said, and then explained what happened with his internship program to bring him home early.

Her mother's brows came together, probably noticing Carly's lack of enthusiasm. "How do you feel about him being back?" The question was standard June Porter–style and probably something she'd learned during Gamblers Anonymous meetings. No judgment, open ended, and didn't give any room for assumptions.

"I don't know. If he'd shown up out of the blue three months ago, I'd have been over the moon. He said all the right things, like how being gone showed him how much I mean to him and when he dated someone else, it never felt the same. That the idea of me dating another man woke him up, and it was a mistake to take a break while he was gone. I think he's being genuine, and there's so much history there. But now, after everything with Brooks . . . I don't know." She leaned right to nudge her mom's shoulder with her own. "I'm sorry if that's not the reaction you hoped for. I know how much you love Benjamin."

They turned a corner and headed toward a small pond toward the back of the neighborhood. "It's not my opinion that matters. Are you still in love with Benjamin?"

Carly had thought of little else in the past few days. "In some ways I think Benjamin's a better fit for me. We know each other so well, and we're comfortable with each other. I know what he expects long term from a relationship and vice versa, and I know we could give that to each other. With him I know exactly what I'm in for."

"Mmm," her mom hummed in response. "That's true. But that's not what I asked."

No, she'd asked if Carly was still in love with him, and that was a question she didn't want to examine. "I know. I *know* that, but isn't all that stuff just as relevant? If you asked me that question about Brooks, I'd say yes, I'm still in love with him. Present tense and probably forever tense. But look what happened when I got involved with him. Everything went straight to hell. I lost my job, possibly my best friend, and got my heart broken." She hadn't realized she'd raised her voice until a few kids looked up from where they were drawing with chalk in their driveway. She waited until they'd passed that house, and said in a lower tone, "None of that would have ever happened if I'd just waited for Benjamin to get back like I'd planned. I never had to risk anything to be with him because he's safe. That's what I want, you know? It's what I need in my life. It's just like you and Lance."

Her mom looked over at her. "What do you mean, like me and Lance?"

"He's just like Benjamin. Solid, stable, and safe. I mean, that's what you like about him, right?"

"No. Not at all," her mom said, surprised. "Those aren't bad things, obviously. But if I made a list of what I like most about him, none of those would be at the top of my list."

Carly turned her entire torso toward her mom, brows raised. "Seriously?"

"Seriously. Whatever gave you that idea?"

"I . . . I don't know," Carly admitted. "I guess I just thought those things would be high on your list, after, well . . ." Yes, they'd come a long way when it came to talking about her mom's past, but it still wasn't easy to just come out and say *after your grossly irresponsible behavior when I was growing up.*

Her mom filled in the blanks. "It's okay. I get it." She said it matter-of-factly, without a trace of defensiveness. "You do have a point, because in most areas of my life now, I loathe taking chances. And based on what I put you through as a kid, I understand why you're the same way. But if you want to know the truth, love is the one place where I feel the exact opposite. I mean, God, think about what a risk it is to give a woman like me a shot. Lance knows all about my past and what it took for me to get clean, and the things I still have to do to make sure I don't fall back into those habits. He knows all of it, and that man still wants to be with me. He thinks I'm worth the risk, and for someone like me, that's the most beautiful thing in the world. His ability to see the good in people, including me . . . That's the stuff at the top of my list."

Carly was dumbfounded. "I had no idea you felt that way." Or how way off the mark she'd been. "You're absolutely worth it, Mom. Of course you are. And I'm so glad you found a man that sees that."

Damn, if she was that wrong about her mom, what else was she wrong about?

"I am, too," her mom said. "And even though I've thought about it a lot over the years, I'm no expert on love, so take what I'm about to say with a grain of salt."

Carly nodded. "Okay."

"I think love is a completely different type of risk. When I went to the casino, the only thing I cared about was what I could win. I didn't care what I was losing in the process of chasing that reward, no matter how high the odds were stacked against me. But with love, it's not as much about what you win if you hedge your bets just right—it's about what you stand to lose if you don't. Instead of thinking about what you could live with in order to simply get by and stick with the status quo, make sure you're not trading that by letting go of something you can't live without."

They reached the tiny pond, where a group of ducks floated gently in the breeze. Carly stopped at the edge and folded her hands together behind her neck, letting her mom's words marinate.

"If anyone knows a thing or two about regret, it's me," her mom continued, coming to a stop beside her. She slipped her hands into her pockets and gazed across the water. "So believe me when I say that's the kind you'll never forgive yourself for."

Carly left her mom's house with a lot more on her mind than she'd arrived with. She was overwhelmed with everything relationship related and opted to take a break from that part of her life and pivot to the other mess: her career.

She had to find a job. She'd spent enough time holed up in her apartment this week, so after swinging by to grab her laptop, she found a local coffee shop for a change of scenery. She ordered a latte and settled at a table in the back corner before pulling up a random job-search website.

She selected her location and typed in "accountant," and in seconds the screen was full of open positions. Carly clicked on the first one—staff accountant at a local Realtor group—but quickly hit the back button when she noticed it was 100 percent in office. Next was Accountant II at one of the major credit unions in the state, but it was only part-time.

The process continued for the better part of an hour, and she couldn't muster even a kernel of enthusiasm for a single one.

Senior tax accountant—seasonal.

Tax manager—not enough experience.

Full-charge bookkeeper—too much experience.

Credit analyst—too stressful.

Payroll clerk—she'd be bored to tears.

When her phone buzzed on the table, she reached for it immediately, so desperate for an interruption she didn't even check who was calling before she answered.

"Carly?"

Her heart squeezed. "Sasha?" She hadn't realized until this moment just how badly she'd missed her friend.

"Are you at home? I'm in the area and thought I'd stop by."

"No, but I'm close. I'm at Elemental."

"Mind if I join you?"

"Not at all," Carly said, closing her laptop. "I'd love to see you. I miss you."

Sasha didn't return the sentiment but said she'd see Carly soon. While she waited, Carly went to the counter to order another drink and a chocolate croissant—Sasha's favorite.

Couldn't hurt, right?

A few minutes later, Sasha came through the doors and headed for Carly's table. Carly turned to the side, knees out from underneath the table, poised to get up and hug her friend if that was the vibe, but Sasha just sat down across from her.

"Ooh, is this for me?" Sasha asked, eyeing the pastry. She dug in before Carly had a chance to respond.

Carly threaded her fingers together in her lap. "How are you?" God, she hated how awkward this felt. She'd never felt awkward around Sasha.

Sasha swallowed and wiped her mouth. "Better than you, probably."

"I . . . What?" There were so many issues she could be referring to, but Carly had no idea which one it was. She obviously hadn't spoken to Sasha about what had gone down over the last week.

Had Brooks?

"I heard you got let go."

"You did? How?" Literally no one knew about that except her mom. She hadn't even told Benjamin what had happened, just that Mode hadn't worked out and she was in the process of looking for something else.

Sasha took another bite, nodding as she chewed. "Mai called me. She gave me the rundown and wanted to make sure the magazine wasn't, like, planning to blacklist Mode or anything. She promised she'd taken appropriate action, and she didn't expect any additional negative publicity to come from it."

"Oh." Carly stared down at the wooden table, wide eyed. "Wow. Okay, then."

She felt Sasha's eyes on her and finally met her friend's gaze. What was Sasha thinking? Did she feel vindicated by what happened? Had she come just to rub Carly's mistake in her face?

Sasha leaned back and propped one arm across the empty chair beside her. "Honestly, what the fuck is that Princeton lady's problem?"

"Oh, thank God," Carly breathed out. Her elbows hit the table and her forehead dropped into her hands. "I thought maybe you came to gloat."

Sasha snorted. "Come on. I might have been mad at you, but you're still my best friend. I came to check on you."

Tears built behind Carly's eyelids. "I'm so glad to hear that." She looked up and reached across the table. "I'm so sorry. I should have talked to you about Brooks before anything happened. I never meant to go behind your back. I think I was just kind of blindsided by all of it, and I definitely never thought he'd feel the same way about me. I got caught up in it and I messed up. I hope you know how important you are to me."

"I do." Sasha grabbed her hand. "I might have overreacted, too. In that moment, I thought you two were just messing around, and was terrified of losing the traction we'd made at the magazine. I was upset because I thought you were being careless, not because I'm against you being together. Actually, the more I think about it, the more sense it makes. You're pretty good for each other."

Well, that was like a punch to the gut.

"I was so upset for you after I got off the phone with Mai," Sasha continued. "And I'm sorry I wasn't there for you when it happened and that you didn't feel like you could call me. But I figure Brooks has been there for you, right? At least one of us has been."

Carly just blinked at her. She pulled back, resting her hands back in her lap. "You . . . you know he broke up with me, right?"

"He *what?*"

"Well, *broke up* probably isn't the right term. We never got around to labeling anything in the first place. But yeah, he, uh, ended things. Monday afternoon."

"Monday afternoon . . ." Sasha repeated, almost to herself. She closed her eyes and shook her head. "That idiot."

"Why do you say that?"

Sasha waved a hand as if it was irrelevant. "Why? Did he give you a reason?"

"He said he needs to work on some things, like dealing with what happened with your parents and how he responds to the things he sees at work. And that he needed to step back from us while he did that."

"Dammit, Brooks," Sasha muttered, sounding irritated and disappointed.

"Hey, I don't hold it against him. He's an adult, and if he needs space to go to therapy or process his emotions differently, that's his decision to make. I get it, and it doesn't make me care about him any less. I want what's best for him. But I'm also not necessarily waiting around until he's ready."

Something like panic filled Sasha's eyes. "But . . . but he loves you."

"I love him, too. That doesn't mean we should be together." It would be nice if things were that easy. "I just . . . I have some things to consider, too, you know? Benjamin came back, and—"

"What?" Sasha shrieked, earning a glare from an older woman sitting behind them. "Benjamin's back?"

"Yes, but I'm gonna stop you right there. Now that Brooks is in the picture, you don't get a say in how I handle Benjamin. You're no longer a neutral party."

She snorted. "Like I ever was."

"Good point." Sasha had never been a fan of Benjamin. "Still. We're not talking about that. It will just confuse me, okay? I need to figure it out on my own."

Sasha practically sank in on herself, the effort to stay quiet almost comical. "Does he want you back?" she blurted.

"No comment."

"Oh God."

Carly shook her head and pushed the plate of food closer. "Finish your croissant."

Sasha nodded like this was an excellent idea and stuffed the rest into her mouth in two bites. When she'd finished, she took a long, slow breath. "You know I just want what's best for you, too, right?"

"I do. But you know what? I've got so many fires in my life right now, let's put relationships on the back burner and focus on my career for a second. Because that's an area where I'll take any and all help you've got."

Her friend pushed the plate aside and rubbed her hands together. "Right. Let's go. What are you thinking? How can I help?"

Carly gestured at her laptop. "I was searching accounting jobs before you showed up, but nothing popped out at me."

"Accounting?" Sasha cried. "You can't go back to accounting. You hated it."

"I didn't *hate* it."

Sasha slow-blinked.

"I didn't! Did I love it? No. But it's definitely not the worst thing I could be doing, and it paid my bills just fine."

"You can't give up on a career in fashion," Sasha said, unmoved. "You can't. It's all you've been working toward, and you can't just throw in the towel at the first setback."

"Getting fired's more than a setback."

Sasha ignored that. "Have you even looked for another stylist job? Or something else like it?"

"No."

"Why not?"

"I don't know. A lot's happened this week, Sash. I'd like *something* in my life to get back to normal."

"Fashion is normal for you." She tapped the top of Carly's laptop with one long fingernail. "Come on, open her up. Let's take a look."

"You realize we're in Oklahoma, right?" Carly said, though she did as she was told. "Not a lot of options in that industry to be had around here."

Sasha cocked her head and lifted one perfectly plucked brow. "You seem to forget who you're talking to. I'm the most connected woman in this city." She cracked her knuckles and leveled Carly with a stare.

"Now, quit whining, pull up Google, and let me work my magic."

CHAPTER THIRTY

Brooks

Guys don't cry at movies.

—Brooks Martin in high school, probably

"Stop fidgeting."

Brooks glanced over at Macy and frowned. They were gathered with Coach's family and friends in a church foyer, waiting to enter the sanctuary for his funeral services. How was she so calm and collected?

He'd been dreading this for days. He'd only attended two memorial services in his life—one for his mom and one for his dad—and few things had brought him the same degree of melancholy. Wasn't Macy thinking about that, too?

"I can't stand funerals," he admitted, ignoring her admonition and shifting on the balls of his feet. He'd loved Coach and wanted to pay his respects, and it was important to show Linda support. But he couldn't help all the memories flooding back, thick with the pain and loss of his teenage and young adult years. "They're so depressing."

Macy glanced at the program she'd grabbed on the way in. "This one's called a *celebration of life*," she said. "Maybe it will be different."

He snorted, skeptical, but as it turned out, she was right. After the doors opened and the crowd filed in, Brooks took in the scene around him.

Nothing was what he'd expected.

Instead of a moody, melodic soundtrack of classical music, they took their seats to the sound of The Who's "Who Are You." Macy glanced at Brooks with a *What the hell?* look on her face, and he just grinned.

"His favorite song," he whispered.

Instead of flower bouquets lining the stage, the banners from his four state basketball championships had been brought in. Poster boards with memorable Coach-isms were posted around the room, some that made Brooks laugh and others that had him hoping no children were in the room. Or if there were, that they couldn't read yet.

The pastor didn't talk long, but when he did, he told a story about the time Coach fell asleep during a men's Bible study and farted so loud he woke himself up. Brooks almost cried he was laughing so hard.

Most of the service consisted of a rotation of speakers, all with positive, funny, and uplifting stories about Coach. A few people choked up once or twice, but for the most part, the afternoon lived up to its name.

A celebration.

Linda was the last to speak, and Brooks tensed up when she stepped to the microphone, anxious on her behalf. The last time he'd spoken to her was when he delivered the news, and he could still hear her sobs. Wasn't it too soon for her to talk about him up there? Would she be able to hold it together?

But her eulogy, if you could even call it that, was the most entertaining of all. She told story after story—of how they met, what he'd been like as a dad, the things he did that drove her crazy, and how he'd always kept her on her toes. Every memory she described was saturated with Coach McKee's trademark wit, kindness, and surprising wisdom.

The service—no, celebration—stood in stark contrast to anything else Brooks had experienced when it came to loss, and it was quite frankly eye opening. He knew Linda wished Coach was still here and would grieve the loss, but even in his absence she could still laugh at the good memories, and think about him and smile. It was beautiful and refreshing.

It was hopeful.

Brooks was reeling by the time he and Macy left two hours later.

"That was incredible," Macy said, voice filled with awe. "That's exactly what I want when I die, okay? I'm putting you in charge."

"Why me?" Brooks sputtered as they made their way across the parking lot. "What about Mark?"

"He's wasn't here. He didn't see it. It's gotta be you, bro. That vibe exactly, you hear me?"

"Okay, yes. Consider it done," he promised.

They reached their cars, parked side by side. He thanked his sister for coming with him, and Macy gave him a hug before she got in her car and drove away. Brooks lowered himself into his own driver's seat and pulled out his phone. He'd put it on silent before the service.

Three missed calls and two texts from Sasha. She must have forgotten where he'd be this afternoon.

Sasha: BENJAMIN IS BACK AND HE'S AFTER YOUR GIRL

Sasha: If you don't pull your head out of your ass and do something about that, I swear to God I'll never forgive you

He pressed the call button, and she answered on the first ring.

"Tell me everything."

Brooks stared at Carly's door for at least three minutes before he got up the nerve to knock. It might not sound like much, but when you

think about a person just staring at a piece of wood, three minutes is a long-ass time.

Ten days had passed since he'd called things off. Ten days since he'd heard her voice, smelled her hair, touched her skin.

Tl;dr—ten days of fucking agony.

He'd sent her a text three days ago after learning about Mode from Sasha. Sasha told me you lost your job, he'd said. i'm so sorry. let me know if there's anything i can do.

Thanks, she'd replied. I've got it figured out.

He'd been relieved she seemed to have some sort of plan, at least. Hopefully, she'd found something even better.

A car alarm went off somewhere in the parking lot, jolting him into action, and he finally rapped his knuckles on the door. A few moments later, she opened it.

"Hi."

"Hey," she said quietly.

She wore black shorts and a cropped T-shirt that left a sliver of skin at her waist on display. She was so beautiful he tucked his hands into his pockets to keep from reaching for her.

"What are you doing here?"

"I was hoping we could talk. Would it be okay if I came in?"

"Sure."

A vestige of hope vibrated through his chest, but he told himself not to get too excited. Her willingness to hear him out was a good sign, but that didn't mean she'd be on board with everything. He paused on the way to the living room to greet Pepper, who shot him a glare that probably said something along the lines of *Where have you been, dickhead?*

He deserved that.

"Want anything to drink? Water, beer?"

"I'm good." He stood from his crouch just as she settled onto the sofa. He sat beside her, careful not to touch her. His heart was trying to lurch from his chest being near her again, like it was finally back where it belonged.

He glanced over at her, meeting the warm brown eyes he'd missed so much. "I found a movie that made me cry."

Her brows rose, either from surprise at the random comment or the fact that he'd actually cried. Probably both. "You did? Which one?"

"*Good Will Hunting*."

She let out a little hum of agreement. "How'd you stumble across that one?"

"I was on a mission. *A Star Is Born* was close, too."

Her face crumpled up, like she wanted to comment on how devastating that movie was, but she seemed to decide against it. "What do you mean, on a mission?"

"I wanted to prove to myself I'm not made of stone." He'd asked James and Jeff (separately—he wasn't sure he ever wanted to experience those two in the same room) if a movie had ever made them cry. James had responded with *The Green Mile*, and Jeff's list had been alarmingly lengthy. It was kind of hard to hide behind the weak excuse that it was just because he was a guy after that.

"Of course you're not. You knew that."

"Maybe." He hadn't been completely sure, to be honest. "But I didn't know if I could ever let go and show it."

"I'm not sure crying when you're watching a movie alone counts as showing it," she pointed out.

"True, but it's more than I've done before. I'm okay with taking small steps as long as I'm going in the right direction."

"Small steps can be good." A long beat of silence followed as he tried to gather the courage to get to the point. Long enough that she asked, "Is that all you came to tell me?"

"No. I mean, that was good and all—it was a relief, to be honest. To cry. I kept going even after the movie was over." He'd cried about his parents, all the patients he'd lost, about the hurt in Carly's voice when he'd told her it was over. "I came because I've been thinking a lot about something else. About the last time we talked and how I said I thought I needed to do this all on my own. I think that was fucking stupid."

Her eyes widened a little, and the tiniest hint of a smile quirked at the corner of her mouth. "Oh, really?"

He ran his palms down his thighs. "Yeah. I went to Coach's funeral a couple of days ago, and it was . . . enlightening."

Her brows came together and her hand came forward as if to touch him, but she seemed to think better of it and dropped it back to her lap. "Oh. I'm so sorry. You didn't go by yourself, did you?"

"Macy went with me."

"I'm glad you weren't alone."

She would have gone if he'd asked her, and he would have liked to have her sitting beside him. But it just didn't seem fair to seek her out for comfort after everything that had happened.

"It wasn't really even a funeral. It was a celebration of life, and the place was packed. Coach touched so many people's lives, and it was like every single one of them showed up. And not just to honor him, but to remember him and share those memories with everyone else. It was like . . . I don't know . . . like a group of people supporting his family and working through the loss together in this really beautiful way. Everyone there had a connection—they knew and loved Coach and were changed by his presence in their lives. And they had the stories to prove it."

Carly smiled. "That sounds like it was really something."

"It was." He dropped his gaze to the floor. "And I started thinking that if I died tomorrow, my funeral would be the exact opposite."

"What do you mean? Tons of people care about you."

"A few people care about me," he corrected. "Not a lot, because I haven't kept in touch with people over the years. And for those I have, I still don't let them too close. It sort of hit me at the funeral that if I keep holding people at arm's length, no one will really know me. I'm not sure that's such a bad thing, because I'm not sure there's anything in here worth getting to know . . . But maybe I should let them be the judge, you know? I don't want to be the one standing in the way if someone wants to try, or if someone decides I'm worth it. Why sabotage my own chance at being able to love and to be loved?"

She smiled then, but it was a small, hesitant one. "Yeah, just sit all the way down, will you?"

That smile set off a chain reaction in his body—amazement, then joy, and dangerously, more hope. "I love you, Carly," he said, voice cracking. He slowly reached for her hand, prepared for her to pull away, but she didn't. "I've been miserable being away from you. I meant what I said before, that I have some work to do. A lot, probably. But I was wrong about something, too. Really wrong."

She kept her gaze locked on his as she threaded their fingers together. "Which part?"

"I was wrong when I said I had to do it alone. I've been alone for so long, and I don't want to live that way anymore. If you're willing to stay with me and give this a shot, that's what I want. It's all I've wanted since the day I saw you at Coffee Slingers. I wanted it every time I went out with a woman who wasn't you, and I wanted it every time I took care of my garden because I wanted to make you proud as much as I wanted to succeed. I wanted it every time you teased me about my favorite jeans and when you put your hands on me, pretending to smooth out my clothes when we both knew you just wanted to touch me."

"I wasn't—"

"Yes, you were."

She bit her lip, pink blooming in her cheeks.

"The first time we slept together shook me to my core. I've never had so much fun and felt so much in the same moment. You made me happy again, Carly. You're sassy and you bring me joy and you make me want to be a better man. I've always been terrified of falling in love because I saw the dark side of it, you know? You know what happened to my dad after my mom died. It really fucked with me. But at Coach's funeral, I saw the complete opposite and watched his wife smile as she remembered the beautiful life they'd shared. I realized that's what I want. I'd rather make memories than never experience them in the first place. And I want to make them with you."

His chest expanded with each word he spoke, and how right they felt. Eyes closed, he took a few breaths to collect himself. "But I also know your ex is back, and unless he's an idiot, he wants to be with you, too. And if you want to be with him, I'll accept that. God knows he's probably less of a mess than I am. But I'm a selfish bastard, and if there's any chance at all you love me and want to be with me too, I had to come tell you how much I want you. Can you forgive me, and give me another chance to be worthy of you?"

CHAPTER THIRTY-ONE

Carly

> The anniversary date you styled me for was absolute perfection. Oliver constantly tells me what a prize I am, but this was one of the first nights in forever I actually felt that way, too. I know my worth comes from many places—the least of which is how I look on the outside—but it sure helps with the positive self-talk I've been working on when I actually believe it. From the bottom of my heart, thank you.
>
> *—Note from Jacque, client, to Carly Porter at Mode Style*

Carly's heart twisted at the unguarded fear in Brooks's eyes. She scooted closer to him, as close as she could without climbing into his lap. It was strange, how he'd become just as familiar to her as Benjamin in just a few short months. In many ways, she felt closer to Brooks than she ever had with Benjamin. She'd let Brooks see far deeper parts of her and shown him a vulnerable side she usually held close.

She tugged his hand into her lap, covering it with both her palms. "I've hardly thought about anything else since Benjamin showed up last week. You and me, me and him. The pros, the cons. The history, the complications, and what makes the most sense for me and my life right now. And no matter which angle I was considering, or how hard I tried to justify going one direction or another, it kept coming down to one thing."

His hazel eyes tracked back and forth between hers, searching her face as if trying to read her mind. The grip on her hand tightened almost imperceptibly, like he wasn't even aware of his body's reaction.

"And that thing is how much I love you."

He swayed toward her, brows pinched as if he was in pain or didn't quite believe it. His lips parted. "You do?"

She reached up and wrapped one hand gently around his neck. "I love you in a way I didn't know was even possible. So much that I told Benjamin it could never work with him, even when I didn't know if you'd ever come back to me. It wouldn't be fair to him. Or me, for that matter." Oh God, she was about to cry. "I used to think playing it safe in every single part of my life—career, finances, relationships—was the key to happiness for me. But now I know it's not. Happiness is making fools of ourselves at trivia and guessing which couples at the bar are on a first date. It's teasing you about your sense of style and getting turned on watching you get dressed. It's being in awe of your intelligence when I hear you on the phone with the hospital, and seeing that look in your eye when I wear those earrings you love. It's your secret smile and knowing I'm the one who put it there. It's the way my heart leaps every time my phone rings and it's you. No one else has ever brought me the kind of joy that you do, Brooks Martin. And all I want is to do the same for you."

He touched his forehead to hers. "God, I adore you," he whispered, and seconds later his mouth was on hers, kissing her softly, reverently. Whispering between touches, pressing words of love into her skin and her soul. "I don't know what I ever did to deserve you. Are you sure about this? About me? No, forget I said that. I'm not questioning it." And he kissed her again, long and deep and thorough.

A wave of dizziness flowed through her, the exhilaration of the moment almost too much to bear. "I'm sure," she breathed, pushing him back against the cushions and climbing onto his lap.

He ran his hands up her thighs and gripped her hips, pulling her closer as he leaned up to catch her lips. When she ran her fingernails through his thick hair and along his scalp, he groaned, a low rumble straight from his chest.

"You're killing me," he rasped, grinding into her and forcing a sharp exhale from her lungs. She slid her hands underneath his shirt, greedy for as much of his warm skin as possible, and went back to his mouth. When she arched into him and attempted to tug his shirt over his head, he put a firm hand on her spine and rotated, flipping her onto her back. He stretched out over her, nestling in between her thighs, and gripped behind her knee to hitch one leg over his hip.

"Oh my *God*."

At the sound of a third voice, Carly jerked her head to the side at the same time Brooks cursed and tried to shield her with his body.

She peeked over Brooks's shoulder to find her best friend standing in the open doorway, one hand over her eyes.

"Sasha!" Carly squeaked. "What, um . . . What are you doing here?"

Brooks dropped his forehead to her collarbone with a groan.

Sasha kept her hand up while she spoke. "I did knock. I feel like it's important that I say that. I came with job news. Obviously I didn't expect to walk in to this, but I'm glad to see you two figured things out. Also, may I suggest locking the door next time you decide to dry hump on the couch?"

"Sorry."

Brooks lifted himself off Carly, looking incredibly disappointed to be doing so, and sat up. Carly passed him a throw pillow, which he gingerly placed on his lap, and then straightened her shirt.

"Is it safe?" Sasha asked.

"Yes. You can look now."

Sasha dropped her hand and marched forward, plopping down on the floor near Carly. She'd brought her laptop and set it on the coffee table. "I have two things to pitch to you."

"Wait," Brooks interrupted. "When you said you had your job stuff figured out, that meant Sasha?"

"Why do you look so surprised?" Sasha objected. "I have excellent ideas."

"The last time you had an idea I had to date half of Oklahoma City and put it on the internet."

"You got Carly out of it, didn't you?"

Carly looked at Brooks. "She has a point."

He just crossed his arms. "Fine. Proceed."

"Okay, so the first one's a temporary option, but it's also the easiest. It could be a nice gig for a few months until you figure something else out."

"Okay, what is it?"

"Come work for me."

Carly frowned. "How, exactly?"

"I'll hire you as a fashion columnist. It wouldn't pay enough to be something you'd want long term, but I talked to Macy and we think having you work on a couple of pieces about boutique shopping in Oklahoma City or how to put together a capsule wardrobe would be well received by readers."

"Really? You'd do that for me?"

"You let me use your friends-and-family discount at Jenni Kayne every year, don't you?"

Carly laughed. "I'm not sure those are the same, but I love where your head's at. It sounds like something I'd like, but the only problem is I'm not sure I'm any good at writing."

"I read that *Gossip Girl* fan fiction you wrote in high school, remember? It was top notch." She wagged her eyebrows. "Spicy, too."

"You wrote spicy *Gossip Girl* fan fiction?" Brooks echoed. "Can I read it?"

"No."

"What? Why not?"

"It's embarrassing!"

"Come on. Please?"

"No." Carly widened her eyes at Sasha. "Can we move on?"

"Yes, let's," Sasha agreed, fairly vibrating with energy. "I'm hoping you'll pass on that idea anyway, after you hear this one. I'm really excited about it and I think it's perfect for you. But I know you and you're probably gonna think I'm out of my mind to even suggest it, so just hear me out, okay?"

Carly and Brooks shared a wary glance. "I'm listening."

Sasha typed something into the search bar on her computer, and once she'd found what she was looking for, turned it back to face Carly.

It took Carly a few seconds to figure out what she was looking at: the website for Backstitch, a self-described high-fashion resale clothing store based out of Tennessee.

"I know you have a thing about budget shopping," Sasha said, tone high and cautious like she was afraid Carly might bolt any second. It was too early for that, though, because Carly had no idea what this shop had to do with her job prospects. "And that you love the concepts of resale and consignment to reduce clothing waste. A friend of mine from college was from Nashville, and her sister owns this place. I don't even remember when, but somehow through the years I ended up following their Instagram account. When I was taking a break from scouring the city for stylist jobs for you, I came across one of their posts, and apparently they started up a franchise model a while back. In the last five years, they've opened fourteen stores across the country. Cool, huh?"

Carly clicked on the About Us page and skimmed the summary of the store and the types of merchandise they sold. "It is," she said, and pointed at one of the photos. "And look at this stuff. It's so cute . . . Gah, look at that handbag! I would totally shop here."

"Right? Anyway, so I did some research and there's nothing like this in the OKC Metro. We've got thrift stores, of course, and consignment stores, but they have mostly children's stuff or styles for, um . . . the more *seasoned* demographic. But nothing to hit the college-age and young professional demographic, or people looking for higher-end designer pieces but can't afford the brand-new price tag."

Carly thought about that for a moment. "You're right. There's not really any good resale shops for that kind of thing." She scoured estate sales and online marketplaces like Facebook and Poshmark for those pieces, but it would be awesome to have a physical location to browse.

"Exactly. It's an unmet need in the community that *you* could fill. If you click on that place that says 'Franchise'—yeah, right there—I mean, look at that. It walks through the entire process of starting your own Backstitch store. Financial requirements to start up, on-site training for new franchisees, and the levels of support they offer from the home store after a new location is up and running. It's literally everything you'd want to know before starting your own store."

"Wait," Carly said, pushing the computer back. "Are you suggesting that I, someone who has never run a business in my life, open up my own clothing store?"

Sasha nodded, unperturbed by Carly's incredulous tone. "Why not? You're perfect for this. You've got the qualities that can't be taught—a natural eye and the ability to connect with people. For the business part they literally help you every step of the way. Check out the on-site training program for complete beginners—it's six months long! On site! It's basically a mini-internship where they teach you everything from retail and consignment models to purchasing and employee management. And when it's over, they're just a phone call away if you hit a snag and need advice."

Carly stared at the screen and their statement of dedication to sustainability, shaking her head. She had to admit she was curious, but at the same time the idea was completely preposterous. Maybe later—after Sasha left and after she and Brooks spent some quality alone time—she'd sit down with it. Read through the FAQ and check out the pages of some of the franchise stores to see how they were doing. Maybe slide into a DM or two to ask what franchise owners thought about the process and what their backgrounds had been before. Had they all been in retail, or was there someone who'd been able to pull this off without prior experience?

"There's one more thing," Sasha said, index finger in the air. "They only run the six-month training program once a year. I called and they had a last-minute cancellation, so there's an open spot with your name on it. And that friend of mine from college, Riza, has a vacant garage apartment you could stay in. So you wouldn't need to pay rent while you were there, either!"

Carly put her hands up. "Whoa, whoa, whoa. You think I should *move* to Nashville for six months?" She shot a glance at Brooks, who'd gone quiet.

"I think you should seriously consider it. Oh, and they need to know by next week."

"You're out of your mind."

"Maybe. But you're intrigued by the idea, I can tell."

"Of course I'm intrigued, but it's also ridiculous. It's impossible. There's no way I could move for six months."

"Why not? You don't have a job."

"Wow. Okay, what about the cost? I don't have that kind of money."

"You've got four times that amount in your savings account."

"How the hell do you know that?"

"That doesn't matter. What's the point of saving money if you won't let yourself use it when you need it? This could be the start of a brand-new career, Carly. Something incredible that *you* get to build, run exactly how you want, and that will be a return on that investment a dozen times over. Every single store they've franchised has been in the black within the first year, and it's something you'd love doing. I swear, it felt like fate when I came across that post. Everything about this has Carly Porter written all over it."

"You seem awfully optimistic."

"I told you I was excited about it."

Carly rested her chin in her palm, regarding the website. She leaned her head to the side and caught Brooks's eye. "What do you think about all this?" she asked quietly.

"It's unexpected, that's for sure," he said, voice low. "And different. But my opinion isn't what matters, here."

There's no way he'd get behind this. It hadn't even been a half hour since they got back together—he wouldn't want her to move out of state.

"I'd like to hear it all the same."

"Are you sure?"

"Yes."

"Okay," he said, scanning her face. "Well, the thing is, I've never forgotten the look on your face when we were on that pretend date and you told me about shopping with younger people who can't spend a lot of money. I don't think I've seen you look that excited since."

She wasn't expecting him to say that. "Not even when you rolled up your sleeves for me?"

He laughed. "This was enthusiastic excited, not turned-on excited. I like both."

"Equally?"

A beat passed and one corner of his mouth lifted. "No."

"Ew," Sasha put in.

"This idea is huge, and it feels completely out of left field. I get that. I also know change is scary," Brooks said, leaning forward to tuck a piece of hair behind her ear. "But this literally sounds like a dream job for you. You'd get to curate your own store full of clothes to sell and help style people that came into shop. I think you might love that, and you'd be fucking awesome at it. You're smart, hardworking, and creative, and when you want to, you can do anything you put your mind to."

"Yes, the only things needed to start and run a small business," she said dryly.

"What else is there? Money?"

It was no small concern, especially for someone who hadn't grown up with it. "For one. Did you see the recommended cash on hand for start-up? That's separate from the training program, and I definitely don't have the money to do that on my own. The thought of taking out a loan is just . . ." She shuddered.

"You're looking at a guy whose career was made possible with loans."

"That's different."

"How?"

"I don't know. I don't know that much about small business loans, but school loans seem different."

"So let's go to a bank and talk about it. Learn the similarities and differences and see what you think after that. My neighbor owns a local appliance store, and I'm sure he'd be happy to talk you through how he got started. Nothing wrong with asking questions just to see, right?"

"Maybe." Her shoulders dipped. "I also lack any business acumen."

"You're a CPA, so I doubt that. But even so, that's what the training's for, right? And the ongoing support from the flagship group. It sounds like they've got a pretty sophisticated system going."

She tilted her head as she regarded him, thoughtful. "You're saying a lot of reasonable things."

"The same things I was saying," Sasha grumbled.

Carly didn't look away from Brooks when she said, "Sounds better coming out of his mouth."

Brooks grinned and took her hand, weaving his fingers between hers. "What's the worst that could happen?"

"I could fail."

"So what?" Sasha cut in. "Everybody fails. Nobody wants to, but at least it means you tried. I'd rather give something my all and miss the mark than never try at all, wouldn't you?"

"Not when it comes to something this important."

"Okay, so let's say you do. You fail. You'd be out of a job, but spoiler alert: You're there now. You've already been there, and look at you. It's not the end of the world that you thought it would be. You're regrouping, surrounded by your people, and you're figuring something else out. You'd do that again. But none of that matters because you won't fail. My gut tells me this will work, Carly. And my gut is never wrong."

Carly and Brooks laughed. Loud. She could think of three instances of Sasha's faulty gut off the top of her head, and she'd bet a lot of money Brooks could do the same.

"Alright," Sasha muttered. She stood and pushed her laptop closed, then grabbed it and propped her other fist on her hip. "You're both assholes."

"No, wait." Carly scrambled to her feet and threw her arms around Sasha. "I'm sorry. Thank you. Really. I can't believe you did all this for me."

Sasha was quiet for a moment. "And?"

"And you're the best friend a girl could ask for. I love you more than life itself."

"And what about my ideas?"

"You're brilliant. Best ideas in the history of the world."

Sasha pulled back to eye her. "And you'll at least think about it? Backstitch?"

Carly dropped her arms in defeat and smiled. "I'll think about it."

"Good. I'll send you all the info I gathered so far and leave you two to whatever it was you were doing before I showed up. But please for the love of God, come lock the door after me."

"Don't worry, I won't make that mistake again," Carly said.

"One week, you hear me?" Sasha called out as she walked to the door. "One week!"

CHAPTER THIRTY-TWO

Brooks

If you ever find me down, check the service schedule, and if Dr. Martin's not on, call him in. I don't want anyone else taking care of me.

—Charge nurse, 4W ICU, University Hospital

Carly closed (and locked) the door and came back to the couch. After she sat, Brooks pulled her into his side and brought her legs across his lap.

"What are you thinking?" he asked.

"At this point, I don't even know."

"Understandable."

She laid her head against his shoulder, absentmindedly tracing a finger in zigzags across his chest.

"What other options have you considered? Job-wise?" He hated that he hadn't been around to help her work through this in the days after she'd been fired.

"I started looking for new accounting jobs," she said. "And I know Bailey would take me back if I asked. I left on good terms."

He put a gentle hand across hers, flattening her palm on his chest. "If you think going back to accounting is the right call, I'll support you. Whatever you decide. But I worry that's not where your heart is."

"It's not." She tipped her head back so she could look at him. "You know how when you were talking about how you ended up in medicine, you said it was the perfect career because it combined your talents and your passion?"

"Yes."

"I'm good at accounting, but it doesn't get me excited. I don't look forward to it or think about how I might change up the way I arrange spreadsheets after I get off."

"Really? A good spreadsheet really gets me going."

She pinched him, and he laughed. "But the work I did at Mode? I loved every second of it. The flexibility, the creativity, the transformations. I get hyped up when I'm just scrolling on Pinterest and come across a sweater I love or a style that inspires me, and thinking about which client I could share it with. When Sasha was talking about Backstitch just now, it was like this weirdly perfect combination of everything I'm good at and love."

"I thought the same thing. So why don't you just sit with it for a day or two? It's a lot to consider, and it's smart to ask more questions and do some research. But if your gut reaction is positive, it's worth exploring, right?"

Her brow furrowed, and she bit her lip. "Maybe . . . but, Nashville? For six months? We literally just talked about trying this thing between us again. How can I just up and leave? What if . . . I don't know, what if we don't survive it?"

"Hey." He gripped her chin between his thumb and forefinger. "If you decide to do this, I won't lie and say I won't hate it when you're gone, but it's gonna take something a lot bigger than that to get rid of me, Carly Porter. I won't make the mistake of letting you go again."

"I was in another relationship where someone left temporarily for a job," she pointed out. "Didn't work out so well."

Yeah, because Benjamin was a dumbass, he wanted to say. "It did for me."

That earned him a tiny laugh. He'd take it.

"I'm not Benjamin. I want you to do what you need to do for your career, and if you go I'll be thinking of you, and yes, missing you, the whole time. I'll text you every day and I'll come visit when I'm not on call. Let me show you how much I'm in this with you. Because even if you fell in love with Nashville and didn't want to come back, I'd find a job up there and follow you."

Her cheeks flushed, and God, he'd missed that. "You would?"

"In a heartbeat." He paused. "If you'd want me to."

"Of course I'd want you to. I love you, remember?"

He sat back and tugged her onto his lap. Framing her face with his hands, he whispered one last thing into her mouth before he kissed her, something he planned to keep doing for most of the night. "I love you more."

Three days later, Brooks was finishing up his shift, an unusual sensation stirring beneath his ribs.

It felt like hope.

He walked through the cafeteria, searching the rows of tables and into the various hallways and connected rooms where employees and visitors could take a break. As he neared the back corner, he worried the nurse had been wrong—maybe the kid hadn't come for something to eat.

Brooks really hoped he hadn't left. He wanted to be the one to break the news.

Just before he was about to give up, his eye caught on a thin form hunched over a table next to the vending machines.

The kid was swiping through something on his phone and didn't look up when Brooks approached.

"Hey. Connor, right?"

The kid looked up and blinked at Brooks, then nodded, the circles underneath his eyes darker than any seventeen-year-old's had a right to be. His dark-blond hair was unkempt, and he wore a wrinkled T-shirt, probably from attempting sleep on the rollaway bed in the corner of his dad's hospital room.

"I'm Brooks, one of your dad's doctors."

"I remember you."

"May I sit?"

Connor shrugged, but he locked his phone, which Brooks took as a good sign.

Brooks sat across from him and put his hands on the table for a few seconds, then pulled them into his lap. He should have taken off his white coat, probably. He didn't need to make Connor any more uncomfortable than he already was.

But he was nervous and liked to slide his hands into the oversize coat pockets and sift through the several pens he kept handy.

"How're you doing?"

Connor just sort of stared at him with a slight frown.

Right. Well, that was fair. Brooks hadn't exactly established himself as one of those providers who asked how his patients' families were doing.

"I wanted to talk to you about your dad. I have some good news."

The slightest flicker of something besides wariness flashed across Connor's face, there and gone in an instant. Again, Brooks understood. He'd kept his guard up pretty high, too.

"Your dad's numbers are looking good. He's moving oxygen well, heart is staying strong, and we've been able to wean sedation. We're ready to try extubating, which means we'll take out the tube that's helping him breathe. I'm hopeful he can do it on his own now."

Connor had gone still, his face paling as Brooks spoke. "You . . . you mean he's going to be okay?"

"I can't promise anything, and he still has a long road ahead of him. But things have gone very well in the past few days, and I'm optimistic.

This is a step in the right direction, and I'll do everything I can to help him. Okay?"

Connor's throat worked as he swallowed, and as if in slow motion, his lips turned down and his lids clamped shut as he fell apart. His arms came up to shield his face, and before Brooks knew what he was doing, he'd moved to the other side of the table and pulled the kid close. Connor didn't return the embrace but didn't pull away, instead leaning into Brooks as sobs racked his thin body.

"It's okay," Brooks heard himself say. "You're okay."

"He has to get better," Connor said, voice trembling. "First my mom . . . and I just—I can't . . ." He couldn't finish, tears stealing his breath.

"Yes, you can. I know it doesn't feel like it now, but you'll get through this." Brooks's own voice shook as he recalled the words Coach had once said to him when he felt so out of control and out of hope. "I lost my mom when I was young. So believe it or not, I know how you're feeling right now. Like the whole world is ending."

Connor nodded against his shoulder.

"Just take it one day at a time, okay? And when you feel like you can't breathe, talk to someone. Do you have someone like that? That you trust and you can go to?"

He sniffed. "My aunt and uncle. And my cousin Brady."

"Good. And I know you don't know me, but you can talk to me, too, if you want. I may not know what to say, but I've been in your shoes. And I'll always be honest with you. Okay?"

"Okay."

For several minutes they remained like that, Brooks the steady presence for once. The one holding strong for someone who needed him. He kept his arm around Connor as his tears slowed and his shoulders relaxed.

"It's okay." Coach's voice broke, and Brooks cried harder. "You're okay. I've got you, son."

"I hate this," he hiccuped. "I hate it."

"I know."

"I can't do this."

"Yes, you can." Coach grabbed him by the shoulders and looked him in the eye, his own eyes red-rimmed. "I know it doesn't feel like it now. But you can do this. You will."

And he had. He'd made it through somehow, and Connor would, too.

Eventually, Connor's uncle had called, looking for him, and Brooks made his way back to the ICU. He claimed a free computer at one of the nursing stations and worked on a few patient charts, unaware of the time until a familiar voice floated over him.

"Hey, Dr. Martin."

He looked up and smiled. "Hey, Nikki. How's it going?"

She laughed. "I'm surviving."

"It only gets worse from here," he joked. "But you knew what you were getting into."

"I did," she said with a laugh. "I'm glad I saw you, actually. I've been hoping to run into you."

"Oh? Is there something I can help you with, for the program or something?"

"No, nothing like that. Everything's great. It's, um, it's about you, actually. Remember last month when I told you what I'd heard about you?"

That he was unemotional and detached? He wasn't likely to forget that anytime soon. "I do."

Her eye twitched, almost like a wince. "I just . . . I wanted to say I think I asked the wrong person. Because even though I've only been here a month, that's not what I see at all. I watch people a lot, and I pay attention. And when it comes to you, I see a physician who's so invested in his patients, he comes in to check on them when he doesn't have to. Who has slept in the on-call room with the fellows because he knows sometimes laying eyes on the patient can tell you more than a number in the chart. Who triple- and quadruple-checks blood gases and pressor drips to make sure everything is as it should be and maybe . . . maybe hoping to see things moving in the right direction. I know it doesn't matter what I think—or what any fellows think, for that matter. But that's a physician who cares an awful lot about his patients, and . . . I don't know, I guess I just wanted you to know that."

Brooks just blinked at her, stunned into silence.

Nikki's phone chirped, and she glanced at the screen. "Shoot, I'm late. Schwartz Rounds starts in ten, and I hate sitting in the back." She looked up at him cautiously, almost like she regretted what she'd just said. "I hope I didn't overstep just now. But I'd better get going. See you around, Dr. Martin."

It wasn't until she was almost out of sight that he jolted into action. "Hey, Nikki?"

She stopped in the hallway and turned back. "Yeah?"

"I've got something to finish up here real quick, but I think I might head that way, too. Save me a seat?"

CHAPTER THIRTY-THREE

October 14

Brooks: hi.
Carly: Hi!
Brooks: i miss you
Carly: I've only been gone three days . . .
Brooks: i still miss you
Carly: I miss you more.

October 15

Carly: I just passed a cool-looking coffee shop and it made me think of you.
Brooks: weird, pretty much everything makes me think of you
Carly: Stop being so sweet ❤
Brooks: ok
Carly: But not really because that was lovely and I'll look at that text every hour for the next three days straight.
Brooks: ok 😊

October 17

Carly: My mom says if you want garlic next year, now's the time to plant it
Brooks: on it
Brooks: does garlic shrink into anything i should know about
Carly: hahahahaha

October 30

Brooks: [image]
Carly: What am I looking at?
Carly: Did you try to go shopping by yourself? I thought we talked about that
Brooks: calm down it's my halloween costume
Carly: Ohhh
Brooks: i'm a ninja. my nephews picked it
Carly: Ninja? That's kind of hot
Brooks: are you dressing up?
Carly: All the people at Backstitch are doing character costumes. I picked Ms. Frizzle from The Magic School Bus.
Brooks: yeah i'm gonna need a picture of that
Brooks: and also for you to keep that costume for later
Carly: Really? Ms. Frizzle?
Brooks: i like science
Brooks: don't judge me
Carly: Is it the hair or the crazy dresses?
Brooks: it's all very good

November 6

Brooks: guess what?
Carly: You watched The Notebook again and bawled like a baby?
Brooks: nope

Brooks: i signed up to be on the discussion panel for the next schwartz rounds

Carly: No way, really?

Brooks: yep

Carly: That's so great! What are you talking about?

Brooks: connor's dad was discharged today. walked out of here on his own and everything, and i just thought it would be good to talk about how it felt to be part of his care after what i went through

Carly: I'm so proud of you. I wish I could hug you right now but it'll have to wait until I come visit next weekend

Brooks: i have so many plans for us

Carly: Like what?

Brooks: i feel weird texting it because they mostly involve us being naked

Carly: I'm in.

November 25

Carly: I'm thankful for you, Brooks Martin

Brooks: i'm thankful for you, Carly Porter

December 10

Brooks: jeff got stuck with me on his trivia team again

Carly: Lol how'd that go?

Brooks: i tried to tell him winning wasn't everything. he didn't like that

Carly: I'd be on your team any day.

Brooks: this is why i love you

Brooks: well, one of the many reasons

Carly: 😘

December 25

Brooks: merry Christmas, beautiful

Carly: Merry Christmas. I wish you were here.

Brooks: yeah?

Carly: Always.

Brooks: you'll probably like the present I got you, then

Carly: !!!

Brooks: let me up, will you?

January 16

Carly: I sent you something, did you get it?

Brooks: you mean this?

Brooks: [image]

Brooks: i thought it was for oreo.

Carly: Omggggg he looks SO CUTE

Brooks: he says thank you, he's very warm.

Brooks: but i was kind of sad there was nothing for me . . .

Carly: [image]

Brooks: holy shit

Brooks: how are you so sexy

Brooks: p.s. that's so much better than a sweater

February 14

Carly: HOW ARE WE NOT TOGETHER ON VALENTINE'S DAY??

Brooks: why are you yelling

Carly: BECAUSE IT'S OUR FIRST VALENTINE'S DAY AND WE'RE TOO FAR APART WHY DID I DO THIS I MISS YOU SO MUCH

[incoming FaceTime call from Boy Toy Brooks]

April

A knock sounded below Carly's feet.

She leaped up and jogged down the stairs, opening the door to the garage apartment she'd lived in for the past six months and launching herself at him.

"Whoa." Brooks caught her with a laugh, lifting her feet off the ground as he hauled her up against his chest. She wrapped her arms around his shoulders, and he buried his face in her hair, inhaling deeply.

She hadn't seen him since Christmas, which was too damn long.

She pulled his head down and kissed him. He wasted no time turning up the heat and backed her against the wall next to her door, sliding his tongue in her mouth and sending her stomach into a deep dive.

The side door to the house swung open. "Oh, uh . . . hey, Carly. You've got something on your face."

Brooks backed up and held out his hand. "Steve. Nice to see you again."

"I'd say the same, but you're taking one of my wife's favorite new friends back to Oklahoma tomorrow, so I gotta be honest and say I'm kind of pissed at you. She's gonna be grumpy for like a week."

"Yeah, I'm not sorry to be taking her."

Steve nodded. "Fair." He shifted his gaze to Carly. "We're sad to see you go. What time do you two head back?"

"Not until noon." She'd miss Steve, too. He'd been super friendly from the day she moved in and, as the foodie in the house, had introduced her to all the best places to eat and drink in the neighborhood. "Did Riza mention we're grabbing breakfast in the morning? I hope you can come, too."

"I'm in." He glanced at his phone. "I gotta run, but text me when and where, okay?"

"I will."

Steve turned to his car as she and Brooks climbed the stairs to the small apartment. As soon as the door closed behind them, Brooks came for her again, taking back her attention and stealing her breath. When they finally pulled apart, she led him through the room, weaving around the boxes and rolls of packing tape strewn around the space.

Brooks kept her hand in his. "We're never doing this again."

"What, live in different states?"

"Yeah."

"It wasn't *that* bad."

He stared at her flatly.

"Okay, yes, it was awful." She didn't regret it, though. She'd learned a ton about the resale business, which she'd take back with her to Oklahoma, and she and Brooks had come out of this stronger than ever before. They'd talked every single day while she was gone, a complete one-eighty from how things had been with Ben when he'd done the same. Everything about this experience had been different.

Brooks slipped his arms around her waist, and his hands dipped low on her back. "Don't get me wrong, I'm so glad you did this. But next time, I'm coming with you."

She slid her hands up and down his chest, wondering if they had time to mess around before the dinner reservations she'd made. She'd wanted to go to her favorite restaurant one last time . . . but he smelled so good and filled out that shirt so damn well. "You'd do that?"

He dipped his head and kissed her deeply. "I'd follow you anywhere."

She hummed happily against his mouth.

A few moments later, he pulled back, a strange look on his face. Sweet but almost . . . nervous? "When we get back, want to head straight to my place?"

She didn't follow. "Sure. He's playing it cool, but I know Pepper's been dying to see Oreo. Why make them wait?"

He rubbed his jaw. "I meant, like, take all your stuff there. For good. What would you think about moving in with me?"

Her heart lurched into her throat. "Really?"

His gorgeous eyes searched hers as he nodded.

"You're sure?"

"I've never been so sure of anything."

She grinned, grabbing his hand and swinging it side to side. "Okay, but I have rules."

"I'm sure you do."

"Wanna hear them?"

"They won't change my mind, but okay."

"We make the bed when we get up."

He rolled his eyes. "Fine."

"I get to paint the bistro set on the porch any color I choose."

"Have at it."

"Tuesday nights are movie nights."

"Unless the Thunder are playing."

"Deal." She squinted while she thought. "Oh, and you have to donate the jeans."

He stilled. "What?"

She narrowed her eyes. "You haven't been wearing them while I've been gone, have you? You promised."

"No." He looked away. "It's just . . ."

She frowned and stepped closer to peer into his face. "What is it?"

"They sort of have sentimental value to me now. When I see them in my closet, I think of you. How we met, the way you stole them and then lied about it, and that time things got hot when I found them again. I love every memory attached to them, and I don't think I can stomach giving them away."

"Are you trying to make me cry?"

"Not like that's hard to do."

"Fine! You can keep the jeans, you big softy."

He looked so damn happy. "Good. Anything else?"

"Yeah." She gazed up at him, heart bursting. "Promise you'll love me forever."

His smile faded into something serious and fierce. "I don't usually make promises," he said, reaching up to trail his thumb across her cheek. "But for that, I'll make an exception."

EPILOGUE

"Okay, everyone!" The guy onstage boomed into the mic. "Before you turn in your trivia cards, we have a surprise tonight. There's a bonus round!"

An excited murmur swept through the sizable room. Fassler Hall was packed tonight, and Brooks was coming out of his skin with anticipation. He cast a covert glance at Sasha and Macy, who had teamed up with Kendall for trivia tonight.

Macy kept her expression neutral, but Sasha couldn't contain her excitement and covered her mouth to muffle a squeal. How she'd kept it all a secret for this long without ruining everything, he'd never know.

Carly was oblivious, chatting excitedly with Jeff, who had become one of Brooks's favorite people.

"Ooh, a bonus round?" she was saying. "Have they ever done that before?"

"Nope," Jeff said with confidence. As often as he went to trivia nights around town, the man would know.

She looked at Brooks and smiled. He leaned over and kissed her, amazed that he didn't sense even a sliver of nerves for what he was about to do.

It just felt right. That was all there was to it.

The moderator tapped the mic, and everyone's attention returned to him. He flicked a look at Brooks that wouldn't have been noticeable to anyone else. "Alright. Even though this is a bonus round, same rules apply, so no cheating!" He cleared his throat. "And also, I'd like to invite a guest to come up to the mic and ask the questions this time. Y'all are probably tired of hearing my boring-ass voice all night."

A few people shouted the affirmative while others murmured in confusion. Brooks stood up and made his way to the stage, careful not to look at her as he went.

All night, he hadn't been nervous. Not even a little bit. But that was before he stood elevated and on display in front of eighty people.

He cleared his throat. "Thanks, Tommy." He gave an awkward little wave. "I'm, um, Brooks, and I'll be leading the bonus round tonight. There are four questions. Good luck, everyone."

Understandably, everyone still seemed confused as hell. Well, everyone except Sasha and Macy. He didn't know how Carly looked because he still couldn't bring himself to look at her yet or he'd lose it.

Confusion or not, winning was still king, so each team had their assigned recorder ready with pencil in hand.

"Question one: Who is the owner of Backstitch, OKC's up-and-coming, hottest new resale clothing store, set to open next spring?" He looked at her then, and it took her a second to process the question. He ignored the buzz around the room and stepped off the stage when her eyes met his, a slight frown between her brows.

"Question two." He began weaving through the tables. "When did Brooks Martin fall in love with Carly Porter?"

Her gaze was locked on his now, her features transforming. She blinked several times and her lips curved up.

"Question three: Which of Carly's body parts is Brooks's favorite?"

By now the audience had caught on and was watching them as he closed in on her, a slight laugh and a few whistles piercing the air. He was close enough now to see the tears welling in her eyes even as she cocked a single brow at that question.

"Number four is a yes-or-no question." He stopped in front of her and dropped to one knee. "What was Carly's answer when Brooks asked her to marry him?"

Her left hand covered her mouth, and the other arm extended to wrap her hand around his propped knee. "Oh my gosh," she whispered.

"Carly." His voice suddenly felt thick. "I love you. You're th—Jeff, you okay, man?"

Jeff blinked rapidly and swiped at his eyes. "Sure. Yeah, I'm fine, whatever. Keep going."

Carly smiled behind her hand, her eyes going wide with humor as tears spilled over.

"Right. Carly, you're the most unbelievable woman I've ever met. Never in my wildest dreams would I have ever thought there was anyone on this earth so perfect for me. I know you're not a big believer in that kind of thing, but I know without a doubt I'll never love anyone the way I love you. I've never met a woman who makes me laugh like you, who challenges me like you, and who drives me out of my damn mind the way you do. Especially when you wear those red strappy sandal things."

The room was as quiet as he'd ever heard it, except for some guy in the back who yelled, "Get 'er done!"

He ignored that.

"There's something about you that I'll never get over. Ever. I don't know what I ever did to deserve you, but I want you to be mine forever and let me love you until the day I stop breathing. So I have this question to ask: Will you marry me?"

Tears streamed down her face (and Sasha's and Macy's and Jeff's) and she nodded, grabbing his hand as they stood and he wrapped her in his arms. She grabbed his face and kissed him.

"What's the answer?" someone yelled from the back.

"Yes!" Carly tipped her head back. "I said yes!"

Everyone cheered, the sound thundering through his body as he held her close, grinning like a fool and certain he'd never been this happy.

After celebrating with his sisters and their friends for what felt like forever, Brooks finally got Carly the hell out of there and took her back to their house. Other than demanding the answers to the other questions (when he fell in love with her: the day he found the jeans in her closet; and which body part was his favorite: her eyes), she stared at the ring the entire ride home and yanked him up against the front door with her before he could even get it open.

"I love you so much," she said into his mouth. "I can't believe you."

Her lips and hands were everywhere, and he had trouble forming a coherent response.

Finally, he got her inside before the neighbors got an eyeful, and she paused in the entryway. "So, um . . ."

He raised his brows. "So?"

She folded her hands behind her back. "I know we haven't done it in a while, but . . . I'm sort of in the mood for . . . you know." She shot him a meaningful look.

He grinned. "Yeah?"

She bit her lip and nodded.

"Get your ass in the bedroom, then," he said, locking the door and tossing his keys on the table. "I'll get the jeans and meet you there."

ACKNOWLEDGMENTS

I'm thankful for every member of the publishing team that made this book happen. Thank you to my agent, Kim Lionetti, for finding this book a home, and to editors Lauren Plude and Selina MacLemore for helping me rethink Brooks and convince me to be a little tougher on Carly (we all know if left to my own devices, Allison Ashley books would be pure banter + flirting + kisses with zero conflict whatsoever). Thank you to the copyeditors, proofreaders, art department, and the many others I will probably never meet. And to the marketing team at Montlake, the exceptional publicity group with BookSparks, and my saviors, Booked with the Emilys—thank you for helping the right readers find my books.

This is the first book I've written that's set in my home state. To be honest, I have a love/hate relationship with living in Oklahoma, but I tried to inject many of the things I love in the setting of this book. Barrios is a real restaurant that has the best margaritas; we really do have a climbing gym in an old grain silo; and as I write this, the Thunder are #1 in the Western Conference. Coffee Slingers and Elemental are top-notch coffee shops, and definitely check out First Friday at Paseo if you're ever here in the summer. If you're ever in the OKC area, hit me up and I'll tell you the best places to go.

As always, to the romance readers of the world, I hope you never stop loving books about love. We need them now more than ever.

ABOUT THE AUTHOR

Photo © 2019 Ashley Porton

Allison Ashley is the author of *If Tomorrow Never Comes*, *The Roommate Pact*, *Would You Rather*, *Home Sweet Mess*, and *Perfect Distraction*. She is a science geek who enjoys coffee, craft beer, baking, and love stories. When Allison is not working at her day job as a clinical oncology pharmacist, she pens contemporary romances, usually with a medical twist. She lives in Oklahoma with her family and beloved rescue dog. For more information, visit www.authorallisonashley.com.